An excerpt from *Just a* 

"They haven't mad

"Who?"

Soren didn't need the answer to that question. He knew. Without hesitation, and not knowing why, he shoved his chair back and took off, striding around the tables at a pace just short of a run.

As he stormed up the stairs, Soren asked himself what he was doing, why he was so desperate to get to Eliot and what he thought he could contribute. He'd kissed her goodbye nearly a decade ago, the spicy taste of her mouth lingering for hours, days. He hadn't spoken to or seen her since.

So why was he thundering up the staff staircase?

He didn't know, but wild horses couldn't pull his feet off the stairs. Seeing the door that would take him onto the right floor, he stepped into the hallway.

Where the bride sorta, kinda, looked like Eliot.

Okay, her face was hidden behind a waist-length veil, but this wooden, tense woman looked like a cartoonish version of the woman he'd known in France. Her face was alabaster white. Her blue eyes, normally electric, were dull. Her dress was an abomination of lace and beads.

She still looked best, as he remembered her, wearing a pair of loose, short denim cutoffs and a bold tangerine bikini, with her damp hair tumbling down her back and her bright blue eyes looking over her sand-dusted shoulder...

* * *

An excerpt from *Their Temporary Arrangement*

Ru stared at Fox, flabbergasted. "I'm sorry... What did you say?"

Fox didn't drop his eyes from hers. "You heard me." He didn't change his stance, but Ru felt tension invade his muscles. "I want to employ you. You are the first person who's lessened my load and not added to it in six weeks. You're also the first woman whose mouth I desperately want to kiss."

What the hell? Had she, somehow, stepped into an alternate reality?

Ru swallowed and dragged her gaze up his body.

Don't do it, Ru. You need the job, the money, to get away. Do not jeopardize this opportunity.

But want, need and recklessness swamped her, and her feet carried her to him, stepping between his long legs. She placed her hands on his shoulders and inhaled his sexy scent, her eyes not breaking contact with his...

* * *

JOSS WOOD

JUST A LITTLE JILTED
&
THEIR TEMPORARY ARRANGEMENT

HARLEQUIN

DESIRE

If you purchased this book without a cover you should be aware that this book is stolen property. It was reported as "unsold and destroyed" to the publisher, and neither the author nor the publisher has received any payment for this "stripped book."

Recycling programs for this product may not exist in your area.

ISBN-13: 978-1-335-45756-1

Just a Little Jilted & Their Temporary Arrangement

Copyright © 2023 by Harlequin Enterprises ULC

Just a Little Jilted
Copyright © 2023 by Joss Wood

Their Temporary Arrangement
Copyright © 2023 by Joss Wood

All rights reserved. No part of this book may be used or reproduced in any manner whatsoever without written permission except in the case of brief quotations embodied in critical articles and reviews.

This is a work of fiction. Names, characters, places and incidents are either the product of the author's imagination or are used fictitiously. Any resemblance to actual persons, living or dead, businesses, companies, events or locales is entirely coincidental.

For questions and comments about the quality of this book, please contact us at CustomerService@Harlequin.com.

Harlequin Enterprises ULC
22 Adelaide St. West, 41st Floor
Toronto, Ontario M5H 4E3, Canada
www.Harlequin.com

Printed in U.S.A.

CONTENTS

Joss Wood loves books, coffee and traveling—especially to the wild places of southern Africa and, well, anywhere. She's a wife and a mom to two young adults. She's also a slave to two cats and a dog the size of a small cow. After a career in local economic development and business, Joss writes full-time from her home in KwaZulu-Natal, South Africa.

Books by Joss Wood

Harlequin Desire

Crossing Two Little Lines

Dynasties: DNA Dilemma

Secrets of a Bad Reputation
Wrong Brother, Right Kiss
Lost and Found Heir
The Secret Heir Returns

Dynasties: Calcott Manor

Just a Little Jilted
Their Temporary Arrangement

Visit the Author Profile page
at Harlequin.com for more titles.

You can also find Joss Wood on Facebook,
along with other Harlequin Desire authors,
at Facebook.com/HarlequinDesireAuthors.

Dear Reader,

Welcome to Hatfield, Connecticut, and the first book of my new Dynasties series.

Eliot Gamble has just been fired—as a supermodel and then by her famous fiancé minutes before their wedding ceremony. She is *not* having a good day.

Soren Grantham is heading to his billionaire grandmother's estate in Connecticut. As a celebrated Olympian, he's deciding whether to continue swimming or to retire at the peak of his career. But what will he do? Who will he be?

At lunch with his cousins, Soren hears news from Calcott Manor. Not only is his grandmother refusing to write her will but the recipient of his cousin Malcolm's liver is visiting Avangeline. What does she want? Soren, already on his way to Calcott Manor, vows to find out.

About to leave, Soren hears that the woman he had an affair with years before has been jilted in the ballroom upstairs. Soren spirits Eliot out of the hotel, away from the buzzing paparazzi, and takes her with him to Calcott Manor.

He's simply rescuing her, right? There's no way that they are running straight into love...

Happy reading!

Joss

Connect with me!

Facebook: JossWoodAuthor
Twitter: @JossWoodBooks
BookBub: JossWood
Goodreads: Joss_Wood

JUST A LITTLE JILTED

One

It is summer and I, Avangeline, am eighty-two years old. I am standing in God's waiting room. I know and accept this... There are only two certainties in life, some wit opined, and that's death and taxes. Death will come sooner than I like and, dear God, I've paid a lot of taxes.

Then again, I've made a lot of money. Billions...

But how much, I keep wondering, is a secret worth? Do I get a discount if I have two?

"World's smallest pair of handcuffs, honey."

Eliot Stone, her face covered by her veil, looked through the six-inch strip of the car's open window into the tanned face of a bicycle courier, gray hair peeking out from under her bicycle helmet.

She frowned, unsure whether the courier was talking to her or not. But when the biker placed her fingers on the edge of the limousine's window for balance and looked straight into her eyes, Eliot had no doubt she was the focus of her attention.

"Are you talking about marriage?" Eliot asked her, fascinated by the wisdom she saw in those deep brown eyes. The woman had clearly seen a lot of life, and not all of it had been good.

"Fancy day, fancy dress, fancy shoes, I bet. But it doesn't mean nothin' when you look so unhappy, girl."

"That's more than enough," Ursula Stone muttered, leaning across Eliot to jab a scarlet nail on the button to raise the window. She scowled at Eliot. "I told you not to open the window, Eliot!"

"I just wanted some fresh air," Eliot replied, watching as the cyclist ducked in and out of traffic, her slight figure bobbing and weaving. The older woman lifted her middle finger when a truck nearly cut her off, and Eliot managed a small smile, enjoying her in-your-face confidence.

Where else but in New York would someone presume to tell a bride on her wedding day that she looked unhappy?

Ursula—Eliot hadn't called the woman "Mom" since her early teens—turned to the videographer and photographer who sat on the bench seat at right angles to them. "Mark that exchange to be deleted," she barked.

They nodded, knowing Ursula was very much in charge of this production. She and DeShawn's manager had negotiated a deal to sell their wedding photographs to a popular fashion magazine and the video—from the rehearsal dinner to them arriving at their honeymoon destination—to a popular entertainment network. Their exchanged vows would be seen by millions of people around the world.

All Eliot had wanted was a small wedding, with a handful of close friends. On a private beach somewhere, far from the intrusive lenses of the world's press. Her wishes had been, as they often were, ignored.

"Your dress turned out rather well," Ursula stated, pursing her thin lips. "Of course, there's nothing we can do about the fact that you are so overweight, but we can photoshop the images to make you look normal."

This *was* her normal weight, Eliot wanted to shout. This was a good weight, a healthy weight—but she knew that nothing she said would change Ursula's mind. She was, in Ursula's view, fat.

And, unfortunately, the fashion world she'd been a part of for so much of her life—and the casting agents and creative directors, the designers—agreed. While the industry now occasionally featured plus-size models in their campaigns, they didn't make allowances for once skinny models who'd picked up weight. Her face and body were her brand…

DeShawn, her long-term partner and fiancé, had liked the original version of her brand and wasn't thrilled when her ranking as one of the world's top supermodels plummeted.

Frozen to her seat, she stared down at her magnificent engagement ring, which she'd moved to her right hand in anticipation of receiving DeShawn's wedding band. Her engagement ring was a flawless, princess-cut, two-million-dollar, fourteen-carat diamond ring. And she hated it. It was too cold and too ostentatious and, because she'd picked up weight since he'd bought it for her, the band cut into the flesh on her ring finger. Last night she'd had to use soap and a lot of pulling and tugging to transfer it from one hand to the other.

Eliot rested her head back against the leather headrest and wished changing ring sizes was the worst of her problems. Her modeling contracts had dried up, and her mother/manager/agent nagged her incessantly about returning her previous, waif-like weight. DeShawn emailed her diets and exercise regimes and, on his orders, his PA booked her into a "fat clinic," another passive-aggressive way of telling her that she was no longer attractive, that her weight was an issue.

At least now there was a medical explanation. When the weight gain had started, along with the exhaustion, sore muscles and brain fog she'd experienced over the past year, Ursula had been quick to blame it on laziness and lack of discipline. It had taken an official doctor's diagnosis to convince her that something more was going on—specifically, the lack of thyroid hormones in Eliot's system. She now took a daily replacement hormone, was more energetic and her mind felt clearer, but she hadn't managed to shed the excess pounds.

The truth was, she didn't want to go back to her old

size. She wasn't a naturally skinny model and the older she got, the more she needed to play the restrict-my-calories game. Despite her diagnosis, she felt heathier than she had been since her early twenties. She felt more positive, her energy levels had increased and she and woke up feeling refreshed. Not fixating on food came with more benefits than she'd ever realized.

But, of course, there were drawbacks, too. Because her increased size was a big-*freakin'*-deal to her image-conscious loved ones.

They loved the supermodel look, the too-thin clotheshorse who strutted down the catwalks of Milan, London and Paris. They wanted the old Eliot— the lingerie model, the one with the sunken eyes and collarbones, the jutting hip bones and the twig-like legs. She knew she'd never again feature in an international lingerie campaign, stride down a catwalk or appear nearly nude on billboards in Times Square.

Starring in the wedding video and the ten-page spread in *Vogue Magazine* would, most likely, be her last big campaign…

Campaign? God, this was her *wedding* she was talking about.

No, it was her mother's wedding, not hers. She pretty much hated everything about it, from the five hundred guests, to the black-and-white theme, to the choice to not actually walk up the aisle of a church. And the rotten cherry on top of the awful sundae was that they were getting married at the Forrester-Grantham Hotel, which brought back too many memories of Soren Grantham, the man with whom she'd spent three magical nights at a private villa in Ville-franche-sur-Mer. Those sun-drenched days on the French Riviera were the last time she remembered being seen. And heard.

As herself, and not just as a pretty face. Soren had focused all his attention on her, had listened to her…

That mental and emotional connection, along with toe-curling, earthshaking sex, had made him ghosting her all the more baffling. Never hearing from him again hurt far more than it should've for what was, at its core, an ultra-brief affair.

She didn't want to think of Soren today. Not on her wedding day.

So it really would have helped if her mother had chosen a hotel that *didn't* have his name right above the door.

"How are you feeling, Eliot?" the videographer asked her.

She looked into the camera and didn't flinch when the camera's flash hit her eyes. She was far too professional for that.

She knew the answer he wanted… She was feeling excited, a little giddy, hopeful for this new chapter in her life. That she couldn't wait to be DeShawn's wife. She opened her mouth to answer him, wanting to tell him that none of this felt real, that she felt like she was shooting a commercial or starring in a short film for some luxury brand. She was desperate for someone to yell, "Cut!"

How would they react if she told them she was

acting her ass off, the star of a production she felt no connection to?

The hero/bridegroom felt like a stranger, just another man who'd snagged the lead role. She hadn't chosen the costumes; instead of the poofy, princess-style dress, she'd wanted something a little more unusual, more boho. She didn't know three-quarters of the cast, and the guest list was populated by people who were barely more than acquaintances. She'd wanted wildflowers but got white roses. She'd just wanted Madigan as a bridesmaid, but she had five more acquaintances—dark haired models—who'd walk up the fake aisle in front of her and pose in her wedding day pictures.

She hadn't been heard when she gave input into her own wedding day… She was *never* heard. No one saw past her pretty face and her 34-23-33 breasts, waist and hips. Though, these days, she was more of a size 36- 26-36.

Eliot had allowed herself to be overruled, to be persuaded into what everyone else thought was best, because giving people what they wanted—her mother, the casting directors, the heads of campaigns—was her job. They asked her for a look, a walk, or a pose and she obliged.

And over the years, her need to please had spilled over into her personal life and here she was, the leading lady playing her role and feeling disconnected on what was supposed to be the happiest day of her life.

And soon she'd place her wrists in, like that bike

courier had said, the world's smallest pair of hand-cuffs.

The limo slowed down, and Eliot lifted her head to look out the window, realizing they'd reached the fancy portico of the Forrester-Grantham Hotel. A doorman, dressed in a top hat and tails, stepped forward to open the door to the limo.

Looking past him, Eliot caught a glimpse of a tall, broad-shouldered man walking up the steps to the lobby. His back was to her, but the shape of his head, the nut-brown hair and his swimmer's build reminded her of Soren.

Then again, all tall, broad, dark-haired men did.

With him, so long ago, she'd felt like herself, the very best version of who she was. But then he'd left, and it felt like the person she was with him was swamped by the Eliot people needed and wanted her to be.

She'd waited a few weeks to see if he'd get in touch again, tell her that he wanted more than a fling, but when he didn't, she'd moved on, dating extensively. Then, shortly after her twenty-fifth birthday, De-Shawn swept her off her feet, and within months they were living together. Admittedly, they'd never been an emotionally intense couple, but they'd gotten along well enough…before her health issues started. Over the past year, their relationship had cracked, then fractured. Instead of talking, trying to find a solution to their ever-increasing distance, they'd slapped a Band-Aid over what was a gaping wound.

She because she was a people pleaser, he because…
God, she had no idea why.

With DeShawn, she felt like another record label,
another Grammy, another acquisition or status sym-
bol. Another accessory, the star on top of his Christmas tree, or a luxurious but unneeded birthday
present—not necessary but a nice addition.

Occasionally noticed, rarely admired and sometimes half-heartedly played with but not, on any level,
needed. Or considered. Or valued.

Surely she was worth more?

And why was she only admitting all this to herself
minutes before she was expected to say, "I do"?

As yet another stretch limousine pulled up under
the impressive portico, Soren Grantham greeted the
doorman and stepped into the impressive bi-level
lobby. The Forrester-Grantham Hotel oozed old-world
charm from the grand chandeliers to the impressive,
wide staircase that dominated the lobby, reminiscent
of English country houses. It was a landmark hotel
on Madison Avenue, and a home away from home
for European aristocracy, international politicians,
celebrities and powerful captains of industry.

"Soren!"

Turning at the sound of his name, Soren greeted
the head concierge with a smile. Garth was in his
sixties now and he'd started as a table clearer in
Avangeline's nearly forty years ago, employed by
his grandmother when he was just sixteen years old.

"You look stressed," Garth told him, dropping the

plummy accent he used with the other guests and allowing traces of his Brooklyn roots to slide into his speech.

"I'm fine, Garth," he told him, ignoring the curious glances from many of the guests walking through the busy lobby.

"Are they here yet?" Soren asked after a few minutes of catching up.

"They are waiting for you in Avangeline's," Garth replied.

Soren looked right. Jack had sent him photos of the recently redecorated restaurant named after his grandmother, and he liked the light and fresh colors of cream and duck egg blue. It was the second time Avangeline's had been renovated in ten years by Fox and Jack and he preferred this look to the gray and gold it had been before.

When their grandmother had owned it, her signature colors had been pink and green, very eighties and, in his opinion, horrible. Bad décor or not, the famous restaurant had started his grandmother's meteoric rise to become one of the world's top restauranteurs and hoteliers. At the height of her power, she'd owned a chain of exceptional establishments around the world. This hotel was the only one she'd kept, renting it out to a consortium to manage after she sold her empire to focus on her grandchildren following the deaths of her sons and their wives.

Hard to believe he'd lost his folks twenty-five years ago, when he was just nine.

Garth pulled him back to the present. "Shall I show you through?"

"No, don't bother…" Soren caught the disappointment in Garth's eyes. He wanted to show everyone in the hotel and restaurant—some of the richest and most powerful people in the country—that he, Garth Gosling, was on friendly terms with one of the most celebrated sportsmen in the world. He didn't need to be wearing his stack of Olympic swimming medals to draw attention. He was recognized everywhere he went, especially here, on his home turf.

"Lead on," Soren told Garth, sliding his hands into the pockets of his dark gray pants.

Garth's chest puffed out, Soren noticed, amused, as the man led him to where Jack, Fox and Merrick sat.

Jack and Fox—and Malcolm, when he was alive—were Soren's cousins, but having been raised by their grandmother after being orphaned young, they considered themselves brothers in every way that counted. Merrick, the son of Avangeline's housekeeper, was another, albeit non-blood, brother.

Malcolm should be here… It was incredibly unfair that the best of them, their leader, their brightest star, had lost his life in a high-speed bike accident just short of his twenty-fifth birthday.

Soren swallowed the lump in his throat as his brothers stood up and manly hugs were exchanged, backs slapped. Soren chose to sit with his back to the room and immediately released a long sigh. Around these men he could be himself, relax, chill.

They, along with Avangeline and Jacinda, Merrick's

mom, were the only people he trusted. Ever. The only people he could love. Because love, unfortunately, was synonymous with loss. In his mind, it was always better to hold back than to run the risk of loving someone and having them leave you.

"We've just ordered, Soren," Jack told him. "What would you like to eat?"

It was day one of his three-week break from training and he didn't need as many calories as he normally did. He ordered a normal portion and three sets of eyebrows rose.

"Are you ill?" Merrick asked him.

"If I retire, I'm going to have to learn to start eating like a normal person," he said, testing the waters. Retirement was constantly on his mind, but he hadn't broached the idea with his family before...

"No way are you ready to retire," Fox scoffed, sounding dismissive.

Jack shook his head. "What would you do with yourself?" he demanded. It was a fair question and Soren didn't know the answer.

"You've got far too much gas in your tank to think about giving up swimming," Merrick said, adding his two cents' worth.

Because they didn't think he was being serious, and he didn't correct them, they swiftly moved on to another subject.

Soren sighed. He found expressing himself difficult so didn't tell them that, before he renewed team and sponsorship deals, he was taking a break, to give himself time to decide whether he was going to commit to another two years of competitive swimming. Only his trainer and business manager knew he was considering walking away from his career while he was at the top of his game.

After winning just one medal in the 2012 Olympic Games—as part of a medley—he'd annihilated his competition in the 2016 Games, taking home three gold medals. After doubling his Olympic medal haul in Tokyo in 2021 and setting two new world records, he was thinking it might be time to throw in the towel. He was having to train harder and longer to maintain his form, stay fit and hit his times. His body was aging and by the time 2024 rolled around, he suspected he might struggle to stay competitive. Maybe it was time to accept that his life as a world-class swimmer was winding down…

But accepting that was tricky when he had no idea what came next, or who he'd be in his post-swimming life. Swimming was all he knew; he didn't have much of a life—or any life—outside of the sport. When he wasn't in the water, he was in the gym or catching up on his sleep. He had the occasional one-night stand with other athletes who treated the act as he did: it was a way to scratch an itch, an hour or two of pleasure in between training sessions.

He needed to have another plan in place before he walked away from his career—something he could throw his considerable energy into.

His brothers, if he asked them, would make a place for him in their astonishingly successful organizations. But he didn't want a handout. Like his grandmother, he liked to see the fruits of his labor, and to stand and fall by his own efforts.

He should be able to talk to his brothers about this, but he found articulating his thoughts difficult. Soren, preferring to keep his thoughts in his head, only spoke when he felt it worth it to do so—and he especially struggled when it came to a conversation about anything deep or meaningful. Emotional intimacy was terrifying. There was a reason why he was called Ice Man by his swimming colleagues. He wasn't the least bit warm. Or approachable.

There had only been one person, outside of his family, who'd made a crack in the sheet of ice he'd built around himself...

Jack glanced at his watch and shifted in his seat. "Got someplace you need to be?" Fox asked him.

"We have the Stone-Connell wedding starting in twenty minutes in the Cairanne Ballroom," Jack replied. "It's been touted as the wedding of the year, and I need to touch base with the event staff a bit later."

The hotel was one of the city's top wedding venues, a favorite amongst New York A-listers.

Wait, hold on, did he say *Stone*? Soren frowned. "Are you talking about Eliot Stone, the supermodel?"

"Yeah, that's right. She's marrying DeShawn Connell, the music producer, this afternoon," Fox confirmed.

Eliot was getting married? What the hell? That was all kinds of wrong.

Soren sat back, feeling like he'd just done a ten-mile training session at speed, short of breath and chest heaving. Why was he reacting like this? He'd said goodbye to her eight years ago—after three days of sun, sea and stunning sex in the south of France—at Paris's Charles de Gaulle Airport and then, through sheer necessity, put her out of his mind.

He hadn't seen or spoken to her since then and did not have the right to be upset about her marrying anyone else.

But he was, dammit. She'd been the only one outside of his family to crack his icy layer...and wasn't that the reason he'd ghosted her? Because she was the only woman who could distract him from his training, from his goal of becoming one of the best Olympians of all time?

"Anyway, we need to talk about Avangeline," Fox said, resting his forearms on the table. "I'm worried about her."

It took all of Soren's effort to turn his attention from Elliot's imminent marriage to his octogenarian grandmother.

"We asked her lawyer to talk to her about writing her will but Avangeline refused to see him," Jack told them, looking concerned.

Soren sighed, worried for his brothers. It had been Malcolm's idea to reestablish the chain of restaurants Avangeline had sold off when she'd taken them in—and she'd gifted Mal, Fox and Jack with this hotel and loaned them the start-up capital to renovate and reinvent the business. She had a loan account with the company, owned shares and was a director. Avangeline had also loaned Merrick the capital to establish his wildly popular chain of food trucks serving healthy fast food across the US and Europe. Like the others, there were implications for Merrick if Avangeline died intestate. Without her leaving specific instructions, his brothers' companies would be tied up in legal red tape for years.

"She's dealt with lawyers all her life. She knows how important it is to cross the *i*'s and cross the *t*'s," Jack muttered.

"That's not all of it," Merrick said. The apprehension in his eyes had hairs rising on the back of Soren's neck. Somehow, he knew that whatever Merrick said next would have a huge impact on his family going forward.

"I took a call from Mom a short while ago. She said Avangeline has company at the moment," Merrick stated. "And her guest is the recipient of Mal's donated liver. This Alyson Garwood might be someone preying on Avangeline, angling for money."

Soren saw anxiety flash in Merrick's eyes and he frowned, instantly on high alert. Fox was the powerhouse of their foursome, the guy who got things done. Jack was the negotiator, the face of Grantham International, and Soren was the introvert, the loner. Merrick, especially after Malcolm's death, saw himself as their protector, the guy who would step in front of a bullet for his non-blood brothers.

And Merrick was, uncharacteristically, jumpy.

"What else, Merrick?" Soren demanded.

Merrick ran his hand over the lower portion of his face, a gesture that revealed his unease.

"Personally, I think it's bullshit but apparently this woman claims—"

They all waited for Merrick to continue. Then waited some more.

"Well, what did she say?' Fox demanded.

Merrick shook his head. "I genuinely think it's better you hear it from her, not me. It concerns your brother."

Fox glared at him. "Stop talking crap, Merrick. Malcolm was as much your brother as he was ours."

A mixture of gratitude and sadness appeared in Merrick's eyes. "Normally, I'd agree with you but this is on a deeper, weirder level. I think you should hear what she has to say from her mouth, not mine."

"Since Malcolm is acting mysterious, someone needs to go to Calcott Manor and see what's going on," Fox said, his expression grim.

"We can't, Fox. We've got functions to oversee and a hotel to run. And we have a board meeting first thing in the morning," Jack replied.

"On a Sunday?" Merrick asked.

"It was the only time we could all be present for the next three months," Fox explained.

"It needs to be you or Fox, Jack," Merrick said.

They seemed to have forgotten that Soren was on a break. He trained in Florida but he'd planned on heading to Calcott Manor anyway, as he explained to his brothers. "I'll go up this afternoon, see what's going on. I'll confront this Garwood woman and see what has Merrick spooked," he told them, rolling his eyes at Merrick. "And I'll try to speak to our stubborn grandmother about making a will."

He took in their relieved expressions and the easing of tense shoulders, and was glad he could help, just a little. He wasn't a part of their businesses but he'd step up for his family whenever they needed him to.

He'd move mountains for them if he could. And even if he couldn't, he'd find a way.

Tenacity, perseverance and determination—he had more than his fair share of all of those, he thought, tucking into his lobster-and-prawn ravioli pasta. . He didn't fail, it wasn't in his nature and he'd get to the bottom of whatever was happening at Calcott Manor. Of that, he had no doubt.

Soren was just one bite into his meal when all hell broke loose.

Two

"Shit, they haven't made it down the aisle," Jack muttered, staring at his phone in horror.

"Who?" Merrick asked.

Soren didn't need the answer to that question; he knew. Without hesitation or an explanation, and not even knowing why, he shoved his chair back and took off, heading out of the restaurant and toward a cleverly concealed staff door past the entrance to Avangeline's. Finding the hidden lever, he walked into a very prosaic hallway filled with a set of boring stairs. Going down would lead to the kitchens and the underground parking area. Two floors up were the ballrooms, the smaller of which was, as Jack told them earlier, being used as a chapel for the wedding. No doubt the adjoining ballroom was the venue for the reception.

As he stormed up the stairs, Soren asked himself what he was doing, why he was so desperate to get to Eliot, and what he thought he could contribute. He'd kissed her goodbye nearly a decade ago, her scent and the spicy taste of her mouth lingering for hours, days. He hadn't spoken to or seen her since.

So why was he thundering up the staff staircase?

He didn't know but wild horses couldn't make him change direction. Seeing the door that would take him onto the right floor, he stepped into the hallway and carnage—of the wedding kind.

Soren moved back to plaster himself against the nearest wall as DeShawn Connell passed him with a foot to spare, his eyebrows lowered into a scowl. His braids touched his shoulders and the large diamond in his earlobe winked. Soren looked around. Two young flower girls—six or seven, maybe?—sat cross-legged on the carpet at the end of the hallway, playing with the black ribbons on their white dresses. An enormous, lily-filled bouquet sat on a gateleg table and a tall, willowy brunette dressed in a sleek black dress had one arm around the bride's waist…a bride who, sorta, kinda, looked like Eliot.

That wooden, tense woman looked like a caricature of the woman he'd known in France. Through her filmy veil he noticed her too-pale face and her lips were the wrong shade of red. Her blue eyes, normally electric, were dull and lifeless and her long blond hair had been blow-dried, straightened and then twisted into a series of overly elaborate knots. It looked more like a wig than the silky locks he once ran his hands through. Her dress was an abomination of lace and beads, with a puffball skirt made from a material that looked shockingly expensive but also heavy and stiff.

Having spent a lot of time online—torturing himself—he'd seen pictures of her in ball gowns and bikinis, outrageous catwalk couture outfits and elegant, designer creations for red carpet events. But she still looked best as he remembered her, wearing a pair of loose, short denim cutoffs and a bold tangerine bikini, with her damp hair tumbling down her back and her bright blue eyes looking over her sand-dusted shoulder. Eliot didn't need makeup, accessories or to be photoshopped— she was naturally beautiful.

Soren looked around. A member of the hotel staff, a worried-looking woman dressed in corporate black and holding a clipboard, stood next to the flower girls, while a woman who could only be Eliot's mother— same blond hair, facial features and blue eyes—stood shoulder to shoulder with DeShawn. Right: it was obvious where her loyalties lay.

Off to the side stood a guy with a video camera in his hands, recording it all with the gleeful grin of a man with a front-row seat to the juiciest celebrity debacle of the decade.

" I've decided to call the wedding off, Eliot. You're not the girl I want to marry. Not anymore," DeShawn stated in his deep, rich voice.

His pronouncement sent a shock wave through the hallway and everyone, including Eliot, tensed.

Her face lost its last vestige of color. "You *don't* want to marry me?" she asked, in a shaky voice.

DeShawn rubbed the back of his neck. "No, I don't. I've had my doubts for a while but they've just gotten stronger over the last six months or so," he admitted. What the hell was wrong with the guy? Soren asked himself. Didn't he realize how lucky he was that she'd said yes?

He expected the first hot response to come from Eliot, but it was her mom who released the first barrage of vitriol—aimed in the dead-wrong direction. Middle-aged, and super-thin, the icy blonde walked up to Eliot and grabbed her shoulders in a claw-like grip, her face ugly with anger.

"After all the work, all the money we spent, the publicity, how could you do this? This is your fault. You are a fat embarrassment!"

Whoa, hold on. Eliot was not fat. She wasn't even in the ballpark. And even if she had been, who the hell cared? And this was her wedding day! Weren't people supposed to be, at the very least, nice to the bride?

And how was this her fault when it was Connell who wanted out?

"Ursula, stop," the dark-haired maid of honor murmured. "Take a deep breath and calm down. Let's find out what's happening before we jump to any—"

"Do you see what you've done?" the older woman screamed at Eliot. "You pushed him away, you idiot!"

"Ursula, seriously!" The brunette pushed heavy bangs out of her eyes and Soren recognized her as another model, a friend of Eliot's. Marnie, Mattie… No, Madigan. Madigan Something.

Eliot, he noticed, just ignored her mother and kept her eyes on DeShawn's face.

"Carry on, DeShawn," Eliot murmured, still looking like she was cast from marble. "You were saying that you don't want to marry me. Care to explain?"

DeShawn ran a finger around the collar of his shirt. "When we got together, you were a supermodel, but you haven't done any significant campaigns in nearly a year. We don't have anything in common anymore. You don't come to my gigs or jam sessions and I can't remember when last you were in a club. You never want to do anything *fun*…"

Soren had never had more fun in his life than those days he'd spent with Eliot—but they'd been low-key days, spent on the beach, or in bed, or sharing a quiet meal somewhere intimate and relaxed. Nothing glitzy or glamorous or shallow or fake.

He clearly remembered Eliot telling him she hated the celeb scene, that she loved staying at home, keeping it casual with a few good friends rather than being out and about. She loathed being photographed when she wasn't working and didn't enjoy public events or cocktail parties. After having her drink spiked when she was younger and being rescued by a friend, she detested clubs with a passion bordering on pathological.

"And you know, the weight thing, it's a problem."

He saw devastation flicker in her eyes and Soren clenched his fists. What a prick! Despite the awful dress and ridiculous hair, she was the most beautiful bride he'd ever seen. Didn't Connell have eyes in his head? Were they working? And what was their obsession with her fuller curves?

"DeShawn, seriously!" Madigan shouted and pulled Eliot close. Soren saw the fine tremors racking her bare arms, her wobbly chin and her frantically bobbing throat. She was on the verge of losing it and he didn't blame her.

That asshole videographer took a step closer, capturing every pixel of her devastation…and that was the last straw for Soren.

He wasn't the type to walk into drama—if anything he walked away from it, as fast as he could—but there was no way he was going to let Eliot be emotionally eviscerated on camera for everyone to see. Eliot needed to get out of there.

He walked up to the party, half pushed himself between her and DeShawn—taking real pleasure in hip-checking the cameraman, making him stumble—and held out his hand to her. "Come with me, Eliot."

Eliot didn't acknowledge his words and didn't drop her eyes from DeShawn.

"Who the hell are you, dude?" DeShawn demanded.

Soren ignored him. DeShawn knew who he was. His face, thanks to a number of celebrity endorsements, was instantly recognizable. Soren darted a quick look at Madigan, caught her eye and saw her quick nod. Soren took Madigan's place and snaked his arm around Eliot's waist, pulling her to him. She was tall but was still a few inches shorter than him and right now, she felt fragile.

"Come with me, Eliot," he told her, knowing he needed to be commanding to get her feet to move.

"You can't leave," DeShawn shouted, suddenly realizing that she was leaving with another man. "*I'm* the one who's supposed to be leaving!"

Soren blistered him with a hot glare. "Go right ahead. Start there," he said and pointed to the closed door leading to the ballroom. "Since you were the one to call the wedding off, you can tell your guests, and the press, that the wedding is not going ahead. And now, it's time for Eliot to leave," Soren snapped.

He started to move, walking Eliot away. At the service door—there was no way he was taking her through the public spaces of the Forrester-Grantham Hotel—he looked back at DeShawn. "Be a gentleman and make her look good, Connell. You owe her that for being an absolute prick and for not calling it off sooner."

Soren led Eliot into the plain, dull hallway. He locked the door behind him and looked at the narrow set of stairs. He picked up her veil and tossed it over her head, before putting his hand on her lower back to gesture for her to start walking down.

She'd yet to acknowledge his presence, or ask why

he was there. She was in shock, Soren decided. Who wouldn't be after a morning like hers?

Eliot slowly shook her head. "Those stairs look steep and I don't want to trip in my heels. My skirt is too heavy and my train, which is stuck in the door, is too long."

Soren looked back, saw that the end of her train had gotten jammed in the door, and quietly cursed. DeShawn and her mother were both pounding the thin wooden paneling, shouting at him to flip the lock.

Not a chance in hell.

No, he'd have to get rid of six feet of material another way. He turned her around and inspected the back of her dress. After tugging on the train, he realized it was attached by a row of tiny, hidden buttons that could only be undone by skilled, nimble and preferably small fingers. His were not.

"Do you want to talk to Connell again? To try and sort this out?" Soren asked her. He didn't think she did but thought he should check.

"God, no!"

Good enough for him. She wouldn't be needing the dress again so there was no need to keep up appearances anymore. He gave the train a sharp tug and buttons flew to ping off the linoleum floor. He ripped at the fabric again and the train fell to the floor...

"That's high-grade silk sewn with platinum thread," Eliot whispered, staring down at the material on the floor. "The metallic thread makes it shimmer."

He was about to tell her how little he cared but

caught the shock in her eyes. The tears in her eyes had nothing to do with the damaged train but with this train wreck of a day. Instead of speaking, he gathered a handful of her skirt at the back of her legs and lifted the fabric off the floor. He pulled his eyes off her sexy shoes—a complicated confection of soft leather and beads—and the tanned skin of her amazing legs thinking she could now move more freely.

"Let's go, Eliot. On the way I'll make arrangements for a private car to pick us up at one of the service entrances," he said as they started down the stairs.

"Where are we going?" she asked, her voice reed thin.

He took a moment to answer her, thinking. He assumed the news that the wedding was off had already reached the press and he had no doubt the paparazzi, who had already gathered to witness the wedding, would be waiting for her outside the hotel and the apartment she shared with Connell. Sensing blood in the water, the sharks wouldn't be kind. If Connell allowed her into their shared home, and that was doubtful, she wouldn't be able to leave for days, possibly a week or more without being mobbed. Her phone would ring off the hook, her inbox would fill up with emails and everyone who had the smallest connection to her would want a piece of her—or have a story to sell.

That was what happened when you lived your life in the public eye. He didn't want that for her after this car crash of a wedding and he could think of only one place where she could, to a large extent, be safe from the flashing cameras and in-your-face questions.

"I'm taking you to my grandmother's estate in Connecticut. It's gated, has tons of security and you'll be out of the public eye there," Soren told her, in the gentlest voice he could muster. "Is that okay with you?"

Eliot nodded, just once, and continued her descent down the stairs, with him following and taking most of the weight of her surprisingly heavy dress. At the landing to the next floor, she turned to look up at him, her face even whiter than it had been before.

"Why are you here? What the hell just happened?" she softly asked.

Soren wanted to tell her that she'd dodged a bullet but didn't think she wanted to hear that. Not right now, at least. Probably not ever.

"You just got jilted, Eliot."

When they finally got off the death trap stairs, Soren led her on a fast, twisty path through the bowels of the hotel and down many narrow hallways, still helping her with her heavy skirt. Her mind felt fuzzy and she couldn't believe she was running away from her wedding with Soren Grantham, the man she'd never been able to forget. Why was he there? Had she really been jilted? What was happening? But Soren's quick pace didn't allow for any questions.

Her fingers cramping from holding up the front of her dress, they stepped into yet another kitchen, where pastry chefs placed tiny cakes, sandwiches and petit fours on silver stands for afternoon tea, an institution at the Forrester-Grantham hotel.

A thin chef, wearing a ridiculously tall hat, took one look at her and grimaced, hopefully in sympathy. He picked up a tray of tiny, mirror-glazed chocolate cakes and thrust it at Eliot. "Girl," he said, snapping his fingers, "you look like you need chocolate."

Eliot took a cake and popped it into her mouth, her eyes closing as the twin delights of buttery cake and dark chocolate hit her mouth. "I thought I needed wine but I need ten more of these."

Eliot shoved in another morsel, tasting dark, rich chocolate and a little burst of orange on her tongue. "So good," she muttered, as Soren's hand on her back pushed her along. The cakes gave her a small sugar rush and the veil of shock started to lift. She looked around and saw she was in a storage room containing, yes—awesome!—boxes of wine.

"Chocolate and wine," she said, a little dreamily. "I could live down here."

Soren, his eyes on the screen of his phone, didn't respond. He just pulled her over to an exit, plugged in a code and, when he heard the locks disengage, pushed open the heavy door. Eliot stepped onto a small loading dock in a narrow, empty and very dingy ally.

"Where are we?" Eliot asked.

"This is the original loading dock for the hotel."

Soren dropped her skirt and she felt the heavy pull

of the fabric biting into her shoulders. She'd never really liked this dress, but now she hated it. She watched as Soren slid his hands into the pockets of his dark gray pants. His open-necked linen shirt was pale cream and untucked, sleeves rolled up his arms.

"Why are we here?" Eliot asked, trying to make sense of all the twists and turns of her crappy day.

"My brother Jack is arranging for one of his minions to deliver a car for us here," Soren explained.

Eliot looked at him, taking in his hyper-masculine face, with thick eyebrows over those deep green eyes. He was tanned and, when he spoke, his teeth flashed white. With his amazing swimmer's body, wide shoulders, slim hips and long legs, she could see why he was frequently asked to feature on the cover of magazines and to endorse sporting wear and male grooming products.

And why she was so attracted to him so long ago.

If anything, he was better looking than he'd been eight years ago. Age had added character to his face, though his expression seemed more guarded.

But that could be because he'd just picked up a jilted bride and didn't know how to handle her.

She didn't blame him; she didn't know how to handle the situation either. She hadn't read the What-To-Do-If-Your-Wedding-Is-Called-Off-At-The-Last-Minute guidebook.

"Why are you doing this?" Eliot demanded.

"Did you want to walk out through the main lobby

of one of the city's most fashionable hotels in your wedding dress, missing your train?"

"No, of course not," she muttered. "You know what I'm asking, Soren! Why did you run to my rescue? How did you even *know* something was wrong?"

Something flickered in Soren's eyes but she couldn't identify the emotion before his mask of imperturbability returned. "I was having lunch with my brothers, who own this hotel. They got word that you hadn't made it down the aisle and the wedding wasn't going to plan. I came up, saw the drama and decided you needed a getaway plan." He gestured to the keypad on the closed door behind him. "If you like, I can return you to the melee."

Eliot shuddered. "It's just that, of all the people in the world, you're the last person I expected to run to my aid…"

"Because I didn't contact you after Villefranche-sur-Mer."

Well, at least he wasn't going to pretend their sun-filled interlude was a product of her imagination. She was already having a bad day—she'd just been jilted, her mother was on-the-point-of-exploding furious and she'd just paid thirty thousand dollars for a dress that was, essentially, ruined—so she might as well satisfy her curiosity and find out why he'd ghosted her the way he had.

Things couldn't, after all, get much worse.

"Why did you?" she demanded.

Soren's eyes locked on to hers, wariness in those deep green depths. "Eliot, you've just been dumped, minutes before you were about to walk up the aisle. Let's park that conversation for now, okay?"

She narrowed her eyes, and shook her head, wincing when a hairpin dug into her skull. She tried to push her fingers into her hair to get to the pin but didn't get very far because of the tight, complicated knots were cemented in place with buckets of hair spray and gel. Currently, her hair held more product than a hairdresser's salon. But the pins were making her headache worse so they had to come out.

Now.

Patting her head, she found and pulled out one pin, felt a heavy curl fall, and pulled out another. "No, I want an explanation. Why did you say that we'd see each other again and then change your mind?"

Soren's chest rose and fell. "Eliot…"

She pointed a hairpin at him. "Don't *Eliot* me. I want an explanation. I deserve one, dammit!"

The thing was, she wasn't heartbroken or hurt by today's events, just…well, *relieved*. The fallout over being jilted would be horrendous, she accepted that, but it would eventually blow over. But it was small beer compared to the scandal of marrying, leaving and divorcing DeShawn. Because that was where they'd been heading…

Why didn't she have the courage to call off the wedding herself?

She hadn't had the guts to do that—shame on her— but she *could* demand some answers from Soren right now.

A heavy mass of hair fell into her hand in a tangle

of sticky curls and knots. With the bulk of her hair falling to one side, she had to tilt her head to see, making her feel like a quizzical bird.

"Give me an explanation I can believe, Grantham."

She stood on the grimy loading dock, her eyes on his face, a part of her holding her breath as she waited for his reply. He had the sexiest mouth; his bottom lip was fuller than his top lip, and he had just the right amount of stubble covering his lower face—short enough to look like he'd forgotten to shave for a couple of days, but long enough so it wouldn't scratch. He knew how to use that mouth, Eliot remembered. And not just on *her* mouth…

"You were a distraction I couldn't afford."

Eliot, caught up in the lusty memory, blinked, trying to make sense of his words. Distraction…blah blah…afford.

She ran a hand over her face. "Sorry?"

Soren frowned. "I was going back into training and I needed to give my career everything I had. I didn't have space for you."

Ooh, ouch. Eliot's hands returned to her hair. Ouch because the knots were tangled, double ouch on being a distraction.

"I wasn't asking you to marry me and give me babies, Grantham," Eliot retorted. "I was thinking more about text messages, emails, the occasional dinner. Dammit, this hair!"

"Why are we talking about France when you've just been jilted, Eliot?" Soren demanded, moving closer to her and batting her hands away. He went to work on the biggest knot in her hair and she stood still, sucking in her breath every time his fingers brushed her neck, sending sparks dashing along her skin.

Eliot felt off-balance at his presence. She inhaled his scent—something lemony, a little woodsy—and resisted the urge to pull his collar aside and bury her nose where the big muscles of his shoulders met his strong neck.

If she undid a button, she could slide her hand into his shirt and cover his pec, swipe her thumb across his flat nipple.

If she pulled up his shirt, her fingers could drift across his ladder-like, hard-as-rock abs, drift down lower to where she could see the way his erection strained against the fabric of his pants. It soothed her battered ego to realize that he wanted her, just like she wanted him.

Eliot felt her heavy hair tumble down her back, and when she tipped her face up to look at Soren, he'd lost his shield of impassivity and his eyes burned with green fire from beneath lowered lids. She saw the muscle ticking in his jaw, and caught his whispered *"Shit, I shouldn't."*

When his hand curled around her neck and his thumb tipped her jaw up, she knew he was going to kiss her.

Standing on a grubby loading dock in her now-wrinkled wedding dress, she wanted him to…

She'd never wanted anything more.

Soren's tongue swept between her parted lips, branding, rediscovering, wiping away any questions and thoughts of "What the hell am I doing?" All that mattered was that she was in his arms, that she was feeling *something*...

Something hot, something intense, something... real. That for the first time in months, years, she felt connected, *alive*...

Soren yanked the heavy silk of her skirt up and, with the material falling over his wrist and arm, ran his hand up her thigh, palmed her butt with a big, broad—dare she say it?—masterful hand. He shoved his other hand into the hair at the back of her head and angled her face to receive his heated, not-gonna-stop kiss. Tongues danced as he devoured her mouth, relearning and rediscovering her, pulling her against his hard body.

Inspired by his passion and turned on both by his touch and by his groans of appreciation, Eliot did as she wanted and pulled his shirt up so that she could stroke his fire-hot body. *So solid*, she thought. Muscular, but not in a bodybuilder, show-offy type of way... just a body conditioned to be as fast and as powerful as it could be. Her fingers reacquainted themselves with the rows of his six-pack and the long muscles that covered his hips, then brushed over the hard erection that tented his pants.

No one but Soren had ever made her feel like this, exhilarated and on fire, like she was dancing along the edge of a volcano or surfing the bands of a hurricane. Flying, swooping, *living*. How could she have settled for less than this? Soren pulled his mouth off hers, stepping back. He pushed a hand through his dark hair and released a low, frustrated groan. She blinked at him, trying to make sense of the last few minutes.

"What's wrong?' she asked, feeling like she was standing on a creaky, coming-apart life raft in a turbulent sea.

"What's *wrong*?" Soren repeated. "Well, let's see. I last saw you eight years ago. Twenty minutes after meeting you again, I'm fighting the urge to take you up against a dirty wall in a disgusting alley, thinking how I can make it work with you in that ridiculous dress!"

It shocked Eliot that she wasn't opposed to that idea. She wanted Soren. It was very obvious that her raging attraction to the blasted man hadn't dissipated in the years they'd spent apart or been tamed by her long engagement and non-wedding. Or even by the events of the day. And, hell yeah, she loved seeing the look of desire on his sexy face, knowing how much he wanted her, even though she wore a stupid dress and was larger than before.

"Don't give me an 'I'm up for that' look!" Soren shouted at her. "You've just walked away from your wedding, your life has been turned upside down and I took advantage of you when you looked at me with those incredible eyes..."

Oh, wait, hold on. She wasn't an unwilling participant…

"And, as the cherry on this shit show, my brother has been standing there for God knows how long!" Soren roared.

"And I could've been a reporter for all the attention you two paid me," someone said from behind her, a bite in his voice.

Soren swore and Eliot noticed the uncharacteristic flush on his cheekbones. They'd lost control and he clearly hated it. She wasn't crazy about the notion either. And he was right. They shouldn't have kissed where anyone could stumble across them. Correction: they shouldn't have kissed *at all*. Eliot turned around to see a tall blonde standing next to the driver's door of a luxurious black SUV with tinted windows.

"I'm Jack Grantham," he said, moving away from the car. "I'm sorry about your wedding."

Eliot, feeling like she was sitting on the point of a spinning top, released a long sigh. She was minutes into being jilted, was still in her awful wedding dress and had kissed another man. What else was today going to throw at her?

Soren took her hand in his and helped her down the loading dock's steep stairs. She stumbled, he cursed and he bunched her skirt in his hand to keep her from tripping. "I hate this dress," he muttered.

She did, too, and she couldn't wait to get rid of it. At the bottom of the steps, Soren took the keys from his brother's hand. "Thanks, Jack."

Eliot caught the thunderous scowl Jack sent Soren. "Do you two even know each other?"

Soren nodded. "France, nearly a decade ago. We spent some time together. Had an affair."

Eliot closed her eyes at his terse, but true, statement.

"Well, that goes a little way to explaining why you shot out of the restaurant and why you kissed the jilted bride." Jack nailed Soren with a hard stare. "You really need to talk more, Soren."

Jack turned his attention to her, and she swallowed at the sympathy she saw in his eyes. "Are you okay, Eliot?"

Eliot nodded, her fingers drifting across her forehead. "It's been quite a day," she answered.

"If my brother took advantage of your emotional state, I'll thump him for you," Jack offered, his tone calm but his eyes showing sincere protectiveness.

Eliot immediately shook her head. "No need. I was a… God, how embarrassing is this?" She took a deep breath and pushed out her words. "I was, um, willing. We have…chemistry."

"Happy now, white knight?" Soren demanded.

"Bite me," Jack snapped back, still unhappy. "It shouldn't have happened, and you know it."

They stared at each other and after a few seconds, Soren's shoulders slumped. "You're right," Soren replied, remorse in his eyes.

The brothers exchanged another long look, but Jack eventually nodded, and a little tension left Soren's body.

"What's going on upstairs?" Soren asked, in his water-rolling-over-gravel voice.

"Connell is hiding out in the honeymoon suite, and your mother is with him, Eliot."

"Of course she is," Eliot muttered, not surprised. Ursula wasn't someone she could rely on to stand behind her.

"They are with Connell's publicist, trying to do damage control because—" Jack grimaced "—the word is already out about your split. Someone filmed the scene in the hallway and uploaded it."

"The videographer," Soren said with a groan. "Dammit, I should have taken that camera."

God, she'd forgotten about the two guys who'd been in her face all day. Eliot guessed that when their footage was released into the world, it would be riveting entertainment. Who didn't like drama? "In fairness, it could also have been one of my bridesmaids," she admitted.

"Nice friends you've got," Soren muttered.

Eliot was too tired to explain that her mother had chosen her bridesmaids, except for Madigan. If she did, she'd have to explain why she didn't stick up for herself, why she didn't put her foot down, why she felt like her life was one long commercial shoot and that she'd allowed other people to make important decisions for her. That she'd been no more effective than a leaf bobbing on a stormy sea.

Well, that was all over now. She needed to take control and that meant figuring out what came next.

"Wherever you go, you're going to be mobbed by the press and paparazzi," Jack explained. "It's already a huge story and it's just going to get bigger. I suggest you avoid your apartment for a while."

Soren tossed the car keys from one hand to the other. "I'm going to take her to Calcott Manor," he told Jack. He sounded reluctant and a little pissed off and his tone shot steel into Eliot's spine.

Huh, so that's what it felt like to have a backbone. "I don't need you to do anything you don't want to do," she told Soren in her iciest voice. Running away with Soren wasn't a realistic option anyway.

She had to face the fallout eventually—now was as good a time as any. "Jack, if you'll take me up to the honeymoon suite, preferably via the hidden corridors so I can dodge the paps, then I'll deal with De-Shawn and my mother."

Soren made a face. "How do you see that conversation going?"

"I imagine that after we yell at each other for a while, we can move on to practical matters such as returning gifts, sending personal notes of apology and issuing a press release."

"I'm afraid that's not possible," Jack said, sounding genuinely apologetic as he held up his phone. "I just got a text from the front desk. DeShawn called down and told them that you aren't allowed back into the suite he booked and paid for."

Right, so talking wasn't an option.

There had to be another solution. "I'm pretty sure

my friend Madigan is still around. If you can find her, she'll take me to her place."

Jack shook his head. "She's already made her escape—I saw her when I was leaving. And I don't think you should go anywhere on your own. Madigan was mobbed by journalists and I'm pretty sure they'll be covering her place, too. As she is your best friend, it's the most logical place for you to go.

"As for the paparazzi, they would kill for a photo of you looking like that," Jack added.

She couldn't look that bad, could she? Jack answered her unspoken question by opening the camera app on his phone and handing her the screen. She stared at the screen and gasped, thinking that she looked like a Halloween ghoul bride. Her hair was a tangle of curls and knots, sticking wildly in every direction. Her smoky eye makeup was too dark, as was her lipstick and, apart from two prominent strips of blush, her skin was ashen.

Looking down, she noted that her dress was wrinkled, the hem grubby. She looked like she'd been dragged through a bush backward. Why, with her looking like this, had Soren kissed her?

She thrust the phone back to Jack. "You're right, I'd hate anyone to see me looking like this."

Jack nodded. "So, let's make sure that doesn't happen, okay?" Eliot appreciated his practicality and low-energy vibe. He was good-looking, too. So why did Soren set off fireworks inside her every time their eyes met? It made no sense.

Then again, nothing about this day did.

"I had my security team toss the press out of the hotel, but they are building up outside all the entrances and exits. Some are even hanging around the service doors. It's not going to be long before they find this one," Jack explained.

"We should go, then," Soren said, walking around the car to open the passenger door for Eliot. "They have no reason to link me to Eliot and they won't know where she's gone."

Jack grimaced. "Too late for that," he explained. "Your grim face is all over that video. You two are linked and the press is wondering why you were there and about your connection to Eliot. And if there are any pictures of your time together in France, they'll dig those up and publish them."

There were, Eliot recalled, images of them dancing together at the Ambassador's Ball, sliding into a car together. She had copies of those photographs in a memory box at the back of her closet.

Soren slapped his hand against his forehead and released a tortured groan. "Can this day get any worse?"

Jack sent Eliot a sympathetic smile. "The best option is to go to Calcott Manor and hide out there until the furor dies down."

Eliot gestured to her dress. "I can't arrive at your grandmother's house looking like this."

"Okay, then let's swing by your place, and pick up your clothes, your makeup, some shoes. Let's give the press what they want—a picture of you and me, together."

Eliot scowled at Soren. "There's no need to be so sarcastic," she told him.

Soren looked down the alley and exchanged a worried glance with Jack. "We can sort out clothes and your stuff later, Eliot. Just get in the damn car... please."

It was the *please* that did it. It was only one word but within it, she heard concern, frustration, and a little bit of panic. He was bossy and sarcastic and radiated annoyance, but she was sure he wanted to shield her from the press and any further distress.

And really, what choice did she have?

Thanking Jack, she approached the car and tried to work out how to get herself and her massive dress into the high seat. Soren rolled his eyes and told her to put her back to the SUV. She did and he gripped her waist, easily lifting her onto the seat. He bundled most of her voluminous skirt onto her lap. "Promise me that the next time you get married, you won't wear something so damn pointless and unsuitable."

She released a nervous laugh. "You think I'm going to do this again? After such a stupid, crazy day?"

Soren just stared at her. "Promise me," he commanded.

It was Eliot's turn to roll her eyes. "I promise to never wear the equivalent of Marie Antoinette's ball gown again."

"Good enough," Soren said, before slamming the door closed, catching a wad of material as he did it. Eliot didn't bother to pull it out. She had, after all, bigger things to worry about.

Like kissing her brief ex shortly after she was due to get married. And liking it a lot.

Who *did* that?

Apparently, she did.

Three

Ten minutes after leaving the hotel, they ran into slow traffic. Soren was grateful for the darkly tinted windows that afforded them the privacy they needed. Seeing that they weren't going anywhere for a couple of minutes, he picked up his phone and logged into the app that tracked his social media coverage. As soon as the latest info popped up on the screen, his heart sank to his toes.

Instagram, Facebook and Twitter were blowing up with mentions of him and, as per usual, the reports were only about 40 percent correct. Along with the video, there were numerous photos of the wedding party in the hallway and quite a few of him standing next to Eliot, his arm around her waist. And yep, the photos of them dancing at the US embassy ball in

Paris had resurfaced. So much for his initial plan to drive past his Manhattan apartment to pick up some clothes before they headed to Calcott Manor.

Although few people had his address, he had no doubt that an intrepid and persistent reporter would've ferreted out where he lived and that several photographers were over there hoping for a money-earning shot.

If he and Eliot were going to be able to think, breathe and have some space, they both needed to get out of town, as quickly as possible. Soren turned to look at Eliot, who'd rested her head against the window and was staring out at the busy streets. Despite her tangled hair, messy makeup and her haunted eyes, she still looked stunning.

Eliot, he decided, looked best with no makeup. He liked seeing the spray of freckles across her nose and along her cheekbones. Without the skill of makeup artists, he could see that her nose was a little off-center and her lips were a natural shade of pink.

But it was her eyes that caused his knees to melt and his heartbeat to accelerate. When she was relaxed, and happy, they were the electric blue of a neon sign, bright and bold. Dark eyebrows and lashes were a stunning contrast to the intense color. Soren swallowed and tightened his grip on his phone, reluctantly admitting that, despite her sad eyes and god-awful dress, he was even more attracted to her right now than he had been eight years ago. And he'd been plenty attracted to her then.

Too much so…

He'd told her the truth earlier about his reason for not contacting her again. He'd never met anyone, before or after her, who could distract him from his training, someone who could pull him away from the pool—and it had shocked and scared him. He'd needed to be completely focused on his sport back then. With his future up in the air, he had even less room in his life for distractions now.

He had some hard decisions to make, and a life to examine.

And he was a jerk for kissing a recently jilted bride. What had he been thinking? But he hadn't been able to resist her when she'd lifted her face, silently telling him she needed his mouth on hers.

But he was too old and too much a man of the world to read anything into that kiss. She was vulnerable and upset, jilted, hurt and feeling less than. It was natural for her to want to be wanted, to want to see if she was desired, still attractive.

Her fire-hot response hadn't been personal…

But hell, it felt like it was.

Eliot sighed, turning to look at him. "Anything I should know?" she quietly asked, nodding at his phone.

"It's a big story and the response is what you'd expect," Soren admitted. "There's nothing that can't wait, though."

Eliot's deep sigh filled the car. "I should go back."

"Tell me where you want to go and I'll take you,"

Soren told her. His words were a calculated risk. Both he and Jack had told her she was out of options but she needed to figure that out herself.

"I don't know," Eliot admitted.

"Well, while you're figuring it out, consider this. Wherever you go, I do, too, Eliot. I'm not leaving you alone," Soren told her, his tone resolute. "And I'd prefer not to be photographed again today."

Contrition flashed across her face. "Hell, Soren, I didn't even think of that. I've been so wrapped up in myself that I didn't realize how this will affect you. I'm so sorry you got dragged into all my drama. I bet you're probably wishing you'd just stayed at your lunch and left me to fend for myself."

Previous lover or not, nobody should ever have to deal with what she'd experienced on their own. How could he have left her there, to be insulted by her mom and slapped by her ex's insensitivity with a camera in her face to capture her misery for the world's entertainment?

"My choice, El. I walked away with you."

"Thank you," Eliot murmured. "I'm glad you were there. If you hadn't been I might've found myself running through the hotel in an expensive gown and shoes, tripping over my train."

Soren placed his hand on her knee, his eyes connecting with all that blue. He started to lean toward her but pulled himself back when he realized he'd been going in for a kiss. *For crap's sake, Grantham! What the hell is wrong with you?*

"Going to Calcott Manor is the best option," he gruffly told her.

It was also where he most needed to be right now. Calcott Manor was his refuge, the hundred-acre estate was where he felt most comfortable. As a child, he'd bounced from city to city, hotel to hotel. He was never sure where he was or what he was supposed to be doing. His parents had loved that luxurious, transient lifestyle, but he'd hated it. He liked structure, order and stability.

Not a fan of change, he felt like the uncertainty of life was battering him from all sides today. Eliot had dropped back into his world at a time when he needed to focus all his concentration on his career and what to do about it.

To stay or to move on? To put his body through hell for two more years or ease off? Staying was the easier choice. He knew what he was doing in the pool and at meets, in that strange world of chlorinated water and stopwatches and judges. He knew how things worked, and what he needed to do at every hour of the day to be the best of the best. He was cold, driven and determined; there was a reason why he had the nickname Ice Man.

But training was becoming more and more of a slog, and maintaining his times was a bitch of epic proportions. And still, he didn't know if he could stop.

He didn't know whether he could be someone other than a world-class athlete and was terrified of what that entailed.

Apart from not knowing how he was going to fill his hours, if he gave up swimming he'd have the time to feel, to remember, to think. When he was swimming, he'd trained himself not to think of Malcolm, to recall memories of his parents or to indulge in what-ifs and might-have-beens. He freely admitted, if only to himself, that he used swimming to self-medicate himself into numbness, and used his devotion to his sport to avoid relationships—both platonic and sexual. He didn't have the time or energy to be a good friend, or to give a woman what she needed…

Besides, losing another person he loved would, he was convinced, mentally destroy him.

"I'm not sure about going to your grandmother's house, Soren. I've never met her and I'm sure she doesn't want a stranger around," Eliot said, interrupting his thoughts.

As a semi-recluse, he knew Avangeline wouldn't want Eliot, a stranger, moving into her home. Luckily, there was a better option. "There's a small guesthouse on the grounds that's quite a way from the house. But it was recently hired out to Paz Conway, the sculptor."

"I know him," Eliot stated. "He does those fantastic, huge sculptures that are twenty feet tall."

"Mmm, apparently, he's attempting his biggest commission yet and his studio is too small so he's renting one of the barns. The point is…my grandmother is used to having people she doesn't know well living on the grounds. She loans out the guesthouse all the time."

"But you just said it's occupied, so won't I still be in the way?"

"Not at all, there's also a two-bedroom apartment above the huge garage. Once I explain the circumstances, I'm sure Avangeline won't object to you staying there temporarily."

Eliot wrinkled her nose. "I still feel like I should stick around and help sort out the train wreck I left behind."

That wasn't a good idea. "Your mother is your manager, isn't she?" When she nodded, he spoke again. "Well, let her manage this. It's what you pay her for. And, if you deal with her by email, you won't have to listen to her yelling at you."

He had only vague memories of his mom, who'd been ditzy but sweet. Mostly, he'd been raised by Jacinda and Avangeline, both of whom rarely raised their voices. And if they did, it was to criticize his and his brothers actions, not their self-identity.

God, they'd lucked out when his sixty-plus grandmother stepped in to raise them. He adored Avangeline and desperately hoped that, in her desire to feel connected to Malcolm, she wasn't falling prey to a con woman. Especially since she'd yet to make her will.

Which was another headache. Not for him, admittedly. Unlike his brothers, he didn't have massive companies where Avangeline was both a shareholder and director. If she died without leaving clear directions on how to dispose of her shares in their organizations, his siblings would be in a world of hurt.

Eliot looked down at her twisted hands, deep in thought. "I don't have any clothes, even shoes. Or a credit card or a phone. Or my medication."

His breath caught in his throat. What was wrong with her that she needed to take medicine? But she answered his question before he could ask. "I take medicine for my thyroid condition. I have the prescription saved on my cloud, so I can get it refilled, but I need a pharmacy sooner rather than later. I can miss one day but wouldn't like to miss more."

Knowing thyroid conditions could be well managed with proper treatment, Soren relaxed. "When we get to Hatfield, I'll drop you off at Calcott Manor and I'll go into town and pick up your meds and some clothes for you, enough to get you through a couple of days. When the dust settles, we can decide on your next move, whether that's staying there or going back to the city."

Eliot thanked him. "You're going to a lot of trouble for me, Soren."

He shrugged. "I'd like to think you'd do the same for me if you found me in a similar situation."

Nobody would ever have to pick up the pieces of his broken wedding. He was perfectly content living his life solo. Hours in the pool made him very comfortable with his own company.

Eliot nodded, slipped out of her wedding shoes and looked down at her bare feet. Her toes were a pretty shell pink, and she had the tiniest hearts dotted on the nail of her biggest toe. Cute. Inappropriate now, but cute.

Eliot wiggled her feet and groaned with relief. That sound reminded him of the noise she'd make when he slid into her, indescribably warm and impossibly wet. The fabric across his crotch tightened and he resisted the urge to bang his forehead on the steering wheel.

"Traffic is moving," Eliot told him and he faced forward, his foot easing down on the accelerator. She turned to look at him, her expression intense. "Are you sure you want to take me home, Soren?"

Yes, no… *God.*

All he knew for sure was that since laying eyes on her, his life was ten times more complicated than it had been before.

And that he wasn't trying very hard to rid himself of the source of the complication.

Forty minutes later Soren stopped at a pair of wrought iron gates and punched in the code on the freestanding panel. Within seconds the gates opened. Eliot expected to immediately see buildings but it was a while before she saw a stone house. It would, she thought, leaning forward, have magnificent views of the estate's long, private beach.

The house was two stories of lovely and had a wraparound veranda on both levels. Swaths of emerald lawn were edged by beautifully and thoughtfully planted beds, the white roses, cream lilies and green shrubs making a restful palette. Eliot looked around but didn't see a garage. It had to be out of sight, maybe behind that small stand of trees. Eliot glanced down and wished that she was arriving at his grandmother's house in something other than a crushed, dirt-edged wedding dress. This was not how she wanted to meet Soren's grandmother.

Or, to be fair, anyone else.

As they approached the small driveway, Eliot took a deep breath, expecting Soren to slow down. But instead of stopping, he carried on past the house, turned left to climb a long hill and sped around a corner.

And Eliot's eyebrows shot up into her hair.

The house she'd just passed, that lovely building, wasn't the main deal after all. *This* was. Like the other house, it was built in a soft gray stone but Eliot could immediately see that this house had some age to it. It oozed history from every brick and window. Most of the front of the building was covered in thick ivy, the exact color of Soren's eyes and trimmed back to let light into the many windows. The structure was colossal, of the type built to house an enormous multigenerational family. It went on, as far as Eliot could see, for ages.

Soren slowed down to give her a chance to take in the house and park-like gardens. "Welcome to Calcott Manor," he said. "This is home."

Home? He called this place *home*? Eliot had money—quite a bit of it actually—and had friends with far bigger bank accounts. She'd visited many exceptional homes across the world, but this was a property on a scale she'd never seen before. It was drop-her-jaw huge.

"The original house was built in the late nineteenth century and it's been added to over the years. Avangeline bought the property more than twenty-five years ago and has made improvements," Soren told her, gently accelerating to steer the car toward a huge garage now visible a fair distance from the house. "It has over a hundred acres of woods, pastures and, obviously, the beach."

"How many rooms?" Eliot asked, lifting her hand to her neck.

He sent her an amused glance. "Do you want the Realtor's pitch?"

She thought she might so she nodded.

Soren gave his answer some thought. "Right, let's see. For starters, there's a guest home—the one we passed—and the apartment over the garage. Ten en suite bedrooms in the main house, plus a three-bed apartment Jacinda uses. God knows how many bathrooms. Lots of period details including stained glass windows and imported marble. As for facilities, there's an indoor Olympic-sized pool and an outside pool, too. Gym and sauna, tennis court. Horse barns and greenhouses."

Soren slid the car into the only empty parking bay in the garage—the rest of the space was taken up by two Mercs, a Rolls-Royce, a vintage Jaguar, a handful of dirt bikes, a Land Cruiser and a nifty golf cart.

"Jack texted to let me know that he'd called ahead and spoke to Avangeline, telling her the circumstances of your unplanned arrival. She's agreed to you moving into the apartment up there." He pointed to the staircase. "You'll be comfortable there. I'll show you up and then I'll head into town and get you some clothes. Jacinda should have set it up for you with fresh towels and sheets, and some food in the fridge."

Eliot held up her hand, feeling emotionally battered. "Jacinda is the housekeeper, right?" She thought she remembered Soren talking about her but France was so long ago.

Soren tipped his flat hand up and down. "That's such a limited word for what she does and for someone who is such an integral part of Calcott Manor and our lives," Soren explained. "Jace does look after the house and the estate but she's also Avangeline's companion and our second parent.

"She came to Calcott Manor shortly after Avangeline purchased the place, she was a single mom with a boy our age. Merrick was raised with us and we consider them family. Merrick is as much Avangeline's grandson as I am."

Eliot was fascinated by the family they'd made, born out of the depths of grief. Despite just being the two of them, she and her mom weren't close—hell, they barely tolerated each other.

What made a family? Eliot didn't know but she'd wanted one for as long as she could remember—people to call her own, children to love, little people to love her back. And her need to be part of a family group, to belong, had led to her nearly marrying a man who did not love, respect or need her.

"You look shattered," Soren said, his tone gentle.

Eliot nodded. "I am."

And she couldn't wait to get out of this heavy, hot, horrible gown. It felt like it was strangling her, bit by bit. Eliot touched her forehead, conscious of the pounding ache behind her eyes. Frankly, she was done with today.

It had been horrible on so many levels. The only highlight was that she wasn't married. Well, that and Soren's kiss. She still couldn't believe that in the middle of her train wreck non-wedding, she'd all but inhaled the guy she'd never forgotten.

She wanted to kiss him again.

And do so much more. *You'd tired, Eliot, not thinking straight.*

Soren opened her car door and held out his hand to her to help her down from her seat. She gathered her skirts and bunched them in her hand, exposing her legs and designer shoes. She dropped to the ground but Soren kept her hands in his, and she looked up at him as his deep green eyes locked on hers. She thought she saw a flicker of appreciation in his eyes but it was gone so quickly she couldn't be sure.

"How are you doing, Eliot?"

She wanted to toss her head and tell him that she was fine, but she didn't have the energy to lie. "I'm feeling numb, stupid, a little silly. Tired. So very tired," she admitted. "A tired that goes beyond exhaustion."

He lifted his hand to brush his thumb over her cheekbone. "Mental exhaustion is a bitch."

She heard a note in his voice that suggested that he understood on a soul-deep, intensely personal level. "Let's get you upstairs and you can have a shower."

Soren's hand covered her cheek, his thumb swiping her bottom lip. Eliot licked her lips and all thoughts about her wedding vanished, her tiredness instantly forgotten. When Soren touched her, she felt she was plugged into a charging station, energy flowing into her flat batteries.

And when he looked at her like he couldn't get enough of her, like she was the person who hung the stars, who made the sun rise every day, her blood turned syrupy and her womb clenched in delicious anticipation.

And she couldn't help placing her hand on his chest and pushing up onto her toes. Soren's mouth on hers simply made sense when nothing much in her life did. Her lips touched his and she rested her hands on his shoulders, pushing her breasts into his hard chest. The instant their lips connected, a white-hot bolt of lust shot through her, igniting every nerve ending in her body. The world stopped turning. Every living creature stopped breathing. Birds were rendered silent, waves stopped crashing onto beaches and the earth halted its progress around the sun.

Needing more, to take this deeper, she probed the seam of his mouth but his lips didn't open.

His lips didn't open…

Eliot kept her mouth on his but opened her eyes, feeling stupid. She was kissing him but his arms weren't pulling her closer and his lips weren't moving…

He wasn't reciprocating… *Shit.*

Eliot dropped back onto her heels and ducked her head, feeling small and stupid. Right, another embarrassment in a series of embarrassments on what had to be the crappiest day of her life.

Let's just go through the highlights, shall we? She'd been jilted by her long-term partner, a man who valued looks above loyalty and appearances above promises. Her mother, once again, hadn't shown her a whiff of maternal support. She was then rescued by the man who ghosted her years earlier, the one who'd simply slid out of her life because he was far too busy and important and driven and ambitious to give her the courtesy of dumping her over the phone or by email. How could she be so stupid to kiss him twice, to be so…so melty when she stepped into his arms?

What was wrong with her? Was she that desperate for love and affection that she'd take it wherever it was offered? Even when it *wasn't* offered?

Eliot stiffened, stepped back and wrapped her arms around her torso, feeling humiliated.

"Eliot—" Soren touched her arm but she jerked away.

He immediately dropped his hands and stepped back to give her some space.

She lifted her head and tried to toss her hair, which didn't move. She turned and started to walk away, only to catch the toe of her shoe in the hem of her skirt. She stumbled but Soren's hand gripped her elbow and stopped her from heading straight to the ground. "Hold on a second, Eliot—"

Eliot, on the point of tears, stared down at the tarmac, still feeling like she was being buffeted by a hundred-miles-an-hour wind. "I just want to climb into a bed, Soren, any bed. Alone."

Soren lifted her chin to force her to look at him. She saw regret in his eyes and, worse, sympathy.

"Our kiss earlier shouldn't have happened, Eliot, and I'm sorry it did. Not because I don't find you attractive—I always have—but because you are in a bad place and I should never have taken advantage. Honestly, I was way out of line earlier and I wasn't going to compound that mistake by kissing you again." He pushed an agitated hand through his dark hair. "You've had an exceptionally hard day, you're emotionally shattered and you're looking for comfort, a distraction, which is understandable. But if things went any further between us then you'd regret it in the morning and I think you have enough to deal with without adding regret to the pile of misery."

She looked into his green eyes and sighed, his words sinking in. Unfortunately, he had a point... a few points, actually. Why *did* she wanted to kiss him—make love to him—on what should be one of the worst days of her life? Was she just using the memories of their old attraction as a way to hide from the confusion and grief she knew she should be experiencing but wasn't?

"Soren!"

They both sprang around at someone calling his name and Eliot saw an elderly lady, her hand tucked into the arm of a tall, slim woman. While the older woman was dressed in a white shirtwaist dress with sleeves that hit her elbows, paired with a stunning necklace of huge, perfectly matched natural pearls, the younger woman, around Eliot's age, wore a sleeveless maxi dress, and flat-soled sandals.

Eliot felt Soren tense and turned to look at him, surprised to see him regarding the younger woman like she was a snake about to strike.

"Avangeline," Soren murmured. In a few strides, he crossed the space between them and hauled the white-haired woman into his arms, lifting her off her feet.

"Put me down, you big oaf!" she muttered in her very posh, very English accent while swatting his shoulder with her bony hand.

Soren put her back on her feet but gathered her close, resting his dark head against his grandmother's.

"It's good to have you home," Avangeline murmured, patting his cheek before stepping back from Soren. "How long are you staying?"

Soren shrugged. "I'll be in and out for about three weeks."

Avangeline's eyebrows rose. She narrowed her

eyes. Eliot realized that they were the same color as Soren's, and capable of just as intense a stare. "How long will I have the pleasure of your company, Soren? I presume you are heading right back to Florida to resume training?"

"I'm taking a vacation," Soren replied, trying to sound casual and missing by a mile.

"You hate vacations," Avangeline countered. "What aren't you telling me, Soren Caleb?"

Soren pulled up a smile but it didn't touch his eyes. "Lots, I expect." He pulled his gaze off Avangeline and when he looked at the younger woman, he nailed her with eyes the color of frozen green marble. "You're Alyson Garwood."

She didn't look away, and Eliot admired the way she pushed back her shoulders and straightened her spine, despite Soren's very obvious antagonism. Why was he hostile? What was his problem with this woman?

"I am," Alyson replied, her pleasant expression not changing.

"I hear you've moved into Calcott Manor with Avangeline." Soren spat out the words. Despite standing there in her huge gown, Eliot had been forgotten. And that was strange because Soren had excellent manners.

"Avangeline was kind enough to invite me and I accepted," Alyson replied.

"Right. What else have you asked for? A car, cash, an art piece or two?" Wow. The legendary Ice Man was on the edge of losing his cool and that was very surprising indeed.

"That's enough, Soren," Avangeline snapped.

Holy hell! What was going on here? Eliot felt like she was about to witness a duel, or whatever the modern equivalent was. But instead of escalating the argument, Alyson just gently smiled and looked away from him to rest her lovely eyes on Eliot's face. Those eyes were a deep gray purple, beautiful and unusual, and filled with remarkable compassion. It was obvious that she recognized Eliot but her expression didn't change. "You look like you've had a very hard day. I'm very sorry."

Her expression held sympathy but not pity, empathy but not malice. "Thank you," Eliot murmured, a lump forming in her throat.

"I'm Aly," she said. Turning to Avangeline, she spoke again. "Avangeline, this is Eliot Stone."

"Welcome to Calcott Manor, Miss Stone—"

"Please call me Eliot," she interjected.

Avangeline inclined her aristocratic head. And that wasn't a figure of speech. Eliot recalled reading—or maybe Soren had told her—that this small, elderly woman had been born into the British aristocracy and was officially, legally, a lady. She was also a friend of the queen.

Avangeline had attended all the royal weddings and had spent time with Queen Liz at Balmoral. The mind boggled.

"You must have a thumping headache, Eliot," Aly

told her. "And I bet you could do with a cup of tea. Or a huge glass of wine."

Oh, she liked this woman. Instinctively and immediately—but it was obvious, by his deep glower, that Soren did not.

"Why don't you take Eliot upstairs to the apartment, Soren? While Eliot has a long soak, I will go back to the house and grab something of mine for her to wear. We're about the same size," Aly suggested. "Later I'll go into town and pick up some clothes for you, Eliot."

Oh, God, a bath sounded like bliss. "That's very kind of you," Eliot told her. "But I also need some medication, if you wouldn't mind picking that up, too."

"Sure," Aly easily agreed.

"I'll go into town and get what she needs," Soren snapped at Aly, folding his big arms across his chest.

"Sure, if you'd like to." Aly nodded. "Jacinta's just come back from Hatfield and the place is already filling up with reporters, they know to look for you here. They will start camping out at the gates soon. You can go into Hatfield and have cameras shoved in your face, or you can allow me to go, someone who won't grab any attention at all."

Soren looked like he'd swallowed a fly. Or swallowed a spider that swallowed the fly. Aly had neatly boxed him into a corner and he didn't like being there. Game, set and match to her.

"I don't like you," Soren rudely told her. "Neither do any of my brothers."

"Soren!" Avangeline said, shocked.

Aly sent him a small, sad smile. "I don't expect you to, Soren. I don't expect any of you to understand why I'm here and what I want to achieve by staying with Avangeline."

"So you admit to having an ulterior motive!" Soren crowed.

"Don't we all, Soren? But does it mean that ulterior motive has to be anything harmful?" Aly demanded, before turning her attention back to Eliot. "I do hope you feel better soon, Eliot. I'm going to go now, partly because Soren looks like his head is about to explode, but also because I need to fetch you those clothes before I go into town. Are you coming, Avangeline?"

"I am," Avangeline replied, sliding her hand into the crook of Aly's elbow. She gave Soren a pointed look. "I expect you for dinner, young man."

Soren opened his mouth to argue with her, then— wisely—snapped it shut without saying a word. Aly and Avangeline turned to walk back up to the house.

After many minutes of silence, Soren looked at her and shook his head. "Don't ask," he warned her.

Eliot, with enough on her plate and feeling like a washed-up, battered piece of flotsam, didn't.

Four

Eliot's day had been a suck-fest but Soren's hadn't been a walk in the park either.

He followed Eliot into the luxurious apartment over the garage, her light, sexy scent lodged in his nose.

Standing in the middle of the fresh blue-and-white beach-themed sitting room, he gripped the bridge of his nose and hauled in a couple of deep breaths. He was debating whether to retire or not—a helluva decision—had met Alyson and had rediscovered, rescued and kissed Eliot—all in the space of a few hours. He was used to performing under pressure but this was ridiculous.

Eliot turned to face him, her long hair in stiff curls, not helped by his big hands pushing into that heavy mass. Her mouth was tight with unhappiness. He shouldn't have kissed her. His actions had been stupid and thoughtless and he was ashamed of his lack of self-control.

Then again, his self-control, and his brain, seemed to melt whenever he came within a mile of the blasted woman.

She could make him do things, and consider things, he never had before. And wasn't that why he ran from her all those years ago? Eliot had been, back when he was younger, his kryptonite. He was older and tougher these days, but she still could mess with his mind.

She was dangerous and he had to be careful around her...

He needed to head over to the main house, give her some time to be alone and settle down. He'd find Jace, say hello, and catch up with her before heading upstairs to shower and change for dinner. Avangeline didn't expect a suit and tie, but she did expect them to make an effort to clean up and be presentable for meals, especially dinner. Like his brothers, he kept a kept a small selection of clothes, mostly shorts and t-shirts, at Calcott Manor and if he needed anything else, he'd raid Jack's closet and wear his designer threads.

Also on his agenda was to get Alyson Garwood alone. Merrick said that there was something he needed to hear from her lips and he was curious as hell as to what that could be. Despite so much happening today, he couldn't forget Merrick's comment about Alyson Garwood having something weird to tell him.

His plan for today had been simple: have lunch with his brothers and then drive to Calcott Manor. He'd talk Avangeline into writing a will, listen to the Garwood woman and dismiss whatever she had to say.

He wasn't a fan of his plans going awry.

Soren felt the buzz of his phone in his pocket and pulled it out to see a text message from Jack.

Tell Eliot to call her mom. She's still at the hotel and is haranguing me for your number. Trying to put out fires here and don't need her in my face.

Soren winced. From the little he'd seen of Eliot's mom, the woman had all the subtlety and charm of a rabid wolverine. Jack, after his help today, didn't need her hassling him.

"Your mother is looking for you," Soren told Eliot.

As expected, she pulled a face. Weren't mothers and daughters supposed to be close? "I'm not interested in talking to her."

Her response wasn't a surprise either. "The thing is, she's driving Jack nuts by nagging him for my number. Just call her, let her know you're okay and get her off my brother's back."

"If I use your phone, she'll have a record of your number."

He shook his head. "My phone number is blocked. It'll come up as a private number."

"Thank God." Eliot released an irritated sigh, took the phone and punched in a number. Putting it on speaker, she placed the phone on the kitchen island

and lifted her skirt to step out of her pretty but impractical shoes.

Eliot's mother answered on the second ring, and the second she heard her daughter's voice, the diatribe began. "Where the hell are you? Do you know what a mess you made of things?"

Soren winced at the shrill voice. "Why are you blaming me?" Eliot asked, lifting her other foot. "De-Shawn is the one who broke off our engagement!"

"Because you drove him to it! How could you let your relationship fall apart like that?" Ursula yelled.

"I'm fine mom, but thanks for asking," Eliot calmly stated, but Soren caught the tightening of her lips and the flash of pain in her eyes.

"When are you coming back to sort out this mess?" Ursula demanded. "Tell me where you are and I'll send a car."

She'll send a *car*? What about jumping into one and fetching her daughter herself? Damn, but this woman was cold. His parents might've been wealthy nomads but he'd never doubted their love. And Avangeline and Jacinda were, along with the gang he grew up with, his biggest supporters. They'd move heaven and earth for him if he asked. Hell, he wouldn't *have* to ask. If they thought he needed them, they'd just show up. He had a family, but it seemed that Eliot's mother was more of a manager than a mom.

"I expect you back in the city tonight, Eliot."

"Not happening, Ursula. And I'll come back when I'm ready." Eliot punched the red button to end the call.

Her eyes clashed with his and she sent him an

embarrassed smile. She gestured to the phone. "My mother, so warm and wonderful."

Soren wondered if Ursula was simply reacting badly to a stressful day. "Is she always like that?"

"Oh, she was quite calm today," Eliot stated. "Even though I didn't deliver my lines, and the shoot was canceled—"

What was she talking about?

He asked and Eliot wrinkled her nose. "I frequently feel like my life is a movie or a commercial… It's hard to explain." She waved her hands around. "Anyway…that was actually Ursula in a pretty good mood. She loves publicity, drama. I'm sure her phone is ringing off the hook with reporters looking for a comment, and friends and industry professionals looking for gossip, and she's reveling in the attention. My mother *adores* attention."

Soren blinked at her calm voice. She was talking about her only family member but she sounded like she was doing nothing more emotional than ordering coffee. Before he could formulate a response, Eliot changed the subject.

"So, do you want to tell me about your strange reaction to Aly?" Eliot asked him, leaning against the white, Italian marble island.

"What are you talking about?" Soren asked, playing dumb.

Eliot narrowed her eyes at him. "I'm talking about your instinctive dislike of Aly. Why? She seems sweet."

"As a rattlesnake," Soren muttered, turning his

back to her. He didn't want to start confiding in Eliot. He opened the fridge. As he expected, there was fresh milk, a fruit platter, cheese, croissants and a chilled bottle of white wine. There was also a small basket of handcrafted Belgian chocolate. Everything a brokenhearted woman needed. Except that Eliot didn't seem brokenhearted and her response to his kiss had been anything but tearful.

"I thought you wanted to have a bath," Soren told her, wanting to change the subject.

"And I'll run one after you explain about Aly."

Soren looked at Eliot, saw the stubborn look on her face and sighed, knowing he needed to tell her something to explain his less-than-welcoming, maybe-quite-rude reaction to Avangeline's guest. She wouldn't move until he did and she needed to take that bath, relax and rest.

"I don't know if you remember that we lost Malcolm, my cousin, ten or so years ago," he quietly stated, feeling the burn of grief in his esophagus.

"In a motorbike accident, wasn't it?"

Soren slammed the fridge door shut and placed his shoulder on the stainless steel surface. "Mmm. He was an organ donor and, as per his wishes, his organs were harvested immediately." A part of him still couldn't believe that Mal was dead, that somebody so bold and vibrant had been whipped away.

"That woman down there—"

"Aly," Eliot interjected.

He knew her name, dammit! He just didn't intend to ever use it. "—received Mal's liver. I heard earlier today that she began corresponding with my grandmother, and that led to them striking up a friendship that resulted in her relocating here for God knows how long. We don't know what her intentions are. We've seen no proof that she even received Mal's liver. We're still waiting for confirmation she's telling the truth."

"Why would she lie?"

Oh, come on! "Why would a thirty-year-old woman strike up a friendship with a billionaire recluse? Money, naturally. She's hoping to get some out of Avangeline."

Eliot frowned. "Maybe she just wants to get to know the family of the person who gave her a second chance at life," Eliot pointed out. "You're being too cynical."

"And you're being naive," Soren snapped back. "I will do anything and everything to protect my grandmother, Eliot."

Avangeline had sold off her billion-dollar empire and turned her life upside down all those years ago to raise four orphaned boys. In a storm-tossed world, she'd been Soren's harbor, his guiding star. He'd never let anyone take advantage of her.

Eliot lifted her hands, then dropped them and shrugged. "Fair enough. But I don't think Aly is going to steal the family silver, Soren."

Maybe, maybe not. But he certainly wasn't going to give her the chance to. He was on con artist watch until one of his brothers could get their ass down here and give him a respite. But if they couldn't, he'd stay here at Calcott Manor until Aly moved on. He had three weeks he'd allotted as vacation time to figure out his next steps professionally. He'd use them here, looking after Avangeline. And when the three weeks were up and he'd decided on his career path, he'd either be retired, with all the time in the world to spend with his grandmother, or he'd move his trainers to Hatfield and train in Calcott Manor's pool, half killing himself to shave a fraction of a second off his times.

Eliot gestured to the hallway. "I'm going to take that bath," Eliot told him. "Is that okay?"

A vision of Eliot, hair wet and water droplets rolling down her fantastic skin, jumped out of his memory bank to ambush him. He recalled her high, perky breasts topped with coral-pink nipples, the row of three freckles to the left of her belly button and her long, streamlined body. He wanted to see her wet again; he desperately wanted to see her naked.

"Soren? Is that okay?"

The note of frustration in her voice jerked him back and he nodded, swallowing hard. "Sure. Do that. But I think I *will* go to town and buy you some clothes."

He wanted to be the person who helped her out, the one she turned to. It was stupid, unnecessary, but he wanted to be the one who was there for her.

Why? He had no damn idea.

Eliot walked away but before disappearing down the hallway, she turned to speak again. "You're being stubborn and you're only going to Hatfield because you don't want Aly doing anything for you."

"But I'm not doing it for her, I'm doing it for *you*, Eliot."

Soren whipped around and saw Aly standing in the doorway, a pile of clothes in her hands. She looked at Eliot, lifted the clothes and placed them on the chair just inside the door. "Jeans, a T-shirt, socks, a sports bra and an old pair of trainers. They aren't designer but they should do for now."

Eliot's smile widened and Soren felt like he'd stepped into the sun. "Honestly, I'm not a brand snob and I'm so grateful," Eliot replied, walking across the room to collect the clothes. "Thank you, Aly."

Eliot borrowed his phone, logged into her cloud, and sent her online prescription to Aly's email address so that she could collect her thyroid medication. "Aly, don't get a lot. I can manage with a toothbrush and some toothpaste, some panties and maybe another T-shirt or two for now," Eliot assured her. "I'll get my friend Madigan to send me down what I need tomorrow or the next day."

"There's a fully stocked range of toiletries in the bathroom," Soren interjected. His grandmother always supplied her guests with everything they could ever need, sourced from some of the best stores in the world.

Eliot acknowledged his statement with a cool nod and smiled at Aly. "Just my meds and a few clothes, Aly. Casual stuff, nothing-fancy. Thank you."

"I'll pay for Aly's clothes," Soren told Aly in a clipped voice as he pulled his wallet out of the back pocket of his pants.

"It's fine," Aly responded. "I have money and Eliot can pay me back."

Soren held out a few bills, far more than was needed, and he and Aly engaged in another stare down. But Aly wasn't any match for Soren and after a few seconds, she took the money with a frustrated sigh.

Eliot knew how she felt.

Aly looked at her watch. "I'll be back in an hour, maybe an hour and a half." She pointed an elegant finger at Eliot. "Pour yourself a huge glass of wine, run yourself an enormous bubble bath and have a good cry."

Eliot nodded. "That sounds like a plan. I might just do that."

But when Aly left, Eliot didn't open the fridge to take out a bottle of wine or ask where she could find a glass. She'd take the bath, but he doubted she'd cry.

Eliot wasn't upset about not getting married.

This was, without doubt, the strangest day of his life.

The next morning, Eliot sat on a stone bench on the edge of Calcott Manor's private beach, the tablet she'd found in the apartment resting on her lap. It was time to face the music and to see the extent of the fallout.

She'd slept a little, a surprise because she hadn't expected to sleep at all. After dozing off around three, she'd awoken a few hours later, made herself some coffee and eaten a few grapes from the amazing fruit platter she'd found in the fridge. Then, taking her second cup of coffee, she tucked the tablet under her arm and wandered down to the beach, enjoying the sound of the waves and the hot, early morning sun on her face.

Despite this beach being private, and a part of the estate, it wasn't empty. There were dog walkers, an elderly couple walking arm in arm along the shoreline and a few enthusiastic joggers. Nobody, thank God, paid any attention to the curly-haired woman dressed in denim shorts and a cropped T-shirt with a ball cap over her eyes.

Eliot picked up the tablet and powered it up, opening the tab to a popular browser. She plugged in her name and a millisecond later, a stream of results hit the screen.

Dumped!

Jilted!

Eliot skimmed through the articles, all of them blaming her. She pulled a face at the unflattering photos, snapped by the photographer Ursula hired to shoot her wedding. Her lips twisted at the oft-quoted comment by DeShawn's best friend and band member, Drew, who expressed sympathy for them both before stabbing her in the heart by saying that DeShawn tried to make their relationship work but Eliot's disinterest in her fiancé and in her work caused her relationship and career to fall apart.

Drew never spoke to the press without DeShawn's permission and his comment was DeShawn's way of justifying jilting her at the last minute. DeShawn was in damage control mode and, because he knew how to work the media, Eliot had no doubt that his image would remain untainted.

Bastard.

Eliot's hand tightened on the tablet as she skimmed through the comments in response to their joint press release, which Ursula had posted without her knowledge or permission. They were as vicious as she'd imagined. And she had a really good imagination. Most castigated her for picking up weight or for not being what DeShawn needed. How crazy was it that her worth and value were measured in dress sizes and pounds? How had the world gotten to this point?

Eliot hugged the tablet to her chest, fully accepting that she was part of the problem, that, as a model, she'd fed the world's unrealistic standards about body size and beauty. And, yes, she'd made money off it. She wasn't an innocent here. She'd profited.

How people looked affected their lives—that was an unfortunate truth. And, up until her thyroid had malfunctioned, she'd won a genetic lottery, having symmetrical features, a long, slender body, pale skin and striking eyes. There were models who didn't fit the mold of tall, white and thin—including women of color, gorgeous women at the top of the game and the occasional plus-size models—but models like her (albeit pre-thyroid) sold products. And the fashion industry obliged by supplying them.

And now, because she didn't fit the image of what they wanted, she'd been tossed out of the sexy girl sandbox. It was so arbitrary and so shallow.

But she'd chosen this life and for too many years, for *most* of her life, she'd lived in the bubble where looks and fashion and how she presented herself were all important.

Her looks were all she had of value to offer her mother. Before she was discovered, she'd been a drain on her mom's meager resources. After her first photoshoot, she became a cash cow, a pretty picture, a talking point and a face and body to be proud of.

Her mother didn't see her as a daughter, or even as a friend. Eliot was a commodity and Ursula didn't bother to engage with her on a personal level. She'd never been seen or listened to. For all her life, whenever she voiced her opinion, her mother either ignored her or dismissed her. She certainly didn't take anything she said into consideration.

Because she wanted to be loved, to be valued, Eliot had always been a people pleaser, hoping that by giving people what they wanted, they'd take the time to know her, understand her and appreciate her.

Madigan was the only person who'd bothered to do that. And, for a few glorious days, Soren.

She'd opted for marriage because DeShawn was, initially, a considerate boyfriend, someone she felt comfortable with. They hadn't used words like *love* very often, but he had talked about commitment and a future together, and she'd thought they wanted the same things—a home, children. She'd fallen into that fantasy because she desperately wanted a family and a place to belong.

Eliot sighed. It was hard to admit, but she was a pushover, someone who bent in whatever direction the wind blew. Her mom and DeShawn rode roughshod over her and, over the years, she'd become more and more emotionally removed from her job and the people populating her world. She was just a body, just a face…a canvas for someone to paint.

To mold.

The problem with being constantly remodeled was that you eventually lost your original shape.

It was past time she discovered herself—what made her happy, sad, excited, mad—because she was done being a mirror to those around her, reflecting the image that made them feel comfortable. That stopped today.

Right damn now.

From this moment on, she'd make decisions based on what felt good to her, what resonated and what felt right rather than trying to please everyone around her.

Her non-wedding was a wake-up call that she had to stop observing life and start *living* it.

Eliot put the tablet down, pulled her heels onto the bench and wrapped her arms around her knees, watching as a swimmer appeared from behind the point of the right-hand side of the bay, easily pulling himself through the calm waters behind the back breakers. She immediately recognized Soren—no other man looked as at-home in the water as he did. He wasn't swimming fast, or slow, but simply seemed to be cruising through the water, just another aquatic creature completely in tune with its environment. After a few minutes, he headed in toward the shore and body surfed a small breaker. Eliot sucked in her breath as she watched him emerge from the sea, stroking back his waterlogged hair.

She felt like she was in an outdoor cinema, watching James Bond emerging from the waves. Soren packed the same punch. He wore board shorts instead of a Speedo, the fabric sticking to his huge thighs. Sunlight caught the droplets of water on his wide shoulders, on those powerful arms, and ran down his chest and over his ripped stomach. He was a man in prime physical condition, probably at the best his body could be.

He was super hot; there was no doubt about that, but his looks and superb physique had never been the bedrock of her attraction to Soren. No, it was his stillness, his self-belief, the way that he never pretended. He didn't court the press and, recently, refused to give personal interviews. He rarely posted on social media and was reputed to be polite but extremely reserved when interacting with everyone from fans to competitors.

Sometimes she still felt like their affair in France had been a step out of time, like a movie she'd watched and couldn't get out of her head. There had been an instant connection, an arc of electricity. Soren didn't leave her side at the embassy party, not talking much but listening intently as she rattled on about her job, traveling, designers…

"Tell me something real," she remembered him asking her, his voice deep and commanding.

She hadn't hesitated. "I'm bored senseless, and I want to leave."

He simply nodded, took her by the hand and walked her away, past the ambassador, past the guards and the other guests into the Parisian night. He drove her to her hotel and waited for her to invite him up to her room. She did—how could she not? Then he proceeded to rearrange, and rock, her world.

The next morning they drove to the French Riviera, to a villa owned by a friend of a friend. They made love often but, over the following few days, they also became friends. Having no shoots scheduled for a week, she blew off her social engagements and after sending her mom a message saying she was fine, she turned off her phone and tossed it into the bedside drawer. He did the same and for three days, they existed in a bubble, cooking, laughing, talking—well, she talked, he listened—and making love. Pretending the world didn't exist.

Then he'd left and dinged her heart by never contacting her again and by ignoring her repeated calls, emails and texts.

For those few days, she had been the complete focus of his attention. Then he'd treated her like she was disposable, something she'd struggled with her whole life. She'd felt like a pampered cat left out in the middle of a torrid thunderstorm.

Soren walked along the beach, looked up and saw her sitting on the bench. He called out a suggestion that she join him and dropped to sit in the sand, his back to her. Sighing, Eliot headed over to stand next to him, looking down at his tanned shoulders and broad back.

Soren patted the sand next to him. "Take a seat."

Eliot sat down and pulled her legs up, resting her

arms on her knees and her chin in her fist. The sun glinted off the water, the still early morning exuding a gentle warmth as a gull swooped down to inspect a heap of seaweed. She couldn't believe that down the beach was the busy town of Hatfield, filled with tourists. The juxtaposition between Manhattan, just forty minutes away, and Hatfield was jarring.

"I thought you normally trained in the pool," Eliot said, breaking their silence.

"I'm not training at the moment," Soren told her, placing his hands behind him and leaning back. "I'm taking a three-week break."

Eliot gave him a confused look. "But isn't this a busy time for you? Shouldn't you be preparing for upcoming meets?"

Soren's expression closed off. "I should," he agreed. He didn't say anything more and Eliot sighed. Yep, that was all he was going to say on that subject. Garrulous he was not.

"Besides, that wasn't training," Soren told her, his words accompanied by a small smile. "It was just a gentle three-mile swim, the equivalent of an easy stroll through the park."

Three miles? Dear God. "What does it feel like?" she asked, envy tinging her words.

Soren turned his head to look at her. "What does what feel like?"

"Swimming."

He stared at her, a small frown pulling his thick eyebrows together. "I don't understan—holy crap, are you telling me that you can't swim?"

She shook her head. "No. I never learned."

"But you've done a million shoots in water… And you went into the sea with me in France."

"When I did those shoots, I only went in up to my knees. My face never got anywhere near the water," Eliot pointed out. "In France, I just hung on to you… You didn't seem to mind."

Heat flashed in his eyes and Eliot knew he was remembering those sunny, sexy days.

"But, surely, as a kid, you went to water parks and pool parties."

He was mistaking her for a kid who grew up with money. Or with a parent who cared enough to entertain her. "Before I was discovered, Ursula worked two jobs and we lived in a shoebox apartment in Queens. Surviving, and paying the rent was a priority. Spending money on fun things like swim lessons was a pipe dream."

Soren's eyes held no judgment. "And after you were discovered, when there *was* money?"

"There was never any time," she explained. "We didn't know how long I'd be in demand, how long this modeling gig would last, so we agreed that I should take any work I was offered, that we should make bank while we could. So that's what we did—I worked, she managed."

Her happiness and mental health hadn't been priorities. Wealth, exposure and fame, in that order, were all that had mattered.

Something as unnecessary to the above as swimming? Not a chance in hell.

But the more she thought about it, the more she wanted to experience the roll of water along her body, the ebb and the bob of the waves. She wanted to taste the saltiness of the ocean, to know whether it felt as silky as it looked.

She turned to look at Soren, who was still looking at her like she was a mermaid with two tails. "How long would it take me to learn to swim?"

"Uh… It depends. First, you learn to float, then you learn to paddle, to become water safe. To do free-style or breaststroke would take more time. But, like everything else, your progress depends on how much you practice."

Eliot tipped her head to the side. "I'm going to learn to swim," she decided, determination coating her words.

"I think that's a very good idea," Soren replied. He hesitated a minute before rumbling out another sentence. "Do you want me to teach you?"

"*You*?" Eliot asked, shocked.

"I've got the time right now and, apparently, I am one of the best swimmers in the world," Soren pointed out, amused. "I do know the basics. I got the medals and everything."

She grinned at his gentle self-mockery. She was tempted to accept his offer, but they'd be nearly naked and they'd be constantly touching. Since their chemistry hadn't faded, maybe it would be better if she hired someone else.

"I'm sure I can find someone in Hatfield who'd

be willing to give me private lessons. Would your grandmother mind if I use her pool?"

"I'm sure she wouldn't," Soren replied, looking disappointed. "You could do that, but whoever you hire would have to fight their way through the reporters still hanging around. They aren't going to leave until they get a glimpse of you. Or better yet, an interview."

She'd rather pull her front teeth out with pliers. "Is your grandmother mad at the intrusion?"

Soren lifted one enormous shoulder. "What intrusion? They aren't on her property so she doesn't care."

Eliot picked up a handful of sand and allowed it to drift through her fingers. "I feel bad for bringing this to her door."

"She's blissfully unaffected and I brought you here because it's secure. Because you're safe here. The grounds are monitored with cameras by an off site security team and if there's an issue, they'll respond immediately. You can relax, and chill. Recover." He gave her an assessing look. "Though I'm not sure how much recovering you are doing. Or need to do."

It was his oblique way of asking what happened and, after all he'd done, he deserved an explanation. Her coming clean might also explain why she responded with such fervor when he kissed her.

But it didn't escape her notice that she, once again, was doing the talking and he the listening.

"I was in the limo, on the way to the hotel, buffed and polished," Eliot told him, her voice low and her words slow. "I felt like I was heading to a shoot, like

I was acting in a commercial. I wasn't scared or excited or nervous or jittery. I didn't feel like a bride."

"I have this idea that you should feel something other than zoned out on your wedding day," she added. She turned her head to look at Soren, whose eyes were on her face, giving her his entire attention. "Don't you think?"

"Sounds about right."

"Getting married felt like just another job. I was going through the motions and I felt so disconnected that I didn't even think to question why he wasn't waiting for me at the altar." Eliot wrapped her arms around her legs, her chin on her knee. "And then he called it off. And all I could think was…'Thank God.' So no, I'm not devastated. I'm simply…" She trailed off.

"You're what?" Soren asked.

She looked out to sea and focused her attention on a ship on the horizon. "I was about to say that I'm back to feeling numb again but that's not true either. It's more like, after living my life anesthetized for years and years, I'm starting to feel pins and needles again. They aren't necessarily pleasant but they are real."

She could feel his eyes on her face but couldn't look at him or see the pity in his eyes. But she still felt the need to explain. "It's sometimes easier just to *not* feel, you know."

His hand came up to gently squeeze the back of her neck, a silent gesture of understanding or support. Or both.

"Are you still in love with him?"

"No. I'm not sure I ever was, really," Eliot quietly replied.

"So what's next for you?" Soren asked. "Any plans?"

Man, she wished she had an idea, just one, even if it was a bad one. Yesterday, she'd planned on becoming a wife, then a mother. Today her future looked hazy and undefined, nebulous. She didn't have a job, a goal or even an idea of what came next. For the first time in forever, she was navigating life without a compass. And that was okay. For now. They sat in silence for a few minutes before he gently bumped her shoulder with his. "So, shall I teach you to swim? It'll give me something to do so I don't mad with boredom while I'm stuck here."

She flinched. It was her fault the paparrazis had painted a target on his back. "I'm sorry you got to be collateral damage. I never meant to drag you into the spotlight with me. I saw the headlines. People are wondering why you are here with me when you should be in Miami, training."

"Yeah, yeah… There will be a lot of speculation about whether I am injured, whether I'm ill, whether I've had a nervous breakdown. Some of the braver souls are even speculating whether I am retiring. Our worlds colliding is what paparazzi and sports journalists dreams are made of. I can't stop them from doing any of that so what's the point of worrying about it?"

Impressed by his self-assurance and confidence, she thought she'd take another stab at finding out why he, workaholic that he was, wasn't in training. Whatever his reason, it wasn't because he needed a vacation. The Ice Man didn't take three-week breaks when he should be in the pool. "Will you tell me the real reason why you are taking time off at a crucial time?"

"Will you tell me why you've been living your life anesthetized?" Soren immediately countered.

He didn't want to answer her question and she didn't want to answer his. Fair enough, but that left a tense silence between them.

Swimming lessons were starting to sound like a good idea after all.

And yeah, she thought that a double Olympic and multi-world champion might be able to teach her that particular life skill. If she could keep her eyes, and hands, off his delicious body…

Five

Later that morning, Eliot stood in the dressing room of the pool house and looked down at the swimsuit in her hand. Aly, very kindly, had picked it up with the rest of her shopping. It was a plain red bikini Eliot was sure was at least one size too small.

It was one thing to prance around in front of stylists, photographers and other models in next to nothing, that was her job and one she'd been good at not so long ago. However, parading her heavier frame in front of a man she was wildly attracted to, someone whose body was sheer perfection, was daunting. He'd known her, made love to her when she was a lot younger—and a lot thinner—and she didn't want him to see the fat roll on her stomach, the cellulite on her thighs or the ever-so-tiny-but-still-there stretch marks she'd acquired over the last year.

Eliot was trying hard not to fat-shame herself but, despite knowing she was too skinny before and was healthier now, she was human and was, like so many other models, insecure.

Eliot stared at herself in the huge mirror that covered one wall of the dressing room, her chest heaving.

"Eliot!" Soren banged on the dressing room door. "What's taking so long?"

Waves of insecurity washed over her like a red, poisonous tide. She couldn't step out of the room with only four small triangles to cover a body that made her feel self-conscious, leaving her feeling raw and exposed and vulnerable. Couldn't bear the thought of being on display in front of Soren, who already saw way too much.

"Look, Soren, I've changed my mind. I don't need to learn how to swim." She'd tried to sound confident and direct but she didn't think she'd managed to pull it off.

When a minute passed and Soren didn't answer, she released a sigh of relief. She was just about to turn to leave when she heard the door opening and she saw him in the floor-to-ceiling mirror. He stood behind her, dressed in the same colorful pair of board shorts from earlier, his broad chest bare. With his strong arms, broad shoulders, a muscled chest and that amazing washboard stomach, he was bodily perfection.

She was…not.

Leaning his shoulder into the wall, his gaze darted from the swimsuit she held in her hand to her denim shorts and pink tank top to her face and back to the swimsuit again. "What's going on, Eliot?"

There was no way she was going to tell him that she had body and insecurity issues, so she tried for a negligent shrug. "The swimsuit isn't the right size."

He nodded to a cupboard behind her. "We keep the cupboard stocked for guests. There are at least five different styles in every size imaginable."

Of course they did. She stared at the floor and her shell-pink toes. "It doesn't matter because I've changed my mind."

"No, you haven't. You want to learn to swim," Soren stated with complete assurance. "Try again."

Eliot threw up her hands. "Why can't you ever take anything I say at face value? Why can't you just let things slide?"

"Because I don't deal in bullshit," Soren whipped back. "Tell me the truth about why you've changed your mind."

To her dismay, her eyes burned with tears and she blinked rapidly, praying they'd evaporate before he saw them. She knew she was being foolish—being insecure about her body was ridiculous and fat-shaming herself was unacceptable—but she couldn't help it. It was what she did, what she'd been taught to do. Her body had always been her tool and now it was no longer up for the job.

Soren stepped forward, frowning. "Jesus, El, are you crying?"

She shook her head, dislodging some strands of hair from the messy knot on top of her head. "No, of course not."

He used his knuckle to tip her chin until she had no choice but to look up. "Is it because of the wedding? Are you upset about the breakup?" he asked, concerned.

Eliot considered lying, taking the easy way out. If she nodded, she knew that Soren would back away, accept the explanation and give her some time and space. But she didn't want to lie to him. Frankly, she didn't think she could.

She had the feeling the Soren would see straight through the lie anyway.

She pushed the balls of her hands into her eyes to push back her tears. "You won't understand, Soren. And I don't think I have the words to explain."

His thumb skated across her cheekbone. "Try."

He stepped to the side and resumed his slouchy stance, his shoulder pushing into the mirror this time. He looked relaxed but Eliot knew he could rocket into action in a heartbeat. He was so physical, Eliot thought. So powerful, his body built for speed.

Eliot sat down on the white bench in front of the mirror and rested her forearms on her knees, looking for her words. How could she explain without sounding narcissistic?

She shrugged. "I'm feeling embarrassed at getting nearly naked in front of you," she quietly admitted.

His eyebrows shot up as he straightened, and surprise skipped across his normally implacable face. He rubbed his jaw, frowning. "I… What? *Why?*"

She stood up and skimmed her hands over her hips. "I've picked up many pounds since you last saw me."

Shock remained in his eyes as his eyes traveled down her body. Despite feeling embarrassed and miserable, desire heated her blood because his stare was anything but judgmental.

"Are you kidding me?" he demanded, his voice hoarse. "You think you are fat?"

"I'm no longer the perfect size four. I'm not even a six. I won't fit into any designer dresses and no one will hire me for swimsuit or lingerie campaigns— hell, any campaigns—unless I get back to my old measurements," she explained. "I'm too big to book."

"It sounds like the fashion industry is a very tough, even brutal world," Soren stated.

"It's a world that routinely tells little girls, teenagers and women you must be skinny and pretty and have long legs and great boobs to feel good about yourself. Some labels have are attempting to rewrite that narrative by booking the occasional gorgeous woman of color or plus-size model—but don't kid yourself, eighty percent of models hired are pretty, skinny white girls."

Eliot pushed her hand into her hair, causing strands to fall down her face. "And, Jesus, I am complicit in promoting all of that. I have been the face of *that*. I've helped reinforce the idea that if you don't look a certain way then you are not good enough.

"I wish I hadn't taken that talent scout's card back when I was fourteen. I wish I had thrown it in the trash and never showed it to my mom. That was my biggest mistake," she continued.

"Why?" Soren asked.

"Ursula grabbed on to this idea of me being a model and, like a dog with lockjaw, wouldn't let go. Within weeks of that chance encounter, I went from a nerdy, goofy kid to a professional model who earned more on one shoot than my mom did in two months. On my second job, I earned more than she did in *six* months. And God, it was so damn confusing.

"Do you have your phone on you? I'll show you." When he handed it over, Eliot did a quick search and found the images from that first year she started modeling. She pulled up a shot of her in a skimpy bikini— butt and boobs out, mouth looking sulky and sexy, her hair tousled.

"Hot, right?" Eliot asked, her tone scathing. He didn't answer, choosing to wait while she pulled up another photo, this one from the cloud, in her folder of personal photos. It showed Eliot in a long, baggy T-shirt, legs draped over the arms of a chair, a cat in her lap and big glasses on her face. She had a zit on her chin, and her hair was flat on one side and a mess on the other. Pretty, sure, in a blond, blue-eyed way, but young—so damn young.

"How old were you here?"

"That was taken two days after my fifteenth birthday." She swiped right to show him the sexy photo. "That shoot happened two days after that photo was taken."

She sighed and dropped her phone. "There are so many photos showing the same contrast—me being a kid, me being a model. In one shoot I'm with a guy in his early twenties—a good eight or ten years older than me—and he has his hands on my ass and his mouth on my neck. At that point, I'd never been kissed. Yet, there we were, looking like he's about to haul me off to bed. The photographer kept yelling at me to make it sexier, steamier—as if I had any idea how to do that. I wanted to die that day."

Soren winced. "Why did you take the assignment?"

She looked at him like he'd just fallen out of a mango tree. "I didn't have a choice in assignments, Soren. They made an offer and my mom accepted. We didn't know if I was a flash in the pan sensation and she was determined to cash in as much as she could. She said yes to everything, and when complained, she told me to just suck it up and deal. Dealing meant I had to cope with situations that made me deeply uncomfortable."

"Is that why you got involved in that campaign to highlight sexual abuse in the modeling world?"

She nodded. "Sexual abuse and harassment are rife in the industry, especially with the younger models who don't have the clout to fight back. I was one of the lucky ones. My mom was always on set when I was younger and nothing like that happened. But anyway, I've gone off the point…"

"Which is?"

She pulled her forefinger through the air in an up and down motion, gesturing to his frame. "My body isn't what it used to be, and when I'm faced with getting nearly naked with one of the best bodies in the world, I'm a little freaked out, okay?"

"No," Soren replied, his tone gentle. "Nothing about this conversation is okay. Stand up."

Eliot did as he asked. She watched in the mirror as he came to stand behind her, his big hands resting on her shoulders. Eliot looked at their reflections, his dark head a stunning contrast to her bright blond hair. Though she was close to six feet, he still topped her by two or three inches. His expression was deadly serious and focused on her.

"Will you trust me, El? Just for the next few minutes?"

Eliot frowned at him. "To do what?"

He shook his head. "Will you trust me, with your body? Will you let me show you what I see?"

His stare didn't waver, and Eliot saw encouragement in his eyes, silently asking her to take a chance. What would he do? What would he say? Could she stand it if he criticized her? She'd heard so much negativity from DeShawn and her mother, but she didn't think she could handle it from Soren.

She started to shake her head but something in

his eyes made her hesitate, made her willing to take a few steps down this path and see where it took her. She nodded once. "But I reserve the right to stop you at any time if I feel uncomfortable."

The relief in Soren's eyes was unmistakable. "That goes without saying."

He stepped back and lifted his knuckles to the tight-with-tension cords in her neck, skating over her skin. "You have the most elegant neck. It was one of the things I first noticed about you. And I adore your skin."

She noticed the brown spot high on her cheek, then the one on her chin. "I look better with makeup."

Soren gently laid his hand over her mouth. "For the next few minutes, will you just listen? I want you to hear my words, let them sink in."

Could she do that? She didn't know. "I can try…"

"Try hard," Soren suggested, dropping his hand to toy with the hem of her shirt. He tugged it up, and when she didn't object, pulled it up and over her head, dropping it to the floor at her feet. In the mirror, she took in her white bra. His tanned hands skated down her ribs, across her stomach and up her arms. Lust heated his eyes and Eliot's breath hitched in her throat. He wasn't speaking, just looking at her with wonder in his eyes, appreciation.

"I love your height, your long arms and legs," Soren murmured, his arms crisscrossing her chest, his forearms pushing into her breasts. "Look how lovely you are, how feminine, how gorgeous you look in my arms."

Eliot looked at their reflections, noticing how much bigger he was than her. The muscles in his arms flexed, and his hands covered a fair bit of her sides. Then his right hand moved to cover her left breast, his hand so tanned against her white underwear.

"I love your breasts. Who wouldn't?"

His hands went to the front clasp of her bra lying above her sternum and with a quick flick of his fingers, he opened the clasp and pulled the cups of her bra away, allowing the garment to slide down her arms. She raised her eyes from her breasts to his face and her breath caught at the admiration on his face. It was blindingly obvious, by his expression, and the hard erection pushing into her back, that Soren very much liked what he saw.

When his fingers drifted over her, she dropped her gaze to see his fingers on her pink, erect nipples. Heat and light and power flashed through her system. "Perfectly round, the same color as your lips," he murmured.

Eliot found herself arching into his hand, but before she could push her nipples against his palms, he dropped his hands, one to lie flat against her stomach, the other to rest on her fleshy hip. She immediately tensed and Soren frowned.

"Trust me, El."

He deftly opened the button to her denim shorts, his fingers working the zipper down. Soren slid his hands between her hips and the fabric, pulling it down by hooking his thumbs into the waistband. The shorts fell to her feet and when she stepped out of them Soren kicked them away. God, look at her. To her eyes, her tummy roll looked enormous, her hips were too round and she didn't even want to look at her butt.

"Stop it, Eliot," Soren's voice held a hint of sharpness, a definite command. "Stop listening to the voices in your head and listen to *me*."

She hauled in some air, released it, and, not able to look at her body, looked at Soren's gorgeous face instead. But Soren wouldn't let her avoid her reflection. "Look at your stomach, sweetheart."

She didn't want to and shook her head. "*Soren…*"

He pushed his fingers between the fabric of her panties and her skin. Shocked, she watched them fall to the floor.

"Yeah, you are carrying a little more weight but who the hell cares? Sure, you don't have a flat stomach anymore and I can no longer see your hip bones but you look better, healthier than you did all those years ago. Rounded, fuller, lovelier. I thought you were beautiful back then, and I find you stunning now."

Eliot gasped, shivering at the need in his voice. "Really?" she asked on a hot, turned-on gasp. Heat pooled between her legs and she watched as her body flushed a pale pink.

"*Really.* Can I show you how beautiful you are?" Soren asked her, his fingers tracing the flesh above her mostly hairless mound.

"How?" The word came out strangled, garbled.

"Watch and you'll see," Soren told her. "Can I?"

How could she say no? Standing in his arms, for the first time in months—years—she felt seen, admired, not as a blank canvas for someone else's creation, but as a work of art in her own right. A beautiful painting, a sensuous sculpture, a delicate handblown piece of glass. Admired in her purest form.

As a woman. As *Eliot*.

Eliot wanted to see herself through his eyes so she nodded and dropped her head back to rest on his shoulder. A long, relieved shudder ran through him and he placed his open mouth on the spot where her shoulder met her neck, gently sucking on her skin. One hand returned to her breast while his other hand dropped lower to explore, stopping briefly when he encountered the tiny, well-groomed triangle of hair. She felt his smile, and their eyes connected in the mirror as his fingers slid between her legs, tracing her feminine lips. She was so wet and so hot and she squirmed, trying to get him to sink his fingers into her.

"Look at how blue your eyes are, El." Eliot reluctantly dragged her gaze up and gasped at the depth of color in her reflected eyes, the blue intensely bold. Her eyes were huge and her skin flushed, making her look like she'd spent the day in the sun.

"Reach up and let your hair down," Soren told her. Eliot pulled the band away, allowing it to fall, so light and so bright, over her shoulders and down her back. Soren immediately buried his nose in the long strands, sighing. "I love your scent, the way the light catches your waves, the softness of your skin.

"Do you know how beautiful you are, Eliot? Look at you, looking so wild and free." Soren's words were accompanied by his finger sliding into her, his thumb brushing her clitoris. "God, you take my breath away. You look like a fierce Viking queen, powerful and ferocious."

Eliot looked at herself, thinking that the woman in the mirror bore no resemblance to the person she normally was. As Soren said, she looked fierce, confident and compelling, a woman who knew what she wanted and how to get it.

A woman on the edge of pleasure, able to reach out and take what she wanted. "More, Soren."

"How much more?" Soren asked her, pushing another finger into her, stretching her. She buzzed at a higher frequency as she felt electricity dance on her skin, the pull of a fantastic orgasm. Eliot lifted her hand to curl it around the back of Soren's neck and watched, fascinated, as his fingers curled into her, his thumb brushing over her most sensitive spot.

She was so close, and time stood still and sensation took over. Soren brushed her clit again, his fingers stretched inside her. Lights flashed behind her eyes when he tugged her nipple between the fingers of his other hand, creating a feedback loop of sensation between her breast and her womb, throwing her over the edge. Shudders rocked her body as she split apart;

colors became sensations, and sensations morphed into pulsing lights behind her eyelids. She wanted to close her eyes but couldn't. She wanted to watch the woman in the mirror as the dark-haired man rocked her to a height she'd never reached before.

She was but not, standing outside of herself and also fully immersed. But, also, at that moment, beautiful. A goddess.

Not because she had symmetrical features or good curves, stunning legs and bright blue eyes, but because, in Soren's arms, she was 100 percent authentically herself.

And Soren, judging by the tortured admiration written all over his face, loved and craved every inch of her body.

When her shudders subsided, Soren rested his temple against her messy hair, pulled his hand away, and crisscrossed her arms across her body again, holding her in that ultra-protective grip. His still hard erection pushed into her butt and lower back and as she came back to herself, she realized that he'd given and given, and had asked for nothing in return.

She met his eyes in the mirror. "We can...you know." She gestured down between his legs.

He shook his head. "This wasn't about me, El. It was my way of showing you that a couple of extra pounds mean jack shit, that you're a stunning woman even if the world, and the people in that world, haven't made you feel that way lately."

Eliot relaxed in his arms and, for just a moment, decided to believe him.

"Thank you," she whispered.

His eyes met hers in the mirror and his lips twitched. "Anytime, sweetheart. Touching you is not, in any way, a hardship. Are you ready to learn to swim now?"

She'd far prefer for him to take her to bed but since swimming that was all he was offering…

Sure.

Jacinda Knowles made her way along the stone path to the barn Paz Conway used as his studio and cursed her pounding heart. She was fifty-two years old and she had no business lusting over a dark-haired, dark-eyed man twelve years younger than her! Good God, he was just six years older than her son! Shouldn't there be a law against menopausal women lusting over totally unsuitable men?

Surely there must be? If only to keep her from making an utter fool of herself.

Cursing herself for being so ridiculous, Jacinda shuffled through the stack of mail in her hand, knowing she could've pushed his letters under the door of the guesthouse for him to find. But no, for some reason she needed to torture herself by heading to the barn and seeing Paz in person.

She was so lame because there was no way that Paz—who was as famous for his oversized sculptors as he was for his affairs with stunning women—would associate her, a menopausal housekeeper with four grown-up sons: one she'd birthed and four she'd adopted into her heart, with bed breaking sex.

Annoyed with herself, Jacinda whipped around, intent on going back to her car and returning to the main house. She'd deliver Conway's mail when she'd corralled her raging hormones. Wasn't her libido supposed to subside around this time of her life? But no, hers was having a second wind…

She'd taken two steps when she bounced off what felt like a brick wall. She yelped, the mail went flying and she waited for her butt to slam into the ground… but that didn't happen because a strong arm encircled her waist. She found herself pressed up against a very firm, very hard and very warm male body.

"Are you okay?" Paz asked, his deep voice directly into her ear.

She nodded, and she looked down at his dark head as he dropped to his haunches to pick up the mail she'd dropped. She was glad to see an occasional strand of gray amongst those black strands, especially since she had more than a few herself. He wore black denim jeans that curved lovingly over an exemplary ass, and his white T-shirt didn't disguise the breadth of his shoulders or the muscles in his arms.

"Sorry, I wasn't looking where I was going," Jacinda said, shoving her shaking hands into the front pockets of her loose jeans.

"No worries," Paz replied, in his broad Australian accent. He flipped through the mail, tucked an envelope under his arm and raised his dark brows at a postcard. He frowned at the writing and Jacinda immediately knew that it was another missive for Avangeline, written, as it always was, in code.

For some reason, Jacinda felt the urge to explain. Why, she had no idea, because this man was only renting Avangeline's guesthouse and barn for the summer. He hadn't exchanged more than two words with his temporary landlord.

"Avangeline's been receiving postcards like that for as long as I have been here and that's over twenty-five years. One every month, always in code," Jacinda told him. "Pretty cool, huh?"

He smiled at her, his black eyes glinting with amusement. "And very frustrating because you have no idea what they say or who they are from."

Busted. Jacinda shrugged. "She pretends like it's nothing more interesting than another bill or a letter from her lawyer. But she always goes straight upstairs whenever she receives one."

"Because she can't wait to decode the message."

Jacinda leaned forward to look at the random letters neatly penned on the expensive card. "It looks like gibberish to me," she confessed.

Paz handed her the bundle of letters and their fingers brushed, sending a fireball of sensation up her arm. God, she had to get herself under control. "It's a variation on the Atbash cipher."

His eyes were gorgeous and he had just the right amount of stubble on his cheeks. His sexy mouth could, she was sure, set hers on fire. Catching herself staring, she blushed. "Sorry...what?"

He folded his arms, and she almost whimpered when his biceps bulged, straining against the sleeves of his T-shirt. "A simple Atbash cipher would swap an *A* for *Z*, a *B* for *Y*, a *C* for *X*... You get the picture."

She stared at him. "How do you know that?" she demanded.

He grinned. "My grandfather introduced me to codes and ciphers as a kid. I recognized it immediately. It's not that sophisticated." He plucked the postcard out of her hand, looked at it for a while, and nodded. "Okay, I think I have it. 'I love her and that's the beginning and end—'"

"'—of everything.'" Jacinda completed his sentence, her hand on her heart.

"F. Scott Fitzgerald," Paz said. "There's a PS as well."

She had no right to know what the PS said, and she wouldn't ask. But her eyebrows did, of their own volition, rise. After a few minutes, he spoke again. "'Forget about me and write your damn will, darling.'"

This person, obviously, knew Avangeline hadn't written her will. Who was he? And what part did he play in the ongoing last-will-and-testament saga?

Paz handed her the postcard, and his slow smile heated her from the inside out. "Avangeline has a lover and has had one for decades. That's pretty... cool."

Jacinda stared at him, guilt rolling over her. They

had no right to decode her employer and friend's messages; it was such a breach of her privacy and her trust. Regret, hot and acidic, rolled over her. "You shouldn't have decoded it. You had no right to do that."

She saw he was about to protest but then he winced, guilt and remorse flashing in his eyes. "You're right, I shouldn't have. But I was trying to impress you."

She stared at him, not understanding his words. "Why would you want to impress me?" she whispered, her fingers crumpling the letters in her hand.

"I've always had a weakness for dark-haired beauties with eyes the color of an Outback sky," Paz told her. He moved closer to her and Jacinda's eyes widened, wondering—hoping—he was about to kiss her. She stood statue still but his lips stopped somewhere close to her ear, his breath warm on her skin.

"Come for dinner one night, *any* night. And then let me take you to bed."

Holy…holy…*what*? Jacinda was still trying to formulate her words, to understand the implications when he kissed her temple and then walked in the direction of the barn.

He was nearly at the big barn doors when she regained her power of speech. "I've got to be at least ten or twelve years older than you, Conway!" she shouted.

He turned to look at her and raised one dark eyebrow. "To quote another famous novelist, Mark Twain, age is mind over matter. If we don't mind, then it doesn't matter." He sent her a look that she swore was hot enough to burn grass, evaporate water and melt glass.

"And I sure as hell don't mind."

With that he disappeared and Jacinda was left standing there, staring at the now empty barn doors.

What the hell just happened?

Six

Eliot was not a natural swimmer.

Soren looked down at her board-stiff body lying on top of the water, his hand under her back to keep her from sinking. Her eyes mirrored the sparkling waters of the outside pool and the red bikini was a perfect complement to her fair skin. Her blond hair trailed through the water but her toes were pointed and every muscle in her body was piano-wire stiff.

"Will you please relax?" Soren growled. "I told you I wouldn't let you go and even if I did, you could put your feet down and they'd hit the bottom of the pool."

Eliot hauled in a deep breath and he watched her perfect breasts—and they were perfect—rise and fall. After rocketing her to an orgasm and not getting off

himself, he needed all his self-control to keep his
hands from wandering, his mouth from plunging.
How could she think she was anything less than sensational? Didn't she have eyes in her head? On the
other hand, he knew a good number of models and
actresses were wildly insecure.

And he hated the fact that the people around her
reinforced her feelings of not being good enough. As
her husband-to-be, DeShawn should've protected her,
reassured her; her mother should've loved her and
built her up instead of dragging her down.

People sucked. Could he be blamed for wanting
to live his life solo?

Soren noticed her hard nipples pushing against
the fabric of her bikini top and swallowed his groan.
Being so close to her body without being allowed to
make love to her was pure torture. It took all his will-
power not to stroke her from tip to toe.

"I can't relax," Eliot whispered, her wide eyes
looking into his mirrored shades.

"Yeah, you can," Soren told her. "Because until
you do, you won't float and you can't swim if you
can't float. So, relax, Stone!"

"Don't quit your day job, Soren," Eliot muttered
before closing her eyes and hauling a deep breath.
Her long eyelashes, free from mascara, lay against
her skin and he noticed the tiniest of scars on her
top lip. Soren watched, fascinated, as she continued
to breathe deeply, and then her shoulders dropped
from around her ears. Her fists unclenched, and her

feet started to point to the sky. He debated whether to let her go but decided to give her another minute or two. When she released a tiny sigh, he finally dropped his hand, allowing her to float. He folded his arms and smiled as she lay there, looking like a glorious starfish.

But then her eyes flew open and she started to flail, her hands banging the water and her head slipping under the surface. He gave her a couple of seconds, wondering if she would remember to stand. When her legs kicked out in panic, he grabbed her by the upper arm and hauled her face above water.

"Why did you let me go?" she yelled at him, terror in her eyes.

"I let you go because you were floating," Soren replied, keeping his voice calm.

She wiped her hand across her eyes. "My face went under the water."

"Yeah, that's what happens when you swim," Soren replied, keeping his tone easy.

"I can't do this, Soren."

Someone had taught this woman to doubt herself, to be scared, and he hated it.

"You can do anything you set your mind to, Eliot," he told her. "For starters, you can put your feet down to stand."

Her feet hit the pool's bottom and she released her grip around his neck. Her eyes widened. A pink flush stained her cheeks as the water hit the top of her chest. "Right, well, don't I feel stupid?"

"A lot of people drown because they panic and don't test whether they can stand. In a lot of cases, they can, they just don't think to try."

"Got it," Eliot muttered. She pushed her hair back and allowed her hand to drift across the surface of the clear, bright water. "Did you learn to swim here, at Calcott Manor? In this pool?"

Soren moved into a deeper part of the pool and started to tread water, just because he could and because his body needed to move. "Not in this pool, no. We only came to live at Calcott Manor when I was nine. I've been led to believe that I could swim before I could walk. My mom taught me the basics—she was a good swimmer herself."

When he was thirteen, and showing promise to be a swimming great, his grandmother commissioned the indoor, Olympic-sized pool. He initially trained with a local club but when his then coach told Avangeline that his talent outstripped his coaching abilities, Avangeline sent him to train three times a week at a training facility in New York City. And specialized coaches had trained him here at Calcott Manor.

Avangeline supplied the money and he put in the effort and all that time spent in the pool had paid off. He'd fulfilled his potential and exceeded even their wildest dreams. And now he was considering whether it was time to retire, whether to go out on a high or to push on and go out on a whimper.

Soren looked at his watch and saw that it was just past eleven thirty. He should be in the gym, lifting weights, doing his usual workout session. His body felt tight from lack of exercise and his mind wanted to jump out of its skull. It was only day three of his forced break—how was he going to fill those empty hours with nothing to do?

He liked structure, being focused and having daily, monthly and yearly goals. He was detail orientated and needed to be busy. Lounging around wasn't his style. His original plan, before he got involved in rescuing the beautiful bride-to-be, had been to spend a few days catching up with Avangeline and Jacinda, and to see if he could try and talk his grandmother into making a will. Then he'd planned on visiting an adventure hot spot: Costa Rica, maybe, or Kauai—somewhere where there were lots of adventures to have, giving him little time to overthink and overanalyze his future while still staying active and occupied.

But the press attention had nixed that plan. And, to be honest, with Eliot dropping back into his life he wasn't going anywhere. Not just yet.

But if he didn't find something to do at Calcott Manor, he was going to start climbing the walls from frustration. He just knew it.

Teaching Eliot to swim was, at least, something to occupy his time. He held his hand palm up and jerked his head at Eliot. "Come on, let's try again."

Eliot looked from his hand to his face and back again. Then she shook her head. "Nope, I'm done for the day."

They'd only been at it for twenty-five or thirty minutes. They hadn't made much progress.

"Learn to float and then you can quit for the day," he told her. He grabbed her under the legs and was about to tip her backward when her eyes met his, and electricity or chemistry or connection arced between them. He held her like that for a few seconds before abruptly dropping her legs and in a swift, sure movement, pulled her to him so that her breasts pushed into his chest…

He didn't hesitate, couldn't. His mouth covered hers and then his tongue slipped past her teeth. Suddenly he was racing his best race, shattering a record, receiving a medal, all at the same time. He was swimming through sunlight, powering through the universe, free and feeling fantastic.

Her mouth was lovely, and her soft hands on his shoulders sent ribbons of pleasure rushing through him. She made a sound deep in the back of her throat and he hardened further, the material of their swimsuits the only barrier between their bare skin. He ran his hand down her back, over her curvy hip, and back up and over her ribs, unable to resist cupping her full breast and finding her nipple with his thumb.

Another rumble of appreciation and she arched into his hand, enjoying his touch.

He knew that if he sank his fingers between her legs, she'd be warm and willing.

Their attraction had always been immediate and hot. Soren was about to take her mouth again, to pull her legs up and around his waist, when he remembered the living room windows of the main house looked down onto the outdoor pool. They could be giving his grandmother, Jace and that grifter, Aly, a peep show. He immediately shriveled at the thought.

And as his passion cooled, he remembered that despite their hot encounter earlier, she'd been through hell lately and he'd be taking advantage if he pushed for more.

Anything that happened between them had to come from her; she needed to be the one setting the pace here.

Dammit.

Soren used both his hands to push back his hair, an action he'd done a million times before—two million. Taking a deep breath, he nodded. "Right, back to what we were doing. Lie on your back and relax."

Eliot started to lean back and he thought that she was about to resume the lesson. But, at the last minute, she shook her head. "I don't want to, not today."

"El, come on," he coaxed.

Determination shone brightly in her incredible eyes. "I'm a people pleaser, Soren. It's why I nearly got married to someone who barely saw me, probably why I've been so very unhappy for so many years. I keep the peace, do what people want and give them what they want and need. I've been doing it since I was fourteen years old and it's, I suppose, a habit.

"But I'm not doing that anymore. I'm going to do

what I want when I want to. And right now, I don't want to be in this pool anymore."

He watched as she walked up the pool's steps and onto the wooden deck. Soren stared at her slim back and her swinging hips and felt a little bemused, a lot disconcerted and even more turned on.

She picked up a towel, wound it around her body, and headed into the pool house to change.

Right, well…

Guess he wasn't giving any more swimming lessons today.

The next day, Soren walked into Avangeline's morning sitting room and found her where he expected her to be, sitting on the couch by the open French doors that led out to her beloved rose garden. A gentle, early morning breeze pulled the scent of the lavender and roses into the room and swirled around him as he took a seat opposite her.

His grandmother's lovely face was deeply lined but she still wore her trademark red lipstick, black-rimmed glasses and a ten-carat diamond ring on her ring finger.

As he waited for Avangeline to pull her attention from her newspaper, he looked around the room, idly noting that the Picasso had changed places with the Rothko and that two irreplaceable Chinese vases had been moved out of the room. Avangeline, who had a passion for antiques, could've lent them to a museum or, for all he knew, sold them for something better or rarer.

Avangeline lowered her newspaper, folded it into a square and laid it on the coffee table in front of her, perfectly aligned with the silver tray holding a carafe of coffee and a single expensive cup and saucer.

Jacinda would be bringing him his coffee soon, in a sturdy mug. He could afford antiques but he preferred to drink out of something simple and solid.

"Good morning, Soren."

"Avangeline," Soren replied. She was always Avangeline, even when they'd been small. "Grandmother," on the very rare occasion, was acceptable.

"So, they sent you first," Avangeline said, her back steel-rod straight and her right foot tucked behind her left calf.

Soren widened his eyes, hoping to convey innocence. "I don't understand what you mean," he answered her.

"You and your brothers got together, decided I was acting out of character and that you needed to take turns to check out the money-grabbing con woman who is trying to take advantage of me," Avangeline crisply stated.

Well, yes. That.

"And to get me to make a will." Avangeline's fingers dug into seat of her cushion.

Soren didn't see any point in dancing around the subject. "Precisely. We don't understand why you are balking," Soren shot back. He leaned forward, sending her a hard look. "You owned and operated a billion-dollar empire, a multi-national company. You understand, better than most, why it's so important to be legally protected, to have clear directives in place for every eventuality. Your lack of action is baffling, Grandmother."

Something flashed in her eyes and Soren frowned, unsure of what he'd seen. His grandmother looked, for a moment, lost and alone. But why?

When she turned her gaze to look at him, her eyes were shuttered and all he saw was flat green. Was that what people saw when they looked into his eyes? Nothing but a barrier, an impenetrable wall of brilliant color?

"I will make a will when I am ready!"

"You are eighty-two years old, Avang—"

"I might be old, Soren, but I haven't lost my mind!"

"Nobody is suggesting that you have. But not making a will and inviting a strange woman into your house are both risky moves," Soren countered. "What do you know about her? What does she want? Why is she here?"

"Ask her yourself."

Avangeline gestured to the high-back couch in the corner. Soren peered over it to see Aly sitting with her back to him, cross-legged on the floor between the couch and the floor-to-ceiling bookcase, family photographs in piles around her. Because it was facing him, he saw the photograph in her hand. It was a favorite of his—the five boys hamming it up on a ski slope when they were all in their teens—and he felt a knife slide into his heart.

He glared at her, hating the thought of a stranger holding his precious memories. "Why do you have those? What are you doing?"

"Looking at photographs and sorting them out, as per Avangeline's instructions," Aly replied, picking up a photograph of his Uncle Jesse standing by his beloved Cessna airplane. The photograph had been taken a few weeks before the crash that made him and his cousins orphans.

Aly picked up the photograph and flicked her thumbnail against the edge. "Was your uncle an experienced pilot?"

Wow, what a weird question. And yes, Jesse had flown since he was a teenager and had many hours in the sky, as he told Aly. "Why do you ask?"

A strange expression crossed Aly's face before she pulled up a polite smile. She shrugged. "Casual question."

No, it wasn't.

"Come and join us, Alyson," Avangeline demanded and Aly immediately rose to her feet and walked around the couch back to where Avangeline sat. She perched on the edge of a white wingback chair and crossed her legs.

Soren squeezed the bridge of his nose, closed his eyes and pulled in a long breath. He needed to get to the bottom of why this woman was in his grandmother's house and report back to the brothers. And then they'd decide on how to deal with her. If she wanted money, they might just pay her off. They were wealthy and sometimes money changing hands was the most expedient, minimal-hassle option.

"Talk," Soren told her, wishing Jacinda would hurry up with his coffee.

Aly sent him a smile that held no amusement. "You should know that I don't respond well to orders, Mr. Grantham. And if this conversation is going to denigrate into you shouting at me, there isn't going to be a conversation at all."

Right. Well, that told him. Soren turned at the sound of Jacinda entering the room, carrying his mug. She looked like she always did, fresh and lovely and much younger than her fifty-plus years. He got up, dropped a kiss on her temple and took his coffee with a grateful smile.

Avangeline might've made the decisions, and taken on the responsibility of raising her four grandsons, but Jacinda had been the person they ran to when they were feeling scared or unsure, the person they called in the middle of the night when they needed a lift home, got into trouble or when they were feeling sick or sad.

He, and his brothers, worshipped the ground she walked on. "Morning, Jace."

Jacinda placed her hand on his cheek. "Baby boy," she murmured. "You look tired. Stressed."

She'd always been able to see through his impenetrable shell to see what was roiling below the surface. "I'm dealing with…things," he said.

Things like whether he should reinvent his life or not. And his fire-hot attraction to Eliot…

"You'll work it out," Jacinda told him with complete conviction.

She sat down on the couch next to Avangeline and Soren resumed his seat. He took a grateful sip of his coffee and placed it on the table. Right, it was time to learn who this Aly person was and what she was doing here.

Avangeline took Aly's hand, a gesture that surprised him. While Jacinda doled out hugs and kisses on a routine basis—much to their outward teenage disgust—Avangeline usually kept her distance. Their grandmother loved them but she expected them to know it without resorting to public displays of affection, so seeing her being physically affectionate was a surprise.

"Go on, darling. He won't bite." She glared at Soren. "Or at least, he'd better not."

Soren spread his hands. Okay, Avangeline was firmly in Camp Aly and, judging by the worry on Jacinda's face when she looked at Aly, so was she. This woman must have a hell of a story to tell.

If it was true.

Aly played with the hem on her shorts and her sandal-covered foot jerked up and down. "When I was in my late teens, I needed a liver transplant," she quietly told him.

That sounded grim, Soren silently admitted.

"I contracted hepatitis C and I was in a dire way.

Long story short, I received your brother's liver. It's been ten years since my operation," Aly said, darting a look at Avangeline. His grandmother squeezed her hand again in encouragement. "I reached out to Avangeline because I wanted to say thank you, to thank your grandmother...

"I mean, I'm not glad he died, I'm glad—God—this is always so hard."

"Alyson, none of us wanted Malcolm to die. But we're glad some good came of his death," Avangeline stated, her voice firm.

Soren stared at her, still unsure where this was going. They knew that Aly was one of Malcolm's organ recipients—or at least, that that was what she was claiming. None of this was news. And none of it explained why she had moved in.

Surely they could've had an awkward lunch or corresponded via email.

"There's something else..." Aly said, her words running together. She scrunched her eyes shut and wrinkled her nose and Soren braced for a request for money, a hand-me-the-moon demand probably packaged around some sob story that she'd already shared with the others.

Was this the story Merrick had mentioned? The one that he needed to hear in person?

Soren turned back to Aly and rolled his finger in a silent command for her to continue.

"So, along with Malcolm's liver, I also inherited some of his memories."

Soren blinked, hearing the words but unable to make sense of them. What the *fuck* did that even mean? How can someone inherit a memory? That was completely insane.

"What?" Soren demanded.

Aly rubbed the back of her head. "Do you want the simple or the medical explanation?" Aly asked him.

"Give me an explanation I'll believe," Soren said, pushing the words through his teeth.

"So, there's this phenomenon in medical circles called cellular memory theory. It's this idea that memories, quirks and personality traits can be stored in places apart from the brain. That they can be stored in individual cells or life-giving organs. There are documented cases from all over the world of this happening," Aly added.

Soren could not believe he was sitting here, listening to this bullshit.

He shook his head and looked at Avangeline. "I know that you miss Malcolm, Avangeline, and that his death rocked you. I get that, but this is ludicrous."

The bright spark in her eyes, the force and determination he remembered so well but hadn't seen for a while, pinned him to his seat. "You will stay, and you will hear her out."

He was a grown man, someone who didn't take orders from anyone, ever. Except, apparently, his grandmother, because his butt remained glued to his chair.

Aly sent him a sympathetic smile. "I know how strange this sounds, Soren, I *do*. I don't blame you for being skeptical. I've spent so much time trying to find a different explanation for what's happening to me but I can't."

Soren rubbed his forehead with his fingertips. He might as well listen to her story and then he could give his brothers the whole picture. At least he got understood why Merrick hadn't been willing to explain when they'd had their lunch together.

"I feel things, things I shouldn't. I remember things I shouldn't, know subjects I shouldn't," Aly said, pushing her hair off her forehead.

"Tell her about your new love of speed," Avangeline urged Aly.

Aly hesitated before shrugging. "I was eighteen when I contracted hep C. Before that, I was fearful of cars, and of being in a car. Someone close to me died in a horrific accident a few years earlier, and I hated cars. I didn't even want to learn to drive. It was something close to a phobia," Aly admitted.

"One of the first things I did after my surgery recovery was to get my driver's license, and I quickly racked up speeding tickets. I went on an advanced driving course, did a basic mechanics course and learned how to ride a motorbike. I adore speed"

He didn't say anything, forcing Aly to fill in the blanks. "Your brother, so your grandmother says, was a real gearhead. He loved everything to do with engines and bikes and cars."

Yeah, so? So did tens of millions of people who had no connection to his family at all. As for her developing a new interest after surgery… Well, people grew and changed, especially after big changes in their lives like an organ transplant. That's what could've happened to her. Or maybe this wasn't even true—she could've read about Mal's love for cars online and learned enough to have an "in."

"I only started having an affinity with cars after my transplant, Soren."

Soren stared at her. "That's all you've got?" he demanded, his tone scathing. "Seriously, that's *it*?"

Aly pulled a face. "No, I'm now messy and I used to be tidy. I seem to have an affinity for candy of all types, and, before the transplants, I didn't eat, or even like, sugar."

Malcolm constantly craved sugar and had packets of candy in his pockets, in his car, in his laptop case and in a hundred different hiding places in his house and office. But it was another lucky guess. It *had* to be.

"I'm not buying any of this." Soren shrugged. He looked at Aly, knowing he had his race-day face on, the one that commentators said intimidated the hell out of his competitors. It wasn't something he cultivated; it was just his default expression when he was completely focused on an outcome. And right now his goal was to get this charlatan out of his grandmother's house.

"How much do you want?" he demanded.

"Fifty million," Aly shot back.

Soren nodded. That was her starting offer, which

probably meant she'd take a tenth of that. Or a twentieth. "If you leave within the next thirty minutes, I won't press charges for fraud and misrepresentation."

"Press charges?" Aly asked, her eyes darting between his and Avangeline's. "Why would you... Dear God, you thought I was being *serious*?"

"Soren has always been a rather serious boy," Avangeline added. She sounded disapproving, but he wasn't going to apologize for it. Life was goddamn serious. He'd lost his entire family in the blink of an eye, went from being an only child into a family with three other boys, and from the age of thirteen, dedicated his life to his sport.

"I don't want Avangeline's money, Soren—or yours," Aly told him. She rose to her feet and pushed her hands into the pockets of her shorts. "I just want to get to know Malcolm's family a little, that's all."

Feeling the urge to run from this woman, he pushed himself to his feet, determined to put as much distance between them as fast as he could. It had been hard enough to lose Mal, but having some crackpot, bullshit charlatan spouting nonsense at him was a step too far.

He should never have left Florida, never should have stopped training. In the pool, everything was regimented and controlled. Between Eliot and this BS, he was so far out of his comfort zone that he wasn't sure he'd be able to find his way back.

His grandmother pushed herself to her feet and her eyes turned ice cold. "How dare you think that I'm stupid enough to be conned, Soren! I might not run an international company anymore but do credit me for retaining a few of my marbles!"

He saw Jacinda wince and knew he was in serious trouble. Oh well, it wouldn't be the first time. He and his brothers had all been on the sharp end of his grandmother's tongue on various occasions. The others had experienced it more than him—he'd had minimal time to get into trouble—but he recognized the signs.

"As soon as I heard this story, I contacted a private investigator and had her investigate Alyson's life, telling her I wanted to know everything about her. It's all true."

"Including the fact that she's inherited Malcolm's love of engines?" Soren retorted. "Candies? Beer?"

Avangeline's eyes narrowed. "This is still my house and I will still make decisions as to who stays in it. Furthermore, I will make a will when I want to and I will decide who gets what."

Well, he couldn't get in much more trouble than he already was, so in for a penny and all that. "I don't give a damn who you leave your assets to, as long as you leave clear instructions. So will you, please, write it already? If you die without one, you'll be leaving us, especially my brothers, with a hell of a headache."

Jacinda closed her eyes and shook her head. "Soren, darling."

Soren shrugged. He and his grandmother had always been brutally honest with each other. It wasn't always comfortable but he knew he could rely on her to give him the absolute truth, and she knew that he would do the same.

He didn't like this situation with Aly and, in case Avangeline was in any doubt of that, he told her so again.

"Your concern," Avangeline said, her tone winter cold and desert dry, "is noted." She nodded to the door. "Please feel free to remove yourself from my company."

"Maybe I should go," Aly suggested, looking anguished. If she was acting, she was good at it.

Avangeline pointed a still, elegant finger at her. "You are going nowhere, my girl. Soren is going to walk away and, sometime later, he will return with an apology." She tipped her head to the side. "It'll probably be ridiculously insincere but his brothers will make him say it because if he doesn't, *he* will be the one leaving. They'll want him here until they can get down here to help him keep an eye on me and, hopefully, chase you away." She smiled at Aly. "Don't let them bully you, Aly dear."

Soren rolled his eyes. But, to be honest, Avangeline had called it correctly. That was exactly what would happen.

Soren looked at his grandmother—really looked—surprised by what he saw. Over the last two or three years they'd noticed, along with a tendency to be agoraphobic, a decline in her normally stylish personal standards. Instead of the ill-fitting clothes he recalled from recent visits, she wore a fitted dress with boldly patterned orange poppies. Instead of just wearing lipstick, he now noticed that she'd put on some foundation and some blusher. Diamond studs glinted in her earlobes and her hair had been recently styled. She looked ten years younger and a hundred times better.

Aly might have an agenda—what it was he wasn't sure—but, since she was the anomaly in his grandmother's world, she'd brought life back into Avangeline's world. But he didn't like Aly's so-called connection to Malcolm or the ridiculous claims about inheriting traits and tastes from him. And if she was using the memory of his dead cousin/brother to feather her nest, he'd rip her apart.

Mal was the best of them—his mentor, confidant, and best friend—and for as long as he could draw breath, he'd protect his memory and legacy.

Avangeline

I know that I need a will, goddamn it! I'm not a bloody idiot. But I can't make one, not yet. I can't bear to put down what is being demanded on paper, but if I do not, the ramifications will be enormous...emotionally and financially. What level of hell is this? Sixteen?

I got a postcard today. For just a minute, maybe two, my dodgy old heart skipped and jumped like it did when we were young.

Seven

In the indoor swimming pool, attached to the east wing of the house, Eliot sat on the edge of the lounger and watched Soren cut through the clear water, powering his way from one end to the other. There was something about his style, and his focus that suggested he was swimming with a purpose. Eliot wondered if he was aware that he was breaking his self-imposed ban on training.

She'd been in the rose garden when she saw him, fury and fear on his face, exit the manor house. He'd rested his hands on the veranda's low stone wall and dropped his head between his arms, and his mouth had moved in what she presumed were silent curses. Then he'd disappeared back inside, looking thoroughly annoyed and more than a little off-balance.

Shrugging, she'd continued walking through Avangeline's garden, enjoying the luxurious beds, the unusual plants and, yes, the peace.

She couldn't remember when last she'd experienced such quiet. Oh, she occasionally heard the sweet call of a gull now and again, the crash of a wave or the distant sound of a tractor, but what she didn't hear were those city sounds—the constant wash of traffic, horns, sirens and people being busy.

She'd never felt so relaxed as she did here at Calcott Manor.

She'd been lucky to land here after her non-wedding debacle, to find herself in such beautiful surroundings. She'd already been here for a couple of days and had settled in nicely. Madigan, bless her, had contacted DeShawn's assistant and reclaimed everything from the apartment she and DeShawn had shared. Most it was being stored in Madigan's apartment until Eliot could figure out her next steps, but her friend had packed a few bags for her and had them sent to Connecticut. She now had her clothes, toiletries and, crucially, her phone and her credit cards. She could go anywhere in the world if she wanted to.

Knowing that, how much longer could she take advantage of Avangeline's hospitality? Another few days, maybe even a week? Or maybe she should just ask Avangeline directly? Truth was, the elderly woman intimidated the hell out of her. The previous evening Soren had told her his grandmother's history, explained how Avangeline had been born into an influential aristocratic family, how she took a smallish loan and parlayed it into a multi-billion international business.

Avangeline took on the business world and won. And when everything changed and she lost both of her sons in a flash, she'd faced new challenges head-on, her chin raised. She wasn't the avoiding-your-mother-and-ex-fiancé-and-the-world type, which made Eliot wonder if she should return to the city instead of hiding out here. She sighed, remembering the number of notifications on her phone. In amongst a few genuine outreaches of sympathy from people she knew were requests for TV and print interviews, forwarded by her mother who'd resumed talking to her now that every talk show host, or entertainment journalist, wanted to interview her.

Beyond the imposing gates of Calcott Manor, the real world still churned and burned, consuming news at a ferocious pace. She didn't know how she'd fit into that world, how to navigate it now that she wasn't attached to modeling or DeShawn—the two forces that had defined her life for the past several years. Did she want to go back there? What should she do? Who would she be?

Last night she'd spent an hour on the phone with Madigan. They'd spent fifteen minutes talking about the non-wedding and forty-five minutes talking about what the future held in store for Eliot. They didn't come up with any definite answers, but she'd gotten far more support from her best friend than she had from her manager, who also happened to be her mother.

Then again, support required talking, communicating honestly, and she and her mom were not close. But, at some point soon, she needed to make some decisions, to figure out her path forward. Eliot nibbled the inside of her cheek, wondering whether she should do that here or in Manhattan.

Returning to the city was what she was expected to do, not what she *wanted* to do. What she wanted to do—right now, today and tomorrow—was to explore the estate, sit on the beach, tip her face to the sun and listen to the wind in the trees.

For now, and for as long as it took, she was only going to listen to what her heart wanted and what her soul needed. Yes, she needed to figure out a life plan, a way forward, but she knew she also needed to nourish herself. If she didn't, she just might fade away.

Eliot had left the rose garden and ambled through the herb garden and on to the vegetable garden, unable to resist plucking a ripe tomato off the vine and biting down. It had tasted of sunshine and she'd closed her eyes as she chewed, enjoying the heat of the fruit's flesh, the juiciness. Snagging another one, she had eaten it as she carried on walking...

Then she'd passed by the windows of the room housing the indoor pool and seen Soren, dressed only in a Speedo, standing on a starting block at one side of the pool. She'd watched, entranced, as he stretched his big body from side to side, arching his back and rotating his neck. He'd done some complicated arm stretches and then, without warning, dived into the pool, doing that underwater dolphin kick she'd recognized from all the videos she watched. He'd popped up and then he'd been streaking through the water at a steady pace, doing quick turns and powering to the other end.

Unable to walk away, she'd slipped inside and found the lounger placed between two huge pots containing squat palms, hidden out-of-sight from both the windows and the door. She'd sat down, leaned back, and watched him swim.

It was strange how comfortable she felt with Soren. Around him, she didn't worry whether her hair was a mess or what she wore, or whether he'd approve of her opinions. No, he allowed—*demanded!*—authenticity. The freedom to be herself was a novelty and was completely addictive.

But Soren couldn't give her more than this moment in time, the space to collect herself. He wasn't interested in a relationship, and not only was she recently unengaged, but she was emotionally vulnerable...

Not because her heart was broken or because she missed DeShawn, but because her attitude about her life had shifted. She needed to figure out exactly where she fit into the world, and what she could offer it, without the complication of a new relationship. Sex was one thing...

But allowing feelings to grow and flourish would be idiotic.

After what seemed like twenty minutes, Eliot started feeling thirsty and when she glanced at her watch, she realized double the amount of time had passed. She looked at Soren and realized his pace hadn't changed; he was still streaking through the water.

Not training, her ass.

Standing up, she walked to the side of the pool and waited for him to notice her. He eventually did, stopping halfway through his lap to scowl up at her.

"Nobody interrupts me when I'm training."

"You're not supposed to be training," Eliot pointed out. "You're on vacation."

Irritation flickered across his face as he realized he'd been caught out. "Uh…"

She pointed to a spot next to him. "Pool, water, and you're swimming in it."

Soren mouthed what she knew to be an f-bomb and swum over to the side of the pool, effortlessly hauling himself out of it. Ignoring her, he walked over to the back of the room, disappeared through a door, and came back with a towel and two bottles of water.

Soren handed her a water, wrapped the towel around his waist—God, his muscles had muscles—and took a long sip from his bottle. He lowered it and used it to gesture to the pool. "That's where I go to think," he said.

Eliot resumed her seat on the lounger and Soren sat down next to her, his towel-covered thigh pushing into hers. His wet shoulder caused her shirt to dampen and she smelled chlorine and the rich scent that was pure Soren.

Eliot watched as his knee jiggled up and down, and he opened and closed his fist. He was rattled and that amazed her. Nothing ever seemed to faze him, but right now, he seemed jumpy and ill at ease.

But she wouldn't ask for an explanation. Soren would either tell her or he wouldn't. Since he was a guy who rarely dished out personal information, she didn't expect him to confide in her.

"Have you ever heard about people undergoing an organ transplant and then inheriting the personality traits of the person whose organ they received?"

Because it wasn't anywhere close to what she expected to hear—which had been nothing—Eliot took a moment to catch up. And then another moment to seriously consider his words. And no, she hadn't heard about it. But it sounded fascinating.

Soren explained the concept and she listened, riveted by the subject but equally entranced by the sound of his deep, lovely voice as he spoke.

"It's called inherited cellular memory. I looked it up. Some doctors believe in it, even more doctors think it's a load of bullshit."

"I can understand why," Eliot said. "It's quite a concept."

"But? I can hear the 'but' in your tone."

"*But* science is still evolving. Just because we can't understand or prove something doesn't mean it's not true. A lot that we accept now was considered nonsense when it was first introduced." Eliot stared at him, connecting the dots. "Are we talking about Aly?"

"I've just heard that, along with receiving Mal's liver, she also got his love of cars and candy." He twisted his lips. "And she got all that when she took his liver! His liver, for God's sake!"

Eliot smiled, amused. "Would you find it easier to buy into this if Aly received his heart?"

"I… No…" He rubbed his hand over his face. "I don't know. Everything about this conversation is absurd!"

Eliot watched a bead of water run down his shoulder and dip into the muscle of his bicep. "Does your grandmother believe her?"

Soren's frustration was evident in his loud huff. "Yep. So does Jace. But they both want a tangible connection to Malcolm. They still miss him terribly."

"That makes it sound like you don't," Eliot softly said, knowing that nothing was further from the truth.

Soren closed his eyes, pain etched on his face. "Of course I miss him. He was the best of us."

"Why? What was so marvelous about him?" she asked.

Soren rubbed his hands up and down his thighs, still visibly agitated. "He was smart and athletic and charismatic and good-looking. A real leader, and pretty much perfect, you know?"

He said that with complete conviction.

"I don't think he was—perfect, that is. Nobody is," Eliot softly stated.

"He came pretty damn close," Soren retorted. "It was his idea to try and restart our grandmother's business, his fire that got it off the ground. Malcolm convinced the initial investors, including Avangeline, to look at the project. Jack and Fox are phenomenal businessmen, don't get me wrong, but Malcolm was like the Pied Piper. People followed where he wanted to go. He was that dynamic, that charismatic." A small smile touched Soren's face. "Had he lived, I have no doubt he'd be president of the world by now."

Eliot bit her lip, thinking Soren had a whole lot of hero worship going on. Which was sweet but, she was sure, probably misplaced. Oh, she had no doubt Malcolm had been fantastically dynamic and ferociously intelligent, but he couldn't have been the perfect guy Soren painted.

It was important to her to see people as they were, not how they were portrayed to be. "Now, tell me one of his faults."

Soren whipped his head to frown at her. "What?"

"Tell me something that annoyed you about him," Eliot insisted. "An irritating quirk, or a horrible habit or something that made you want to punch him."

Soren sat up rigidly straight, his expression remote. "I don't believe in talking badly about the dead. And I won't criticize him when he's not here to defend himself."

Eliot knew that he was about to walk away so she

put her hand on his arm, hoping to keep him in place so she could explain. "Soren, I wasn't asking you to criticize your cousin. I just wanted you to tell me something to round out his character for me because, right now, he's flat, uninteresting. Our quirks and our faults are what make us human, what make us real. The man you're describing is perfect but perfect is *boring*."

He looked confused, but at least he wasn't angry anymore. After a moment, he shrugged. "He was awful when he had a cold, a minor sore throat or even a shallow cut. He'd whimper and moan and demand attention. It drove me up the wall. Avangeline and Jacinda would fuss around him and he loved it. The more demanding he was, the more they fussed," Soren told her. "But God forbid if I wanted to miss a training session! I needed a doctor's note and had to be on the point of death. I trained through pulled muscles, colds and even a chest infection once. God, he was such a baby!"

There you go, Eliot thought. *He wasn't such a paragon after all.* "What else?" she softly asked.

"He had this super annoying habit of thinking that everything of ours was his, too, and he'd take our stuff without asking. It used to make us so angry… Hell, I'd forgotten about that," Soren said, a small smile on his lips. "He wouldn't eat tomatoes but he ate ketchup with everything. He had an obsession with Eminem and would play his albums at top volume on repeat."

"Tell me more," Eliot encouraged.

"He used to swim and he was good. I beat him the first time when I was ten and he was twelve. I hit the wall and I slapped my fingers against my forehead in an *L*-for-loser sign, unbelievably happy about smokin' his ass. When I settled down, he told me, completely seriously, that he didn't mind losing to me because I was so talented. That he was so proud of me and that I could beat anyone, anywhere."

Eliot swallowed at the emotion in his voice.

"At my next meet, Mal was there and I looked at him when I was on the starting block. He gave me the same loser sign I'd given him. I broke two new state records that day. He did that at every race of mine he ever attended.

"I still do it before every race. It's my way of calming myself, of connecting to him."

She finally knew the secret to his strange habit of pulling that sign before every race, something no one else understood. Eliot felt honored and touched that he'd shared something so personal with her.

"Despite being a great entrepreneur, he was unbelievably disorganized. And untidy—" Soren went on from there, warming to the subject as he talked so fast he tripped over his words, suddenly overflowing with little details he wanted to share.

This was how she wanted to be remembered, Eliot thought—with quirks and flaws, three- or four-dimensional as opposed to one.

Few people knew her and if she died tomorrow,

she'd be remembered as someone who used to have a lovely face and stunning body. It wasn't enough. She wanted someone to know that she devoured Christmas movies year-round, that she funneled money to anti-poaching efforts to stop the demise of rhinos in Southern Africa. That she never remembered to put the lids back on jars properly and frequently found herself sweeping up glass shards when they dropped out of her hands. Someone should know she hated sushi and that she was quite adept at rescuing spiders, but that moths terrified her.

She was so sick of being a manipulated image, a blank canvas.

"I guess it's easy to remember only the good," Soren conceded.

"We tend to hyper-inflate our good memories and downplay the more realistic memories. I think that's natural," Eliot shrugged. "But I think that remembering our loved ones with their quirks and flaws makes them more real. It means we're remembering the whole person, not just the highlights reel."

"I never thought about it like that," Soren said, his tone subdued. He stared down at his long feet, his massive shoulders rounded. "I still miss him. He was my biggest supporter. No matter what was going on in his life, he made the effort to crisscross the country, and the world, to be at my most important races. At the end of every race, I *still* look up from the water into the stands, hoping to see his face."

Eliot rubbed her hand over the middle of his back,

her heart aching for him. She considered saying something about Mal watching him from wherever he was but decided to remain quiet instead, hoping silence offered more comfort than clichés.

After a minute Soren turned to look at her. His grief had receded and he'd regained his flat, cool expression. How she wished he'd permanently drop his Ice Man facade around her and be the passionate, open person she sometimes glimpsed. She wanted to reconnect with *that* Soren, wonderful and warm.

How she wished they could go back...

Her heart thumped and her stomach clenched and she realized that her statement wasn't true. She didn't want to be the girl she'd been in Villefranche-sur-Mer, the one who'd been so acquiescent, happy to fall in line with whatever Soren suggested. She recalled being so tired after dinner one night she could barely keep her eyes open but instead of going to bed, she'd eagerly agreed to go out to eat. Despite not being able to swim, she'd climbed into her kayak—wearing a life vest; she wasn't stupid—and followed Soren up and down the French coast. She'd accompanied him on an early morning run when she hated jogging and had pretended to love modern art at a gallery in the village, even though none of it made any sense to her.

She was over that.

"You've gone quiet," Soren said.

She shrugged.

"Something on your mind?" he asked.

She wanted to dump on him, to get his realistic,

non-emotional take on her overwhelming feelings, but there was a chance she'd take whatever he said and be overly influenced by it, falling in line with his suggestions and not bothering to take the time to work out for herself what she truly wanted.

She shook her head and tried to smile. Then she made the mistake of looking into his face, her eyes connecting with his. Green hit blue. Then his eyes dropped to her mouth, and Eliot could practically taste his kiss, feel his big hands on her body.

His eyes slammed into hers again and she sucked in a breath. A minute ago, they'd been connecting emotionally and mentally, and now all she could think was that she wanted his big hands on her, that the world would stop spinning if he didn't kiss her. How did they go from zero to sixty in five seconds flat?

Soren turned, placed one hand on the cushion behind him and faced her, lifting his hand to place it on her cheek, his thumb sliding across her lower lip. The smell of chlorine, mingling with deodorant and hot, aroused male hit her nose. Lust, warm and thick as molasses, slid into her veins and pooled between her legs. She wished she could hide her reaction from him but her nipples pushed against the fabric of her bra and T-shirt, and she knew her face and neck were blush-pink. Despite being unable to pull her eyes from his, she was conscious of the erection tenting his towel, the tension in his muscled body.

Soren continued to look at her, desire bright in his eyes, his gaze alternating between her eyes, her body, and her mouth. He painted her skin with heat, every pass causing another chemical reaction on her skin. How could he ratchet her up this much with little more than a hot look and his thumb pressing down her bottom lip?

She didn't know how long it took for his sexy mouth to drop onto hers—could have been minutes, felt like days—but then his hand slid down her neck, down her chest, and onto her waist, pulling her closer to his hard, naked torso. His tongue flicked at the seam of her lips and she opened without a second thought... Kissing Soren was what she wanted to do.

If she could call what they were doing kissing. The word seemed so high school for an action that realigned her world. When she was alone she recalled each occasion their mouths met, but her imagination fell far short of the reality of having his mouth fused to hers. He claimed her, marked her. This was a hallucinogenic kiss, bolder, hotter and wetter than before.

Everything was more grown-up, several degrees more intense than what they'd shared nearly a decade before. Soren's body was bigger, his hands more assured and his mouth more demanding, and she was left in no doubt that she was what he wanted. His hand moved across her body without hesitation and settled on her breast, teasing her nipple with the rough, sexy strokes of his thumb.

"I want you, El."

She nodded, unable to speak.

"Do you want this? Me? Are you in a position,

after all you've been through lately, to make that decision?"

Easily. There was no reason why she couldn't share this moment with Soren. She was single, she was a consenting adult and she was allowed to feel lust, attraction and desire. She was the captain of her ship and right now, all she wanted was to touch Soren.

"I'm not heartbroken or on the rebound, Soren, I promise you. I'm not looking for a way to escape or to use you for revenge. I just want you, just like before."

"Thank God," Soren muttered, closing his eyes in relief. Eliot arched her back and lifted her hands, patting the space between them to find his chest. Once she made contact, she knew she was home.

Her fingers danced down his smooth skin and drifted across the ridges of his stomach, hesitating when she came to the top edge of the towel. He groaned, a sexy, guttural sound deep in the back of his throat, and she tugged the towel apart, her hand skating over his hard shaft. Annoyed by the barrier of his swimsuit, she slid her hand under the fabric and encircled him with her hand, teasing his length.

Soren surged to his feet, bent down, and gripped her biceps, easily rearranging her so that she lay back on the lounger, hidden between the two potted plants. He placed his hands on either side of her head, staring down at her, his expression fierce with need. Ducking his head, his mouth connected with hers...sweet and hot and sexy and... *Dear Lord.*

This was going to end with them both getting naked, right here. Right now.

But, before they lost their minds, someone needed to be sensible. "Will anyone see us?" she asked.

"The ground staff takes Mondays off," Soren replied, his hand playing with the hem of her T-shirt. "The others are in the house."

People could leave the house...but that was a chance she'd take. And besides, they were hidden if anyone stepped into the pool house. Well, mostly hidden.

"We don't have any protection," Soren said, his words followed by a low groan.

Eliot forced herself to think. "We're covered by my IUD. And I'm clean."

"Me too," Soren replied, his eyes clashing with hers. "Are we doing this, Eliot? Can I make love to you?"

"Absolutely," Eliot murmured, knowing he was exactly what she needed. Eliot wasn't sure how he whisked her shirt and shorts away or how she came to be nearly naked in no time at all, and frankly, she didn't care. All she knew was that her nipple was in Soren's mouth, his hand was between her legs and he'd turned her brain to liquid sunshine.

She'd kissed guys before and made love to a few, and her reactions ranged from a mild buzz to a heated storm. But nobody had ever turned her into a supernova like Soren did. Nobody had ever come close to making her feel like there was nothing else she'd rather do than be touched, stroked and kissed by him.

Soren's hand ran up her butt, over her hip, and down the front triangle of her blueberry-colored panties. "Pretty, El."

It would be so much nicer if he got rid of that tiny scrap of material. Taking control, she pushed her hand down her hips to shimmy off her panties, and his eyes took in her naked body. Thinking she needed more action and less looking, she pushed her hands back under the waistband of his Speedo and tugged the garment down his hips. She sighed when his erection broke free, long and hard and so masculine that her breath caught in her throat.

Eliot wrapped her hand around him and Soren growled his approval. Soren pulled back, his eyes intensely focused. "I need to make you mine again. Just for this moment, this step out of time."

She hesitated, her brain rejoining the party. Making love to him wouldn't be smart, not when she knew she wouldn't be able to keep him. She'd been naive last time—she wasn't anymore.

But her body overruled her brain. There was no way she was walking away from him without having this first. Needing him, Eliot lifted her lips to his and slipped her tongue inside his mouth to tangle with his. She heard another deep growl, felt his fingertips pushing into the skin of her hips.

"No promises, Eliot," Soren muttered, pulling

away from her mouth to speak against her ear. "Don't ask me for anything else but this."

Eliot nodded her agreement, knowing she'd never ask him for anything he wasn't willing to give. Besides, how did she know what to ask for when she didn't know who she was or what she wanted?

Soren's hand slid between her legs and Eliot shuddered. *Oh, God, yes. There. Just like that.*

"Do you like that, sweetheart?"

"So good." Eliot spiraled on a band of pure, undiluted pleasure and lifted her head, seeking Soren's mouth. He kissed her, his lips demanding. Soren lifted her thigh over his hips and plunged inside her.

This was the best idea ever. Why had she even hesitated?

"Soren," Eliot murmured, her face in his neck, trying to hold on. Her entire focus was on what Soren was doing to her, what he was making her feel—she'd never believed it could be this magical, this intense.

Soren clasped her face in one hand, using his thumb to lift her jaw so that their eyes clashed and held.

Eliot sighed when he pushed a little deeper, a little further. She wanted more; she needed every bit of him. "So good. No, amazing."

"It's going to get better. Hold on."

"Can't. Need to let go… Oh, *Gawd.*"

As she hovered on the edge of that abyss, Soren stopped moving. Eliot whimpered and ground down on him. She thought she heard Soren's small chuckle but then he was moving, sliding in and out of her, the base of his shaft rubbing her clit, and she was flying. A kaleidoscope flashed behind her eyes and it was…

Stars and candy and electricity and fun and…

Mind-blowing. Tears pricked her eyes and she ducked her head so that Soren wouldn't see the emotion dancing in her eyes and across her face. This was only supposed to be about good sex—great sex—but an insistent voice deep inside stated this was more, that it always had been. And she was a fool if she thought they could be bed buddies and brush this off.

This is Soren, your hottest fantasy, the guy you've never been able to forget. Someone you came close to falling in love with…

Eliot pulled those thoughts back and pushed them into a dark cupboard. Her feel-good hormones were working overtime and her serotonin levels were making her far too mushy. She could not allow herself to blur the lines between sex and love, to mix friendship and good memories to make one confusing stew.

Sex was sex, nothing more.

She wouldn't let thoughts of love and forever mess with her mind. She was smarter than that.

Or she was trying to be.

Eight

"You've been avoiding me."

Jacinda, repotting a root-bound tub of thyme in the greenhouse, spun around and dropped her trowel. She stared at Paz, dressed in a pair of black chinos and a very stylish untucked lemon-green shirt, the cuffs rolled up to show his ropy forearms.

She, on the other hand, was a mess. Intending to spend most of the afternoon in the greenhouse, she'd pulled on a ragged pair of shorts and a stain-splattered tank top, while her hair was pinned in a messy bun on top of her head. Thanks to the humidity in the greenhouse, she was sure she'd sweated off every last bit of makeup she put on this morning. And if there were any traces left, it would be freely running mascara, with the end result that she probably now looked like a raccoon.

Awesome.

"What are you doing here, Conway?" she asked, bending down to pick up her trowel. It was only after she straightened and saw the appreciation on his face that she realized that she'd just given him a very good view of her covered-in-plain-cotton boobs.

Paz walked toward her and he lifted his hand to brush his thumb over her cheekbone. "You have a streak of dirt," he told her.

"I'm pretty much dirty everywhere," she said, pointing to the tub of thyme with her trowel. "Gardening is messy work. You, on the other hand, do not look like you have been working today at all."

"I had lunch in the city with my agent," Paz told her. "She's nagging me about whether my commission will be finished on time."

"Will it?" Jacinda asked, interested. "And can I see it?"

"No. And I'd be ahead of schedule if I weren't distracted by thoughts of the beauty on my doorstep," Paz told her, his mouth lifting in a what-can-you-do smile.

Jacinda's mouth opened and closed, not knowing how to respond. She'd never encountered anyone as smooth-talking as Paz and she didn't know how to take him. Was he mocking her? Toying with her? Or was he simply one of those super-direct men who stated what he wanted?

She didn't know and she cursed her lack of experience. She'd had a couple of relationships over the years. None of them went anywhere, but all her lovers were simple men—nice men, men who didn't make her feel like she was tiptoeing along the edge of a black hole, waiting to be sucked in and away.

"I see the crowds at the gate have dissipated a bit. Is the model still in residence?" Paz asked, pushing his hands into the pockets of his pants.

"Eliot? Yes, she is," Jacinda told him, moving a strand of hair out of her eyes. She knew that Paz operated in A-list society, the same circles as Eliot. "Have you met her before?"

Paz nodded. "Ages ago and it was brief. But she seemed nice."

"She's very nice," Jacinda told him firmly. She'd shared a meal with Eliot and Soren, and Eliot was more down-to-earth than she'd expected. "And I think she's just right for my boy."

Paz frowned. "Your boy?"

Right, she had the perfect opportunity to show Paz how unsuited she was for him. Not that there was any realistic chance of anything happening. "Soren Grantham, the Olympian? I helped raise him, and his cousins, when both sets of their parents died when they were young. My son Merrick is the same age. They all grew up together."

"Four boys—you must've had nerves of steel," Paz commented.

"Five. Malcolm died ten years ago," Jacinda said, her voice cracking.

He ran his hand down her arm, from shoulder to hand. "I'm so sorry, sweetheart."

She nodded her thanks.

"How old were you when you had Merrick?" Paz asked, after sliding his hands back into his pockets.

"Eighteen," she admitted. "He's not that much younger than you."

"Nice try but I'm still not put off," he told her, his voice sending shivers down her spine. God, she wanted his lips on her skin, his hands on her body…

"Any more postcards?"

She blinked, flustered. Talking to him was like trying to hold a conversation while riding a roller coaster. She didn't know which way was up. "No," she replied, biting her lip. She'd thought about them a lot. Avangeline and her postcards had taken up a lot of mental energy lately.

"What is it?" he asked, his eyes laser sharp.

He was the only person she could talk to about this. And she instinctively trusted him not to repeat what she said to anybody. "Avangeline's grandsons are wanting her to make a will, and she hasn't yet. I'm wondering if her mystery lover is the reason why?"

"I'm not following you," Paz replied, frowning.

"Well, it's obvious that they've kept their relationship secret for decades. What if she wants to name him in the will but he won't let her because he doesn't want their relationship to come to light?"

"That's quite a reach, Jacinda."

She liked hearing her name on his lips. "But it's the only thing I can think of that even vaguely explains why she won't make a will. Avangeline is the smartest, most practical woman I know. It's not like her to leave this undone." She heard the frustration in her voice and internally grimaced. She plucked at the dead leaves on the thyme plant. "Do you think I should tell the boys about the postcards?"

He placed his hand on her shoulder and Jacinda was instantly comforted by his touch. "No, I don't. I shouldn't have read that message. It was wrong of me. It's her secret and she has the right to disclose it as and when she sees fit." His thumb skimmed over her exposed collarbone. "See you at seven. I'm cooking risotto."

"Okay…" Jacinda murmured as he turned to walk away. "Wait, *what*? No, I'm not coming to dinner."

His smile belonged on the face of a swashbuckling pirate or a loveable rogue. "Yeah, you are. See you later."

Jacinda, frustrated at him—or her reaction to him—threw the trowel in the general direction of his departing back, missing him by a mile.

The sound of his deep laughter stayed with her for the rest of the day.

After dinner on the ten-day anniversary of Eliot's non-wedding, Soren picked up a bottle of wine and two glasses and carried them through to the extensive balcony flowing from the sitting room of the apartment. He sat down next to Eliot on the two-person pool lounger, swinging his legs up. He handed her a glass of wine and leaned back to look up at the star-studded sky.

Thanks to a famous Broadway star being admitted into rehab, the news cycle had finally moved on and the press had decamped back to the city, allowing them the opportunity to leave the estate and explore the Connecticut coast. They'd eaten lunch in a seaside diner in a small town north of Hatfield and he'd given Eliot another swimming lesson in a deserted tidal pool they'd found as they drove along the rocky shore.

After returning from today's excursion, he did a light gym routine and a short, slow two-mile swim, mostly to keep his muscles warm and his fitness steady. It was common knowledge that swimmers started losing time and strength—their edge—after not training for two to three weeks so the time was fast approaching when he'd need to make a decision.

To resume training or to retire?

The idea of retirement still scared him. He couldn't fathom not having a plan for his future. What would he do with so much free time, and the lack of a routine? And really, what else *could* he do but swim? Unlike Fox and Jack, he'd never been an amazing student and he didn't have the charisma and outgoing nature that had made Mal everyone's favorite.

His cousins were reinventing the concept of fine

dining, switching it up, and were known to be powerhouses in the industry. So, in a completely different way, was Merrick with his fleet of food trucks. They each had found their lane in the food industry but he'd never been into food. To him, it was mostly just fuel to make him faster, stronger. Apart from the fact that he didn't want, or need, his brothers to create a job for him, he couldn't see himself sitting behind a desk from nine to five. His head, he was sure, would explode.

He'd always thought that swimming was his love and his passion, but maybe it was more of a security blanket, a place he could retreat to when the real world became too tough and, well, real. As a kid, mourning his parents, the pool was where he went to cry, tears mingling with chlorine as he swam through his grief. When Mal died, he did the same.

After Mal passed, he dropped even deeper in the world of times and sprints, records and medals. He ran from the pool to the gym and back to the pool, limiting socializing to nothing more than the odd evening for no-strings sex. He knew that swimming was great self-medication for his grief, that it required all his focus and energy to shave a second here, another half-second there. Did he use swimming as a shield, and an excuse not to have a relationship? Of course he did; after all the loss he'd experienced, why would he want to risk loving and losing someone again?

There'd only ever been one person who had the power to distract him...

And he was in danger of being distracted by her again. Being with Eliot was easy, nondemanding, and whenever he felt restless, like he should be doing something, he looked at her and the ants crawling under his skin settled down. He'd only ever felt that at ease in the water—and the feeling was dangerously addictive.

Eliot, dammit, could become a factor in his whether-to-retire-or-not decision. If he carried on swimming and seeing her, she'd be a disruption as she'd never be far from his thoughts. He couldn't afford to have her in his head—wondering when he'd see her next, recalling their conversations, remembering the incredible sex they'd shared—while he was training; he needed to be intensely focused on the next race, on hitting is times.

He was very sure that he couldn't maintain the necessary focus to win races if half his mind was on Eliot. And if he couldn't be the best, what was the point of carrying on?

But if he gave up swimming, what then? What was on the other side of the pool? He'd seen swimmers who'd retired—people who weren't as focused as him—spiral into dark places, lose themselves when they lost their identity and lost the security training gave. There was a good chance that when he stopped, the ghosts he'd been running from—loss and grief—would finally catch him.

He released a long sigh and silently cursed when Eliot turned to look at him, her brows lifting. Three, two, one…

"Something on your mind?" she asked.

"I'm good."

"I don't think you are, actually," Eliot replied, her tone holding a touch of asperity. She took a sip of wine before resting the glass on her bent knee. "I know you are struggling with something and I wish you'd talk to me."

Crap. A part of him wished he could open up and tell her what was going on in his head, but he was no good at talking, and he far preferred to work out his problems solo. Even as a kid, before and after his parents died, he'd had a hard time expressing himself. He'd learned that if he took his time formulating a response, a parent and, later, a cousin usually answered for him. It became easier not to talk.

"I told you about Aly," he pointed out. "A little bit about Malcolm."

"Barely anything," Eliot scoffed. "That was the tippiest-tip of the iceberg, Ice Man."

But she didn't realize that it was more than he'd ever shared with anyone, since Malcolm. Soren had been with his trainer for years and he never spoke to her about anything personal. They talked times and training, but they weren't friends.

He didn't have friends. Friends could die, leave, betray you.

Yet he wanted to talk to Eliot about his current dilemma, maybe because she was also at a crossroads and struggling to see what was next in her life. Along with his career choices, he wanted to tell her about his fears about the future and how much he missed his oldest brother.

But he didn't know where to start…

"Do you have any idea what you want to do next?" he asked, thinking his question was a good way to, maybe, steer the conversation around to his career.

She shrugged, and casually draped her leg over his. His hand came to rest on the top of her thigh, a movement that seemed more natural than breathing.

"Well, unless I drop a lot of weight, my modeling career is over. And losing the weight doesn't seem likely without some extreme measures. Apparently, hypothyroidism slows your metabolism and makes it harder to shed pounds. My TSH levels are fine now. I'm not tired all the time and the headaches are gone but those extra pounds have hung around."

"You're not fat…" Soren told her, prepared, once again, to tell her that she looked healthy and lovely—stunning, in fact.

"I know I'm not, but I'm not skinny enough to model."

Was money an issue? He knew that she'd earned a fortune, but fortunes could easily be spent. "Do you need to work? Do you need to earn?"

She wrinkled her nose. "I've invested well and I'm pretty comfortable. Obviously, I'm my mother's biggest client but she has other models she represents, so she'll be fine."

He linked her fingers in his. "If you lost the weight, would you go back?"

Eliot pulled a face and was silent for so long that he didn't think she was going to answer his question. But finally, she spoke.

"I've been thinking about that since leaving Manhattan. I've also been thinking about DeShawn's expectations, my mother's and the world's. My expectations of myself. About the world of fashion and beauty I've been a part of for so long. I'm trying to look at it with honesty. Trying to look at myself honestly."

"And?"

"I made choices. I did campaigns that put me in the spotlight and earned me a lot of money. And I liked the money, the ego boost, the fame. I flew high and fast and too close to the sun. Then my thyroid kicked out, I picked up weight and everyone who I thought valued me dropped me like a stone," Eliot continued. Her honesty made him feel slightly uncomfortable and he questioned whether he had the strength to look at his situation with as much candor as she did.

"Being dropped didn't surprise me, not really, as I know a few models who only picked up work after losing ten pounds in a week due to a stomach bug. The industry wants what it wants and that's skinny, pretty white girls."

She rubbed her hands up and down her face and when she lowered them, he saw the misery on her face. "I was the image of what way too many girls thought they wanted to be. But what they don't know is that being a model is damn hard, not because of the work or unending travel but because you are so easily replaceable. They think that great hair and a small waist and thin legs will make them happy but they don't realize that we models have all that, and a lot more, yet we are all incredibly insecure. We're insecure because we know our value is based on something that's a lucky break—genetics. Being pretty isn't a skill. It's not something I've worked hard at."

Eliot jumped up from the couch and paced the area next to him, her long legs eating up the space. One stride, two, turn.

"Modeling has given me so much, but it hasn't always made me feel fulfilled. I want to do something that excites me, Soren, something that makes me want to leap out of bed in the morning. I want to be happy."

He swung his legs off the lounger, placed his hands behind him and leaned back. "I don't think we can be happy all the time, sweetheart. I don't think life works that way."

"Does swimming make you happy?"

That was a hell of a question. Had anyone else asked it, he would've answered with a blithe comment that he wouldn't have pursued it so long if it didn't. But swimming was, like so many other solo sports, 90 percent training for 10 percent glory. If that.

"Being a success makes me happy," he admitted.

"But you're a success because of years and years of hard work, because you push your body, because of honing your talent. I'm a success because of my genes," Eliot said, bitterly. "My validation came via how I looked, not who I am."

Eliot placed her hands on her sternum and looked at him with big, wide, scared eyes. Her fear was a reflection of his, except that she was far braver when it came to showing hers than he was. "I want to feel validated for something more than just my looks, Soren. Something...*else*."

"Do you know what?" he gently asked. "Marriage? A family?"

She didn't answer him, and that in itself was an answer. Soren responded by reaching for the hem of her low-riding denim shorts, his fingers sliding between the fabric and her warm, warm skin. Unable to look at her, he rested his forehead on her breastbone, his hands holding her thighs. She was so courageous, so honest and so direct in what she wanted.

He, on the other hand, couldn't be that open, even when he wanted to. He was, by nature, too reserved, too introspective.

She dropped her eyes. "Up until now, I thought that was what I needed to validate me. I thought both would make me happy."

His head shot up at her unexpected words. "I'm sorry... I don't understand."

"I need to be happy with myself before I can be happy with someone else, Soren. I need to know and accept that my self-worth isn't based on being important to someone else, being the center of their world.

I need to be the best version of myself and I need to stop looking at myself through everyone else's eyes."

That made a lot of sense, and was profoundly sensible. But how did he fit into the new picture she was painting of her life? And could he ever be as honest with her as she was being with him?

Nine

What was it about this man who made her feel real, who forced her—by not saying a damn thing—to be truthful? Who made her feel secure enough to say things to him that she'd barely voiced to herself, let alone to anyone else?

Eliot wrapped her arms around Soren's head, wishing she had the same effect on him as he did on her. But Soren was still a closed book, a tightly shut vault. She wasn't even sure that it was by choice—he just didn't seem to know any other way to be. The thought made her indescribably sad...

Soren lifted his head and tipped it back to look up into her eyes. "I'm trying to decide whether to retire or not."

Right. So he wasn't always a tightly locked vault.

His words slammed into her and she took an involuntary step back, but his arms tightened around her to hold her in place. Needing to look at him, she dropped to her haunches and rested her hands on his knees, shocked.

"Can I ask why?"

He rested his arms on his thighs and she sank back to sit on her heels, keeping her hands on his knees, needing the connection and thinking that maybe he did, too.

He swallowed and when he spoke, he sounded like he was pushing stones up through his throat. "I'm getting old. It's getting harder to keep up my times. I hate to lose and it's getting much harder to win. Those medals I won in Tokyo?"

"Mmm?"

"They said that I made it look easy but, God, those were the hardest races of my life. I nearly killed myself to win."

She rubbed her thumb on the top of his wrist, silently encouraging him to continue talking. "My sponsors want me to sign a new deal, and if I accept, it'll mean committing to swim for another two years. Two years ago, that decision was easy to make, but things have changed. It's the Olympics in three years and it'll kill me if I don't qualify—"

"Of course you'll qualify!" Eliot protested. She couldn't imagine the USA swim team without Soren in it.

He managed a wry smile. "Honey, I appreciate

the support but the reality is that I probably won't. There are kids out there who are nipping at my heels, kids who are eighteen, twenty...*young*, with their best years still ahead of them. I am no longer young."

Eliot bit her bottom lip, nodding slowly. She understood where he was coming from: both their careers had short life spans and they were on the tail end of theirs. No, hers had expired.

"Have you spoken to your brothers about this?" Eliot asked him.

"I mentioned it, and they brushed me off," Soren replied with a quick shrug.

She narrowed her eyes at him. "Did you raise the subject as a throwaway comment?"

"What do you mean?"

"You're not a talker, Soren," Eliot said. "And you tend to toss around quick, sarcastic comments people don't take seriously. So, did you sit down with them and say, 'Guys, listen to me, I need your advice. I'm thinking about retiring—what do you think?' Did you say that?"

She saw the flash of guilt in his eyes and had her answer. "They are busy people..."

"They are *your* brothers. If you asked for their time, they'd give it."

"I never asked for Malcolm's time, but he always seemed to know when I needed it," Soren muttered.

Malcolm seemed like a great guy but, to her, Soren still had him on a pedestal. "Well, your brothers aren't mind readers and they can't help you unless you ask for it." His expression turned stubborn and she decided to change track before he shut down. "What does your trainer think?"

"She thinks I'm having a confidence crisis and that I have another four years in me, that I can maintain and even improve my times. My business manager says that I am bankable, and that I should capitalize on my fame while I have it. As we know, a swimmer's fame is fleeting."

"But you don't care about the fame," Eliot said. "Do you need the money?"

He shook his head. "I've made good money from swimming and from sponsorship deals. I'm the grandson of one of the wealthiest women in the country and if that wasn't enough, Avangeline gifted each of us with a trust fund. I have enough money for several lifetimes."

"So what are you going to do?" Eliot softly asked him.

He stared down at his hands, tension radiating from his taut muscles. "If I was brave, I'd make an announcement, pull out, go out at the top of my game…"

She cocked her head. "But?"

His eyes met hers and his forest green eyes held layers of pain. He shook his head and shrugged.

"But?" she prompted again.

"But I'm *scared*. If I retired, I don't know what I'd do, how I'd fill my time," he whispered, every word uttered with extreme reluctance. "Up to now, my days have all been mapped out. I'm always preparing for the next swim meet, the next goal, the next record to break. What's on the other side of that?"

"Just thinking about it is putting you outside your comfort zone, isn't it?" she murmured. She knew how frightening it could be—she'd been living there for a while now.

"I'm terrified, El," he softly admitted, and it broke her heart to hear this strong, tough, smart guy admit to something so personal, to be so vulnerable.

Eliot looked at his big hands, the ones that knew how to touch her, how to comfort and to soothe. It was her turn, through words, and later with her touch, to do the same for him.

"Soren, you know fear. You deal with it all the time," she said. He didn't raise his head but she knew he was listening. "Once, a long time ago, you publicly admitted to being terrified every time you step up onto the blocks and I believe that's true. You said fear motivates you, but you won't let it beat you, that your job is to dive into your lane and kick that fear's ass by breaking a record or two.

"Changing careers is just another starting block, another fight between you and fear," she added, letting her fingers rest on his wrist, her thumb drawing patterns on his skin.

"But what do you think I should do?"

Oh no, this was his journey and he needed to map his own path. "That's up to you, Soren," she murmured. "But what I can do, right now, is love you."

She felt him tense, knew that he was wondering

how to take that sentence. She suspected he would take her words as an offer on her part to make love to him, and yeah, that's where they were going. But silently, somewhere deep in her soul, she knew that she loved him, and probably had from the first night they'd spent together in Paris.

He saw her; he saw past her pretty face and sexy body to the goofy, nerdy, vulnerable woman she was beneath her cut-glass cheekbones, bright hair and blue eyes. He knew her, was the first man to take the time to pull off the pretty wrapping paper and dig into the layers below.

And maybe he did love her, just a little. Knowing how private Soren was, how introspective, she knew she had to mean something to him in order for him to reveal his dilemma, to let her inside his head. He didn't do that with everyone…

He didn't do it with *anyone*. She was special. She felt it in his touch, in the way he looked at her sometimes, like she was an unexpected, amazing gift. It was in his touch, in that singular smile he gave her, the way he kissed her…

Did he know? Did he suspect? She couldn't be sure, but she didn't care. She loved him and Soren deserved to be loved.

But she knew he wasn't ready to hear any declarations. She could see he was feeling overwhelmed and emotionally whipped. He needed to get out of his head, just for a little while.

And Eliot knew the perfect way to do that…

Rising, she placed her hands on his tense shoulders, grazed his chin with her lips and slowly moved on to his mouth. The night, warm and fragrant, shimmered with desire, with that buzzy emotional connection that lifted and strengthened lust into something deeper and bolder.

She felt his sigh against her lips and one of Soren's hands landed on her bottom while the other curled around her neck. Tongues tangled and hands rubbed at the barrier of T-shirts and shorts. Under the hand she'd placed on his chest, his heart thumped, fast but steady.

Eliot murmured in dismay when Soren pulled away to rest his forehead on hers. He tangled his fist in her hair and tipped her head up so he could look into her eyes.

"I need you, Eliot. I want you so much."

For a man who never expressed his feelings, it was almost—*almost*—a declaration of love. "I'm yours, Soren." And she always would be.

Her eyes drifted closed and her lips parted as she tipped her head to allow him access to her neck, then to the very sensitive spot in the hollow of her throat. He pushed his hand up under her T-shirt and pulled it up her stomach, then over her head. Easily, quickly, he found her nipple with his clever fingers, pulling it to a hard nub. Eliot desperately wanted his lips, his tongue and his teeth there, needed his kisses on the inside of her thigh, closing over her feminine places. But that was for later. Right now, they could take the time, let love and desire build to a fever pitch. This was, after all, a night to remember.

Eliot helped him remove his shirt, ran her hand over his hard stomach and slid her fingers under the waistband of his tailored shorts. He helped her flip open the button, and she pulled down the zipper and glided the tips of her fingers over his erection. It was a gentle touch, but Eliot felt him shudder, tasted his groan and, feeling invincible and utterly feminine, she circled his girth, and dragged her thumb over his tip. Eliot didn't think it possible that his kiss could deepen, that her desire could expand, but they both did and a fireball threatened to roll over her.

"I can't take much more, El. I need to be inside you," Soren muttered as Eliot touched his collarbone with her tongue and inhaled the scent of his masculine skin.

Soren's hand skimmed over her hip and moved across the zipper of her shorts. His thumb landed far down on her mound and she gasped when his fingers pushed the fabric of her thin cotton shorts into her most sensitive spot.

"I need you naked," Soren informed her, his voice growly. He spun her around, looking for the side-zipper to her shorts. He found it quickly and Eliot felt a warm breeze on her skin. She took in a sharp gulp of air when Soren's hot mouth touched the base of her spine as her shorts dropped to the floor.

This was better than she could have imagined. Soren unclasped her bra and it fell to the floor in a pretty puddle of deep purple lace; her thong followed and she stood naked, her back to his chest, his lips on her neck.

"You're so beautiful. Inside even more than out. Funny, smart, so very honest and brave."

It was the perfect compliment, another way he showed her that he saw her, knew what she needed to hear.

Soren turned her around and watched her with lust-filled eyes as he dropped his hands to push his shorts down his hips. Eliot stepped back to look at him, tall and built and looking oh-so-fine in a pair of plain black tight trunks, strained by his very impressive erection.

Seconds later the last piece of his clothing was on the floor and his arms were banded around her thighs. He lifted her against his body, his cock probing her slick, wet folds. Their eyes were level as he surged into her. He was hard, powerful and amazing and she felt complete, fulfilled.

"So wet…so lovely and warm."

Eliot moaned as she linked her arms around his muscled neck. Her clitoris brushed against his groin as he pulled her even closer. But there was no way they could continue making love standing up. Soren was strong but she wasn't a lightweight. A second later, she forgot her concerns as he moved inside her, flinging her into a dizzying, color-filled world of light and sensation and color.

She lifted her hips and Soren demanded she give

him her mouth. Eliot obeyed his command and pressed her lips against his and their tongues swirled and curled as he pumped his hips.

Eliot barely felt him lowering her to the pool lounger, only vaguely aware of the cool material against her back. Her heart and mind and body were full of Soren, and she was too immersed in what he was doing to her, how he made her feel, to be very aware of anything that wasn't him. She was concentrated pleasure…needing that ultimate release, so she lifted her hips, increasing the rhythm.

"Harder, Soren, more," she demanded and he immediately responded, pumping into her faster and harder, pistoning his hips. She didn't think she could take much more but knew she would. Nothing felt as good as Soren did…

She transformed into a ball of pure sensation and bucked and strained, digging her heels into his back, determined to wring every ounce of pleasure from this moment.

Reaching, reaching, and then exploding, shimmering, flying, Eliot shattered into shards of intense light. She danced and flew and then something deep inside her pulled the pieces back together and slotted them back into place. She knew rather than felt that Soren had followed her over the edge; she could hear him panting in her ear. As the world slowly started to make sense again, she felt the aftershocks rippling through his body, the softening of his erection inside her.

But he didn't pull away and Eliot lost track of time. She wasn't sure how long they lay there, Soren's weight on her, her hand drawing random patterns on his back. She just knew that this was where she wanted to be, in his arms, at his side.

In his life.

"Are you sure you want to do this?"

Eliot, wearing what she had told him was a vintage Halston, off the shoulder and in an intense red, turned her eyes on him. She looked fantastic, but she was in model mode, hair styled and makeup perfect. He far preferred her tangled hair and natural face, the sand-on-her-skin look.

Eliot shrugged. "You need a date and we have to come out of hiding some time," she said. "Obviously, by attending this function with you for—what is it again?"

"A ball to raise funds for once competitive sportsmen and women who now find themselves in need," Soren explained.

"Right. Well, by attending it as your date, we will be linked together," Eliot completed her thought.

He had no problem with that. "We've been linked together since I walked you out of the hotel, El. You and I, in the celebrity world, are old news already."

She looked out of the window of the limo he'd hired and sighed. "I guess."

They were approaching the outskirts of New York City and Soren started to knot the tie he'd earlier draped around his neck. This ball was black-tie and he wore an Armani tuxedo, choosing a plain black silk Hermès tie as he hated bow ties with a passion.

He flipped the ends with practiced ease, thinking about how this was the first time Eliot was returning to Manhattan since her abortive wedding. He got the sense she'd prefer to be sitting on the deck of the apartment or lying on a blanket on the beach, but they both knew it was time to show their faces so that they could all move on.

It was time for her to emerge from her self-imposed cocoon, and this Sportsman's Benefit Ball was a great vehicle for her to do that—big enough to attract attention, but not so big that she'd be bombarded.

She'd still have to put up with some questions, of course. He found himself wondering what her answers would be. He knew she'd been exploring her options lately, thinking about what her future held. She'd been offered the opportunity to audition for a small role on a sitcom but she'd told him she wasn't interested in acting. She'd had a video call with a famous yoga teacher, asking her if she'd be interested in joining his studio and documenting her yoga journey. That had been a hard no, as had the offer for her to appear on a reality series in the jungles of Costa Rica. She'd appeared gratified that there was still interest in her, but none of the offers themselves had piqued her interest.

Like him, she seemed no closer to discovering a way forward.

As for him, he was enjoying his vacation time more than he'd expected—but that was only because Eliot was at Calcott Manor. Honestly, doing nothing was starting to pall. He needed to go back to his routine and knowing what his day entailed.

His desire for structure had deep roots, going back long before he'd lost his parents. His father's role in Forrester-Grantham International demanded that he fly all over the world, all the time, and Soren and his mother accompanied his dad wherever he went. Years of going to bed in a hotel room in a different city every week had, to a kid who'd simply wanted his own bedroom, his own things, taken its toll. He'd wanted to be like his cousins, who went to the same school every day, played Little League and soccer, and had sleepovers.

His education had been erratic—long spells of inactivity punctuated by intense weeks of schooling by tutors when they thought he was falling behind—and he had been constantly in the company of adults.

Stability, a home, his own bedroom, the normality of going to school daily and seeing the same people regularly had finally come when he was nine, but at a hell of a price: the death of his parents. Little wonder that when he did finally start school, it had been difficult for him to adjust. Outside of his family, he hadn't related to kids his age and while he wasn't bullied, he was ignored.

Swimming, that solitary pursuit, suited him perfectly. He became good at it, then great at it and now he was the best in the world. And he was thinking of chucking it in.

"Are your brothers going to be there tonight?" Eliot asked, playing with the clasp of her tiny clutch bag. What was the point of carrying something so small?

"I asked my manager to send them an invitation," he replied. "I forgot to ask whether they'd be attending. My trainer and manager are going to be there and they *will* take the opportunity to pull me away for a private conversation about my future."

Eliot pulled a face. "Do you know what you are going to tell them?"

Yes. No... He didn't know. "Not yet."

Soren leaned forward, rested his arms on his thighs, and allowed his arms to dangle between his legs.

He needed to find something that gave him the same satisfaction swimming did, but he couldn't think of anything that would give him the same thrill, that would capture his attention and focus.

Until he found out what he wanted to do, *what* he could do, he should stick with what he knew and was good at. But, maybe, he should stop making his sport his whole life, his every thought. Maybe he could find more balance: pick up a hobby, pick up a new skill, start a relationship...

Start a relationship? He was in a relationship already, and it was one that he didn't want to end. He wanted to see more of Eliot, to enjoy her lovely body but also to further explore her fascinating mind. At some point he'd have to give up swimming; he wouldn't have a choice, and even if the time wasn't now, maybe he start making time for a life outside of the pool. He could spend time with his brothers, look for a business he could start or buy, and spend time, depending on where she went and what she did, with Eliot.

Mostly Eliot.

Yes, he was worried about her being a distraction, but he could control the impact she had on his life. The upside of this plan was that, if he allowed his world to expand, his transition into the post-swimming world would be more of an elegant roll than a graceless tumble.

Sure, the thought of committing himself to swimming for another two years made his stomach burn and churn (and the thought of giving it up made his throat and lungs close) but the prospect of having Eliot in his life made him feel settled and safe, calm and in control.

She was, he decided, the one thing he knew for certain that he wanted more of—the only thing he absolutely couldn't give up.

Ten

Eliot looked around the star-studded ballroom and frowned when she couldn't see Soren. Picking up a glass of champagne, she skirted a group of basketball players, smiled at a PGA Grand Slam winner and admired the dress of a tiny gymnast.

She was conscious of many eyes following her and she'd already had to bat off a few people who'd expressed far too much interest in her future. She'd yet to stumble on what she most wanted to do, but she had no intention of discussing the difficult issue of what came next with strangers.

She was heading for the balcony to meet Soren after a bathroom break. Stepping through the open doors onto the deep balcony of the hotel—not the Forrester-Grantham this time—she saw Soren standing at the far end, talking to three equally tall, broad-shouldered men.

Eliot stopped and placed her hand on her stomach, conscious of a flutter of nerves. She was about to meet his brothers, three daunting, powerful men who, she was sure, had doubts about Soren hooking up with her after her car-wreck wedding.

Eliot hauled in a deep breath, straightened her shoulders and walked over to the group, taking strength in Soren's encouraging smile. He held out his hand and introduced her to Fox and Merrick while Jack, whom she had met before, simply said hello.

They were perfectly polite, but she saw the suspicion in their eyes and felt their lack of warmth. Eliot tried not to take it personally; she knew they were all protective of each other, and her relationship with Soren was both quick and unconventional.

Fox pushed back the lapels of his jacket to slide his hands into the pockets of his tuxedo pants. "Have you made any progress in our quest to get Avangeline to write her will?" he asked Soren, who shook his head.

"None at all. She gets irate every time I mention it," Soren replied. "Jace says she also gets her head bitten off whenever she raises the subject."

"I don't understand it," Fox murmured. "She's the last person in the world I expected to leave such a loose end untied."

"How's her health, mental and physical?" Jack asked Soren. "Did you notice anything different about her when you returned home?"

Soren's fingers moved up and down Eliot's bare back. "I think she looks and sounds better than the last time I saw her, not so low. She seems to be enjoying Aly's company."

Three sets of eyes darkened with annoyance. "Seriously?" Fox demanded.

"Are Jace and Avangeline still buying her BS about Mal and inheriting his personality traits?" Jack asked after Soren nodded.

"Seems like it," Soren said.

Eliot fought the urge to speak up in Aly's defense. She wasn't completely on board with the concept of cellular memory, and she needed to know more about it before she decided one way or the other. But she did believe Aly was completely sincere and only had good intentions for Avangeline and the others. She opened her mouth to speak, but swallowed her words, sensing that her opinion wouldn't be welcomed by the others.

From there, the conversation drifted in other directions, mostly revolving around the various athletes who were in attendance. Then one of the others mentioned something about a basketball coach across the room who was planning to retire after his next season, and Eliot felt Soren stiffening, and his hand dropping away. He shifted away from her and she turned to look at him, and saw him take a deep breath.

Holy hell, he was going to talk to his brothers about his dilemma. She knew this was hard for him, that he found it difficult to talk about his inner world.

She linked her fingers with his, squeezing his hand in support.

"I need to tell you guys something," Soren said, his voice cracking, just a little.

Fox looked at their linked hands and raised his eyebrows. "I think it's a bit early to make any big decisions, bro."

Eliot clicked on to his meaning before Soren did and was blushing brightly by the time Soren started glaring at his brother. Fox Grantham had a reputation for not pulling his punches, and for being the grumpiest of the brothers, but she didn't need him jumping to conclusions.

"This is not about me," Eliot said, her voice cool.

"Of course it's not about Eliot," Soren firmly stated, pushing an agitated hand through his hair. Eliot told herself not to overreact to his automatic dismissal, but she couldn't stop herself from pulling her hand from his and schooling her face in an I-don't-care expression. The urge to run was strong, but she knew doing that would make her look like a spoiled child. No, she'd stand here and pretend that she suddenly didn't have a million doubts about where they were going, and whether they'd be traveling together.

Was this madness? How could she possibly be feeling this much for Soren so soon? She'd been about to marry another man a short time ago. Was it even possible to fall in love with someone new so quickly?

Short answer: yes.

"I'm toying with the idea of ending my career as a competitive swimmer," Soren stated.

There was a long silence, only broken by Fox's harsh "Explain."

"I've been struggling to make up my mind between swimming for two more years or going out now, at the top of my game."

"You mean, like *quit*?" Fox demanded, sounding annoyed.

"There's a difference between retiring and quitting, Fox!" Soren replied, sounding aggravated.

Merrick, obviously the peacemaker, held up his hand. "What's the motivation behind this, Soren?"

Soren turned to look at the glinting lights of the Manhattan skyline. "It's been at the back of my mind since Tokyo. I thought taking a vacation would allow me time to think. Unfortunately, my business manager grabbed me a few minutes ago and told me my sponsors want an immediate answer. I have thirty-six hours to give them an answer. It's a two-year sponsorship deal, if I accept."

Eliot stared at him, a sense of unease growing. She'd sensed that he was beginning to reconcile himself to retiring, but that wasn't how this sounded. Did he really want to stay in the game for two more years? Soren wasn't someone who could compartmentalize his life. His career required total dedication, intense concentration and single-minded focus. There was no place for her in his life if he remained a professional swimmer.

Her gut twisted.

She'd thought she'd have more time with him. More time to love him, more time to talk to him, more time to make him see that he needed her in his life, as she needed him in hers.

It felt like he was drifting away from her, that he'd left no place for her in his life.

"Two years isn't that long, is it?" Merrick asked.

"It is when you are a competitive swimmer, when you are already training twice as hard as you used to just in order to keep making your times, when your body is tired," Eliot said, unable to stay quiet.

"El…" Soren murmured, a quiet demand that she not interfere.

"With respect, this is a conversation between us brothers," Fox told her. "You're not family."

Eliot looked at Soren, waiting for him to defend her right to be there, but when he didn't, she closed her eyes. She thought they'd come to a point of having the right to express an opinion, while he obviously thought their relationship was still a temporary deal.

She was thinking of their future together, while he was only thinking of his.

A subtle but hugely important distinction. *Right.*

Eliot glanced at the door, desperate to leave, but Soren held her in place with an arm around her waist. She didn't want to pull away and draw attention to herself—she didn't want him to see how hurt she was. No, she'd wait until she got the opportunity to walk away with a little dignity.

"Why on earth do you want to give up something you've worked so hard at for so long, Soren?" Jack asked, his tone measured and calm. "And what does your trainer think?"

"She thinks I've still got it but I don't know if I do."

"Maybe you should trust her," Fox suggested, still sounding annoyed.

"Fox…" Merrick warned him.

Fox turned his turbulent gaze from Soren to Merrick and back to Soren again. "No, I'm not going to stand here and tell him it's okay to walk away from his career, not when he has a chance to go higher and faster. We are Granthams. We don't give up, *ever*."

Was this guy for real? Did he have any idea what Soren put himself through mentally and physically to remain at the top of his game? Did he know how tiring it was, how scary it was for Soren to face the prospect of staying in swimming too long, working himself to the bone only to see himself slip in the rankings, no matter how hard he tried to stay on top?

"If you did retire, what would you do, Soren?" Merrick asked. Like Jack, he was calm, trying to help Soren with his dilemma and trying not to allow emotion to color his response.

But his question was Soren's Achilles' heel, something he couldn't answer.

"I don't know," Soren reluctantly admitted.

Jack and Merrick winced and Fox threw up his hands.

"Well, maybe you should figure that out first be-

fore you throw it all away, hotshot. All of us are work-
aholics but you are possibly the worst at dealing with
downtime." Fox flicked a glance at Eliot before returning to look at Soren. "You've been distracted
lately, but we're talking about your *life*, bro. Swimming is what you do, who you are."

Oh, no, that was a step too far. She wasn't going
to stand here and listen to this nonsense for a minute
more. "That's such BS," she stated, her voice strong
and sure.

"Again, Ms. Stone, you're not fam—"

"Oh, shut up, Fox. Who made you boss of the
world?" Eliot snapped, pleased when his mouth
dropped open in shock. Yeah, she had a voice and
an opinion. And this was the man she loved, and he
was getting crap advice and unfair pressure from the
people who were supposed to have his back.

To hell with what she should and shouldn't say,
she was trusting her gut here.

"I am Soren's friend, someone who has his best interests at heart, so I'm entitled to an opinion, despite
not being a Grantham. And in my opinion, you're
talking out of your ass and being—I hope uninten-
tionally—cruel. We are not what we *do*, for God's
sake! Soren isn't *only* a swimmer, and being an Olympic champion and world record holder isn't *all* he is
capable of! He can be anything, do anything, try anything he wants to and I know he'd be a success at it.

"Do you know why?" she demanded, looking from
shocked face to shocked face. "Because he's got heart

and drive and buckets of persistence. We don't need to be one-dimensional, to only be good at one thing. If swimming doesn't make Soren happy anymore, then he doesn't have to carry on doing it just because he's the best in the world. He is allowed to walk away, to try something new."

"I know that you and Soren have spent a lot of time together lately, Eliot," Jack said, sounding like he was doing his best to be ultra-reasonable, "but we've known him all his life."

"And that's the problem!" Eliot retorted. "You look at him and see who he was five years ago—or ten, or fifteen. You're not seeing who he is now."

She continued, trying to remain calm. "More than anything else, I want Soren to be happy, to wake up excited, to be filled with joy. And I don't think swimming does that for him anymore."

"I just think—"

"Hey, I am standing right here!" Soren said on a half shout, loud enough for people to look over to them. "Stop talking around me, dammit."

Fair enough, Eliot conceded. She looked at him and saw the confusion in his eyes, his tumultuous expression. She placed a hand on his arm and squeezed. "I don't think you are ready to make a decision yet, Soren, so please, ask for more time from your sponsors."

"I can't keep putting them off forever," Soren snapped, tense and frustrated. "And I can't give up swimming until I have something else in place, Eliot. I can't do *nothing*."

His eyes connected with her and she saw that she'd lost him. Not that she'd ever had him...

No, she'd lost the possibility of what they could be, what they could mean to each other. How they could be the missing puzzle pieces in each other's lives. He was choosing the certainty of swimming over the prospect of what they could build together. He was choosing to give in to fear instead of fighting it.

"You can," she insisted, not ready to give up. "You can take more time off and we can be together. We can start something new, something else."

Soren gripped the railing of the balcony, and she knew that under his tux, his muscles were tight with tension. "I can't bumble along until something falls into my lap! I can't just live my life like I'm on vacation. While it has been fun the past few weeks, it's not real life! It has no purpose!"

"Being together like this is a step out of time, I get that," she countered, desperate. She was vaguely aware that his brothers had stepped away to give them a little privacy for this conversation.

Good of them.

"The last weeks have been wonderful, but I know it isn't real life. And I do understand that you need to do something. But swimming doesn't make you excited anymore and I've seen you lighten up around me. You are more relaxed, and so much happier."

"I've been banging one of the most beautiful women in the world. Of course I have a smile on my face!"

Nothing he could've said at that moment could've hurt her more. He'd taken what they had and reduced it to her looks, to her body, to the pleasure he took in both. The pain was fast and intense and threatened to drop her to her knees.

"Jesus, I didn't mean it like that," Soren muttered, rubbing his jaw.

"Maybe not, but you went there anyway—and you did it to put some distance between us," Eliot said, her words sounding wooden.

That was okay, because she felt like she was stiffening up from the inside out, going back to that place where she was just a spectator in her own life. She felt herself start to disengage, retreat and shut down. *No!*

She *absolutely* refused to go back there, to that awful place where she couldn't, or wouldn't, feel. She pushed away the temptation to slide into numbness and gathered her courage. This might hurt—no, it would definitely hurt—but she was done pretending, done with accepting what people handed her. She was going after what *she* wanted.

He'd either give it to her or not. Probably not. But she'd rather hear that from his mouth than spend the rest of her life regretting the chances she didn't take.

"I'd like to explore life with you and I'd like us to start that journey on an equal footing, both of us starting a new path. If you decide that swimming competitively is what you want to do then I know there isn't space for me in your schedule. If you decided to leave..." she closed her eyes, feeling like a leaf on a storm-tossed sea.

"We don't have to know what we are doing or where we are going but I know I want to live my life with you in it," she told him, a little desperately. "I'm in love with you, I want us to work."

"Love? After such a short time?" He shook his head. "You're asking me to give up all my training—"

"I didn't—"

"You said that there wasn't space for you unless I stopped swimming so, at the very least, you are implying that I should give it up to take a chance on *love*? On someone I haven't spent more than a month with?"

She was splintering inside. Couldn't someone, just once, see that she was worth taking a risk on? That she had something to offer, love to give?

"This is madness, Eliot!" Soren's voice rose. "Seventeen days ago you were walking up the aisle about to marry someone else!"

That was a low blow and she told him that. "Don't throw that in my face, you jerk! This has nothing to do with him and then and everything to do with you, me and now!"

He shook his head, stubbornness turning his expression hard. "It's too soon."

"You're looking for a reason, a excuse. You are feeding your fears, Soren," Eliot countered.

"How can you ask me to give everything up to take a chance on someone who could leave me?"

"I'm not going to leave you, I lov—"

"You can't promise me that!" Soren shouted, interrupting her. "You can't promise that you'll always be around, that nothing will happen!"

"Nobody can promise that," Eliot quietly told him. "But I can promise to love you as hard as I can, for as long as life allows me to do that."

Soren linked his hands behind his neck, his eyes wild. "Let me carry on swimming, but be in my life. Let's try it that way."

Eliot knew what he was asking: that she tailor her schedule—and life—to be available for him in the few hours he could spare for her between training and meets. That was what she'd been prepared to do for DeShawn but it was no longer an option, she needed to make life choices that worked for her.

She knew, because she now knew herself better than she ever did, that waiting around for Soren to *see* her, to give her time and attention, would emotionally eviscerate her.

No, they needed to start this new adventure together, on equal terms, or not at all.

That was the only way they could work.

"I'm not going to play second fiddle to you and your career. I'm not going to sit by and wait, wringing my hands, hoping that you look up from the water at some point and see me, see what I need. I want a career, purpose and to do something important. I also want and deserve a family. A husband who is committed to being there and present as much as possible.

I want a lover and a friend. I want babies and dogs and pets and… I want *you*. But I'm greedy. I want it all. I've always been prepared to settle for what the world and the people who are supposed to love me can give me, but I won't do that anymore. Not again. I won't settle for less than I deserve."

"Eliot—" Soren muttered. "Don't do this. Don't walk out of my life."

Eliot shook her head. "Then don't put what you no longer love above someone who loves you."

As long as she lived, she knew she'd never forget the despair in his eyes, the jostling between hope and fear. But fear, as she knew it would, turned his eyes to a flat green-gray and she knew she'd lost. He didn't even need to say anything.

Tears, hot and acidic, filled up her suddenly empty heart. "I never had a chance, did I? I was conning myself that you would put me above your need to feel safe, to feel secure, to feel in control."

His mouth opened and closed, and she knew he was looking for words, but he didn't need to. Everything important had been said.

She lifted her hand and dashed the tears off her cheeks. "I can't settle, Soren, and if you loved me the way I love you, you wouldn't ask me to," she told him.

"You can't ask me to give up everything that makes sense to me, everything that's safe, to take a leap with someone I barely know."

They were both right.

And both wrong.

But they were definitely at an impasse.

Knowing that nothing would be solved now or, possibly, ever, Eliot walked back into the ballroom and headed for the exit.

Pushing away her tears, she walked toward the elevator bank, trying to think. She couldn't go back to Calcott Manor with Soren—she'd rather eat fire ants. Madigan was in Hong Kong, doing a shoot, so she couldn't go to her place. And she couldn't get a hotel room for the night—she hadn't brought her wallet with her to the ball. Everything she needed was in Avangeline's above-the-garage apartment.

She'd go down to the concierge desk and ask them to call her mother. She'd ask her to book and pay for a ride to her mom's place. However it panned out, it was going to be a long night.

Eliot stepped into the elevator, stared at the floor and took a deep breath, knowing that if she allowed her tears to fall, they'd never stop.

"I'm sorry I was a bastard back there."

Eliot lifted her head at the deep voice and turned to see that Fox Grantham had entered the elevator with her. "Do you make a habit of it?" she asked, her tone icy.

"Habit of what?"

"Thinking the worst of people?"

Fox winced. "Yeah, I probably do." She was surprised by his honesty. "I'm super protective of my family. I apologize, Ms. Stone."

He sounded sincere and Eliot didn't have the energy to be angry with him. She had too many other emotions—disappointment, sadness, loss—rolling around her system to be overly bothered by him.

"Do you really think Soren giving up his sport is the best thing for him to do?" Fox asked as they stepped into the busy hotel lobby.

She shook her head, no longer sure. "I don't know, Fox. But neither do I think it's good for him to keep swimming only because he's scared of having time on his hands. I genuinely believe he can do anything, be anything—he has so much to give, in and out of the water, but I can't make him believe that. He has to see that himself."

If she accepted that she wasn't one-dimensional, then neither was Soren. She realized it; he didn't.

"Could you not compromise, give him a year or two, and help him find the next thing that sets his soul on fire?" Fox asked. "Why does he have to give up swimming right now to be with you?"

He held up a hand when she frowned at him, both oblivious to the people passing them.

"No, don't respond yet. Take a minute and think about it. You're asking him to choose between something he loves, has always loved—"

"*Does* he still love it, Fox? Did he ever? Or does he just do it because he's good at it?"

Fox rubbed his chin. "To be honest, I don't know."

She didn't either.

"But what I'm really asking is why does he have

to choose between you and his sport? Can't he have both?"

Eliot opened her mouth to reply but no words came out.

"Why does it have to be everything or nothing?" He touched her shoulder, squeezed and let it go. "That's a hell of an ask, Eliot."

Rightly or wrongly, she wanted *one* person— Soren—to make that call, to put her first. To make her his highest priority.

She knew how dedicated she was, how focused he could be and swimming would be his priority, she would be the third wheel always butting in, demanding attention.

Oh, God, was she being unfair? Was she assuming too much, not giving him enough credit? Maybe he was he genuine in his desire to find a more balanced work-home life.

Maybe picking swimming didn't mean not picking her.

Was she asking him to sacrifice everything so that she could be sure—and to prove to herself—that she was worthy of that grand gesture?

Fox placed his hand on her back and nodded to the doors of the hotel. She shook her head.

"I need to call my mom, then get a cab over to her place," she told him. "I'm not going back to Calcott Manor tonight."

"I'll arrange your transport," he said. As they stepped out of the perfumed, expensive lobby, a black

Range Rover pulled up beside them. Fox reached for the back passenger door and gestured for Eliot to enter its expensive interior.

"Doug, my driver, will take you where you want to go and you are welcome to use the car phone," Fox told her. He stood between the door and the car, a faint smile on his face. "I hope we meet again, Eliot. You and I, I think, could become friends."

He shut the car door before she had a chance to reply and the driver steered the car toward the exit and glided into traffic.

And away from Soren.

Eleven

"Can I join you?"

Soren, sitting on the edge of the outdoor pool, his calves in the water, looked up to see Aly standing next to him. He hadn't heard her approach and he felt a spurt of annoyance.

He wanted—no, he needed—to be alone. Plus, Aly had moved a few notches up on his shit list because she'd been the one to pack up Eliot's stuff and deliver it to her in Manhattan. He didn't care that Eliot must have asked her to do it—he was too caught up in resenting the fact that Aly had taken away what might have been his last chance to see Eliot again.

She must've caught something on his face because she grimaced and turned to leave. He closed his eyes, feeling like a jerk. This wasn't his pool, and Avangeline's guest had every right to use it whenever she wanted to.

He called Aly back and gestured to the pool. "Go for it."

Aly sent him an uncertain look but dropped her sarong and did a neat dive into the pool, striking out for the other end. She was a good swimmer, he noticed, unlike Eliot who was all long legs and floppy arms in the water.

God, he missed her.

Instead of moving back into his suite of rooms in the main house, he was still sleeping in the apartment, using the bed they'd shared. In that room, he could still smell her scent, and memories of the way she loved him rolled over him.

He missed her every hour, every minute and in every way. He missed her low, sexy laugh and her silky skin, her bright eyes and her long toes. He missed the way she bashed her pillow three times before she fell asleep, how her legs ended up entangled in his in the night. The way she kissed, the way she looked at him like he was the answer to every question she'd ever had...

He longed for her, loved her, but still couldn't decide what to do with his life. She was asking him to give up everything, to start a new life with her with no safety net, to sacrifice his career based on a three-week relationship.

That was crazy, and too big an ask. What if it

didn't work out? What if she changed her mind in six months, in a year? In five? In ten?

Risking his heart and losing her was a horrible possibility but giving up his career as well? That was two hundred steps too far.

But every time he, almost, made up his mind to keep swimming, to sign another two-year contract, he hesitated. He'd never vacillated this much in his life.

Aly hauled herself out of the water to sit next to him. "It's strange to see you outside the water, not in it," she commented.

Soren leaned back on his hands, rotating his feet in the water. He closed his eyes and tipped his face up to the sun, wondering what Eliot was doing, how she was feeling. As long as he lived, he wouldn't ever forget the devastation in her eyes just before she walked away from him and out of that ballroom.

The desolation he put there.

"Aren't you supposed to be in the city, signing a contract with your sponsor? Your negotiation window must be up."

Soren turned to look at her, irritation in his eyes. Aly winced. "Sorry, your grandmother talks to me. If it's any consolation, she's also told me that Fox has fired another personal assistant and that Jack flew to London this morning."

"You and my grandmother have become good friends," Soren commented. "Avangeline doesn't usually talk to people."

"She says you two are alike, and that it takes a

crowbar to get anything out of either of you," Aly said. "So, why are you here and not dashing your signature across a page?"

"I asked for more time and my sponsor gave me until the end of the week. If I can't give them an answer by Friday, they'll find someone else to sponsor," Soren admitted.

Aly dropped backed into the water, her arms resting on the lip of the pool, her face turned up to him. "Why is it such a difficult decision to make?"

"Because I'm choosing between my career and Eliot," Soren admitted, wondering why he was talking to a woman he didn't like, someone he didn't trust. Someone who spouted crap about inheriting some of Mal's personality traits along with his liver. But maybe an outsider would look at the situation differently, toss in a solution he hadn't considered.

"If Eliot wasn't in the picture, what would your decision be?"

"I don't know. That's why I decided to take some time off—so I could decide. But then I spent all my time with Eliot instead," Soren muttered.

"Okay, but giving up swimming was always a possibility, right? I mean, if it wasn't, then you wouldn't have opted to take a vacation."

"Fair enough," Soren conceded.

"So, are you more freaked out now than you were three weeks ago?"

He thought about it. "Yeah, I guess."

"So what's changed?" Aly asked, her unusual purple-gray eyes somber. She didn't wait for his answer. "You met Eliot. Could it be that you are using going back to training as a security blanket because you are scared of what's happening between you?"

"Men don't get scared," Soren automatically replied.

Aly rolled her eyes and he knew he deserved it. "Men are the biggest 'fraidy cats out there!"

Aly pushed away from the wall to tread water. "This water is delicious. So, another question…"

"God, you're full of them today," Soren snapped.

"Well, since you haven't got up and walked away, you can't be that annoyed with me," Aly pointed out. "So, say you go back to swimming and in two years you retire… What will be different retiring then instead of now?"

"I'll be older and slower," Soren stated, his tone glum.

"You will also be alone. Eliot might've moved on, be in a relationship with someone else, or even married. Is another two years of training, pushing your body, hours of lonely hours in the pool worth the risk of losing her forever? Will you regret that?"

Of course he would. And that was why he'd asked her whether he could swim and be with her—but she'd blown his suggestion out of the water.

"Why do I have to give everything up?" he asked. "Why does it have to be all or nothing? She's not asking for us to date each other—she wants *everything*. The ring and the babies and the pets and the house…"

"I like a girl who knows what she wants," Aly stated, her eyes laughing.

"It's too much, too soon!"

"If you don't want that, then walk away, go back to Miami and don't give her another thought," Aly blithely told him. When he didn't answer her, she released a low, "Mmm".

He shoved his hands into his hair, frustrated. "Just say it, Aly."

"If you didn't want that, you'd have told her so, straight up. You're not the type to waffle, Soren. So, is it possible that you do want what she's offering but you're scared to reach out and take it? Scared that if you do, she'll disappear on you?"

Maybe. Possibly. *Yes*.

Fear... It was like a choke chain around his neck, holding him back. Fear to give up swimming because he didn't know what the future held, fear to go all in with Eliot because he was frightened something would happen to her, fear she'd change her mind about him, that she'd fall out of love. He liked certainty and he liked structure, liked having his life in boxes, organized and in place.

Eliot was someone who rearranged his boxes, rubbed out lines and added in squiggles where there should be right angles.

But she also added color and laughter and fun. He smiled more with her, laughed more and talked more. He was a better person without all those rigid boxes and not-to-be-crossed lines.

"I can live without swimming, can deal with months of rediscovering what I want to do with the rest of my life," Soren spoke slowly, the thick fog in his head clearing. "But I can't—won't—live my life without Eliot. I walked away from her once and I missed out on eight years with her. I'm not going to make the same stupid mistake again."

"That's excellent news," Aly said, grinning. Then she frowned.

"Problem?" Soren asked, standing up.

She looked puzzled. "I have the craziest impulse to do something I've never done in my life," she said, sounding confused.

"What?" Soren asked a little impatiently, eager to end this conversation and get to Eliot.

"I feel a fool but…" Aly lifted her hand to her face and spread out her fingers in an *L*, which she held to her forehead. "I have no idea why I need to do this—but I do. Even though I do not, in any way, think you are a loser.

"I also have this burning urge to tell you I'm proud of you."

Soren's knees wobbled, and he dropped to his haunches, placing his hand on the deck to keep his balance. Jesus… *Malcolm*. He could've dismissed her gesture, but her follow up statement about being proud of him sent chills racing up and down his spine. She'd connected the sign with his words.

Nobody but Eliot knew the link and she would never, no matter what happened between them, betray him by telling anyone something so personal about him and Malcolm.

Mal's sign. Mal's words.

God.

Aly dropped her hand and quickly swum over to the side, concern on her face. "Soren, you're as white as a sheet. Are you okay?" she asked.

"That… You… The loser sign…" He could barely get the words out his throat was so tight. "Malcolm did that—."

Aly's eyes widened in shock. "What does it mean? I mean, it's one thing to inherit his sweet tooth and his love for cars but if you tell me that he's insulting you, via me, then I'm going to lose it."

Soren laughed before holding out a hand to Aly, easily pulling her out of the pool. "No, he most definitely wasn't insulting me."

Somehow, through Aly, his brother had let him know that he loved him, that everything would be fine.

Aly shook her head, bemused. "If you say so," she said, not convinced. She bit her bottom lip and looked down at her bare feet, her expression turning thoughtful. She looked past his shoulder, rocked on her heels and pushed her hand through her wet hair.

"What is it, Aly?" he asked, pushing down his impatience. He needed to get to Eliot—she was his highest priority—but she wouldn't be happy with him if he blew off someone he knew she'd come to see as a friend.

"This is a difficult question but it's something that's been bugging me… The plane crash that caused your parents' death?"

Why the hell was she bringing this up now? It happened so long ago. "Yeah? What about it?"

"Did Malcolm ever say anything about it?"

"Like what?" Soren asked, looking at his watch, finding it hard to concentrate on her question. It would take him forty minutes, maybe a little more to get to New York, and then he still had to track Eliot down. He didn't want to scour New York looking for her. He would, but he didn't want to.

Aly's damp and gentle punch landed on his bicep. "Go, Soren, my—" she hesitated "—curiosity can wait. Go find your girl."

He grinned at her, dropped a kiss on the top of her head and made a quick getaway. As far as he was concerned, anybody and everything could wait.

Eliot was all that mattered.

Eliot had no idea why she was in the Forrester-Grantham's award-winning bar at five thirty in the afternoon. Maybe it was because the walls of her mother's apartment were beginning to close in on her, because it was too hot to walk in Central Park and because she wasn't in the mood to go shopping. Or see a movie or talk to anyone.

Maybe it was because this hotel was the closest thing she had to a link, tenuous though it was, to Soren.

Whatever the reason, she'd been sitting at this table for over ninety minutes, nursing the same glass of tepid white wine. She was surprised she hadn't been tossed out to make room for guests who were waiting for a table in the busy bar. But no, the waiters left her alone to stare out of the window at the busy street outside, her thoughts a million miles away.

She had to snap out of this slump soon. She couldn't keep walking around in a fog of despair, a miasma of depression. This was how she should've felt when DeShawn called off their wedding, but she was finally there, miserable and heartbroken.

Three weeks later and with the wrong man…

Or the right man at the wrong time.

Eliot sighed. She didn't blame Soren for being so reluctant to trust that their relationship could last. Who fell in love so quickly and so completely? He was a cautious guy—life had taught him to be that way—so she couldn't expect him to jump feetfirst into a relationship with a woman who'd just called off her society wedding.

Why had she mentioned marriage and babies and pets? Why did she ask that he give up his career for her? What had come over her? She still believed she had the right to have it all, her career and a purpose and a family, but maybe she shouldn't have suggested—implied— that he give up his career for her.

Eliot resisted the urge to bury her face in her hands or bang her forehead against the round table. Why hadn't she taken Soren up on his offer to date while he continued his career? Anything would be better than not having him in her life at all. Now she had nothing…and it was killing her.

Eliot pushed her fingertips into her forehead, hoping to rub away the dull headache that had taken up permanent residence in her skull. She had to get over him, move on. And that would be a lot easier if she found something to do, a way to occupy her time.

Oh…and because it was important to emotional growth. She couldn't make Soren love her but she could sort out her life, get it on some sort of track.

She wanted, and needed, to do something relevant, important, something that changed lives. Something to do with fashion—it was what she knew—but what? Should she consider starting a fashion line or her own agency. Could she be an agent? Mmm, neither option grabbed her.

She could launch a clothing or accessory line, but that seemed too easy, and well, inauthentic. She wanted more than just her name out there.

What had she wanted when she was fourteen and starting as a model? she wondered. What had she most needed when she was eighteen and going to jobs and parties, flying all over the world on a few hours' notice? What had she wished for she was tired of smiling, when her feet were hurting, when she was arguing with her mother?

She'd wanted a friend, but more than that, she'd *needed* a mentor. How many times had she wished she had someone she could talk to, could turn to for help and advice? In fact, she and Madigan had had a few conversations about how they wished they'd had a big sister in the industry, someone who knew their world inside out and who would be on their side, helping to protect themselves from pitfalls.

She and Madigan had tried to be there for the younger models but fame and success were hard-to-breach barriers between the superstars and the girls, and guys, just starting out.

But what if that relationship was formalized? Eliot sat up straighter, excitement skipping through her. You couldn't monetize or sell friendship, but it could be done on a mentorship basis, with older models taking on younger models. There were also models going through hard times who might need advice. She could form a support group, with monthly meetings—via video conferencing or in person—and one-on-one mentoring. The group could also be a lobby group and engage the industry heavyweights on issues such as diversity, sexual harassment and body positivity.

Madigan would sign up to be a mentor; that she knew. There were a couple of the older models who would as well, and she knew of a dozen retired models who might give of their time. The trick would be getting her younger colleagues to ask for help, or to sign up for a mentor.

It would take more thought—she needed to speak to Madigan and her former colleagues to get their input—but this was the first work-related idea she'd felt excited about for months, even years. Her heart felt warm and her brain was alive with possibilities...

Eliot grabbed her phone, opened an app and started to type notes, getting her ideas down. It might not work, but at least she was doing something important. Something that was needed. Something exciting...

So exciting that when Soren took the seat next to her, she looked at him and blurted out the news. "I want to set up a formalized support group for people in the beauty/fashion industry, specifically younger or at-risk models—an organization where they can connect with mentors, have someone to talk them through the rough and ugly bits of our industry, from getting rejected for a campaign to being hit on by a photographer or stylist."

"I think that's an awesome idea," he said, placing his elbows on the table. He smiled at her, his eyes full of love. Eliot held up her finger and jotted another idea on her notebook app. Soren hadn't dismissed her idea; he thought it awesome...

Soren was...

...*here.*

Sitting next to her.

Eliot looked up and blinked, her world coming into focus. Why was Soren here when he should be celebrating his brand-new sponsorship deal with his business manager or his brothers?

"What are you doing here?" she asked, confused.

"Looking for you," Soren replied, thanking the waitress when she placed an icy beer in front of him.

"How did you know I was here?" she asked, putting her phone down on the table. She clenched her fists to stop them from shaking.

"I had just started tracking you down when I got a text from Fox, telling me you were in the bar. He told me to get my ass over here."

He'd been looking for her...

"Why did you want to see me?" she asked. "Have you signed your new contract? Is that what you've come to tell me?"

He took a sip of his beer and shook his head. "No, I managed to squeeze a few more days out of my sponsors before making a final decision. My new deadline is Friday."

Friday... So he hadn't signed anything. And even if he had, she doubted there was a clause in there that stated he couldn't spend any free time he had with her.

"I'll spend as much time with you as I can. I'll move to Miami to be with you while you train." Eliot pushed the words out in a hot, fast rush. "I'd like to try and establish this support group, maybe as a foundation or a nonprofit organization, so I'll need to spend some time here since this is where most models are based, but I'll do whatever it takes to stay in your life. I had no right to ask you to give it all up, no right at all."

She looked at him and sighed at his impassive expression. Would she ever be able to read him? But then a small smile touched the corner of his lips, and his eyes lightened to a rich, bold green, the color of the rarest Colombian emeralds.

"That means a lot to me, El."

But was it enough? She didn't know. Soren tapped the side of his glass with his index finger, his brow furrowed in a frown. "But I don't think it will work."

She scrunched up her eyes as her heart fell like a steel anvil to the floor. She'd pushed too hard, demanded too much, and now it was definitely over. God, she couldn't stand it...

Eliot stood up and groped for her bag, pulling it off the back of her chair. "Okay, good to know," she said, through blurry eyes. "I'm so sorry for pushing, Soren."

She'd taken two unsteady steps when his words reached her. "Where the hell are you going, Eliot?"

She stopped and lifted her shoulders to her ears. With her back to him, she brushed the tears off her cheeks and pulled up a smile as she turned around. "Home," she admitted, "to try and work out how to live in this world without you in it. *Again*. So far, I'm not doing such a good job figuring it out."

"Me neither," Soren softly said. He held out his hand, broad and strong. "Come here, sweetheart."

She knew there were eyes on them, could feel the room watching them, and wouldn't be surprised if a couple of those eyes belonged to his brothers. But she couldn't look around; she only had eyes for the man dressed in tailored shorts, leather flip-flops and an open-necked, cobalt blue button-down shirt. The dress code for this bar was strict—a jacket and tie were required—and Eliot knew there was no way that Soren would've gained admittance had he not been a Grantham.

And, possibly, because Fox knew she was here.

Eliot looked at his hand, ignored it, and walked back to the table. She placed her elbows on its surface and rubbed her forehead. "I'd like to go, Soren. I have a headache."

"I'm retiring from swimming, Eliot. I thought it important that you be the first to hear my decision."

Eliot lifted her head to meet his eyes, hearing the words but not understanding the meaning. "I…ah… Why?"

"Because I was being ruled by fear, too scared to discover what was on the other side of being a world-class swimmer," Soren softly admitted. "Because you made me realize that swimming is what I do, not who I am."

"Who are you, Soren?" Eliot asked him, her eyes glued to his.

"I'm the man who loves you, who wants to spend the rest of his life with you, loving you. Having babies, adopting rescue pets and making a home." He pulled her closer and rested his forehead against hers. "I'll find something to do, some way to keep myself occupied. I'll have to or I'll go mad. It will be something that pushes me, that demands that I strive for excellence, but it won't be the be-all and end-all. *You* are, Eliot. Loving you is what I most want to do," Soren quietly added.

Eliot felt her heart settle and her soul sigh. Standing in this bar with Soren, she was home, the only place she wanted to be. It didn't matter what they did, or where they lived—being together was all that was important. "I love you," she murmured. "Do you mean it?"

"With all my heart," Soren said, before touching his lips to his. There was passion there—there always would be—but this was a kiss full of promise, with hints of the future, a here-she-is and there-you-are and *finally!* kiss. It was both a start and an end: a start of the rest of their lives with each other and the end to being alone.

Eliot pulled back and lifted her hand to lay her palm on his face. "Are you sure? Because if you aren't, that's okay. You can swim and I'll be there while you do it."

He shook his head. "I want us to start something new together, both of us in the same, what-the-hell-comes-next boat." He smiled and nodded at her phone. "But you seem to be ahead of me there—As in most things... I think I am going to spend my life trying to keep up with you."

"My support group is still just an idea," Eliot babbled, scared at the spark of hope burning in her chest.

"Tell me more," he gently commanded.

Eliot stood between his legs, enjoying his arms around her as she quickly explained, not wanting to go into too much detail. Soren tipped his head to the side. "I think there's a gap for mentorship in sports as well. So much pressure is put on kids…on everyone. I might hijack your idea, El."

Sports stars and models, both in the public eye and required to be nothing less than flawless. And that quest for perfection was hard to cope with, to maintain. "There's nobody else I'd love to work with more than you, Soren. But, right now, it's just a nebulous idea and I need to make sure that you are fully comfortable giving up swimming."

"I am fully comfortable giving up swimming," Soren replied, smiling. "Do you want to keep your surname? Or would you prefer to be called Eliot Stone-Grantham?"

She blinked, his words sinking in and settling. Her eyes widened, and her brain short-circuited. "What are you asking me, Soren?"

"I told you… I want babies and a home, and pets. And you as my wife." Soren lifted her left hand and kissed her fingers. His lips rested on her ring finger longer than the others. "Let me put a ring on this finger, Eliot. Be mine."

"When?" Eliot asked, the sound of her heartbeat roaring in her ears.

"As soon as possible," Soren told her. "We got engaged in three weeks. Let's try and break that record by getting married in under two."

She overexaggerated her wince. "I don't think so, Soren. It'll take time to make another puffball dress, and I don't think the Forrester-Grantham has an opening to hold a ball for our thousand-plus guests."

He dropped a kiss on her neck, just below her ear, and she shivered. "Honey, it's all up to you. All I ask is that, in two weeks' time, you become my wife."

"We can get married on the beach at Calcott Manor at sunset, with a handful of guests, or in a cathedral with half of Manhattan there," he told her, sounding determined. "You can wear denim shorts and a tank top, be barefoot or be in a bikini for all I care, but there will be a preacher and there will be promises made. Clear?"

She draped her arms around his neck and swiped her mouth across his. "Perfectly. I love the idea of being married on the beach but I think I can do better than shorts and a tank top or a bikini."

"Just be there for me, El. That's all I need."

Eliot pulled back to look into his eyes, intense with emotion. "I promise I always will be, Soren. Now, tomorrow, always. You are my person."

"And I am yours," Soren whispered before deepening their kiss. He pulled her flush against him and they sank into passion, reveling in being together, in finding each other, in knowing that they were never going to be alone again.

Then Fox's deep voice broke into their romantic moment…

"Okay, stop before I throw a bucket of water over you! God, you came close to blistering the wallpaper and blowing out a couple of lights."

Eliot laughed at her soon-to-be brother-in-law before raising her eyebrows at Soren. "That sounds like a challenge, darling."

"Accepted. You know how competitive I am," Soren said, laughing as he bent her over his arm and dropped them into another wall-scorching, need-a-fire-hydrant kiss.

* * * * *

Don't miss the next story in the
Dynasties: Calcott Manor series!

Their Temporary Arrangement

Available Spring 2023!

Dear Reader,

Welcome back to Hatfield, Connecticut!

Hospitality billionaire Fox Grantham accepts that he is difficult to work with, but after losing many assistants, he's at his wit's end. To add to his frustration, his brothers insist he relocate to Calcott Manor as he needs to convince his grandmother to make a will and keep an eye on her guest, the recipient of his dead brother's liver.

Ru Osman was abducted when she was three and her parents are ridiculously overprotective, resulting in her becoming a world traveler, refusing to be controlled. She's back in NYC and needs a job to earn money to return to traveling. She hears Fox Grantham needs a PA and talks her way into his office. How hard can the job be?

Ru accompanies Fox to Calcott Manor and they sleep together, telling each other they can separate work and sex. As they grow closer, they keep reminding each other this is a going-nowhere relationship and it will end when Ru returns to her travels.

But can they plan a life together that suits both of their personalities and ambitions? Read on to find out.

Happy reading!

Joss

Connect with me!

Facebook: JossWoodAuthor
Twitter: @JossWoodBooks
BookBub: JossWood
Goodreads: Joss_Wood

THEIR TEMPORARY
ARRANGEMENT

One

Oh, how they would laugh to find out what a pickle, I, Lady Avangeline Forrester-Grantham, have found myself in. Old friends—though there aren't that many left anymore—would snicker, and the press would salivate.

It is becoming harder and harder to keep the truth from Jack, Fox, Soren and Merrick. They have the write-your-will bit between their teeth and they won't give in until I do as they ask. I have raised stubborn, determined men, something I always took pride in doing.

At this point in my life, their pinprick focus and sharp intelligence is a pain in my blue-blooded bottom.

But I will handle this, just like I've handled everything else that's been thrown at me.
We don't buckle. We don't bend.

"**W**hy did you leave your last permanent job?"

"I stole some money and failed a drug test."

Fox Grantham looked at the blonde sitting opposite him. Right—if this latest candidate to be his personal assistant wasn't joking, then hers had to be the dumbest response he'd ever heard when interviewing someone for a job.

He glanced down at her résumé sitting on top of a pile of folders—he hadn't seen the surface of his desk since Dot left six weeks ago—and flipped to the second page. She was too young, in age and experience, and she didn't have any of the organizational, personal and computer skills he needed. He wondered what his HR department was thinking sending him the applicant, then remembered they weren't in a position to cherry-pick.

His fault, not theirs.

He dismissed her and gripped the bridge of his nose, trying to find the energy to get up and make himself a cup of coffee. He'd had his HR manager contact three of New York's best recruitment agencies, but they were scraping the bottom of the barrel if the last candidate was all they could come up with. Then again, in the six weeks since Dot retired, he had gone through nine temps. He was, as the owner of one of the agencies told him this morning, a difficult and demanding client.

Sure, he expected his assistants to work long hours and he didn't engage in personal conversations, but he paid exceedingly well and offered incredible benefits. That had to count for something, surely?

Damn you, Dot. He'd worked with her for over a decade, and her resignation had come as a blow. His sixty-year-old PA had the physical energy to keep up with him, the mental acuity to follow his rapid-fire thought processes and the skills of a master logistician. He couldn't see why she couldn't keep working for him after getting married. Dot had told him, with a roll of her eyes, that her new husband—six weeks from meeting to marriage! Madness—objected to her working ten-hour days and most weekends.

Reason eighty-two why Fox thought marriage, relationships and commitment were a bad idea. The fact that he'd lost his fantastic PA because she'd chosen a personal relationship over him annoyed him intensely.

"Oh, God, it's glowering."

Fox looked up as Jack walked into his office, his brother's hands pushed into the pockets of his suit pants. Despite it being early evening, Jack looked like he'd just rolled in from a fashion shoot for *GQ*. His gray designer suit was exquisitely tailored to fit his broad shoulders and looked freshly pressed. His gray-and-mint-green-patterned tie was perfectly knotted. Mr. Perfection always looked like a million dollars and never, unlike Fox, lost his cool. Those were two of the many reasons why Jack was the public face of Grantham International, the multinational company he, Jack and their late brother, Malcolm, had established years ago.

"What's the problem, Fox?"

"Stupid people. Every day, the stupid get stupider," Fox answered.

"Or you get more impatient," Jack pointed out, walking over to his window to look down at the ant-size cars zooming down 5th Avenue. Or, because this was New York and traffic was horrendous, crawling.

Jack made a fair point, Fox conceded. Instead of gaining more patience as he aged, he seemed to be losing chunks of it every year. By the time he was forty, in five years, he might qualify for entry into the *Guinness World Records* book for the most impatient person alive.

It wasn't something to be proud of but… *God.* He didn't have time to waste explaining to an endless string of assistants, each more inept than the last, what he wanted and how he wanted it done. Dot, damn her, just knew.

"I see Soren and Eliot's engagement has caused a stir online," Jack said. Fox darted him a quick look. Sometimes Jack's expression was so imperturbable that even Fox, who knew him best, was uncertain of the emotion behind his calm words.

That wasn't a problem anyone had with him. People never had any doubt about the way he felt. He wasn't known for pussyfooting around.

"I like her," Fox stated, leaning back in his chair and linking his hands over his flat stomach. Their cousin Soren, raised with them by their grandmother when all their parents were killed in a plane crash when they were kids, was more of a brother than a cousin. "I think she's good for Soren."

"High praise, since you don't like fashion models."

"I'm sure there are many as lovely, grounded, down-to-earth and sensible as Eliot," Fox said. "But I've only met the ones who are bat-shit crazy."

Jack chuckled. "I still can't believe Soren is retiring from swimming."

Honestly, Fox couldn't, either. After winning a slew of gold medals in the latest Olympics and breaking a couple of world records, Soren had decided to quit the pool, start up a foundation and marry a jilted bride, the ex-supermodel Eliot Stone. And all in under a month. His head spun just thinking about it.

Growing up, he, Jack, Malcolm and Merrick—another brother by choice, the son of Avangeline's housekeeper—had been fascinated by the food and hospitality industry. He, Malcolm and Jack had reignited the empire their grandmother had retired from to raise them, and Merrick had set up his chain of massively successful food trucks and diners, specializing in healthy fast food. But Soren, the outlier that he was, considered food fuel and didn't know the difference between a spice and an herb. Swimming had been his focus, and he'd pursued it with the single-minded dedication every Grantham shared. But now that focus had shifted to his foundation.

Fox was glad that Soren had a foundation to set up and work to do. The Grantham boys tended to get into trouble when they had time on their hands.

Jack walked over to the chair and sat down, undoing the button of his jacket. He pushed back his sleeve and Fox noticed that he wore a pair of simple platinum cuff links that had once belonged to their father. He was glad Jack got some use out of their parents' vast collection of jewelry. Fox never touched it—but then, he didn't have the emotional connection to his parents' memory Jack did. After all, he knew things about his allegedly perfect parents—gorgeous, successful, crazy in love—Jack didn't.

Their mother's rings and necklaces, bracelets, and earrings would stay in the safe-deposit box until Jack married, and then the stunning collection could be passed on to his wife and maybe a daughter. There was no doubt that his mom's stunning, brilliant-cut, ten-carat Colombian emerald engagement ring would be passed on to Jack's future wife. It had, briefly, adorned the left hand of Mal's fiancée, Peyton, but she'd returned it after his death.

All Fox wanted from the collection was a magnificent nine-carat black opal ring, a gift to his mother she had never received. He had no one to give it to, never would have, but since he'd first seen it a decade ago, the stone—bloodred but flashing with vibrant streaks of blue, purple and green—had fascinated him.

"Have you heard from Peyton lately?" Fox asked, sitting up and putting his elbows on his desk. Their relationship with Mal's ex had turned frosty after his death, but Jack had extended an olive branch last year.

A strong emotion he couldn't identify jumped into Jack's eyes, and Fox cocked his head, intrigued. And was he a shade paler than he was before? *Hello...* His brother had the best poker face he'd ever encountered, and he never gave anything away, ever. So why had the mere mention of Mal's ex caused such a reaction? What had he missed here?

He was about to demand an answer when Merrick walked into his office, dressed as he always was in chino pants and an untucked button-down shirt. Merrick's Native American ancestry could be picked up in his coal-black hair, his high cheekbones, straight nose and heavy eyebrows. His eyes were his mother's, the bright blue of an Irish sky. Merrick, constantly on the road, operated his business virtually but used their conference room for meetings.

"Mom wants me to ask you whether you've lost the ability to use the phone," Merrick said as he took the chair next to Jack, pulling his ankle up onto his opposite knee.

Fox winced. "I'll call her tonight," he told Merrick.

"Be prepared to have her nag you about being the next brother to temporarily relocate to Calcott Manor," Merrick warned him. "She told me that if we are determined to keep an eye on Avangeline and her new guest, then she wants you to be the next up to bat."

"Why me?" Fox demanded, gesturing to his messy desk. He couldn't relocate to his grandmother's estate—not when he had a company to run and a PA to hire. His life was in Manhattan. Frankly, he was angling to be the last brother on the roster—or maybe not land on it at all, if one of the others succeeded in their two goals of persuading their grandmother to write a will and to running Aly Garwood off the premises. Soren had taken first crack at it, but no dice. The will remained unwritten, and the scam artist who'd been leading Avangeline on with some BS story was still in residence. It was time for someone else to step up to bat, but why did it have to be him?

"Mom says you are burned-out and that you need to get out of the city before you end up with acute stress disorder or something like that," Merrick casually explained. "I tried to tell her that you've always been a grumpy bastard, but she wouldn't listen to me."

Fox lifted a lazy middle finger and decided that it was in his best interests to change the subject before he found himself buckling under the pressure of Jacinta's wishes.

"So, Soren now seems to think that Aly is the real deal," he stated, still struggling to understand how his levelheaded, pragmatic cousin could have fallen for that hippie-dippy crap. Aly was nothing more than a scam artist, and the story she was peddling couldn't possibly be real.

Yes, it was true that Aly Garwood had received

a transplant of Malcolm's liver on his death, but did she really expect them to believe that she'd also inherited some of their oldest brother's quirks and personality traits? Her so-called proof was that she now liked beer and cars and sweets. Seriously, was that the best she could do? She could have found out any of that on the internet. They were Granthams, heirs to a multibillion-dollar fortune. Fox wouldn't be surprised to find that someone had posted everything about him from the measurement of his inseam to his preferred brand of toothpaste online. Aly would have had no trouble digging up some nuggets on Mal. The real question was, what was she after? That was the question that would drive all the brothers to visit Connecticut if necessary—and they wouldn't stop until they found the real reason why Aly Garwood had insinuated herself into Avangeline's life.

"Soren is looking at everything through rose-colored glasses at the moment," Merrick said. "He spent his trip to visit Avangeline falling in love with Eliot. It's no wonder his head isn't on straight. I'm going to need more proof than what Soren gave us to start believing her."

"Precisely," Jack agreed, and Fox nodded as well. He excelled at skepticism and cynicism: being that way was a damn good way not to get hurt. He'd learned that lesson early, and he'd learned it hard. Nothing was ever, *ever* the way it looked. There was always something lurking beneath the surface, something held back. It was important to keep digging to ensure he was never caught flat-footed or blindsided ever again.

"Moving on from Liver Lady," Merrick said, playing with the laces on his shoes. "One of us—and by one of us, I mean you, Fox—needs to get up to Calcott Manor to keep an eye on the situation there. And to keep working on Avangeline to write her damn will."

Avangeline was in her eighties now, and it would be a nightmare of epic proportions if she died without leaving a will. Since she was a shareholder in Grantham International as well as Merrick's business, anything other than clear allocation of her assets would be a massive roadblock for any business decisions as probate worked its way through the court system and Avangeline's estate was resolved. It would be far easier and cleaner if their grandmother wrote her damn will.

None of them could understand why Avangeline, who'd run a massive empire for forty years and had worked with lawyers her entire life, was balking at such an obvious business reality now. What could be behind this illogical, frankly stupid, streak of stubbornness?

"I can't go up to Calcott Manor," Fox said, gesturing to his desk. "I'd need to take a PA with me, and I don't have one. Right now, I'm keeping my head above water by using Jack's PA for anything urgent."

"And she's had it with you, too," Jack told him.

What? He'd been on his best behavior with her!

"The reason you don't have a PA is because you

are impatient and demanding and you machine-gun instructions. You expect everyone you hire to hit the ground running, without giving them any training, and then you dump a pile of work on their heads and expect it back yesterday."

Yeah, so? Dot had managed brilliantly. "I have a hell of a workload, and I don't have time to babysit anyone," he muttered.

"Well, you're going to have to lower your expectations if you are going to find anyone willing to stick around for more than a day," Jack told him. "Maybe you can find a PA in Hatfield."

Yeah, and he just saw a purple pig fly past his window. If the agencies couldn't find someone in New York City, there was little chance of finding someone up to standard in Hatfield, Connecticut, as he told his brothers.

"God, you can be such a jerk," Merrick cheerfully told him. "How many temps have been through your office since Dot left? Six or seven?"

He shrugged, a little embarrassed to admit to more.

"What's the common denominator?" Jack asked, then continued to speak before Fox could answer. "You. You're the problem, not them."

Fox looked at Merrick, who spread his hands out in a gesture of agreement.

Brilliant.

Jack leaned forward and rested his forearms on his knees, concern in his eyes. Fox recognized his expression. Jack was in white-knight mode, determined to rescue and protect. Except that Fox wasn't a bird with broken wings. He didn't need patching up. He just needed to not go to Calcott Manor and to find a damn assistant.

Like, yesterday....

"We're worried about you," Jack said, tipping his head sideways to include Merrick. "We think you are burned-out, that you are on the verge of a meltdown."

No, he was not. "Look, working long hours is what I do—you know this!"

"These days, you never arrive after six or leave before eight," Jack countered. "That's fourteen hours, minimum."

"What are you, my nanny?" Fox growled.

"When last did you have a date? Sex?" Jack demanded.

Four months ago? Five? He'd had a one-night stand shortly after his fling with Giselle, a prima ballerina with the American Ballet Company. His brothers were his closest friends, but he wasn't going to discuss his sex life—as sad as it was—with them.

"It's just been a hectic time," he explained, hoping to get them off his back. "We opened the hotel in Dubai, a restaurant in Rio—"

"It's no busier than it always is," Jack countered. "You just won't delegate." He slapped his knees and stood up, his expression resolute. "You're going to Calcott Manor for a month, with or without a PA."

"I am not—"

Jack placed his hands on a pile of papers on Fox's

desk and glared at him, anger in his eyes. "Do not test us on this, Fox. We will drag your ass through this hotel and into a taxi if we have to."

No, they wouldn't. Fox started to scoff and looked at Merrick, waiting for him to join him in mocking Jack's dramatics. But Merrick had risen to stand behind Jack, his eyes equally determined. Hell. They were being serious.

Fox rubbed the back of his neck, feeling exhausted. He didn't want to relocate to Hatfield, but neither did he want to argue with his brothers. And he could, at a push, work remotely, without an assistant, for a week or two. After that, he'd either need to find help or come back to the city, but he'd cross that bridge when he came to it.

He moved his mouse and glanced at his huge monitor, quickly pulling up his calendar. Today was Tuesday—he had a few important meetings tomorrow and another on Friday.

"I can drive up on Saturday or Sunday morning, if that suits you two," he suggested snidely, annoyed at being pushed into doing something he didn't want to do.

"That's fine," Jack agreed.

"I was being sarcastic," he muttered.

"We know. You excel at it," Merrick retorted. He looked at Jack and held out his fist, which Jack bumped. "Our work here is done."

"Bastards," Fox told their departing backs. Both of them, as if they'd choreographed the move, put their hands behind their backs and extended their middle finger.

Brothers 1, Fox 0.

So far, so good.

The entrance to the Grantham brothers' office suite, situated on the middle floor of the north wing of the square shaped Forrester-Grantham Hotel, was through a discreet lobby on the side entrance to the iconic building. Just as she had hoped, the receptionist hadn't balked at the fact that she hadn't been preregistered as a visitor. All she had to say was that she was Fox Grantham's latest temp, and the receptionist handed over a visitor's badge without hesitation. She'd also told her that, if she lasted the day, she'd eat her hat.

Oh, Ru Osman intended to last the day, the week, the month. Because if she didn't, she might just murder her parents in their sleep.

Metaphorically, not literally.

Ru pushed a long curl off her cheek and tucked it behind her ear, eyeing the door leading to Fox Grantham's office suite. *He needs a PA*, she told herself, *and you have a master's degree. You can handle this, no problem.* Okay, her degree was in Asian studies but she did have some unusual computer skills.

She'd arrange some meetings, type up some notes and create a couple of spreadsheets. Easy-peasy. She'd rebuilt houses after the Haitian earthquake and worked as a night porter in a busy youth hostel in Athens. She knew how to operate keep things running in busy, chaotic environments, how to keep her cool when she was faced with difficult personalities, how to stay focused and gather the info she needed when she was handed a difficult or challenging task. Surely she could manage a few weeks working for Mr. Gorgeous but Apparently Grumpy?

Ru took a deep breath, opened the door to his office suite and released a long breath to find his luxurious, glass-walled corner office empty. The PA's desk sat in the corner of the outer office, and behind it was a credenza and banks of cupboards. A state-of-the-art computer sat on the desk, and Ru started to salivate.

Despite being a world wanderer, she was a computer geek and had been, once upon a time, a better-than-decent hacker. After having her bells-and-whistles computer stolen in Rome, she'd downgraded to a lightweight, smaller computer that could be tucked into her backpack and kept close with ease. She'd used that machine for years, until it finally gave up the ghost in the humidity of Kuala Lumpur three months ago. She'd also fallen ill with a virus that had kept her in bed for two weeks and low on energy for another six.

The combination of medical bills and being unable to work had decimated her savings, and she'd had no choice but to finally use the open-ended ticket her parents had purchased for her to return to the States. She'd moved back home and promptly moved out a week later, unable to deal with their constant hovering.

"Darling, you are skinny and pale—eat an egg, drink this green smoothie and have an afternoon rest."

"I've updated your résumé, Ru. One of the guys at my club thinks he can swing you a job inputting data for his company."

Ru never took afternoon naps, far preferred gin to green smoothies and knew that she'd never have the patience for a data-entry job. It didn't matter that she was in her late twenties and hadn't lived with them for long time, her parents fussed. The fact that she was back in their city, on home turf, meant that they had first dibs on her time, burying her under a barrage of comments about how she should be safe, avoid rideshares, lock her doors and marry someone who could protect her.

Her phone rang. Ru pulled it out of her bag, scowling at the "The 'Rents" displayed on the screen. How was it that whenever she thought of them, her parents called her? Did they have some kind of Google Alert set on her brain?

Ignoring them would just result in frantic texts along with even more calls, so it was easier and less time consuming to answer so she accepted their video call. "Morning, parents."

Her parents cheerfully greeted her, and Ru smiled at their enthusiasm in spite of herself. Yes, they drove her up the wall, but it was sweet that they were always so happy to talk to her. She was the center of their world, the reason the sun rose and set every day.

"We thought we could meet you somewhere for brunch?" her mom suggested. "Our treat."

Um…she didn't want to lie to them, but neither did she want to tell them she was trying to land this job. They would get overly excited that she was looking for a job in the city, and their hopes would be raised that she might settle down at last. No matter how often she reminded them that she was leaving, they lived in constant hope she'd stick and stay.

"Sorry, Momma, I can't. I have…plans."

Oh, God, that made her sound like she had a date.

"With Scott?" Taranah demanded, excited.

Ru tipped her head back to look at the ceiling. "No, Mom, not with Scott. I keep telling you that nothing will ever happen between Scott and me."

"Why not? You dated him."

She adored her mother, she did, but she really didn't want to explain the concept of friends with benefits to the woman who, genuinely, believed that sex only belonged in the confines of marriage. "Stop nagging her about Scott, Tara," her dad said. "Are you sure you can't join us for brunch, sweetheart?"

"Sorry, Dad. But you and Mom go," she suggested. "Pretend it's a date."

"I hated dating," her father replied morosely.

"Like you can remember that far back, Mazdak," Tara teased, resting her temple on Dad's shoulder. "Okay, honey, come see us soon, okay?"

Ru said goodbye, and their faces left her screen. They loved her and they wanted her, their only child, to be around rather than flitting off to some far-away country. While she was close by, she knew she should spend more time with them. If only they'd be a little less in her face…

"Who the hell are you?"

At the sound of a lovely, rich and deep male voice, Ru turned around slowly, deliberately taking her time. She had to look like she belonged here, like she'd been sent from the recruitment agency. But, dear God, how was she supposed to talk when six feet something of sheer lusciousness stood in the doorway to his office, his dark hair wet with perspiration and his tanned, wide shoulders and huge arms on display? His gym tank top dipped low under his arms and showed off the muscles of his rib cage and the light sprinkling of dark hair on his chest. She couldn't stop her eyes from drifting down, taking in his muscled thighs beneath the hem of his expensive jogging shorts. Strong calves, she noticed, big feet encased in a pricey pair of running shoes.

Yum yum yum…

Out of Breath and Grumpy repeated his question with more force, and Ru jerked out of her reverie—long nose, overlong hair, a sexy bottom lip and a very stubborn chin—and lifted her eyebrows at the annoyance in his eyes. They were a fantastic shade of deep blue, the color of space on a winter's night. Fascinating…

His lips flattened further, and Ru warned herself

to get a grip. Knowing she could show no fear, she sent a very deliberate look at the clock on the wall.

"I'm Ru Osman, and you're late," she told him, knowing that she was taking a huge gamble goading him. But she'd suspected if she showed him a hint of fear, he'd gobble her up and spit her up.

"For your information, I was at my desk at five forty-five this morning," he told her, lifting the bottom of his shirt to wipe his slick face. Ru nearly swallowed her tongue at his six-pack. "You have ten seconds to tell me who you are and why you are in my office," Fox said, hands on his hips.

"I'm from Bednar Recruitment, and I'm on temporary assignment to you."

He cocked his head to the side, and Ru felt like a bug under a magnifying glass. "I thought they weren't prepared to send me any more candidates."

They weren't, but he didn't need to know that. She tried to distract him by changing the subject. "I need a job, and you require a personal assistant. Sounds like we both have what the other needs."

He stared at her, not looking convinced. "What did you say your name was again?" he asked.

"Ru Osman," she replied.

"Experience?" he barked.

"Enough," she shot back, lying through her teeth. "Shouldn't you hit the shower? Or are you intending to work in your gym clothes?" she asked.

"You're bossy," he stated.

"And you're ripe," she countered, although that

wasn't true. Sure, she could smell that he'd exercised, but his scent was a very pleasing combination of perspiration, deodorant and a lemony cologne. Honestly, if she could bottle it, it would be an overnight bestseller.

"Stay there," he barked before walking into his inner office, immediately turning right and disappearing. Intrigued at his vanishing act, she stood up and crossed the room to take a better look. Through the glass walls of his office and in the corner closest to her, she saw a half-open door showing a mirror on the wall. In the reflection, she saw Fox pull off his top, muscles rippling across his shoulders and chest. God, he was...

Ripped. Built. Muscled... All those words applied. He was fantastically sexy, and for the first time in, wow...the first time ever...she wanted to step into that private bathroom, slide her hands under the band of his shorts and explore that long body with her tongue and her teeth. She wanted to taste his mouth, feel his stubble on the sensitive skin of her breasts, his lips on her stomach...she imagined him going even lower.

The sound of voices in the corridor pulled her back, and she lifted her hands to her face, feeling the heat below her fingertips. What was wrong with her? She didn't react this way to men. She was no virgin, and she'd long since mastered the casual fling. Usually, an attractive guy barely caused a blip on her radar. But Fox Grantham was causing her world to spin, wobble and threaten to fly off its axis.

Enough now, you cretin.

Ru shook her head, dropped her hands, and when she looked back at the door to his bathroom, it was shut.

Good. That was good.

Even better was the fact that he hadn't thrown her out of his office or arrested her for trespassing.

Ru paced the outer office, keeping an eye on the bathroom door.

Okay, this had to be the craziest thing she'd done in a while. A long while. She'd talked herself into Fox Grantham's office and lied to the man's face.

She didn't like lying but, unfortunately, she was running out of options. Since arriving back in the States, she'd looked for temporary jobs but hadn't been able to find any that paid enough to make it worth her while. She'd needed a lot of money quickly to pay off her bills and replenish her savings so she could get back to traveling. Flights weren't cheap, and working as Grantham's PA was a good solution.

Because she *needed* to get back to traveling. It wasn't anything as simple as itchy feet or trouble settling down. No, she craved the freedom of travel, the liberty to choose her own direction in life every single day, for the exact same reason that her loving-but-overbearing parents wanted to lock her down and keep her close.

Because that's what happened when you were abducted, the subject of an Amber alert and found two weeks later.

Luckily, she'd been so young, just shy of her third birthday, and remembered little of the entire experience. Her abductor had been a woman with mental health issues who'd been desperate for a child and had treated her like a princess—but the experience had left her whole family, and their friends, traumatized.

Her parents had reacted by battening down the hatches. Their efforts to keep her safe included everything but wrapping her in cotton wool, then bubble wrap, and placing her on a shelf. Ru's response—not just to the experience of being held captive but also to her parents' overprotectiveness—had been to break free the first chance she got and explore the world on her own terms. That was the life she'd chosen, the life she loved…and she wanted to get back to it as soon as possible.

Ru sighed, walked back to the PA's desk and sat down in the chair, easily finding the button to power up the computer.

A box appeared on the log-in screen, and Ru dusted off some of her old, rusty skills to get around it, smirking with satisfaction when she got in barely two minutes later. Ru leaned back in her seat, her eyes flying over the desktop icons. There was a calendar app, a logo with a G and a C intertwined, and a mail app. She opened the calendar app, saw that Fox had an all-day meeting scheduled and, very helpfully, that her predecessor had typed in a list of all the documents he required. Ru did a search for the documents, sent them to the printer and slipped them into a folder she found in the third drawer of her desk.

God bless you, previous PA person. And yes, she totally planned on taking the credit for her predecessor's good work and efficiency.

She eyed the computer, thinking that she had the skills to go snooping. Deciding to be good, she slipped into his office to put the folder on his desk, and, needing something to do, she tidied his very messy desk. Maybe it would earn her extra brownie points. She needed them—because sooner or later, he was going to realize that she had no connection to the recruitment agency after all.

Shellie, a college friend, and owner of the couch she was currently sleeping on, worked at the recruitment agency and had told her about how none of the experienced and smart women she suggested survived more than a week working for Fox Grantham. Complaints ranged from him being demanding to being terse and rude. Some reported him having a hair-trigger temper, though Shellie was convinced that claim was overexaggerated. But Fox Grantham was, she conceded, a handful.

He paid extremely well, far above the average, but he didn't only demand a pound of flesh, he wanted spines and internal organs, too.

Ru's ears had perked up when she heard he paid extremely well. Good money meant that she could be gone by autumn. In Australia, her next stop, she could distance herself from her parents and their anxiety and rid herself of the caged-in feeling she got whenever she came back home.

She often thought that anxiety and fear were the fourth and fifth members of their family.

Two

Fox placed his waterproof cell phone on the shelf out of the direct spray of his shower, ducked under the stream of water and reached for the shampoo.

He didn't know who Ru Osman was, but she hadn't been sent by Bednar Recruitment. Marie Bednar, the owner of the company, was convinced they had no one by that name on their books by that name. Besides, she'd run out of candidates for him to terrorize, she explained, with all the familiarity of someone who'd done business with him, his brother and his father and uncle before him.

Marie didn't pull her punches, and he liked that about her. He recognized that same quality in the woman waiting for him in his office. Only a supremely confident woman would question him about being late and all but order him to take a shower.

She had balls, he admitted. That confidence, and the intelligence in those eyes—the blue-green just a shade deeper than the flash of a tropical parakeet's wing—were both as attractive as hell. She wasn't conventionally pretty, not supermodel gorgeous, but that was fine by him. The most beautiful women he'd dated had all been bat shit. And by dated, he meant taken to bed…

For some reason, they'd all thought a few hours of naked fun entitled them to, at the very least, another date. Every one of them had been pissed to learn that it didn't. Saying goodbye, he recalled, had been a nightmare.

Fox rinsed the shampoo from his hair. No, Ru wasn't cover-girl beautiful, but she was different— unconventionally lovely. Hers was a face you *looked* at and then looked at it again. Her nose was straight, her full mouth a perfect pink, and she had a trio of tiny freckles on her right cheek that drew attention to her beautifully high cheekbones. Her dark eyebrows were strong but beautifully arched, and she had the longest eyelashes he'd ever seen in his life.

As he'd learned from the models, mascara could only do so much.

Her hair tumbled around her face and over her shoulders in thick, loose natural curls, the color a mix of dark blond and caramel brown. She was medium height, slim—maybe a little scrawny—with long

legs and a nice chest. A *very* nice chest. She had deep
dimples, which flashed when she spoke, and a double
dimple on her left cheek when she smiled. The dimple
was unusual and, surprisingly, sexy as hell.

But, God, those eyes.

Fox felt himself rise to the occasion, and he encased his shaft with a soapy hand, idly stroking. He
wondered whether Ru's eyes changed color when she
was aroused—would they deepen to blue or green?—
and whether her nipples were the same color as her
currently painted-in-red lips. Would her body flush
with pleasure when he kissed her hip bone or the inside of her thigh, dipped his tongue into the honey
between her legs? He imagined the slide of her tongue
up his shaft, and he tightened his grip and moved
quicker, the palm of his other hand resting on the
shower wall, as he softly panted. He felt the buildup—
so fast, so intense—and tugged some more, imagining her lips around his head.

The pressure in his balls rocketed up his spine and,
unexpectedly fast, he released, surprised at how fast
it happened. His mouth was dry, and he tipped his
face up to take in some water, stunned by his over-
the-top, very explosive reaction.

What the hell?

He wasn't a choirboy, and, thanks to his busy life,
jerking off was something he did regularly, but he
never fantasized about anyone specific while he did
it. And no idle fantasy had ever given him that super-
quick, intense, out-of-body experience.

Fox washed himself down, rinsed off and shut off the water, resting his forehead on the wet tiles and staring at his big feet, feeling off balance and, frankly, exhausted.

Ru Osman. What had brought her into his life and why was he having such a weird reaction to her? And, most importantly, why was she pretending to be from Bednar Recruitment when she most definitely wasn't?

Fifteen minutes later, Fox walked back into his office, knotting his tie. He stopped next to his desk, glowering at the folder in the center of his uncharacteristically tidy desk. Leaving the knot of his tie hanging a few inches below his open collar, he opened the file and saw copies of his notes for the meeting and all the other documents he needed.

He picked up his head and looked through the glass wall to where his brand-new assistant sat behind her desk, leaning back in her chair, her arms folded and one eyebrow cocked, obviously waiting for his reaction.

A few questions fought for dominance in his head. How could she tidy his desk so quickly, how did she know what he needed for his meeting, who was she and why was she here? And, dammit, how soon could he get her naked and under him?

He rubbed his jaw, thinking he'd better stop that kind of thinking. He didn't have the time or the energy for a fling right now.

Fox pushed a hand through his still-wet hair,

picked up the folder and walked out of his office to slap it on her desk. Ru handed him a slow smile, looking very pleased with herself. "Did I forget something? Was there something else you needed for the meeting?"

She knew there wasn't—she was simply baiting him. "How did you get into the server to access these papers?" he demanded.

Ru wrinkled her nose as she debated how to answer him. "I have certain IT skills that aren't always...well, appreciated."

It wasn't difficult to make the connection.

So she was a hacker. Interesting. "Black or white?" he demanded, expecting her to tell him she was a good guy, a white-hat hacker.

"*Meh*... I'd say gray. I mean, I'm not above sneaking into a system to make my life easier, but I don't steal personal information, Social Security numbers or money."

Right, so not what he'd expected her to say—but it was an answer he liked. Fox respected her honesty. He rarely encountered pure white or black situations and fully believed that most life events fell on the spectrum between the two monochromatic extremes.

He pulled his attention back to what was important, and that was her, working here. "What did you do before, who were your former employers and who will give you a reference?"

She had the audacity to grin at him. "Most recently, I was a barista in Barcelona, a night porter in

Athens and an English teacher in Kuala Lumpur. I could get you their numbers, but I don't think their thoughts on my coffee making, teaching or handing out room keys would interest you."

Ru sat up and pulled the keyboard to her, and her fingers flew across it. Then she spun her screen around for him, and he saw a face he recognized. "Try him."

Derek Cannon? The CEO of Bolivar Interactive? How did she know one of the most famous dot-com guys of their generation?

Calling her bluff, he used his smartphone to search for the number of Bolivar Interactive. Usually, he'd ask his PA to do something like that for him, but currently she was being a pain in his ass.

Putting his phone on speaker mode, Fox gave his name and asked to be put through to Derek's office. Ru held his eyes, and he clocked the glint of mischief in her clear, intense gaze. His call was immediately put through, and Derek's voice, full of joviality, filled the space between them.

"Fox Grantham, it's been an age! How are you?"

Fox swallowed his impatience and went through the motions of a quick catch-up chat. He and Derek knew each other from various A-list social events but had never made it past a casual-acquaintance level.

"Well, I doubt you called just to catch up, so what can I do for you?" Derek finally asked, much to Fox's relief.

"Do you know someone called Ru Osman?" Fox

asked, placing one butt cheek on the corner of her desk and stretching out his leg. He was watching her closely but he couldn't pick up any anxiety in her expression.

"Sure, she did a three-month stint with me back when I first started Bolivar. Seriously talented coder," Derek confirmed.

"So it would seem," Fox muttered. "She wants me to hire her. Any reason why I should? Or shouldn't?"

"She's smart as hell, but don't expect her to stick around. Ru's not good at long term."

He lifted his eyebrow, and Ru's shrug confirmed Derek's assessment.

"Last I heard, she was traveling around the world, picking up work whenever she could and moving on whenever she got bored," Derek mused. "I saw something about her being sick on social media, about her needing to come home because she was running low on cash."

Ru winced, obviously embarrassed. "I have to stop putting every detail of my life on Facebook," she murmured, too low for Derek to hear.

"Anyway, my advice is that if you have the chance to employ Ru, snap her up, even if it's only for a couple of weeks. Ru has a way of making you think outside the box, of upending apple carts. But in a good way, right? If you choose not to hire her, tell her to come back to me. I'm sure I can find something for her."

He heard a note in Derek's voice that suggested more than professional interest and he tensed.

Like hell. Derek went through women faster than light shot through space.

Fox ended the call and slid his phone into his pants pocket.

"It's nice to know I've got options," Ru murmured, leaning back in her chair again and crossing those long, slim legs. He wanted them wide-open and locked around his hips...

Fox gripped the bridge of his nose and shook his head. His morning—his goddamn life—was not going as planned. "Why would a talented coder want to work as a PA?" he demanded. "I pay well, but so does Derek. Why didn't you hit him up for a job and why are you here, harassing me?"

"I haven't done any serious coding for years, and I'm very out of practice. Fifteen-year-olds know more than I do these days, and I would last, maybe, a day working for Derek because I'm so out of touch with new developments."

"It sounds like he believes in you—I get the feeling that he'd be willing to give you the time and resources to catch up."

"Yes, he probably would," Ru agreed. "But that would require me to commit to sticking around long enough to make the investment worth his while. And that's not something I'm interested in doing. Working for you for a month, six weeks, will pay me enough to move on after that."

"To do what? Travel some more?"

"Yes."

Her short answer wasn't enough. He needed more: What country, city, zip code? He wanted to know what she planned on doing when she got there and how she intended to get a job. Where would she look for work? How did it all work? Was she running from something? If so, what?

"Don't you have a meeting to get to? Tick-tock," Ru stated, not even slightly rattled. She tapped the top of her bare wrist with her index finger, suggesting he get a move on. What would it take to see her disconcerted, knocked off balance? She was far too composed, too confident. She reminded him of someone...

Jack. She reminded him of his brother...cool. Unreadable. Unshakable.

So why did he feel the insistent urge to push through her layers to see the truth below? Why her and why now? He rarely—okay, never—felt the tug to go exploring in someone else's life. The last time he dug for the truth, he'd discovered so much more than he needed to know.

Ru glanced at the clock behind him. "Shall I stay or shall I go?"

He didn't want her to leave, not just yet, but neither did he want to make an impulsive decision. The woman had, technically, barged into his life, lied her way into his office and hacked into his system. If he was thinking straight, he'd toss her out on her pretty ass. But, weirdly, he felt compelled to keep her around. Why?

He needed more time to figure it—her—out. But

that was a commodity that was, perpetually, in short supply.

"I'll give you a day's trial, and if you get through it without any major screwups, we will talk again tonight and I will consider hiring you," Fox told her.

Ru wrinkled her nose. "Why on earth wouldn't I get through it?" she asked, sounding genuinely curious.

"Because I am, according to the person who walked out on me two days ago, a demanding son of a bitch with a cold heart and dollar signs in his eyes," Fox retorted. "I'm rude and exacting. And I don't say please and thank you."

Ru shrugged her slim shoulders. "If you are trying to scare me off, it's not working. I'll stick around for the rest of the day."

Fox sighed. A part of him, a part he didn't recognize, really hoped that she could cope with the demands of this job. He'd just found her—he didn't want to have to cut her loose...

But he would. Work was all that was important, and if she wasn't a decent PA, he'd show her the door. He'd had a lot of practice in doing exactly that.

He stood up, tucked his folder under his arm and met those stunning eyes. His heart, stupid thing, did a backflip, and he told it to calm the hell down. This was work, dammit!

"Get a notepad out—there are some in the top drawer. I'll give you a list of what I want you to do today," he ordered her.

"Okay, yes, good idea!"

She grabbed a notepad, flipped it open and dived back into the drawer for a pen. She scribbled on a page to see whether the pen was working, and when she saw it was blue, she yanked the drawer back open and pulled out a red pen. "Much better," she murmured. "I far prefer red ink to blue. It's so much more interesting."

God help him. She was finicky about what color pen she used? Fox wondered how much he'd have to pay Dot to come back.

"You ready?" he demanded, his hands on his hips. She was halfway through her nod when he started to rattle off instructions and her pen flew across the page. Her handwriting, he was interested to see, was even worse than his. He wondered if she'd be able to read her rough scrawl when he was done.

When he was done speaking, Ru nodded with a determined expression on her face. It was a pretty long list, he admitted. If she got through half of it, he'd be impressed. "Are any higher priority than the others?" she asked.

"I mentioned them in order of priority," he replied.

Ru nodded. "Cool."

Cool? Who the hell said cool and when last had he heard it in a corporate environment? Never would be the answer.

"When can I expect you back?"

He wasn't going to give her the opportunity to ditch work early, as so many of his assistants did when they realized he would be out of the office for the rest of the day. "I'll see you back here later," Fox told her. "I shouldn't be too late."

Ru turned her attention to her screen and waved him off. Knowing he couldn't spend any more time with her—why did he want to? —Fox walked into his office and picked up his suit jacket. When he passed her desk again, he said goodbye and she replied with a distracted "'bye."

And he was nearly out of the door when she spoke again. "If you are not back by six, I'm leaving."

Fox resolved to make damn sure that he walked back into his office with thirty seconds to spare.

She would've waited until seven, but he didn't need to know that.

As Fox stepped into the room, Ru made a show of looking at the clock and ducked her head to hide her smile as he glared at her. Damn, he was easy to rile…

And she only did it because if she didn't, the urge to slide her hands around his thick, taut neck, to kiss away the deep furrow between his eyebrows and to massage the stress out of those ripped muscles would overwhelm her.

In between trying to figure out how to accomplish his list of tasks—most of which she'd figured out with the help of Shellie, YouTube, the office's messenger app that let her tap in other assistants and the inter-net—she'd imagined kissing his lips, stroking the tips of her fingers through his soft-looking scruff—

half beard, half stubble—and rubbing his wavy hair between her fingers. God, he was gorgeous, but in a rugged way, a combination of Javier Bardem and Gerard Butler. Not conventionally handsome but attractive in a *please, get into my panties* way.

Keeping her hands off him while being his PA was going to be hella hard. Could PAs be sued for sexual harassment if they made a pass at their boss? She'd have to look that up.

Fox told her to follow him and walked into his office, throwing his folder onto his desk and removing his jacket. He tugged down his tie, undid the top button on his shirt and rolled up his shirtsleeves, exposing his muscled forearms. Moving over to the floor-to-ceiling bookcase in the corner, he opened a cupboard, removed two tumblers and a bottle of scotch whisky. He held up the bottle, his expression a challenge. "Would you like one?"

"Sure. Unless you are planning to use drinking on the job as a reason to get rid of me," Ru said from the doorway.

"I'm a straight shooter. If I want you to go, I won't make up a reason."

Good enough. Ru walked into the room and took the offered drink. He poured whisky into his glass before crossing to the other side of his office to look out on his spectacular view of the city and the edge of Central Park.

"Nice offices," she told him after taking a sip of the smoky drink. The intense flavor hit her tongue, and she held it up to the light, taking in the deep gold color. She took another sip, the flavors rolling over her tongue. "Malt, obviously, maybe apple. Or pear. A touch of dried fruit. It's not Macallan or one of the Glens, but it definitely comes from the Speyside region."

Fox's smile transformed his face, instantly making him look years younger. "I'm impressed. Not many women like whisky and few can identify regions, never mind flavors in whisky."

"I fell in love with Scotland and went on many whisky-tasting tours. But I've never tasted this one before."

"You wouldn't have," Fox informed her. "It's from a distillery my family owns, and we only do small batches. We sell it exclusively through Grantham restaurants and in our hotel bars."

Damn. Going to the bar at one of his luxurious hotels or eating at one of his fine dining restaurants was way beyond her budget.

"How was your meeting?" Ru asked him, watching as he sat on the edge of his wide desk, one knee hitched higher than the other, the fabric of his pants pulling tight across his thigh. *Great legs*, she thought.

Great everything.

Ru took another gulp of her whisky, reminding herself that she was here to work, to earn enough to go back to the life of traveling that she loved. She needed to explore places and people. Sitting in a coffee shop in Naples or on the sidewalk in Hanoi, watching the world go by, was her idea of nirvana. She needed to chase fog, try and capture the sun, taste the air, and meet a culture through its food. Living to her was getting out there...

Seeing. Doing.

Yes, exploring the world could, if one neglected to do proper research and was naïve, be a dangerous pastime—far more dangerous than her parents wanted her life to be—but it was also wondrous, and stimulating, fast and tranquil, exciting and devastating. She adored traveling.

But the strong pull she was feeling to this man also reminded her how lonely that life could be. When her life was constantly on the go, it was hard to form lasting bonds. She'd meet someone she connected with, and then, what seemed like five minutes later, she or they were moving on. Her life was a sad cycle of meeting—friends and lovers—and leaving people, them going left, her going right. And when she did get serious, her relationships deepened quickly, burning brightly, then dying out just as fast.

The deep attraction Fox sparked in her was something she hadn't felt in a long, long time. And it was, dammit, the one attraction that she couldn't afford to let play out. She needed this job too badly to risk screwing it up.

Keep your eyes on the prize, Osman.

"Are you okay?" Fox asked, surprising her a) by noticing that she was miles away and b) with the gentleness of his question.

"I'm fine, thanks," Ru replied, placing her glass on his desk. "How was your day? Do you normally spend all day in one meeting and off-site?"

"No, today was the exception," Fox replied. "I got the emails with your updates throughout the day."

"Sorry, I wasn't able to finish the list."

"No need to apologize—you did well to get through as much as you did."

She was shocked at his comment. He'd told her he was rarely polite, so praise wasn't something she'd expected from him. "Thanks. Does that mean I can come back tomorrow?"

Fox folded his arms, his index finger tapping against his biceps. Ru saw the doubt in his eyes, and her heart plunged to her toes. She saw a no coming, dammit.

"You're obviously intelligent," Fox told her, lifting his hand to push his hair off his forehead.

Ru wrinkled her nose. "But?"

"But you are short term, and I need someone to stick around."

That was an issue. *Think, Osman.* "If you committed to hiring me on for a month, part of my duties could be to find and train someone so that you don't have to," Ru suggested, her mind working a mile a minute. "I'd find you your forever PA."

He stared at her, considering her proposal. "That would be a hell of an incentive for me to hire you," he told her, stretching out his long legs, his fingers gripping the edge of the desk. "But some of the best recruitment companies in the city have tried and failed to find me a PA. What makes you think you can do what they couldn't?"

"Because you've been concentrating on the skills and qualifications of your applicants, not their temperament," Ru told him. Within ten minutes of meeting him, Ru had realized Fox needed someone who could work smart, a person with a mind that could keep up with his. Skills could be learned, but mental speed and acuity? Not so much.

"I'm pretty sure I'll find your someone," she told him with a confidence she didn't actually feel.

She didn't blame him for hesitating—if she was in his position, she'd question her statement, too. What did she know about recruitment? Basically nothing. Ru looked at the door, wondering if she'd bitten off more than she could chew. But no, she wasn't going to throw in the towel before she'd even begun to try.

"I can't understand why you're not jumping on all this," Ru said a minute later when he'd yet to respond.

"Ah, that might be because all I can think about is jumping you."

Say what?

Three

Ru stared at him, flabbergasted.

She wasn't the type men fell over, whom they even looked at twice. She was, at best, an ordinary girl next door. She had nice eyes, and people often commented on her double dimple, but her cheeks were too round, her smile too wide, her nose too long, her chin too pointy.

Too thin, too tall, more of a scarecrow than sexpot. She wasn't putting herself down or judging herself too harshly—she knew that she wasn't a troll or repulsive. She was just a normal, very average-looking woman who rarely—and by rarely, she meant never—caught the eye and attention of gorgeous, successful men. Men like Fox usually dated booby super models and curvy actresses, women who oozed sex appeal from every one of their tight, moisturized pores.

Ru frowned at him. "I'm sorry...what did you say?" she asked, tipping her head to the side.

Fox didn't drop his eyes from hers. "You heard me." He didn't change his stance, but Ru noticed the way that tension had invaded his muscles. "I want to employ you. God knows that I need you—you are the first person who's lessened my load and not added to it in six weeks.

"But you're also the first woman who's ever made me think about bending her over my desk while I was in the middle of a meeting, who caused me to jerk off in the shower minutes after I met you, whose mouth I desperately want to kiss."

What the hell? How strong was that whisky? Or had she, somehow, stepped into an alternate reality? This couldn't be happening to her...

Ru wrenched her eyes off his face, looked down and gasped when she saw incontrovertible proof of his attraction. The fabric of his suit pants was pulled tight across his hard, long, big erection.

She had caused that?

"Uh...um..." What did one say in situations like this? *That's impressive? I like what you made me? Can I touch it?*

She really wanted to touch it.

Ru swallowed, looking for moisture in her mouth, found none and reluctantly—very reluctantly— dragged her gaze up his body. When she hit his eyes, she fell into a vortex of deep blue. He didn't move, but those eyes begged her to come to him, to fit her mouth against his.

Don't do it, Ru. You need the job, the money, to get away. Do not jeopardize this opportunity. But want, need and recklessness swamped her, and her feet carried her to him, stepping between his long legs. She placed her hands on his shoulders and inhaled his sexy scent, her eyes not breaking contact with his.

"If you don't kiss me soon..." Fox warned her, his hands still gripping his desk.

"I don't understand this," Ru whispered, her breath mingling with his. "This isn't what I do."

"You're not doing anything," Fox said through gritted teeth. "And it would be so much better if that luscious mouth of yours made contact with mine."

"You could kiss me," Ru whispered, her mouth a fraction from his.

"I could," Fox agreed. "But what if you kissed me?"

"And if I don't?" Ru asked, her fingers digging into his thickly muscled shoulders.

"I'll cry like a little girl," Fox reluctantly admitted with the smallest of smiles. Then he turned serious again. "If kissing me isn't what you want, then walk away, Ru."

She did want to kiss him, and she'd never been good at resisting temptation. She was the girl who was always up for a new adventure...

Unable to wait for a second longer, Ru placed her mouth on his and gently nibbled. His lips were softer than she expected, and she lifted her hand to touch his face, his stubble tickling the pads of her finger-tips. She felt his sigh, tasted his escaped breath and pushed her tongue between the seam of his lips, melting against him when he allowed her access.

For a couple of seconds—three or four?—he allowed her to explore, but then, in a whirlwind of action, his tongue invaded her mouth and his flat palm pulled against her lower back, pressing her into his erection. He lifted his free hand to hold her head steady, occasionally changing the angle of his kiss.

She'd been kissed before, and, up until now, it had always been a fun experience. But kissing Fox was extraordinary, on another level.

Fun, sure, in a way that diving off a sixty-foot cliff was fun, swimming with great white sharks was fun, heli-skiing was fun. Dangerous, immersive, with the ability to both chill the blood with fear and heat it with excitement.

Ru moaned and wound her arms around his broad back. She needed to feel his skin, so she tugged his shirt from his pants, her hands sliding under the cool cotton to explore his heated body. Her knees melted, just a little, and the heat of his kiss edged up another level. Ru placed one hand flat on his back, her other hand sliding between his lower back and his suit pants, needing more.

She had to stop this. If she didn't, Fox Grantham, her boss of exactly *one* working day, would take her on his desk, or on that sleek couch resting against the opposite wall. She didn't sleep with guys eight hours into knowing them. It took her longer than that.

Much, much longer.

But she was tempted, so very tempted to throw caution to the wind and allow him to strip her down and settle his huge erection between her legs, push inside and make her whole.

She'd sob, she'd scream and cream, she'd fall apart... If his kiss was anything to go by, Fox would be the best sexual encounter of her life.

But, that small voice deep inside her reminded her, when it was done, after they'd scratched that itch, she'd have to face him the next day. And the day after that. The job required them to work in close proximity. How could they do that while acting like nothing happened if she let this go too far?

She was free-spirited, uncontrollable and impulsive but she wasn't an idiot. She knew she couldn't afford to toss aside the best opportunity she'd found for a little, or a lot, of pleasure.

Sex was great, but it only provided a momentary high. Working for Fox was her way to get back to the world. Sex with Fox Grantham would give her a stunning but brief orgasm. The choice was obvious...

Ru put her hands up and stepped back. "We're not doing this," she told Fox, backing away. "Not here, not now."

"Where and when?" Fox asked her, his eyes glittering with frustrated desire. He kept looking at her mouth, and she wished he wouldn't. Yes, she wanted to kiss him again.

No, she wasn't going to give in to that impulse.

She was going to *try* very hard not to.

Fox slapped his hands on his hips, obviously frustrated. "I want you, and you seem to want me. I'm single—" he lifted a brow "—I'm presuming you are, too?"

"Of course I'm single," Ru responded, annoyed. "I wouldn't have kissed you if I wasn't!"

Cynicism turned his eyes a shade darker. "Many women would," Fox replied. "But anyway…you're single, I'm single and we have a crapload of chemistry. So why are we talking and not doing?"

"You need a decent PA. I need a job. A quick bang would put both in jeopardy."

He looked like he was about to argue, but at the last minute, he closed his eyes and gripped the bridge of his nose. She watched him fighting for control. She was, too. But Ru knew she was right—there were far more important things in life than great sex.

Damn, being sensible sucked.

Fox walked over to the credenza where the whisky bottle sat, poured another shot into a clean glass and threw it back. He turned, lifting the bottle in a silent offer, but Ru shook her head. Lust and whisky were a combination that lowered her inhibitions and encouraged stupidity.

She linked her hands behind her back and rocked on her feet. "I really need this job, Fox. So, can I return tomorrow?"

He rubbed the back of his neck and rotated his head, and she caught a flicker in his eyes suggesting pain. She had no doubts that Fox had more knots in his neck and back than an eighteenth-century frigate. A little oil and she could…

Stop!

Really?

"Yeah, I could use you. You're smart and efficient, and I need smart and efficient," Fox said. "The thing is, I won't be in the city from this week onward. Whoever I employ needs to be able to relocate temporarily."

Was he kidding? Getting out of the city, and away from her parents, off Shellie's couch, would be the answer to her prayers! Where was he relocating to? Miami? Cartagena? London?

"My passport is current and I can leave whenever you want," she eagerly told him. "What's the destination?"

Abu Dhabi? Hong Kong? Vancouver?

"Hatfield."

Hatfield? Ru, who had an excellent grasp of places, had never heard the name before. She wrinkled her nose, confused. "Where?"

"Hatfield, Connecticut."

The addition of the state didn't help her at all. "Sorry, I've never heard of it."

Fox crossed the room and dropped into his huge leather office chair. He casually placed his feet on the corner of the desk, and Ru noticed that his navy socks had the Batman logo printed on them. Cute… and unexpected.

"Hatfield is a small town, about forty minutes'

drive from here. On the outskirts of Hatfield is Calcott Manor, where my grandmother lives."

Fox spun around in his chair to look out the window, where dusk was sliding into darkness. It was a magical time of the day, one filled with passion and possibilities, a time that straddled the responsibilities of the day and the delights of the night. His chest lifted as he inhaled, and Ru assumed he was debating how much to tell her.

She wasn't surprised when he chose not to explain the reason behind his relocating. She'd met him this morning, and twelve hours and a scorching kiss did not a relationship make.

"Could you move to Hatfield for the next month? I hope it won't be that long, but I'm not sure how much time I need to achieve my objective."

He sounded like visiting his grandmother was a military campaign, like there was a specific task to be achieved while he stayed in Hatfield. Intriguing.

Apart from the fact that she far preferred the energy of a city to a small town, she couldn't think of a reason not to agree to relocate with him.

"You'd have to organize for me to stay somewhere close to your grandmother's house, and you'd have to pay for my transport to and from work," Ru said, considering the practicalities.

"You'll stay at her house," Fox stated, his tone suggesting she not argue. "I'm sure I can arrange for you to move into the apartment over the garage. I will stay in my suite in the main house, and I'll commandeer the library or one of the studies as my—our—office."

Multiple studies. What was this place—Buckingham Palace? "How big is your grandmother's house?" Ru asked, sitting down on the arm of a visitor's chair.

"It's a hundred-plus-acre estate, with a private beach. Its guest house is currently occupied, but the two-bedroom apartment above the garage is vacant. As for the rest, there are two pools, one Olympic size. Gym and sauna, tennis court. Landscaped gardens, paddocks, stables and indoor arena for training the horses. A walled kitchen garden and a greenhouse. The main house has ten bedrooms with en suite bathrooms, and attached to the house is a three-bed apartment Avangeline added for Jacinta, our very beloved housekeeper."

"So, just a little country cottage then. Nothing special or over-the-top expensive," Ru stated, her tone as dry as she could manage.

The corners of his mouth lifting suggested he was considering a smile. "Exactly. Just your regular run-of-the-mill country cottage."

Yeah, for the sultan of Oman.

Feeling off balanced, Ru moved to sit down on one of the visitors' chairs and tried to ignore the way her lips tingled from his kiss.

"I know a little about your family, from celeb magazines and social columns. Avangeline established a billion-dollar restaurant empire, right? But then she sold it after…" She pulled her words back, remembering the death of his parents and uncle and aunt. But maybe she wasn't supposed to mention that?

"After the plane crash," Fox finished for her. "My

dad was the pilot. They crashed into a mountain
shortly after takeoff. My dad wasn't perfect—far,
far from it," Fox muttered, "but he was a damn good
pilot. It makes no sense."

Ru homed in on the bitterness in his tone. Her curiosity was piqued. His parents had been portrayed
as one of the world's golden couples, devoted to each
other and their three sons. The American dream embodied, they had been good-looking, rich, successful
and crazy in love with each other.

Judging by Fox's comment, there might've been
trouble in paradise. But how would he know that?
He'd been a child at the time of their deaths.

Fox spun around to face her again and rested his
arms on his desk. "The point is, there's space for you
at Calcott Manor. So will you relocate with me, be
my PA there instead of here?"

She wanted to say yes, but they needed to address
the elephant in the room. "Only if you're willing to
forget about what we just did."

He shrugged. "Can we? But know this—whatever
happens between us, I can and will be able to draw
a line between work and play. One will not affect
the other."

She appreciated his realistic attitude. Their unexpected attraction was off-the-charts hectic. It would
be naïve to think that it would just go away. But
as long as it didn't jeopardized her job, she could
deal with it. And she believed him when he said it
wouldn't. Fox seemed to be a straight shooter, someone who said what he meant and did as he said. Just

as she wouldn't sue him for harassment if they hooked up, he wouldn't fire her if she refused his advances.

She could, as much as she could trust anyone, trust that.

"So, are you going to work for me or not?"

Ru stood up and paced the space in front of his desk. She considered asking him for more time to think about his offer—she liked to look at things from all angles—but somehow she knew, subconsciously, that Fox was too impatient for that to happen. She'd just have to think fast, consider the pros and cons, and do it quickly. At first glance, the pros far outweighed the negatives.

Could she push him for one more thing?

"Ru?" Fox prodded, and she blinked.

"I'll be your PA and relocate to Hatfield, but only if you attend a wedding with me on Saturday night," she said, wincing at the desperation she heard in his voice.

Ru wasn't shy, but she normally wasn't audacious, or confident enough, to ask a guy she didn't know, her brand-new boss, for a kickass favor.

But desperate times called for desperate measures, and no one made her desperate like her parents.

Her parents, and Scott's, were determined to rekindle the spark between her and Scott—long dead, never going to happen— who was the son of their oldest, and best, friend.

The weekend wedding of Scott's brother was their big chance. The wedding party would be full of people who'd known her all her life, hovering from all sides, eager to promote a relationship her family thought she needed in order to be safe.

Ru would rather take a long walk off a short pier.

But skipping the wedding completely wasn't an option when she'd known the groom, and his parents, all her life.

But she could put a giant spoke in their let's-get-Ru-to-settle-down wheel…

Bringing a date would throw them into a tizzy of indecision and what-do-we-do-now?

And the fact that Fox was gorgeous and semi-famous was a huge bonus.

He shook his head, and Ru pulled a face. Of course Fox wouldn't come to the wedding with her—why should he? She was sure he had many more exciting ways to spend his Saturday night.

"Why are you putting this job on the line, a job you've gone to great pains to tell me you need, for me to be your plus-one at a wedding?" Fox clarified, his expression puzzled. "What is so important about this wedding that you'd risk that?"

She couldn't tell him that Scott—and her parents and his—wanted to see her with him, living life in a bubble of protection. She hoped that when Scott saw her and Fox together, if he picked up on the chemistry bubbling between him, he would finally, finally realize she wasn't interested in him and he would move on, letting their parents do the same.

And yes, Ru was egotistical and honest enough to admit that she'd love to rock up to the wedding on

Fox's arm and have everyone wonder how she managed to snag the very hot Fox Grantham as her date.

"Is the wedding a deal breaker?" he demanded. "Will you walk away if I say no?"

His question forced her to think, to push her emotions aside. Of course it wasn't. She wasn't going to jeopardize an excellent job, the money she needed, just to have him on her arm at the wedding. She'd handle the weight of family expectations and their collective disappointment, the sighs and the worried glances on her own if she had to. She did, after all, have years of experience in doing just that.

"I'll take the job either way," she told him, resigning herself to attending the wedding alone.

He nodded and linked his hands across his flat stomach. "We'll leave for Connecticut on Sunday morning," he told her. "Now, ask me."

She lifted her hands, not understanding his statement. "I'm sorry?"

"Ask me to be your plus-one at the wedding you obviously don't want to attend alone on Saturday night."

Could he be suggesting that he'd say yes?

Oh, well, nothing ventured, blah blah blah. "Will you be my plus-one at a wedding I don't want to attend, at all, on Saturday night?" she asked quietly, holding her breath.

"Sure." He tossed her a business card—one that, she noted, included what seemed to be his private number. "Send me the details, tell me where to pick you up and at what time, and I'll be there," Fox stated. He picked up a folder, flipped it open and started to read.

She had no idea why he was agreeing to this madness, but she didn't care. "Thank you."

Ru stared at his bent head, trying to make sense of the last half hour. She had a job, was going to leave the city to accompany Fox to Hatfield, Connecticut, and she had a date for the wedding on Saturday?

"That's our evening summarized," Fox agreed, without lifting his head. It was only then that Ru realized she'd spoken her thoughts aloud. "I'd also add that we also nearly nailed each other on my desk, something that might or might not happen again."

"On the desk?" Ru asked, her words a little more than a whisper.

"Desk, chair, wall," Fox replied in his nothing-to-see-here voice. "Now, if you'll leave, I will attempt to get some work done."

"Do you need me to stay?" she asked, praying he wouldn't. She needed some time away from him, time alone, to work through the up and downs of her day.

Fox lifted his head, and when he met her eyes, he look at his desk, then at the chair, then at the wall.

Desk, chair, wall…right, she got it.

Time to go.

Four

They'd agreed Fox could skip the church service and would meet Ru in the bar of the hotel before they moved on to the ballroom for the wedding reception. Ru was running ten minutes late, but when she crossed the lobby, she saw Fox waiting for her by the door to the bar, his shoulder resting against the wall, one ankle crossed over the other, his focus on the phone he held in his hand.

Ru stopped, needing a minute to take him in. He wore a linen jacket, the color falling somewhere between tortilla and tawny, over a blindingly white shirt. She dropped her eyes to take in his coal-black pants and shiny dress shoes. A pocket square peeking out of his jacket pocket picked up shades of blue and black, metallic brown and silver...

Sometime between her leaving him in the office last night and this afternoon, he'd had a haircut and a shave. He had nice ears, she realized, and a strong jaw. With his shorter hair brushed off his face, she could see the triangular shape of his face and his strong neck.

He looked fantastic. Mind-blowing, elastic-melting hot.

A part of her wished he didn't look so stylish, so…so…put together. Sophisticated wasn't her style, so she'd raided Shellie's closet for something cheerful. She'd found a bright pink maxi skirt, patterned with bold roses, and a plain white, off-the-shoulder crop top, showing the world an inch of her stomach. She'd let her hair dry naturally, so it fell in crazy curls down her back and shoulders, and she'd kept her makeup simple—mascara, a little blush, lip gloss. Now she wished she'd opted for a formfitting little black dress and heels, and taken her mom up on her offer to have her hair and makeup professionally styled. Then maybe she'd look like she belonged on Fox's arm.

Ru heard the familiar ring of her phone and pulled it out of her bag with a long sigh. She'd left her parents fifteen minutes ago, for God's sake. Knowing that her mom would just phone again if she sent her to voice mail, she answered her call.

"Where are you? You should be here in the ballroom already. Everyone is asking where you are."

Ru resisted the urge to bang her phone against her forehead. "Mom…"

"Has he stood you up?"

Dear. God.

"That's okay, it's not a big deal," Tara assured her, rattling on. "And don't take it personally, darling—the very rich change their minds at the drop of a hat."

And she knew this how? "Mom..."

Ru gripped the bridge of her nose, and it took a few more *Mom*s before Ru was able to tell her that she hadn't been stood up, that they were downstairs and they'd be up shortly. When Tara asked whether he looked as sexy in real life as he did at red-carpet events, Ru killed the call. Because the answer was *hell to the yes*.

Fox looked up and across the room, and their eyes caught and held. He tucked his phone into the inside pocket of his jacket and straightened, his eyes doing a long, slow slide up and down her body. Despite feeling a little underdressed, her body heated and her skin tingled at the blatant appreciation in his eyes. It seemed he like what he saw...

His reaction to her was incomprehensible. She wasn't his type, she knew this, so why did the air seem to sparkle and shimmer every time they came within fifty feet of each other?

"Ru, there you are!"

Ru closed her eyes in dismay on hearing Scott's voice. Like an annoying mosquito, Scott was unable to leave her alone. He'd hovered last night at the rehearsal dinner, swapping place cards around so that he sat next to her and attempted to monopolize her attention the entire evening. Despite not drinking much, she'd had a pounding headache by the time she left the restaurant.

She'd sat with her parents during the wedding service, grateful Scott was a groomsman. She'd felt his eyes on her during the service, more often than was appropriate. She'd told him she was bringing a date to the reception, but here he was, tracking her down.

She turned and pulled up a weary smile. "Scott, I'm about to meet my date—"

"You can stop pretending, you know. I've already figured out that you don't have a date, you're just trying to make me jealous," he said cheerfully, grabbing her hands. Knowing that he was homing in on her mouth, she whipped her head to the side, dropped her head and his lips met her cheek.

"Old friend, sweetheart?" Ru heard Fox's deep voice over her right shoulder, and she spun around, tugging her hands from Scott's clammy gasp.

His eyes flickered from her to Scott and back again. Ru stepped toward him, placed her hand on his chest and stood on her toes to kiss his cheek. "I am so damn glad you are here," she whispered, holding her cheek against his.

She dropped back and turned away to introduce Fox to Scott, but Fox's hand on her arm tugged her back. She faced him, and he lifted both his hands to cradle her face, his expression soft. "You look absolutely gorgeous, baby."

Ru wanted to thank him but couldn't find the words. Smiling, Fox lowered his head and covered her mouth with his, his thumbs swiping over her cheekbones. It wasn't a hot kiss, but sweet, a *hello, I'm here and you look sensational* kiss.

Um…

This wasn't the reaction she'd expected from her boss, but, yeah, she'd take it. What woman didn't want to be kissed in the middle of a busy lobby on a summer's afternoon by a gorgeous man?

When Fox pulled back, she realized she was holding his strong wrists and her breathing was uneven. She looked up into his dark eyes and caught desire and a hint of amusement. "Strawberry-flavored lip gloss—I haven't tasted that since I was sixteen." He seemed to remember that they were supposed to be a couple and quickly covered up his faux pas. "You've been wearing the mint-flavored one lately."

Good catch, Grantham.

"You know that I'm not good with makeup," Ru admitted. "And that I rarely wear lipstick or makeup."

"As I keep telling you, you don't need to bother. You look fabulous without it."

Wow, he sounded sincere. He looked sincere. Could he actually mean it?

Fox dropped his hands as he looked past her and raised his eyebrows.

Scott was watching them with all the intelligence of a stunned fish. Ru wanted to roll her eyes, but instead she poked his biceps, and when he blinked, she gestured to Fox. "Fox, this is one of my oldest friends, Scott Dean. Scott, this is—"

"Fox Grantham. I'm with Ru." Fox held out his

hand, and Scott reluctantly shook it. Judging by his grimace, Fox squeezed his hand a little too hard.

"You're with… What does that mean?" Scott asked, his hazel eyes dazed. "Are you… Um. You are just her date for the wedding, right?"

Fox clasped his shoulder, squeezing it briefly before slapping his hand between his shoulders. "Nope, sorry. In fact, tomorrow morning, I'm taking her to the coast for the next month or so."

That wasn't, technically, a lie. They were leaving for Hatfield in the morning.

Fox held out his hand, and Ru slipped hers into it. She wasn't one for public displays of affection, so why did his public kiss, and holding his hand, feel so right? This was her boss, not her lover. She'd decided that. Hadn't she?

Scott sent Fox a look that combined pity and malice. "Ah, so you are Ru's way to pass time while she's hanging around on this visit," Scott stated, straightening the boutonniere on his lapel. "Just a heads-up… no matter what she says, she's always going to leave."

Before she could respond, Scott stomped away, visibly upset. What a way to start the evening! Fox had to be wishing that he'd never agreed to give up his Saturday night to be here.

She met his eyes and shrugged. "Sorry."

Fox looked around, a smile on his lips. To anyone paying attention, he looked happy to be here, but Ru saw the irritation in his eyes, the annoyance on his tight lips. He was pissed. And could she blame him?

Ru and Fox followed Scott up the wide stairs that

dominated the lobby to the hotel's main reception room on the second floor. Ru deliberately slowed her steps, and when Scott was out of earshot, she squeezed Fox's hand, causing him to stop and look at her.

She couldn't pretend Scott's outburst hadn't happened. "I'm really sorry about that," she said.

Fox pulled her to the side of the stairs so that a family of five could pass them. "So what am I walking into here?" he demanded.

Ru shook her head in denial. "Nothing you need to worry about, I promise you!" Well, that wasn't completely true. "Not from my side, anyway."

Fox folded his arms and sent her a hard look. "I'm going to need more than that, Ru."

She played with her clutch bag, wishing she was somewhere else, anywhere else. What had she been thinking, dragging Fox into her family drama? "A few years ago, I came home to visit my parents. I was on my way to Costa Rica before my South American journey. I reconnected with Scott—he's the son of my parents' best friends—and we had an affair."

"As people do."

The lack of judgment in Fox's voice made her feel more comfortable about carrying on. "I told him, over and over again, that I was heading out soon, that I wasn't interested in more than what we had, no matter how much pressure I was getting. My parents—and his— were pushing me to settle down, to commit to Scott, to start living a normal life."

"He didn't get the message?"

"He just kept asking for more and thought that I was just playing hard to get. At a family supper, with his parents and mine and the extended family—aunts, uncles, cousins, friends—he proposed. Got down on his knee, arranged for someone to film the whole thing."

"And you said no."

"I said no, but inside I was yelling, 'hell no!' In front of everybody, he accused me of leading him on. The only reason he didn't use the word *cocktease* was because our parents were present."

Fox grimaced. "Ouch."

Yeah, that hadn't been fun. Ru gestured to the second floor. "His parents were livid with me, mine only fractionally less angry. I was very much the bad guy. Since then, I haven't come home for anything but flying visits. But the day after I landed this last time, my mother organized a dinner with the Deans, and Scott was there. I thought, cool, the hatchet has been buried, but a half hour in, I started to understand that they were all hoping that I'd grown up and gotten the travel bug out of my system and that Scott and I would reconnect."

Fox took her hand. "He's persistent, huh?"

"I've told him, and them, a hundred times that I don't want to settle down and I'm not interested in being with him. I don't need him to, like everyone else, wrap me up in a bubble—" Ru snapped her mouth closed, realizing she was on the point of saying too much. She rarely told people about what happened to her when she was little, and her family and friends knew it was a subject that was firmly off-limits. She wanted as few reminders of the past as possible.

But her parents and the Deans, because they'd lived through that awful time too, found that difficult to do.

He nodded, his thumb sliding over her knuckles and sending little bolts of bliss up her arm. "Have you? Gotten the travel bug out of your system?" Fox asked.

"I've still got Australia and New Zealand to explore," Ru told him. "That's where I'm heading in six weeks, and nothing will change my mind."

Fox smiled at her. "You don't need to convince me, Ru. I hear you. I have a limited time with you. I'd love a longtime PA, but I'm not interested in a long-term lover."

Why did his statement send a ripple of sadness through her? That was…weird.

Ru knew she'd far prefer to stay here, talking to Fox, rather than going into the reception, but she had people expecting her to make an appearance. If she didn't, there was a good chance a search party would be dispatched. She pulled a smile onto her face and looked up the stairs.

"By now, Scott will have told everybody we are more than a simple date. And because they go from zero to sixty without thought, you might have to fend off questions about our wedding, where our kids are going to go to school and where we are going to live. Oh, and everyone is going to ask how the hell did you get me to stay in the States when I've been quite vocal about never returning here to live."

Fox shrugged, looking unconcerned. "Do you want to get the I've-moved-on message across to him and your families? Like, *really* get the message across?" he asked her.

She squinted at him, a little scared, a lot intrigued. "I haven't known you for long, but I do not trust that mischievous glint in your eye." And yet, Scott moving on would be utterly wonderful. And what was life without a little risk? "You know what? Go for it. My irritation levels would drop, and I also think it would be good for him to move on, find someone else."

He slid his hands into the pockets of his suit pants and Ru noticed that women of all ages—and a handful of men—sent him *oh, yum* looks as they walked past them, going either up or down the stairs. "I'll do what I can to make the message clear. And if that means I have to cope with a bunch of nosy questions, then so be it. I don't mind if it will help you out."

"Really?" she asked, surprised. Frankly, everything about Fox Grantham surprised her: he wasn't turning out to be the selfish, abrupt, annoying and terse man she'd expected.

Sure she'd only spent three full workdays with him—Wednesday, Thursday and Friday—but working shoulder to shoulder ten hours a day was a crash course in getting to know Fox. She'd quickly realized that while he was frequently terse and abrupt, it was because he had a dozen balls in the air at once and he needed to be completely focused. His get-it-done-now attitude wasn't intended as a personal attack.

He needed someone to work as fast as he did and, more importantly, to understand what he wanted without long explanations on his part. He was hyperfocused and yes, he tended to forget to say please or thank you, but he wasn't harsh, and he didn't blame her for things that weren't her fault. Whenever he threw a task at her that she didn't know how to handle, all she had to do was ask him to slow down, to allow her to catch her breath. Then she asked him to explain, in layman's terms, exactly what he wanted. He'd quickly learned that her asking questions got him what he wanted faster. And so far, he'd never criticized or derided her lack of knowledge.

But she'd never expected him to be this laid-back about acting as her fake boyfriend.

Fox shrugged. "I'm here. I might as well make myself useful," he told her with a slight hitch to his lips. His expression didn't change much, but she saw the amusement in his eyes and knew he was teasing her, inviting her to smile.

"You might as well," Ru cheerfully told him, holding out her hand. "But I want it noted that pretending to be my boyfriend wasn't my idea, and when you find yourself standing in front of a priest with no idea how you got there, don't blame me."

"Duly noted," Fox said wryly.

His mouth curved up, and Ru had to fight her impulse to taste his smile. She wanted to suggest that they blow off this wedding, get a room and spend the rest of the afternoon exploring each other's bodies.

No, bad Ru. That was too impulsive, bordering on reckless. But damn, he was temptation personified.

His eyes, as they sometimes did when they were in the office, warmed with desire. So far, they'd managed to keep their hands off each other, but it hadn't been easy. With every day that passed, their attraction seemed to grow, being fed by denial and anticipation. Ru did not doubt that, sometime soon, they'd lose the battle.

But until then, she was too stubborn to stop fighting.

"God, you are stunning."

Ru blinked at his change of subject, bemused. No, she wasn't, not particularly. She looked like his new PA, except a little better dressed and wearing more makeup than normal.

"...thanks?"

Fox was silent for a couple of seconds. "You don't think I'm being sincere."

Ru shrugged. She wasn't great at accepting compliments, but while she appreciated the gesture, she figured he was only saying what he thought she wanted to hear.

Fox placed his hands on her biceps, gently pulling her closer to his body, and dropped his mouth to her ear. "I could tell you that your body is stunning, slim but strong, and that your mouth makes me want to sin. All true. But your eyes... God, your eyes remind me of the flash of blue-green lightning. Hot, exciting, unexpected."

She closed her eyes, allowing his words to settle on her skin. She swallowed, unable to speak or pull away. His voice was deep, rumbly and sincere, and for the first time, she felt she could rest here and lean on him. Being with him was both exciting and safe, a dichotomy she didn't know how to resolve. She'd never known anyone like him before, someone who was both straightforward and poetic, terse but tender. He confused her. She couldn't tag him with a label, and he refused to fit into a box.

Then again, so did she. They were both, to a degree, outsiders and outliers.

"Shall we go up?" Fox asked. Ru felt the heat of his body so tantalizingly close to hers and resisted the urge to rest her temple on his big shoulder as they started to walk up the stairs. At the entrance to the ballroom, she stopped in front of the six-foot-high seating chart and found her name. She wasn't surprised to find herself—*Ru Osman and guest*—seated at a table to the right of the bridal table, with her parents and some Dean cousins.

A waiter with a tray stood outside the door to the ballroom, and Fox picked up a flute of champagne and handed it to her before taking one for himself. She was about to start the long walk to the front of the room to find her parents and their table when Fox tapped his glass against hers. "Cheers," he said softly.

"Cheers," Ru replied, looking at him over the rim

of her glass, bubbles sliding over her tongue and down her throat.

"So when I said that you look stunning..." he said, pushing her curls off her shoulder with the back of his hand. "I was wrong."

His hand curved around the back of her neck, and he bent his head so that his face rested against hers, his lips close to her ear. "You aren't stunning or even beautiful. You are fucking breathtaking, and I have a deep desire to know how much of me your body can take."

He was the first man who ripped her words away, who could drain her mind of thought. Of reason. Ru stood there, on edge and quivering with need, her body demanding that they find the nearest flat surface so that he could find out the answer to that question.

Fox kissed her cheekbone and the space next to her mouth before pulling back and draining his glass of champagne. "Shall we go inside?"

Not knowing what else to do, still short on words and air, and tingling from tip to toe, Ru did as he asked.

I have a deep desire to know how much of me your body can take? You are fucking breathtaking? What foreign entity had taken over his very rational mind?

Fox leaned his shoulder against the wall and watched Ru being pushed around on the dance floor by Scott, who hadn't stopped talking once since she stepped into his arms two minutes ago. Fox didn't need to hear his words to know what he was saying—

how long have you been together? Is it serious? When did you start seeing him?

Hurt, disappointment and betrayal flickered across his face, and Fox wanted to pull him aside and tell him to grow a pair. Ru had told him, years ago, she wasn't interested, so instead of whining about it, he should pick his face up off the floor and move the hell on.

Fox sighed. It was easy to judge Dean, to think about him instead of dealing with his own craving for Ru or his tumultuous thoughts and feelings. He was cynical and mistrusting, and he never ran his mouth, never told a woman she was breathtaking, never played the white knight and offered to chase unwanted suitors away. If his brothers could see him now...

A) they wouldn't stop laughing their asses off, and b) he'd be ragged on for the rest of his natural life. Or they'd wonder who he was and what he'd done with their naturally uncommunicative, prickly and brutally straightforward sibling.

Fox took a sip of whisky and pushed back the cuffs of his jacket and shirt—he was one of the few who'd yet to shed their jacket and roll up his sleeves—and looked at his watch. It was nearly eleven, and he'd been here for six hours...*six* hours, surrounded by people he didn't know.

It was official—he was losing his goddamn mind!

Fox narrowed his eyes as Scott's hand landed too close to Ru's butt and released a low growl. He

straightened, ready to intervene, but Ru smacked
Scott's hand away. Good for her.

And God, how *long* was this song?

He sighed and ran his hand over the back of his
head, unused to his new hairstyle. He'd gone to quite
a lot of effort—haircut, shave, asking his seldom used
stylist to put together a smart but snappy outfit—to
attend this wedding with a woman he barely knew,
the same woman who would be exiting his life in a
month. He didn't understand any of it. He didn't understand why his brain melted when she looked at
him—and why he'd offered to do things he'd never
usually consider.

What was it about her that had him acting so out
of character?

He looked at Ru, watching her hips move in perfect rhythm to the music, her feet doing a complicated
dance step while Scott blundered his way across the
dance floor, trying to follow her. She had grace and
style, and she was, from the top of her curly head to
her baby toe, an original.

She reminded him, strangely, of his mom. Yeah,
he had some deep-seated issues regarding his mother,
particularly in regard to things he knew about her
that no son should ever know. He didn't, unlike Jack,
worship her memory—the opposite in fact. But even
though he'd only been nine when she died, he did remember her sense of self, of not giving a damn what
anyone thought about her.

And that was how she and Ru were similar. Avangeline had once described his mom as an original, and that's how he saw Ru.

She, like his mom, was different, unusual and fascinating.

Had his dad felt like this on meeting his mom? Was her individuality the reason he'd been so attracted to her? Had he sensed the darkness in her and been attracted to it? Or was it the other way around?

What had happened between them that caused them to take such risks, to color so far over the lines? Was it because, as Avangeline mentioned when speaking about her oldest son, his dad had had a brilliant mind and a low boredom threshold? Everyone said Fox was most like him, in both looks and personality. It was generally accepted, by himself and others, that he was easily bored and moved on quickly from people and situations that didn't hold his attention.

In truth, most of the time, he didn't move on because of boredom but because of suspicion. He couldn't stop looking for hidden motives in every friendship, every romance…and far too often, what he found when he went digging brought the relationship to an end. In more recent years, he'd stopped trying. It wasn't worth the time and effort to find someone he could trust.

And yet here he was, at a wedding because a woman with eyes the color of a tropical parrot's wing had asked him. He needed to be intrigued and challenged and, so far, Ru was doing that.

It wouldn't last. It never did for him. Thank God Ru wasn't interested in anything but work and a fling, and that she was leaving in a month. They could avoid the *what have I done wrong*s and the *I don't understand why you won't let me in*s. But the thought didn't bring the relief he thought it would. If anything, the idea of her leaving made him feel a little nauseous and uncomfortable.

He was used to women falling for him. Getting them into bed wasn't, in any way, difficult. He made no promises, always treated his lovers well and hoped they remembered their encounter with him with fondness. He knew he could get Ru into bed—their attraction was fire hot and instantaneous—but, unlike everyone else, her mind and soul were not easily accessed.

He had so many questions about her. What was behind her need to travel? Why didn't she want to stay in the States? Why was she consumed with being on the move? Why did she equate traveling with freedom? Why did she eschew a career and a comfortable life to live in foreign countries and explore other cultures?

What. Made. Her. Tick?

This was madness, Fox told himself. Why was he torturing himself like this?

Crap, he was overthinking and overreacting.

Fox heard the music change. A cheer went up, and the atmosphere in the room changed. Something was about to happen. But what? The speeches were done, the cake cut, the bride had tossed her bouquet and the formalities of the evening were over. Ru joined him, placing her hand flat on the wall behind her, a rue-ful smile on her face.

Ru took the glass he held out to her—another first, because he didn't share his food or drink—took a sip of whisky and handed it back to him. A few cou-ples, including the bride and groom and Ru's parents, had taken their place on the dance floor, exchanging good-natured heckling. The rest of the guests were starting to drift over to the dance floor to watch the action. "What's happening?"

"Ah, that would be the swing portion of the eve-ning."

As in the dance style? He didn't understand.

"It's a long-held tradition," Ru explained, a trifle wistfully. "At every get-together where there's danc-ing, the Deans, my parents and a few of their other old friends compete for the kudos of being the best dancers on the floor, judged by the audience."

"Your parents are originally from the Middle East, right?"

"All my great-grandparents were born in Iran," Ru explained. "But they weren't raised in the Muslim faith—they were Zoroastrians. We are proud of our heritage but, really, apart from our names, my fam-ily is as American as apple pie."

Fox looked puzzled. "I thought Ru was an English name. I wondered why it didn't end with an e."

"It's short for Rumina, which means *polished* or *brightened*."

Ru gestured to the dance floor. "Anyway, the dance competition has happened for two decades, ever since my parents and their friends met at a dance class. The next generation is carrying on the tradition."

"What's the prize?"

"Just bragging rights at barbecues and dinners," Ru replied, smiling.

He'd been raised by his grandmother and Jacinta, had moved in A-list society. Like their friends, they did formal Thanksgiving and Christmas dinners and attended stylish cocktail parties and fancy dinners at Calcott Manor. This was very out of his comfort zone.

"Have you ever won?" Fox asked her as a good-natured argument broke out on the dance floor over a suitable song.

Ru snorted. "Uh, no. I can swing, but not only am I single, but I'm also never around. This is the first time I've been at a dance-off in years."

"Who's the reigning champ?" Fox asked her.

Ru looked puzzled at the hand he held out. "The bride and groom, actually. They danced at their engagement party and won the hearts and minds of their guests. The oldies say that the vote was rigged, and they are out for revenge. Why are you holding out your hand to me?" she demanded.

This was madness—he hadn't danced swing since high school. But he was naturally athletic and had an eidetic memory; the moves were in his brain. "Let's screw with everyone by winning."

Ru didn't look convinced. "We danced earlier and you were okay…ish. But this is the big-time, Grantham, and the competition is fierce. Do you even *know* how to swing?"

He did.

Her lack of conviction made his competitive spirit kick in. "Back in high school, I had a crush on a girl who was a junior national champion," Fox replied, hearing the first beats of the much-disputed song. "I learned to impress her."

He didn't bother to tell Ru that his crush had asked him to be a stand-in at a competition when her partner broke his ankle. He spent three months in intensive training with one of the best coaches in the country. They didn't place, but he hadn't embarrassed her. But, sadly, long hours spent in a dance studio quickly killed his fascination with the dancer.

Ru grinned and shook her head. "This is such a bad idea," she said, but she allowed him to tug her onto the dance floor. "We haven't practiced, and we don't know the moves."

Fox spun her out, pulled her back in and, with her back to his front, rocked her from side to side. He inhaled her perfume and placed his mouth close to her ear. Her breath hitched at their close contact, and he felt her shiver. "Sure we do. Dancing is just sex standing up. And with our clothes on."

"We haven't had sex," Ru pointed out.

"But we're going to," he told her after he dropped her into a low dip. "And I know it's going to be earth-shattering."

Five

She and Fox managed fourth place in the West Coast swing competition. The bride and groom walked off with honors again, and after that, it was time to leave the wedding. They'd made a hell of an impression—more than she wanted to, to be honest—but now she had to say goodbye to her parents…and tell them that she was leaving town. She'd been putting it off all evening, but she couldn't stall anymore.

They were not going to be happy. To Mazdak and Taranah, her leaving the confines of Bay Ridge, Brooklyn, was problematic, relocating anywhere in the US was concerning, but leaving the country was consistently catastrophic. For now, she only had to deal with a midlevel crisis, Ru reminded herself.

She'd cross the rickety leaving-the-country bridge when she came to it.

She was a grown woman; she had the right to live her life as she saw fit. She would not be ruled by fear, nor would she bow to family pressure or obligation. Neither would she allow herself to be emotionally manipulated.

But, damn, it was hard.

These people loved her, they wanted what was best for her, but they couldn't get past their need for her to be safe, at any cost. In her parents' eyes, danger was everywhere, and they were terrified of losing her again. But her abduction didn't give her parents the right to control her life.

They were, frankly, exhausting. Her parents took up a lot of her mental energy, so much so that she couldn't imagine committing to a man, allowing him into her head and her heart. She couldn't cope with anyone else fussing over her, trying to tell her what to do, how to live her life. Crowding her.

No, it was far easier to be single and unattached. She liked marching to the beat of her own drum.

"Ready to go?" she asked Fox, on a long, frustrated, unreleased sigh.

"Sure. I'll call for my driver," he replied, pushing back his chair. Her mom's head jerked up, and she rose to her feet, the familiar look of concern on her face. *Okay, strap on your seat belt, Osman.*

"Are you heading back to your friend's apartment,

Ru?" her mom asked, walking around the table to stand in front of her. "We'll call for a taxi and travel together."

Even if she hadn't intended on leaving with Fox, sharing a cab with her parents made no sense at all. Shellie's apartment was in Bushwick, a trendy area full of young professionals—and, crucially, in the opposite direction of Bay Ridge, where her parents lived.

And, well, if she and Fox had any plans for some after-wedding fun, her mother had just smacked that idea on the head. "You stay, Mom. There's no point in you rushing home when you are having fun. I'm just going home to pack—" *Just say it, Osman.* "—because I'm leaving tomorrow."

"You're *leaving*?" Taranah demanded, her voice rising to a level just under screech.

Right, she could've broken that news better. Ru winced as her father shot up so quickly that his chair tumbled over.

"I thought you were staying in the country for another month," Taranah said, her hand on her heart and her lipstick a red slash on her now-pale face.

Dammit, Osman. "Sorry, that came out wrong. I'm leaving the city for *Connecticut*. I'm going to be spending a month there."

Her dad shook his head and sent her a weak smile. "Don't be silly. Of course you're not going to Connecticut," he told her. "What on earth would you do there?"

Ru pushed her fingers into her forehead. "I've got a job there," she told them, not wanting to mention that the man she'd been dancing and flirting with all evening was her new employer. Their attraction, and their work dynamic, were too complicated to explain. And why did she need to? She was almost thirty and didn't need their permission.

Her parents exchanged worried looks. "Where are you staying? What job are you be taking? Why didn't you mention this before?"

"We've both been busy, Mom," Ru answered her, weary. "But, just to be clear, I will be working out of the city for the next month, maybe six weeks, so I can earn enough money to fly out again."

"Where to? And what about Fox?" Taranah demanded. "Are you just going to walk away from him, too?"

Oh, God, she'd forgotten that she and Fox were pretending to be in a relationship!

"Ru and I will continue to have a long-distance relationship, and I'll see her when I visit our Australasia restaurants and hotels," Fox said, his voice smooth and convincing as he rejoined their conversation.

"You have interests in Australia?" Ru asked, surprised.

Amusement made his eyes flash. "Quite a few, actually. It won't be difficult to make a detour to see you."

Huh. Sometimes she forgot that Fox was so damn

successful and incredibly wealthy. And, for a moment, she was caught up in the idea of extending this—whatever this was—beyond its one-month expiration date. She'd love to explore the Great Barrier Reef with him, join him for wine tasting in the Barossa Valley, and discover Melbourne or Brisbane with him at her side...

Her imagination was running away with her. She hadn't even slept with the man yet.

She turned back to her family and pushed steel into her spine. "I told all of you that when I returned, I would be leaving again. You *knew* this."

Taranah released a small wail, and her father's expression turned gloomy. "If you'd just agree to live close to us, settle down in the city, you'd have access to your trust fund. You wouldn't have to take jobs in strange places to make ends meet," Taranah insisted.

Connecticut was now strange? Good to know.

Her trust fund had been passed down from her grandfather and was under Taranah's control until Ru turned thirty, unless her parents decided to release it early. She'd have access to millions if she'd just stay, shut up and settle down. Ru wasn't tempted to sacrifice her freedom and step into their sticky web of interference that wore a pretty cloak of concern and protectiveness.

The thought made her shudder.

Taranah sank into her chair and shook her head. Bending her head, she took in a long shuddery breath.

"I just don't understand why you have to be so stubborn and selfish."

Here we go again.

When Taranah got the bit between her teeth there was no stopping her and Ru resigned herself to listening to the oft-repeated litany of why did she had to go and did she understand the hell she put them through? They missed her, they worried about her...

Taranah's words made her feel like she was a bad daughter, an inconsiderate and ungrateful person. If she was better, kinder, she'd stay close by, be around to reassure them, allow them to cosset and protect her. They'd lived a thousand horrible lives in the two weeks she was gone, and she should give them what they needed...

She'd die inside, but—

"Come with me, Ru."

Ru felt Fox's hand encircle hers, and she imagined that connection to be a rope, one that slowly pulled her out of the darkness and into the light. Color slowly started to seep back into the room. The gray roses were actually pink and red; the party lights were gold and not pewter.

Her father wore his usual expression of confusion, her mom one of sad resignation.

Ru looked at the big, tanned hand enclosing hers and then lifted her heavy head to look at Fox. She picked up the curiosity in his eyes but latched onto his steady expression. He was her life raft in this turbulent ocean of emotion.

She licked her lips, her mouth bone-dry.

"Can we go? Right now?" she pleaded.

If she didn't walk away, right now, she might do or say something that would result in her promising to stay in the States and allow her parents to control and interfere in her life. She was feeling sick and sad, immensely guilty, and she'd felt like this often enough for her to know that she needed time and distance, an immediate change of scenery to feel settled and like herself again.

"You've got it," Fox said, picking her bag off her chair and wrapping the strap around his free hand. He bade her parents a curt good-night and led her out of the ballroom and to the bank of elevators. When one appeared, he ushered her inside. After hitting the button for the lobby, he immediately wrapped his arms around her, pulled her into him and rested his chin on her head.

He didn't say a word, and Ru appreciated his silence. At some point, she'd have to give him an explanation, but for now, she was content to rest her cheek against his chest and enjoy his solidity, the barrier his body created between her and the rest of the world.

After leaving the wedding, Fox asked her where she wanted to go. Not being able to face Shellie's couch, she suggested he take her back to his place.

She'd pack in the morning, she decided, as she was used to traveling light. Ru didn't know if they'd end up in bed tonight, but it was a possibility. She did not doubt that tonight—or maybe tomorrow or the day after—they'd be sleeping together. It was predestined, predetermined, something that simply was.

They would, like stars or atoms, collide. It remained to be seen what impact their smashing into each other would have.

In Fox's suite in the Forrester-Grantham Hotel, Ru curled up in the corner of one of his sofas in the smaller living room and took the snifter of brandy Fox held out to her. To her left was a huge window and below her darkness, three sides of the park edged in bright city lights. Fox looked down onto Central Park, and he woke up to one of the most iconic views in the world every day. Lucky guy.

Ru looked around his suite, taking in the modern art and the minimalistic, beautifully designed furniture. She had to look hard to find any personal touches, anything that told her someone other than a transient guest lived here. She found a solid silver frame of five teenage boys standing on a snowy slope, holding ski poles and goggles pushed up into their messy hair. There was another of Fox, Jack, Soren and Merrick, taken a few years ago as they lounged bare-chested on a yacht off what looked to be on the Amalfi Coast.

Good-looking guys, Ru thought, and it took some

effort to pull her gaze off the photo and look for other personal items. She found none.

It was a beautiful apartment, exquisitely decorated with an amazing view, but like its owner, it wasn't cozy.

"Do you like living here?" she asked, wishing she could kick off her shoes and tuck her feet up under her butt.

"It's convenient," he answered, sitting down next to her and stretching out his long legs. "I work long hours, so I appreciate not having any commute. I use the hotel's gym and sauna and order from the room service menu. Or, if it's not on the menu, it's easy enough to ask for the dish to be made and have it delivered. Housekeeping keeps everything clean and does my laundry, and I wake up to a hell of view every morning.

"What's not to like?" Fox blithely added, but Ru heard the forced bonhomie in his voice.

"Right, that makes sense," she replied. "Now tell me the truth."

He darted a look at her, and she was surprised when he lifted his big shoulders, holding them to his ears for a few seconds before dropping them again. "Jack and I both live in the building. His suite is around the corner. When we renovated the hotel, we agreed to design the spaces so that they could be, at a moment's notice and at no expense, converted back into suites suitable for our most valued guests for an emergency booking. That means not putting up our own art, rearranging the furniture or bringing in other pieces. Or changing any of the colors in the room. I've spent many nights in Jack's spare room while someone else used this place for a few days, and he's spent many in mine."

He looked around and frowned. "I love my grandmother's house. It's filled with priceless art and antiques, ceramics and collectibles. She has a history with each object and can tell you, if you ask, why she bought the piece and where. Even if it was passed down to her, she knows where the piece originated. She's connected to her stuff." He waved a hand, encompassing his space. "I have two bedrooms, two sitting rooms, a dining room, a study and a pantry. On the other hand, I can pack up everything that's actually mine in fifteen minutes, and I never forget that I'm living in a hotel. But it's a price I'm willing to pay for the convenience of living above the office."

Fox reached behind her to put his glass on the table and pushed his hand into her hair, his fingers digging into her scalp. Ru purred. His touch felt so good, and she dropped her head, inviting him to use those strong fingers to break down the knots in her neck.

"Want to tell me why your parents had such a strong reaction to you relocating to Hatfield and to you traveling overseas?" he asked after a couple of minutes of bliss.

With her forearms resting on her thighs, her head

still bowed, she turned to look at him. He was only touching her with one hand, and she was melting. God knew what would happen if he used both hands, his teeth and his tongue. She'd probably dissolve into his ridiculously expensive designer sofa. His eyes met hers, and within them, she read desire and need and a fervent wish to see her naked. But underneath the lust, she caught a solid dose of concern and more than a little curiosity. She rarley explained her past, the dreadful thing that happened to her as a child. She didn't want to be the object of someone's pity, to be defined by something that happened to her so long ago. But, for some unexplainable reason, she wanted to tell Fox.

Ru stood up and walked over to the crystal decanters of expensive liquors arrayed on the credenza. Instead of pouring herself another shot of brandy—smoky, expensive, lovely—she put her glass down and turned to face him. She kicked off her shoes and sank her toes into the carpet.

Where to start? How to explain? There was no other option but to dive right in. "A few months after my third birthday, I was abducted."

As expected, Fox shot up, all trace of lazy attraction obliterated. "*What?*"

"My mom was shopping for clothes. I was sleeping in my stroller. My kidnapper walked up next to us with an identical stroller, timed it perfectly, and when my mom looked away, she swapped strollers. When she turned back, I was gone."

He rubbed his jaw, looking shaken. "I have so many questions, but—" he gestured for her to continue "—carry on."

"I wasn't hurt or abused," Ru told him. "I was mostly confused as to why I was in a strange house. My parents brought in the police, and the Deans—including Scott, who was only eleven at the time—threw themselves into organizing search parties and handing out flyers. The police got hold of security footage, but it was grainy and faded and they didn't have any leads."

"God, Ru," Fox said, standing up and walking over to her. He poured a shot of brandy into his glass, tossed it back and offered her a belt. She refused, feeling surprisingly calm. But then, most of her memories were a result of what she'd been told, not what she recalled experiencing. If she felt sad or scared, it was because she'd absorbed those feelings from her parents who, understandably, took a long time to recover.

The only real emotions she could identify from that time were missing her mom, missing her home and feeling bored and frustrated when her captor wouldn't let her out to play.

"How did the police find you?" Fox asked, resting his butt against the credenza, his bicep an inch from her shoulder. They weren't touching, but she felt reassured by his heat and presence.

"They didn't. My return was resolved differently."

He cocked his head in question, so Ru continued. "About a week after I disappeared, somebody contacted Scott's mom—she became my parents' spokesperson, and she appeared on all the news channels, begging for my return—and told her they knew who had me."

"Ransom?"

She shook her head. "No, the person who called knew the kidnapper but didn't know where she, or I, was. They said that they would facilitate my return if the police weren't contacted. Everyone realized fairly early on that the person who kidnapped me was known to my family."

"Who was she?"

"Scott's mom's cousin. She'd visited them about two weeks before I was kidnapped. She met my mom, and me, on a few occasions during her visit."

"Why did she take you?"

"Ah, she was mentally disturbed. She'd had a series of miscarriages and a stillborn daughter, who would've been about my age had she lived. They say she snapped and tried to replace her daughter with me."

"She snapped, but she was lucid enough to find an identical stroller, to keep you hidden for...how long?"

"A little over two weeks. At the start of the second week, my folks knew I was okay, but they didn't know where I was. Eventually, the informant nailed down an address, and the kidnapper agreed to surrender me. My parents picked me up from a house in the Hudson Valley."

"And your kidnapper?" Fox demanded.

"The agreement was that if I was returned safely, my parents wouldn't press charges and she would enter a psychiatric clinic. She did." Ru looked out the window, counting the different shades of yellow lights edging the park and beyond. "A month later, she committed suicide."

He reached for her then, pulling her into his warm embrace. He didn't say that the kidnapper deserved it, or that it was good riddance, or any of the things she'd expected him to say. He just held her, his body warming her from the inside out. After enjoying his hug for several minutes, she pulled back and rested her hands on his arms, enjoying the feeling of his big hands on her hips.

"My parents and the Deans, including Scott, all remember those two weeks like it was yesterday. In their eyes I am still the little girl who was abducted, someone who was lost, then found. They can't stand the idea of me not being close, of not knowing where I am, whether I am safe at all times. Around them, I feel smothered and controlled—which makes me want to run." She held up her fist and then her flat hand and the two connected. "Rock, meet Hard Place.

"I am a better daughter, and friend, when I'm thousands of miles from them," Ru added.

He stroked her hair and stepped away from her.

"Families can be so damn complicated," Fox said, his tone serious.

She'd told him so much, far more than she normally shared, and she wanted to even up the playing field. "Is yours?"

"More than most," Fox replied. His expression closed down, and he edged away from her. When he glanced down at his watch and frowned, Ru knew the bare-their-souls portion of the evening was over. She picked up his hand, looked at his expensive watch and sighed. It was after one. "I'd best get home. Can you call me a taxi?"

Fox shook his head. "It's late, and your parents know you are with me. Stay here tonight—"

That wasn't a good idea. Not tonight, when she was feeling tired and emotional and was in danger of confusing comfort with sex. She wasn't vastly experienced, but she knew enough to walk into a sexual relationship—especially one with her boss—clear-eyed and emotion-free.

Fox spoke before she could. "I'm asking you to stay the night, not have sex. I have a guest bedroom, and I'll get you a T-shirt to sleep in. I'm going to head down to the office for a while. In the morning, we'll go by your friend's place to pick up your stuff. How long will it take you to pack?"

Ridiculously, given her thoughts not a few minutes before, she felt put out he wasn't asking her to sleep with him. Annoyed with herself, she shrugged. "Not long—I travel light," she told him before frowning. "Damn. I might have to borrow a suitcase, because the work clothes I bought won't fit into my backpack."

"You're not going to need work clothes where we are going," Fox told her.

That was the best news she'd heard all day. "I won't?"

"All my meetings will be online, and it's summer on the coast. No one, least of all me, cares if you come to work in shorts and a T-shirt." Excellent news. She rocked shorts and T-shirts.

"And bring a swimsuit. The beach is at the end of the garden, and there are two pools and a hot tub," Fox told her, his voice turning growly. He looked at her mouth and released a long sigh. "Now, because the thought of you in a swimsuit just sent my blood pressure rocketing, I am going to leave."

He pointed down the hallway. "My bedroom is on the right. There's a pile of my clean laundry sitting on the chair in a corner. You'll find a T-shirt there. Towels, toothbrush, everything else you might need is in the bathroom."

She nodded, linking her hands behind her back so that she didn't curl her hand around his neck and pull him down into a kiss. If that happened, neither of them would get any sleep tonight. Though, frankly, she'd gladly sacrifice a night of sleep to experience—

No! She'd had a long and confusing night, had tangled with her parents and had an emotional discussion with Fox. She needed some time and space to put some mental distance between them. She was feeling too emotional, and when sex and feelings clashed, girl-boy situations got messy.

She was only here for a few more weeks—she didn't need messy. She inclined her head. "Thank you. I'll see you in the morning."

Fox brushed past her, but as he did, his pinkie finger caught hers, and he squeezed. It was a tiny touch, small but powerful. He hesitated, squeezed her finger again and walked away.

And Ru spent the rest of the night wondering how so small a touch could keep her awake for so long.

Six

Fox's two-seater Aston Martin Vantage, with its humming growl, attracted attention as they drove through Hatfield, Connecticut. Ru's first impression of the town was that it was vibey, pretty and sophisticated, judging by the number of art galleries, artisanal delis and bakeries they passed. Affluent, too, she thought. Fox's stupidly luxurious car was one of many she'd seen since entering the town's limits.

Fox stopped at a light. Ru followed his gaze to the left and noticed a willowy woman heading toward the coffee shop on the corner. Her red hair glinted with gold in the sunlight, oversize glasses covered her face, and her loose T-shirt and denim shorts couldn't hide her sleek, subtle curves.

She was stunning, Ru admitted. She couldn't blame Fox for looking.

Fox seemed to make a last-minute decision and turned right, pulling into the first open parking space he found. When she looked at him, he cut the engine and pushed his sunglasses up into his hair.

"I just saw an old friend walk into the coffee shop, and I'd like to say hello," he stated, unclipping his seat belt.

Okay, well, he probably didn't need her cramping his style while he renewed old acquaintances. "I'll stay here," she told him, not wanting to be a third wheel.

Fox exited the vehicle and surprised her when he walked around the hood to open her door. "Come and meet my brother's ex-fiancée," he told her. "I think you'll like her."

Ru grabbed her oversize tote and slung the bag over her shoulder as she straightened her aqua-colored T-shirt. Her white capri pants were a little creased, but that couldn't be helped. Fox slammed her door shut and placed his hand low on her back and kept it there as they walked toward the coffee shop, its entrance covered by a rounded, bright purple–and–white–striped portico. The main street was lovely, Ru decided, looking around. The shopkeepers seemed to be competing to see whose hanging baskets were the prettiest, who had the shiniest front door, the most attractive window display.

"Was she engaged to Jack?" Ru asked as he pulled

open the door to the coffee shop and gestured her inside.

Fox allowed the door to close behind them and shook his head. "No, Malcolm."

Ru watched as the redhead looked up at him, flashed a smile and then tried to pull it back, as if she wasn't sure what reaction she'd receive. To both Ru and the other woman's surprise, Fox pulled the redhead into a gentle, cautious hug. His fondness for her couldn't be disputed but she didn't catch anything sexual in their embrace. She got the sense of a man greeting an old friend he hadn't spoken to for a long time.

Not wanting to intrude, Ru moved down the counter and ordered two iced coffees, Fox's with an extra shot of espresso. She handed over some money, gave her name and turned when she felt Fox's hand on her back.

"Ru, meet Peyton. Peyton, this is Ru Osman."

Ru shook Peyton's hand, telling her she was happy to meet her. She was a classic redhead, with porcelain skin, freckles and the most incredible pair of pansy-blue eyes Ru had ever seen. She looked like a fairy princess from an Irish tale.

Ru listened as Peyton and Fox engaged in a brief catch-up session—him explaining that he was working out of Calcott Manor for a month, then asking her when she returned to Hatfield and hearing that she was only in town for the summer. That they knew each other well was indisputable, but Ru sensed that they were both trying too hard to appear jovial and that a lot of water had passed under their respective bridges since the last time they'd spoken.

After five minutes, Peyton told them she had to run, and Ru said goodbye. A moment later, the server called her name.

Ru nudged Fox's arm with his cup, and his hand encircled it. "Thanks," he told her, lifting the straw to his mouth. He looked preoccupied as they made their way back to his car. Ru sipped at her icy drink and wondered if he'd tell her why seeing Peyton had unnerved him. She could only ask, so she did.

"Let's walk." Fox gestured to the small, grassy, tree-filled park across the road, complete with an old-fashioned bandstand. When they reached it, Fox led them to a bench. She sat down, placed her cup next to her and dropped her bag to the ground as Fox stretched out his long, tanned legs. He wore a white linen shirt, cuffs rolled back, navy shorts and de-signer flip-flops. Strong calves, she noticed, and big but elegant feet. Would she find anything she didn't like about this Grantham brother? Talking about his brothers…

"So Peyton was engaged to your brother…" Ru stated, hoping he'd take up where she left off.

Fox's face tightened with grief. "Malcolm. He was the eldest of us, two years older than me. Merrick is the same age as me, and Jack and Soren are roughly eleven months younger.

"Mal was the fearless one of our band of five—

smart, charismatic and dynamic. It was his idea to revive and restore my grandmother's business empire, and he built the foundations of Grantham International. Jack and I might've grown it, but it was his vision and drive that got it off the ground," Fox explained.

"He died awhile back, right? Sorry, I don't remember how he died." Ru asked, hooking her calf under her thigh and turning to face him.

Fox stared at the bandstand, but Ru knew he wasn't looking at the pretty, painted-white structure. "He was killed in a motorcycle accident ten years ago."

Ru winced. "I'm so sorry. That's awful."

"Yeah, it was," Fox said, rubbing his palm up and down his jaw. "Actually, Malcolm is part of the reason I've relocated back to Hatfield for the next month."

"How?"

"When he died, as per his wishes, his organs were donated," Frustration mingled with annoyance in his eyes, and Ru didn't understand why he was irritated by what was a wonderful gesture.

"At the beginning of this year, our octogenarian grandmother, Avangeline, started corresponding with the supposed recipient of Mal's liver. Then she surprised us all by asking the woman to— temporarily, I hope—move in with her."

Supposed? "Do you think she's lying about receiving your brother's organ?"

Fox gripped the bridge of his nose, obviously frustrated. "No, I misspoke. She did receive it—that's been verified."

"So what's the problem?" Ru asked.

"The problem is her moving in with my vulnerable grandmother. It's not like she has nowhere else to go. She's taken a sabbatical from the law practice she works for to move here. If she just wanted to reach out, she could visit her on weekends, call and email. Moving in is a drastic step, and we are not sure of her motives."

Avangeline was one of the wealthiest women in the country, and Ru understood Fox's wariness. What did this woman want? What was her angle?

"The second problem is that she is saying that, along with his liver, she's inherited certain traits and memories of Malcolm's."

Well, that wasn't what she'd expected him to say. How interesting.

"You're supposed to say 'what a crock of shit' or something like that," Fox grumbled.

Having watched a documentary on cellular memory theory—the idea that memories, quirks and personality traits could be stored in organs apart from the brain—Ru knew the medical world had, mostly, debunked the theory, calling it quackery and hype. The theory relied very heavily on anecdotal evidence from people who might not be trustworthy. But she also believed that the body was a far more complex system than scientists realized and just because something couldn't be scientifically proved didn't mean it didn't exist.

In her opinion, she told Fox, old Will Shakespeare had it right when he wrote in *Hamlet*, "'There are more things in heaven and earth, Horatio, than are dreamt of in your philosophy.'"

"You really aren't helping," Fox told her.

She smiled. "Sorry. Is there something else going on with this person—"

"Aly Garwood," Fox interrupted.

"—this Aly Garwood that makes you suspicious of her? Has she asked your grandmother for money? Has anything gone missing from the house?"

"No," Fox admitted. "Per Soren, she and Avangeline seem to be good friends. Even Jacinta, who is the best judge of character I know, seems to love her."

He sounded insulted, and Ru swallowed her smile. "Well, since she's in your grandmother's home at her invitation, I don't know what more you can do other than wait and see." She changed positions and crossed her legs.

"Tell me about Peyton. Was she engaged to Malcolm when he died? And why did I sense like you two weren't completely comfortable with each other?"

He drained his coffee and shook his head, seeming bemused. "You're something else, did you know that? How did you work that out?"

She studied people—it was her favorite thing to do. And in the countries where English wasn't spoken, body language was essential to her navigating the world safely. "What happened?"

"In a nutshell, Malcolm and Peyton's dad, Harry, got involved in a business deal. The deal fell, with Malcolm calling Harry a con man. Peyton stood by her dad, and she and Mal broke up. A few weeks later, Mal died," Fox explained. "Peyton came to his funeral but didn't speak to us. Jack came back here two years ago, and they had dinner or something, paving the way to a reconciliation. Anyway, I'm glad that we spoke. I always liked Peyton."

Ru sorted through all he'd told her, filing away the various bits of information. "Right, Avangeline is your impressive grandmother, her guest is Aly—who received Malcolm's liver—and Jacinta is the housekeeper." She caught Fox's small frown and lifted her eyebrows. "What did I get wrong?"

"Well, Jacinta is the housekeeper and estate manager, but she's so much more. She's been our rock and compass point, my second mother and..." Fox trailed off, looking a little embarrassed at his passionate outburst.

"Noted. Anyone else?"

"Uh, the main guest house is being rented to the artist Paz Conway. He needed a bigger-than-normal barn for his latest oversize commission."

"I love his work," Ru exclaimed, excited. "He had an exhibition in Hong Kong that I went to see."

"I have two of his smaller pieces," Fox admitted.

"They are currently touring the country as part of a traveling exhibition."

"I am so jealous," Ru told him. She shook her cup, sucked up the now-watery coffee and looked up into the trees, sighing softly. This was a very lovely town, and she felt very at home here, despite only arriving a short time ago. She also felt equally comfortable sitting next to this big man on a lazy Sunday morning.

It was a good thing that her stay in Hatfield would be limited to four to six weeks. Any longer and she could find herself in serious trouble...

Maybe even wanting-to-stay trouble.

After settling Ru into the apartment over the garage—strange to think that Soren's fiancée, Eliot, had recently stayed there as well, though they hadn't yet been engaged at the time—Fox walked across to Calcott Manor, skirting around the imposing front of the house to head for the side door that led into the mudroom and kitchen. This was the only door he'd used as a child and teenager, and he hoped he'd find Jacinta in the chef's kitchen, whipping up something amazing for afternoon tea, a custom Avangeline had brought over from England. The world could be ending, but you could always find Avangeline every afternoon in her favorite sitting room, drinking strong tea and eating scones, white-bread sandwiches with their crusts cut off and tiny bites of shortbread.

Fox saw that the kitchen was empty and sighed in disappointment. He'd hoped to have a chance to catch up with Jace before talking to Avangeline. Jacinta was the heartbeat of this house and more of a daughter to his grandmother than a housekeeper. Jace kept a close eye on everybody in the family, including his occasionally difficult grandmother. If something fishy was brewing in the Forrester-Grantham family, Jacinta would know about it first.

Fox looked at his watch—a Patek Philippe he'd bought himself a few months back—and realized it was later than he thought. They'd all be gathered in the blue salon by now. Stepping into the wide hallway, he turned right, idly noticing the Picasso and Degas sketches on the wall to his left. There was a Manet on the opposite wall and a Toulouse-Lautrec farther down. His grandmother loved her art.

Fox turned left, then right, and stepped into the intimate room overlooking his grandmother's rose garden. Avangeline sat in her favorite chair, and Jacinta, who didn't look like she was in her early fifties, sat on the white couch next to a petite woman with chestnut hair. The stranger was the first to notice him. When she lifted her head, her green eyes, the color of an ancient forest of firs, slammed into him. He felt, momentarily, off balance.

What the hell was that about?

Jacinta leaped to her feet and rushed over to him, flinging her arms around him and kissing both his cheeks. He hugged her slim frame, closing his eyes and thinking how lucky he'd been to have this woman in his life. He'd been a spiky and sarcastic kid, rebellious as hell, but no matter what he did or how he acted, Jace never stopped loving him. Nobody was perfect—his parents the least perfect of all—but Jacinta came, in his opinion, pretty damn close.

Fox greeted Avangeline with a brief kiss on her papery-thin cheek—Avangeline wasn't one for open displays of affection—and was introduced to Alyson Garwood, she of the fake memories and sudden addiction to all things that Malcolm liked.

Fox sat down, accepted Jacinta's offer of a cup of coffee and thanked his grandmother for allowing his assistant to move into the garage apartment for the next month.

"First the model, now your assistant. Do you plan on falling in love with her as Soren did Eliot?" Avangeline demanded.

Fox waited for what should be an instantaneous recoil at her suggestion, but to his surprise, it didn't come. Seriously? He couldn't possibly, after just a few days in Ru's company, be thinking that she could be the one to change his mind about commitment and relationships, was he? No, of course not. He simply wanted to sleep with her—he didn't want anything deeper or more intense.

Get a grip, Grantham!

Avangeline narrowed her still-sharp eyes at him when he didn't respond to her question. "So, are you as burned-out as Jacinta insists, or is it just your turn to harangue me about my will and Aly moving in?"

Always blunt, Fox thought, with no small amount

of fondness. It was one of the traits he loved best about Avangeline. He could lie and tell her he did need a break, that he wanted to be here, but he knew his grandmother wouldn't respect him for being less than truthful. "I don't think I am burned-out."

"According to my sources," Jacinta told him, "you have been working fourteen- to sixteen-hour days and you are exhausted. When you are this tired, you lose the little patience you have, and that's why you've gone through so many assistants in so short a period."

Her "sources" had to be Jack, backed up by Merrick. And yeah, it was true that when he was tired and stressed, his patience flew out of the window. But he had a company to run, and that required hard work and long hours. That wasn't stressful—it was just life. If anything, being here would be a greater stressor. Despite all the good memories he had of growing up here with his brothers, the place still made him remember that horrible argument he'd witnessed between his parents more than twenty-five years ago.

It was weird how the memory seemed to work in reverse, how the events of that day became more vivid as he aged instead of the other way around. He now remembered more of his parents' fury and their disdain than he had when he was nine. Or maybe age and greater access to information just meant that he understood their argument better.

He could still see his parents standing in the small living room attached to their bedroom suite, consumed by rage and both screaming, accusing each other of crossing too many lines. The world had thought them to be a perfect couple, deeply in love, but that morning, just a few hours before they died, he'd seen beneath their layers of perfection to the people they were beneath. From that day, he never took anything at face value. He scratched, then dug, needing to understand. There was always something below, something he wasn't being told. He refused to be blindsided ever again.

Their argument, those private revelations, had impacted him deeply and were at the root of why he had so much difficulty letting people in. He had, he admitted, significant trust issues. Because, really, if you couldn't trust your parents to be who you thought they were, whom could you trust?

Fox saw that the trio were waiting for a response, so he just shrugged his shoulders and changed the subject. "I heard you converted Soren to your side," he said to Aly, using his hardest, you-don't-impress-me voice. "Don't expect it to happen with me."

Aly had the temerity to smile at him. "That's what he said," she replied.

In response to her joking tone, frustration rose like a red tide. "What the hell do you want from us, Ms. Garwood?"

Fox saw something flicker in her eyes—sadness or fear?—and narrowed his eyes. She did want something from them—from Avangeline. It might not be money, but it was *something*.

"Just spit it out, Ms. Gar—"

"Fox, enough!" Avangeline's hard voice cut through his sentence. When he turned his head to frown at her, she released a long sigh. "I wish my grandsons would stop treating me like a mad old woman without a brain in her head," she complained. "I do know what I'm doing."

Fox didn't try to hide his disbelief. When you were worth billions, in your twilight years and hadn't yet made a will, he begged to disagree. He thought about explaining, yet again, why her not having a will was a disaster waiting to happen. If she didn't leave specific instructions, it would take years, possibly decades to untangle her estate after her death. It was just a stupid move, which was inexplicable, since his grandmother was one of the smartest women he knew.

There was more to her not writing a will than simple stubbornness…something was wrong. It had to be. But what? He needed to dig into his grandmother's life and try and get to the bottom of why she was acting so irrationally. He'd do the same for Alyson Garwood.

"I don't like that look in your eyes," Avangeline said.

See? He'd said she was smart.

He placed his hand on his heart and tried, probably unsuccessfully, to look innocent. "I'm here because I am burned-out and tired, grandmother."

"Poppycock!" Only English octogenarians, friends of the queen of England, still used that phrase. Though Fox had once, maybe twice, heard Avangeline lose her temper, and she'd let loose with creative curses that would've made a sailor blush.

Avangeline lifted a bony finger and pointed it at his nose. "Stay out of my business, Foxcroft. I've got it well in hand."

Foxcroft? He internally winced at her using his full name. She was being deadly serious about sailing her ship alone…

But, dammit, he owed this woman everything. She had given up her business and career to take in and raise her four grandsons. Now it was their turn to look after her. There would be no solo sailing for Avangeline as long as he lived and breathed.

Seven

Ru lifted her hands off the railing of the apartment's wraparound balcony and dragged her eyes off the rolling, sparkling Atlantic Ocean and the wide, empty private beach. Needing to move, she walked down the balcony, turned the corner and looked right, straight into a huge bedroom dominated by a massive king-size bed. For a moment she thought that the room had no doors, but on closer examination, she realized the doors slid into the walls, creating an illusion of the room being open to the elements. *Nice.*

Ru trailed her fingers over potted, fragrant lavender and brightly colored scented geraniums and stopped at the end of the balcony, which looked onto part of the front facade of Calcott Manor. Her family was wealthy (ish), but they lived in a crowded city and having so much space was mind-bending. Ru didn't think she was the type to be overly impressed by swaths of grass, landscaped gardens and an enormous, soft gray, ivy-covered house but...

Yeah. She was.

Hugely impressed.

Calcott Manor reminded her of the stately houses she'd visited in England, not so much in architecture and age but in presence. Calcott Manor belonged here, right on this spot, reigned over by an old lady with immense style and flair.

Ru danced on the spot. She loved being in a new place and couldn't believe that this insanely lovely estate was where she'd be working for the next month. How lucky was she? The sun was shining, the sky was a perfect shade of blue and she was a long way from the city. And her parents. Awesome.

"Ru?"

Ru spun around and quickly walked onto the main section of the balcony, surprised to see a frustrated-looking Fox stepping out from the sitting room area of the luxurious apartment. She hadn't expected to see him again today. She was, after all, here to work, and entertaining her wasn't something he had to do. But he had an icy bottle of white wine in one hand and two glasses in the other and, yeah, she had no objections to a glass or two.

Or to his company.

"Hey," he said, lifting his hands. "I need wine. Would you like a glass?"

"God, yes."

Ru sat down and lifted her bare heels to rest on the edge of the couch, wrapping her arms around her knees. She watched Fox efficiently remove the cork, noticing the deep furrows in his brow and deep grooves bracketing his mouth. He was a lot tenser now than he'd been before going to say hello to his grandmother and Jacinta.

She wondered if she could, or should, ask him what the problem was. They veered between being employer and employee and friends and potential lovers, and she wasn't sure what hat she should be wearing right now. And if they slept together—when they slept together—the situation would just become more complicated. Where was the line?

"I love my grandmother, but she drives me insane," Fox said, surprising her. He handed her a glass of wine and slumped into the chair opposite her, crossing his long, muscular legs at the ankles.

"Any particular reason?" Ru asked him, keeping her tone light.

"We keep bugging her to write a will, but she refuses to. And if she dies without one, we are going to be in a world of hurt."

Ru was surprised to hear it. Avangeline Forrester-Grantham had the reputation of being one tough cookie. Smart as hell…and smart women didn't make mistakes like not writing a will.

"She's so damn stubborn," Fox muttered, taking a large sip of wine before resting the bowl of his glass on his forehead. "And she hates being told what to do. Maybe if we tell her that we don't care about whether she writes one or not, she might actually write one!"

That sounded like a stretch. "Have you asked her why she's hesitating?"

He looked confused. "I'm sure we have," he answered, not sounding sure at all.

"Maybe you should ask her again," Ru suggested. "Intelligent women don't make dumb decisions unless they have a damn good reason."

Fox stared at her, and she saw that he was turning over her words. "That's a good point, Ru." He pointed his wineglass at her, and his grin wiped away the stress in his eyes. "I knew there was a reason I hired you."

Ru returned his smile, dropped her legs and reached for her wine. After sitting in silence for a few minutes, she posed a question of her own. "What happened to your grandfather? Did you know him?"

"Nah. I think I met him once or twice before my folks died, but he lived on the West Coast and wasn't around much. He and Avangeline divorced when my dad was barely more than a toddler. She raised my dad and my uncle on her own."

"Impressive lady, raising her children and then her grandchildren," Ru mused. Losing her sons and their wives must've been a blow of epic, and horrendous, proportions. How she'd remained standing Ru had no idea.

"She really is. We saw a little of my mom's parents

growing up, but Avangeline wouldn't allow our grand-father, her ex, any contact with us," Fox explained.

"Do you know why?"

He shrugged. "I know they had a nasty divorce. My father only connected with my grandfather after he left college, and that caused a rift between him and Avangeline. He and my grandmother were barely speaking at the time of the crash."

Four people died when the airplane crashed into a mountain shortly after taking off, Ru remembered. "Do they have any idea what caused the crash?"

Fox pushed his hand through his hair. "They don't. The report says that it was pilot error." His eyes turned hard. "Blaming the pilot is what they do when they don't have another explanation."

Ru felt like she was tiptoeing through a minefield. She wanted to know more, but before she could ask a follow-up question, Fox spoke again.

"The plane was a few months old, state-of-the-art. My dad was a brilliant pilot. He went solo at sixteen and clocked plenty of hours in all sorts of planes. He was instrument rated, analytical and so meticulous that he was a pain in the ass when it came to flight checks. He did everything properly in the cockpit—he wasn't a cowboy. I can't believe he did something that resulted in him flying that plane into a mountain."

"Especially since he had his much-loved wife, his twin and his sister-in-law on board," Ru mused. "I have this feeling that you take extra, *extra* care when you have the lives of the people you love most in your hands."

She caught the flash of dismay in Fox's eyes, a hint of disagreement. Ru frowned, wondering where she'd gone wrong. So she asked him.

He waved her question away. "Nope, you're right. He would've taken extra care with the ones he loved," he told her, but his eyes were now a flat blue and the grooves next to his mouth were deeper than before.

She was missing something, something important. "What am I missing, Fox?"

"And I thought that *I* liked to dig," Fox muttered, sounding aggrieved.

Ru winced. Fox owed her no explanations; she had no right to prod and pry. Just because she felt comfortable telling him about her past didn't mean that he had to reciprocate. He was entitled to his privacy. And, unlike her, he had good reason to be careful about what he told to whom and when. Because if he said the wrong thing to the wrong person, private information could be splashed across the internet and headlines would be made. His family was high-profile and interesting, and people paid attention.

Ru wrinkled her nose. "Sorry, I didn't mean to pry. I mean, I did, but I respect your right to privacy."

And she was grateful for the reminder of her place in his life—firmly *outside* the circle of those he trusted. She had no right to push her way in, just because she found herself desperately eager to know what made him tick, what made him mad. What made him sad.

She'd known the guy for only a couple of days, and she was completely hooked and crazy fascinated. This was not good news.

She had to put some distance between them and throw up a wall or two. His reluctance to confide in her was his way of doing exactly that. Clever man.

"What you've read about my parents is wrong. They didn't love each other," Fox told her after a few minutes of surprisingly comfortable silence.

Ru felt the sudden urge to slap her hands over her ears. His statement was too personal, too fascinating, and it pulled her right back in again. She caught the bob of his Adam's apple, the faint sheen on his brow that suggested he was nervous about discussing his family with her...

But he was doing it anyway.

Fox wasn't a guy who opened up easily, so Ru felt honored he was sharing this much with her. Honored. And terrified.

Sitting cross-legged in the chair, she rested her elbows on her knees, her entire focus on the man opposite her. "You were pretty young when they died," Ru said, picking her words with care. "Why do you think that?"

He stood up, walked over to the railing and gripped it, staring out to sea. "I heard them arguing just before they left for the airport. They were flying to Martha's Vineyard for the day and were due to return that night. It was a flight they did often—the four of them would occasionally take the day and hang out, leaving us kids with Avangeline, here at Calcott Manor. She'd just bought the place and hired Jacinta. It was Jace's second or third day on the job. She was waiting downstairs to drive them to the airport. Malcolm was with her—he never missed an opportunity to go to the airfield and help our dad with his preflight checks. He was obsessed with flying, with anything that had an engine, but back then, planes were all he cared about," Fox continued.

"And after the crash?" Ru asked.

"He hated them," Fox replied. "We all did, for a long time. We managed to fly commercial, but it took a long time for any of us to get back into a small plane."

So sad, Ru thought. And so understandable. "So your parents were fighting..." she prompted.

He rubbed the back of his head. "Yeah, right. I was outside with Jack, doing something, and came back inside to get something from our room, I can't remember what. I could hear them screaming at each other when I turned down the hallway, and it was a long hallway."

Ru winced.

"I didn't understand half of what they were talking about at the time, but I put it together when I was older. They were hurling tit for tat accusations, getting very real about each other, their marriage and their sex lives."

Whoa... *What?*

"The only thing they agreed on was that they were both heartily sick of pretending to everyone that they were happily married." Fox pulled a face. "I remember my mom saying it might be better to divorce, because her needs weren't being met. My mother told my dad that she hated him, and he told her that he loathed her..." Fox continued, and Ru knew he was reliving that afternoon in crystal-clear detail.

"I stood there, frozen, my back against the wall," Fox told her. "Then their argument moved onto something that happened in the basement."

Ru was struggling to keep her jaw from dropping. His parents had been portrayed as American's golden couple, pretty and perfect. But, judging by what Fox was saying, that was far from the truth.

She homed in on his last sentence. "Your basement? The one at your home? What happened there?" she asked, fascinated. Did someone throw a dumbbell or a swing a golf club? Did she set fire to his collection of vinyl records or did he destroy her wedding dress?

Fox briefly closed his eyes, his tanned face pale in the late-afternoon sunlight. "As I discovered in my early twenties, The Basement is a New York club."

Oh, Ru thought, that made sense. They must've had a cracking fight in the club, just like thousands of couples did, every night across the world.

"The Basement is a pick-a-partner-out-of-a-hat, mix-and-match S&M club."

It took her twenty seconds to make sense of his

sentence. She lifted her fingers to her mouth and shook her head. "You mean they...um..."

Fox closed his eyes. "Oh, yeah, it was their thing. So much so that they owned the building, the bar, the club itself. The ownership was hidden under layers of red tape, but I traced it back to them eventually."

Ru wrinkled her nose, feeling uncomfortable. Look, she knew these things happened. It wasn't a scene that had ever interested her, but she tried not to judge what other people were into. "People have needs. Sometimes those needs are not...*vanilla.*"

Fox looked like he wanted to roll his eyes. "I know that, Ru. While I'd much rather not know anything about my parents' private life, I do understand that they had the right to do what they wanted, as long as they were on the same page."

Then she was missing something major here. To keep him talking, Ru asked another question. "How did you find out about the...uh, this club?"

Fox turned around, his hands gripping the railing behind him. "I was up in the attics one day when I was in my early twenties, just looking at all their stuff, and I came across a box with stuff from my mom's desk. I found her day planner from the month before the crash. It had numerous entries of the letters *T* and *B*, at least a couple a week. At the front of the planner was a phone number next to the letters and another phone number, with the name Tommy. I called the first number. It was out of service, but the second reached Tommy. I asked him how he knew my mother, and he hung up on me."

Ru, fascinated, couldn't take his eyes off him. "I kept calling. He kept hanging up. I became obsessed with finding out who he was, so I hired a private investigator to find him."

Judging by the bleakness she saw in his eyes, sometimes, especially when it came to kids and parents, knowledge was *not* a good thing.

"You found out something about the Basement that you didn't like," Ru stated, not needing to frame it as a question.

Fox looked gutted. "According to Tommy, who was the manager of the place, sometimes the patrons got bored with each other, and they... God, how do I put this? They brought in sex workers through a pimp Tommy knew. Sometimes the sex workers were on the young side..."

Ru felt her throat close up. "Kids?"

"No, older teenagers, seventeen, eighteen, nineteen—but that's bad enough."

Ru held her hand up to her throat, feeling a little sick. "God, Fox."

"Unfortunately, that's not where this sordid tale ends. According to Tommy, my mom—bright, bold, the epitome of the all-American girl—was a lot more into the dark side of sex than my dad and wanted to go deeper into that world, explore things that were, frankly, very dangerous. She'd met some people in a dark web chat room, and she wanted to invite them to the club. My father refused—he said it was too dangerous. Tommy was in the room when my dad told my mom he was going to close the place down, that they were done with that world. My mom, apparently, lost it. She tried to claw him, slap him. She told him she'd leak photographs of him to the press...

"He was vice president of Forrester-Grantham, one of the most respected companies in the world. His mother was and still is a good friend of the queen, and they all had celebrities, captains of industry, politicians and royals on speed dial. My parents were good friends with all the power couples on the East Coast—hell, in the country. They were looked up to, idolized, written about and photographed."

Yeah, that would be bad. "A compromising photo of either of them would've created a media shit storm."

"Of epic proportions," Fox agreed. "The Basement argument happened a week before the plane crash."

Twenty-six years ago. "It's amazing that no one from the club ever spilled the beans about their involvement."

"Not really," Fox explained. "Real names weren't used, and faces were always masked. The clients stayed anonymous. Tommy was a former drug user and would've been—would still be—easy to discredit. And something he said suggested they made it worth his while to keep quiet."

It was, possibly, the most unbelievable and bizarre story she'd ever heard. Yet she believed every word that came out of Fox's mouth. Then another, more shocking thought, popped into her brain. "Who else knows about your parents' extracurricular...thing, Fox? Who else knows about their failing marriage?"

He met her eyes, but his gaze slid away. "You."

Sorry? What?

Ru placed her palm over her mouth as shock coursed through her. No. Way. "You never told your brothers?"

Fox rolled his eyes at her. "Of course not! Nor did I tell my grandmother. How could I? How would I?" He linked his hands behind his head, his expression stormy.

Right, of course, he couldn't tell his brothers, not if he could barely think about it himself. And why would he want to? Why would any child want to know that much about their parents' private lives, especially if it shattered their view of people they'd always looked up to? She couldn't think of anything worse. Fox had been protecting his brothers, especially Jack, by keeping this knowledge from them, but he'd paid a high price. Fox's recollections of the couple everyone viewed as ideal were tinged by the knowledge he was never meant to have.

How...horrible, Ru decided. Just awful.

She didn't stop to think; she simply stood up and swiftly walked over to him, sliding her arms around his waist to lay her head on his chest. She hugged him as tightly as she could, wishing she could take his pain away and make him feel not quite so alone.

He'd lived with this secret for so long, and it had to have flayed his soul.

"I'm so sorry, Fox. Nobody needs to know such intimate details about their parents," she murmured. "But, even worse maybe, is that you know everything the world thought, and thinks, about their marriage wasn't true at the end."

Under her hands, his body was ironing-board stiff. "That's why I always need to dig, to understand, to scratch away until I get to the truth whenever I think someone might be hiding something from me. I will never accept what's presented to me, because I always think there's more…and usually I'm right."

She now understood why he was never satisfied with the status quo. But she didn't know why he'd shared all this with her, someone who was just a few steps away from being a stranger.

"Why would you trust me with that knowledge?" she asked him, stepping back but leaving her hands on his chest.

"Do you plan to sell it to a sleazy tabloid?" Fox asked her, looking down at her.

"Of course not! I won't tell anybody, and I am very good at keeping secrets, Fox. I'll keep yours."

"Of course you will," he agreed, stepping away. "Because if you tried to sell the story, they'd ask you for proof. You have none, and without any, they'd send you on your way. Even the sleazier publications know better than to cross the Granthams without rock-solid proof, because I'd sue the publication, and you, into oblivion."

Right. Okay, then. Ru lifted her hands off her chest and stepped back, feeling hurt and irritated. "Why did you do that?" she demanded.

"Do what?"

"Your voice became colder, and I felt like you'd taken a dozen steps away from me. We've had a pretty intense, emotional conversation. Do you deliberately retreat to put some distance between us?"

"Yes."

She'd never expected him to admit that so easily. And now, having received an answer she hadn't anticipated, she didn't know what to do or say. So she said nothing and kept her view on the ocean. This man was complicated and intense, frustrating and exciting, and she didn't know how to handle him. She was so out of her comfort zone...

Ru felt Fox's hands on her shoulders and felt him pull her hair off her neck to place a kiss on her nape. She told herself to ignore the tingle, that it was just sexual attraction, that he was trying to distract her. But instead of kissing her again, he wound his arms around her waist and rested his chin in her hair, seemingly content to simply hold her.

"There's something about you, Ru Osman, that makes me tell you things. And that's damn scary," Fox murmured. "I look into your eyes and words bubble up, as well as memories and feelings I've kept locked away for a long time. I don't like it."

She couldn't blame him out for that—she wasn't completely comfortable with their connection, either. But it couldn't be denied that something was brewing between them. And, like him, she'd shared intimate details about her past, about her abduction, a topic she'd never broached with anyone else. They were each other's truth drug.

"I'm leaving the States in a month, Fox. I'm not staying here," she told him, needing to remind him— and herself—that no matter what, she was leaving. "I'm not looking for a relationship. I won't be controlled or corralled."

"Is that what you think a relationship is?" he asked.

"Isn't it?" she asked, twisting and tipping her head to look up at him.

"I have no damn idea," he admitted. "I'm too busy to have one, knowing that I need time to strip people apart to see what they are hiding."

God, they were a pair. "I'm not going to fall for you, Fox," Ru warned him.

"Good. I'm not going to fall for you, either."

He'd barely finished his sentence when he spun her around and his mouth settled on hers, taking her by surprise. Passion ignited between them, wild and uncontrollable, and when Fox probed the seam of her mouth with his tongue, she opened up, releasing a little gasp when his tongue stroked hers. Something bright, hot and white flashed through her system, supercharging and heating her blood, sending pure energy into every cell and atom.

Standing here, engulfed by him, was the most alive she'd ever felt. It was both wonderful and utterly terrifying. If she didn't stop kissing him, this would be the night they'd end up rolling around that big bed... naked.

Fox cupped the back of her head with his big hand, holding her head in place, his mouth devastating her common sense. *It's just sex*, she desperately told herself. *You're a grown woman—you're allowed to want this. To want him. It's a simple, physical release. Neither of you is prepared to put your hearts on the line, so where's the problem? You. Want. Him.*

"I want you," Fox said, pulling away to mutter the words, verbalizing her thoughts. He placed his hand on her breast, looking down when her nipple spiked his palm. "I want to strip you naked and kiss every inch of you before sliding inside you and making you mine."

Mine... She liked the sound of that. She shouldn't, but she did.

He ran his fingers over her nipple, curled his hand around her breast. How was she supposed to think when he touched her like that, when he dropped sexy little kisses on her jaw, on her cheekbone? Breathing wasn't even that important, she decided, as his lips hovered over her mouth, heavy with the promise of pleasure to come.

"Forget that I am your boss, that we seem to tell each other things we shouldn't, that you are going and I am staying. Just take the moment and be mine. Be with me."

She could resist confidence and charm, but sincerity—the hitch of emotion in his deep voice, the suggestion of desperation—was much harder to resist. Ru stood on her tiptoes so that her mouth was aligned with his. Then she gently, so very gently, bit down on his bottom lip. "Make me yours, Fox. Be mine."

He pulled back, blue eyes glowing. "Just for now," he clarified.

"Just for now."

Then he kissed her, kissed her like the fate of the world rested on the fact that he got it right, and their surroundings faded away. Now was later, later had no meaning and time stood still as Ru gave him the gift of her body.

That much she could handle...

Eight

She couldn't handle it, Ru decided, as a deliciously naked Fox kissed her hip bone and ran his tongue along the edge of her pink lace panties. He rubbed his nose across her still-covered mound and Ru thought this was it, this was when he'd pull down her panties and bury his face between her legs, giving her what she needed. What she craved.

But no, Fox was now moving up her body…

She tapped his shoulder. "Wrong direction," she muttered, surprised she'd managed to form words despite the way his touch drained her brainpower. "South, not north."

She felt his grin against her rib cage. "I have an excellent sense of direction," Fox told her before pulling her nipple into his mouth, rolling it between his teeth. Ru arched her back, once more flying down that highway of energy and pleasure. God, he was good at this...

But while she loved the fact he'd traced his tongue up and down her spine, nibbled her rib cage, painted kisses on her stomach and hip bone, worshipped her breasts and mouth, she was more than ready for the main event. His fingers deep in her, his mouth on her clitoris, his erection buried deep. Moving, rushing, flying, falling...

Ru closed her eyes, but she could still see his face, masculine and rugged, a perfect counterpoint to her feminine features. Everything about them was opposite: his confidence versus her shyness in bed, her lilting and his deep voice, his strength, her softness. Ru rubbed her hand over his sexy, firm butt, enjoying his low moan. That moan turned to a gasp when she pushed her fingernails into his skin, and she lifted her hips to grind her core against his shaft, sighing when his cock hardened even further.

"Touch me, Fox," she begged.

He pushed her hair off her forehead, his expression soft. "I need you so much, don't doubt that. But I want to take it slow. We only get one time to do this for the first time. I want to savor every stroke, every kiss... I want to watch you fall apart."

His thumbs stroked the cords of her neck, and Ru kissed his mouth again, sucking and teasing his bottom lip. She pulled back to see his satisfied, cocky

smile. God, his confidence turned her on: he had excellent bedroom skills, and he knew it.

"You are so lovely and sexy. Even if you have no
idea that you are," Fox murmured, running his hands
over her rib cage and down her sides, across her ab-
domen, his mouth following the same path down her
body. He finally, finally pulled her panties down and
off, tossing them to the floor. Fox gently spread her
thighs. After looking down with heavy-lidded eyes,
he ducked his head and placed his mouth over her.

She'd never felt completely comfortable with such
intimacy, but Fox made her feel lovely and special,
like he wanted nothing more than to feed her pleasure. Her hand came to rest on his head, holding him
in place as she lifted her hips, needing more of his
tongue, lips and heat.

Fox looked up at her, his eyes the color of the blue
tiles found everywhere in Morocco, bold and brilliant. "You are so wet for me," he told her, his voice
guttural with desire.

"Fox…"

He placed his thumb on her clit, and Ru nearly
launched herself off the bed. "The way you say my
name…"

"Fox…" she drawled, loving the power she had
over him. The power he had over her. "Get inside me."

He moved to her side, braced on his arm, and lowered his head to kiss her. She wanted him joined with
her but couldn't deny his kisses were intoxicating, her
taste on his lips deeply erotic. With every stroke of his

tongue and movement of his lips, he overloaded her senses even further. He moved his hand to her breast and stroked her nipple. He took it in his mouth and, at the same time, spread her thighs further open with his knee and probed her entrance with his erection. His eyes met hers, silently looking for permission.

Ru licked her lips and nodded.

"I don't have a condom," Fox told her, scrunching his eyes closed before cursing. "I mean, I do, but it's in my room...shit."

She was so close to what she knew would be an amazing orgasm, the best sexual experience of her life, and she was not going to put it on hold. "I'm on the pill and I had some tests done when I came back a few weeks ago," she told him. "And it's been a while."

He stared down at her, his head seemingly at war with his libido. *Please don't insist on a condom. Please trust me on this*, she silently begged him.

"'m clean too and I always use a condom. I never take chances, but I can't wait to have you," he told her as he settled himself between her legs, his erection stretching and filling those empty spaces with light and pleasure.

"You are so hot and so tight." Fox waited for her to adjust to him, keeping his pace slow and steady. Ru heard the distant sound of the sea above her loud pants, surprised she could think of anything but her need for him to move, to make her his. But despite lifting her hips, he wouldn't be rushed, and it took far too many lust-soaked minutes until he was as deep as he could go inside her.

She wished he'd move and told him so.

"We only have one first time," Fox whispered in her ear. "Only one time when everything is brand-new. I really want to take my time."

"You're killing me," Ru told him, sounding needy and desperate even to her own ears.

Fox gripped her hips and rocked, keeping his pace steady. How could he remain so in control? She didn't need slow—she needed wild and wicked, crazy, roll-around-the-bed sex.

Enough now.

Lifting her hand, Ru grabbed his chin and forced him to look down at her. His eyebrows lifted, and she swore she saw amusement in his eyes.

"Stop messing around and take me, dammit."

He grinned, his expression devilish. "Are you sure you want that? Sure that you can handle that?" he demanded, his expression turning serious. Ru touched her top lip with her tongue and nodded. Fox didn't hesitate a moment longer; he simply slid his hand under her bottom and launched her up while he thrust into her. When he pulled back, Ru dug her finger-nails into his ass and raised her hips, reveling in his heat and his power.

Ru found his rhythm and immediately loved it, her hips rocking and rolling in time with his. She felt the building pressure, the amalgamation of color behind her eyes, her whole body desperate for that some-times-elusive orgasm. If she lost it now...

Then it rolled over her, color and heat and pleasure, and she spun into it, allowing it to rip her apart in the best way possible. She heard Fox groan her name, his voice ragged. She felt his shudder under her hands and a pulse deep inside her. Then his face was in her neck, his breath loud in her ear.

There was, she thought as her hand skimmed over his hot shoulder, down his spine, only one first time together.

And, yeah, it had been better than amazing.

Okay, inviting Paz to dinner had been, technically, Jacinta's idea, but Avangeline loved art and artists and had happily agreed to have her temporary tenant, the world-famous sculptor, over for a meal. Besides, having enjoyed his risotto a few weeks back, Jace knew she owed him dinner.

It was only polite to reciprocate.

But, unlike him, she didn't feel comfortable inviting him to her apartment within Calcott Manor, to entertain him alone in her private space filled with comfortable couches and throw rugs, photos of her boys in every stage of their journey to adulthood and framed examples of their terrible artwork. Her apartment was where she'd raised Merrick—and the four Grantham boys—where she'd overseen homework and refereed arguments, baked cookies, and listened to teenage angst.

Despite now having grown-up sons, she still regarded her apartment as her mommy space.

Avangeline had provided the boys with the money, the opportunities they needed to find success—Jace was deeply grateful to her for treating Merrick as one of her own—and paid for their superb education, but Jace was the one who picked up the rest of the slack. She was their sounding board, their conscience, the person who demanded discipline and accountability, who kept their feet on the ground. She held hands, wiped away tears, calmed tempers and pulled them back into line...

They said that sometimes it wasn't what you did that was important but who you raised, and Jacinta knew that her greatest accomplishment was raising five well-adjusted, successful, decent men.

But she saw herself clearly: coming from a dirt-poor family, she was well-read but not college educated. She'd had a child in her teens and had struggled for years to support herself and Merrick. That kind of strain left its mark on a person, mentally aging them before their time. And she was twelve years older than Paz, who had constant access to the most glamorous, elegant, sophisticated women the world had to offer.

Jace was a country girl, as deeply rooted at Calcott Manor as Avangeline. She knew about growth seasons and timber prices, polytunnels, and how to fix a fence...

Paz lived and worked in Soho. In the articles she'd read about him, she'd learned that he loved the city and fed off its energy, and he'd said he couldn't imagine living and working anywhere else. And then on top of that, he had an advanced degree in philosophy and was as often lauded for his intelligence as he was for his art.

They said opposites attract, but this was ridiculous.

She was diametrically opposite to the young, sexy, successful women Paz normally dated. His previous girlfriends included esteemed art scholars, museum curators and professors as well as a string of ballet dancers and opera singers. He was attracted to the educated, the smart, the arty, the successful.

And also, so he said, to her. Was she just convenient? A way to pass time? To alleviate his boredom while he was out in the countryside, far from everything the big city had to offer? Until she had answers to some of her questions, possibly all of them, she'd avoid being alone with him.

"Are you going to stand there or are you going to come inside?"

Jace straightened, cursing the fact Paz had caught her loitering at the door of the huge barn he'd rented to construct his latest oversize commission. She squinted into the barn, trying to decipher the tangle of metal in front of her, not able to imagine what it might be. Was it a woman bending over, or a horse? She couldn't tell and didn't want to reveal her ignorance by asking, so she kept quiet.

Instead, she made the mistake of looking at him and, literally, lost her breath. Dammit, she was fifty-something years old. She'd raised five boys and buried one. She shouldn't feel so jittery when confronted with a half-naked man. He was shirtless, his skin glistening with perspiration. His battered jeans rode low on his hips, revealing a flat stomach, sexy hip muscles and a dark happy trail that disappeared beneath the waistband of his pants. She couldn't help noticing that the soft material of his pants cupped a very nice-looking package...

Jacinta slapped her hand over her eyes. Dear God, when had she started noticing a man's package?

Jacinta heard his footsteps coming closer, and she blushed when he peeled her fingers from her eyes. Feeling hot and oh so bothered, she tipped her head back to look at him, taking in the amusement in his eyes and his mischievous expression. His thumb brushed her jaw, and she shivered.

"I don't mind you looking," he told her, his voice low and surprisingly gentle. "Want to see more?"

She did. She really did. Jacinta started to nod and then violently shook her head. What the hell was she thinking? She was not going to sleep with this man. At least, she didn't think so.

Paz lowered his head to nibble her mouth, and Jace was unable to bring herself to pull away. If he'd done anything but play with her mouth, gently sucking her lower lip between his and flicking his tongue against her lips, she would've immediately pulled away. But his touch was so gentle, so exploratory that she put her hand on one hot, bare pec, the heat of his skin branding her hand.

"It's taking all I have not to back you against the wall and kiss you until you are breathless," Paz muttered, his words bouncing off her lips. "I'd love to strip you naked, plunge inside you."

He was so raw, so in-your-face, so open about what he wanted. His honesty scared her. She didn't understand him, nor his attraction to her. And because she couldn't understand it, she did what she always did—she retreated.

Jace ducked to the side and took a few steps back, jamming her hands into the back pockets of her knee-length jean shorts. She rocked on her heels and traced a floorboard with the sole of her slip-on sandal. She felt so out of her depth and ridiculously naive. Unsophisticated. Why hadn't she dated a little more, had a bit more bed-based fun? If she had, then she'd know how to handle this intense man and his deal-with-it honesty.

"Too much?" Paz said before releasing a long sigh. He slipped his hands into the front pockets of his jeans. The action lowered the waistband, and Jace nearly whimpered when she realized he wasn't wearing any underwear.

"What brings you by, sweetheart?"

It took her a little time to drag her eyes up. Nobody'd ever called her sweetheart before, and she liked hearing the endearment on his lips. It made her feel warm... seen. Jace pushed her hand into her thick black hair and pushed the wavy strands back, trying to get her brain to work with her and not against her. "Uh… I've come to invite you for a meal."

His smile dropped ten years off his face. "It's been two weeks, three days, and ten hours since I had you over for a meal. I was wondering if you'd ever reciprocate. When? Where?" he asked. "Will I get to see you naked afterward?"

Jace narrowed her eyes at his cockiness. "I'm inviting you to dinner with Avangeline, her grandson Fox, his assistant, Ru, and Avangeline's guest, Aly Garwood."

His face fell, obviously disappointed. "So I won't get to see you naked?" he asked, his expression woebegone but also amused. Yeah, he wanted her and was letting her know, but she didn't feel pressured.

"Tempting but…no," she replied, keeping her tone light.

If they had dinner alone, she might end up becoming the main course. A prospect that was, at the moment, more terrifying than it was thrilling.

"So, dinner?" Jace crisply asked him. "Yes or no?"

"If it's the only way I'm going to get to see you," he replied, sounding annoyed.

Because she'd raised boys, she immediately recognized the source of his irritation. Paz didn't like not getting his way. Too bad, how sad. Moving closer to him, she lifted her hand to pat his cheek. "Not always getting what you want is good for personal growth, Conway."

He grabbed her hand and laid a hot, open-mouth kiss in the center of her palm, his eyes boring into hers. "I always get what I want, Jacinta. Eventually. And I want you."

Damn, she thought, as a shiver ran down her spine. There was a good possibility of that actually happening.

A sexy sculptor on a mission was very difficult to resist.

"Chase down the revised blueprints for the renovation of the Edinburgh hotel, and I need projected cash flows from Jason," Fox said, not bothering to look up from his monitor.

Who was Jason again?

"Is Jason your chief financial officer?" Ru asked him from her desk in the corner of one of the reception rooms in Calcott Manor. Fox's desk—a lot older, bigger and messier—sat under the window, on the opposite side of the cream-and-mint room. He was far away enough for him to have a private conversation without her hearing every word, close enough for him to call out instructions at her.

Which he did, a lot. Ru had now been working with him for two weeks and had been living at Calcott Manor for ten days. As hard as she tried to separate her emotions, she was finding it increasingly difficult to be the dispassionate personal assistant during the day—biting her tongue didn't come naturally to her—and the passionate lover at night. It was becoming harder to flip the switch from work to sex, from employee to lover. Did that mean that she was sliding deeper into this situation? Was she feeling more emotional about Fox than what was healthy?

Was her imagination playing tricks on her? Was she making more of this than was there because she—miraculously—had yet to feel hemmed in by him, controlled in any way? Last night she'd told him she needed a night on her own, and he'd quickly agreed to allow her some space. And the other evening, when she told him she was going into Hatfield—not informing him she was joining Aly for cocktails, then supper—he hadn't questioned whom she was meeting, where she was going or what time she'd be back. Ru appreciated him allowing her space to move.

But that could be because he primarily saw them as work colleagues who were enjoying some after-work-hours fun. Maybe he didn't ask for more details because he didn't care.

If she was catching feelings, and God, she prayed she wasn't, then it was on her. Three weeks. She just had to play it cool for another twenty-one days and she could leave…

Leave him. Leave the country.

Ru felt a burning sensation between her ribs and pushed her fist into her sternum, hoping to ease the pain. No, she wasn't going to allow him to affect her like this. Work and sex, that's all they were doing here. She would not let her feelings get involved.

Besides, Fox was the last person in the world that

she should fall for. Even if he was interested in a relationship—and he wasn't, as he'd reminded her a few times! — he was an alpha male, a guy who liked calling the shots in bed and out. He might be hands-off when it came to her time and her choices right now, but she couldn't imagine him being as laid-back in a committed relationship. She refused to be controlled, to be told what to do, where to go, how to be. If she ever fell in love, it would be with an easygoing guy who'd allow her the freedom she so desperately needed.

"Yes, Jason is my... Are you even listening to me?"

Ru blinked, and his gorgeous face came into focus. She saw his frown, the flash of frustration in his eyes, and shrugged. "Sorry, I blanked out. Blueprints and cash flow, got it."

Fox leaned back in his chair and linked his fingers over his stomach. "How are you doing with your quest to find me a PA?" he asked, his question coming from out of the blue.

Oh, she hadn't even started looking for her replacement. And she couldn't leave his employ until she found someone to replace her—that was the deal.

But with that said, why was he asking? Was he unhappy with her work? Was he feeling frustrated? Just today, there had been a few tasks she hadn't understood, things she needed him to explain. Alien concepts, business terms she'd never heard of. He'd answered all her questions, but her lack of knowledge made it clear, once again, that she didn't have all the skills he needed for an assistant who was anything other than temporary.

"I'm on it," she lied.

"No hurry." He tipped his head to the side, his amused expression suggesting that he knew she was lying.

He smiled at her. "I'm rather enjoying this visit to Calcott Manor," he added, his voice containing threads of amusement and desire, "and I'm enjoying having you around."

That might be true, but Ru knew that, even if their situation were different, her taking a permanent position as his long-term PA wouldn't be feasible. Out here in Hatfield, Fox wasn't working the same long hours he did in Manhattan, and his pace wasn't nearly as fast. He was, surprisingly, taking it easy. For the last few days, they'd only worked mornings and had skipped off to the beach after lunch to explore the pretty Connecticut coastline, or to do a beach and forest hike. He seemed to only be dealing with his most pressing projects, responding to the most urgent inquiries.

And Ru was, just barely, managing to keep on top of it all. When he went back to Manhattan and to being Fox the Furious and Fast, rejuvenated and raring to go, she knew she couldn't cope with his work demands. She simply didn't have all the skills he needed. He needed another Dot, Ru thought. But she didn't know where to look for a clone of his previous PA.

But maybe, Ru thought, Dot did. Had Fox asked his old PA to find him a new one, or to train someone new? Probably not. And because, as Fox told her, Dot had been planning her wedding and moving house when she left his employ, she likely hadn't thought to offer. But maybe her life had settled down and she could give Ru some input on how and where she could find a Dot 2.0.

Ru dropped her eyes, returning her attention to her monitor, conscious of his eyes on her. Of course he wanted her to stick around—he was getting the best of both worlds, a reasonably intelligent PA and a lover he seemed to enjoy. And while he was having his cake and eating it, she was, too. The job was difficult but rewarding and certainly paid her very well—and outside working hours, she was enjoying some of the best sex of her life. It had been, still was, her choice to sleep with him. She wasn't, in any way, being coerced into sharing his bed. She could stop sleeping with him at any time, and her job wouldn't be jeopardized. She knew that, *trusted* that.

She was the one getting emotionally jumbled up, blurring the lines, complicating what was supposed to be a simple arrangement. And she had to stop it, right now.

She would *not* be the woman who demanded the goalposts be moved simply because her feelings had rocked up, uninvited, to the party. She would not be the woman who ignored reality and wished for the impossible.

Ru heard her phone beep with a message and dived on it, thankful for the reprieve. She picked it up and winced when she saw it was from her mother. Actually, seeing that it was just ten in the morning, and this was her first message today, she was doing well. She'd had two from her dad already. And none from Scott since the wedding, which was, in her mind, a big win.

We impulsively decided to drive to Hatfield and we want to see you. Where can we meet?

Ru released an audible groan. Her parents weren't impulsive people—any trips out of the city demanded days of discussion, route planning and area research. Nope, this "impulsive" trip had likely been in the works since she'd told her parents she was relocating to Hatfield. She'd also told them she was, temporarily, helping Fox by working as his PA.

At least this time she had a decent excuse to blow them off. I'm working, Mom. Sorry.

Her mother must have been watching her phone, because a message popped up on her screen seconds later. We realized that. We've made reservations at the Willow Tree for seven thirty. I'm sure you and Fox will be done with work by then?

Ru dropped her head to the desk and banged her forehead against her keyboard, no doubt sending a string of incomprehensible nonsense across her screen.

Ru heard the scrape of Fox's chair on the wooden floor, his heavy footsteps as he crossed the room to her. She sighed when his hand gripped her neck, his strong fingers immediately finding and digging into the knots. "What's the problem, Ru?"

Ru patted her desk and, without lifting her head, picked up her phone and held it over her shoulder. He took it with his free hand, his other hand still massaging her neck. "Nice place to eat" was his only comment.

Ru reluctantly sat up, and Fox moved to sit on the edge of her desk, facing her. "They are coming to check up on me."

"I figured."

"And on you. And on the state of our relationship," she gabbled.

"We don't have a relationship," Fox pointed out—unnecessarily in her opinion. He knew that, she knew that—he didn't need to keep repeating it.

Ru glared at him. "I know that, but they don't!"

"I suppose you want me to come to dinner with you?" Yeah, she'd heard no enthusiasm in his question.

No, she didn't, not if he was going to resent being there. She would rather go by herself than feel like he was doing her an enormous favor.

"No, please don't bother," she told him, keeping her tone businesslike. "I'll tell them that you have a meeting with people in another time zone. That you'll join us later if the meeting doesn't run too long."

He nodded and then scrubbed his hands up and

down his face. He stared down at his shoes and rubbed his hand along his jaw. "Look, Ru, I just... I..."

Wow, Fox Grantham short on words. That had to be a first.

He dropped an F-bomb and met her eyes, his expression rueful. "Look, I don't want to be a dick, but we agreed that our fake relationship for your family's sake was a one-night deal."

It had been. He'd attended the wedding with her, had acted like her significant other, and that had been that. Their arrangement did not include subsequent meals with her overprotective parents. She could, and would, handle them on her own. She'd been doing it for a long time. When it came to Fox, sex and work was all they had. They both wanted it that way.

Both of them. Definitely.

"It's fine, Fox," she told him before leaning back in her chair. She crossed her legs and gestured to her desk. "I've got a lot to do..." she hinted.

His eyes met hers, a little confused, a lot wary. He looked like he was about to say something personal. Ru hoped he wouldn't. If he referred to their nonexistent relationship one more time, she might just brain him with the heavy-duty stapler to the right of her screen. She got it, she did. She didn't need him to remind her.

Thankfully, Fox took her hint and stood up. She watched him as he returned to his desk and dropped into his chair. She pulled up her email program, conscious of his eyes on her face. She bit her lip and started to compose her email to the CFO, ignoring him.

Work now.

Sex later.

That was all they had going on.

But she was terrified that this one, supposedly simple, choice could change her thoughts, her attitude to relationships. And her destiny.

Nine

He'd been an ass earlier, Fox conceded, as he paid the bill for their dinner at the Willow Tree, Hatfield's most exclusive restaurant. He'd had a nice evening and a very decent meal. Ru's parents were cosmopolitan, well-read people—her dad was also funny as hell, her mom innately charming—and he'd enjoyed himself more than he expected to.

He'd arrived at the restaurant a half hour late, much to Ru's astonishment. Before greeting her parents and apologizing for his tardiness, he kissed Ru's mouth and tasted her shock and a hint of gratitude. Throughout the evening, it had felt natural to hold her hand, to put his arm around her shoulder. He'd never been into public displays of affection, but touching Ru was instinctive—half the time he only realized his hand was on her knee or he was stroking her arm when he needed both hands.

As for being an ass, he shouldn't have made such an issue about going to dinner, insisting *yet again* that they weren't in a relationship. She knew the parameters—he didn't need to keep reminding her. But there was a better-than-good chance he kept repeating it in order to remind himself, not her. The thought made him press the nib of the pen deeper into the flimsy credit card receipt, tearing the slip as he dashed his signature across it.

She stood on the other side of the glass door to the restaurant, her hand tucked into the crook of her dad's elbow, her head on his shoulder. Despite her frustration with their overbearing ways—thankfully, there had been only a few references to her staying Stateside this evening, and none were pointed enough to start a fight between them—he knew Ru loved her parents, and their adoration of her was obvious, even if it wasn't always expressed in the healthiest way. But even that was understandable, given what they'd gone through. There could be nothing worse than not knowing where your child was and whether she was safe.

But he also understood Ru's need to live her life on her own terms. Maybe, with some in-depth dialogue and clear boundaries in place, they could find a solution that didn't necessitate her living halfway across the world. And didn't he sound like a life coach?

But, Fox suspected, the only thing that would give

her parents true peace of mind was knowing that Ru had someone in her life, someone to rely on, to protect her. Someone, at the very least, who knew where she was, what she was doing, where she was supposed to be. Oh, not the minutiae of her day, but in a general "hey, I'm going out for a drink with my girlfriends, I'll be back by midnight" terms. Someone who'd know where to start looking if something went horribly wrong again. With her hopping from country to country, city to city on a whim, how could they rest easy knowing that if the unimaginable happened to her again, they wouldn't know how to find her or where to look?

But Ru was a free spirit, and the quickest way to lose her was to try and control her. She refused to be a victim, and he admired that about her. She had the choice to live a comfortable, protected, easy, and financially secure life, but she'd chosen to do something different, to make her own way, to taste the world.

She was unusual, Fox silently admitted as he slowly slid his card back into its slot in his wallet. She was funny, brave and outspoken, bold and sometimes belligerent. Best of all, he didn't intimidate her. And because she gave as good as she got, he was far more relaxed working with her than he normally was. Which actually made him nicer to be around. More than one person had hinted on it in the teleconference meetings he'd had since coming to Connecticut.

Jack flat out asked him what he'd done with his

grumpy bastard of a brother and Merrick sent him a thermometer so that he could check his temperature.

Assholes.

When he and Ru left work behind them, things just got better. Sometimes they ate together, and sometimes he ate with his grandmother, Jacinta and Alyson—his grandmother had banned him from discussing her lack of a will and Aly's connection to Malcolm, so their meals were pleasant enough—but he always ended up in the apartment she occupied at some point during the night. And before, after and sometimes between their lovemaking sessions, they talked. About movies and books and politics, sports and travel. Neither of them raised the deep issues—his parents, their secrets or her abduction—but he sensed that if one of them did, the other would listen.

Sometimes, he still found it impossible to believe that this woman, dressed in a creamy white, short-sleeved polka dot–print dress that hit her ankles—how could something that long and simple look so sexy on her?—knew his darkest secrets, the ones he'd do anything to keep. Yet her knowledge of his parents' vices didn't cause him a moment of lost sleep. He knew without hesitation that she'd never repeat to another living soul anything he told her. And that meant that he trusted her…on some level, at least.

Any type of trust was so damn rare. The only people he truly trusted were his brothers, Avangeline and Jacinta. Family, in other words.

The people he loved…

Ru turned her head to look at him, and her soft smile, the deepening of those double dimples, hit him like a fist in his stomach. Fox swallowed the lump in his throat as he stepped through the door the maître d' opened. Ru left her father's side and slipped her hand into his, turning her face to look up at him. "I'm with you, Fox. I took a cab so I could have a glass of wine or two."

He squeezed her fingers and held out his hand for her dad to shake. "It was good to see you again, sir." After dropping Mazdak's hand, Fox kissed Taranah's cheek, and she gave him a small hug. He waved away her thanks for joining them and paying for dinner. It had been, he assured her with complete sincerity, a lovely evening.

After Ru hugged her parents and said good night, they stood on the sidewalk and watched them cross the road to make the short walk back to their hotel. Ru reached for his hand again, his slim fingers sliding between his. "Thank you for coming," she told him quietly. "I appreciate it."

He turned his head to drop a kiss on her hair. "I had fun," he told her. He took a deep breath and released the words he knew he had to say. "I'm sorry I was an ass earlier."

He hoped she wouldn't ask him to explain *why* he had been an ass, and, because she was completely wonderful and didn't play games, she didn't. Neither did she let him off the hook. "Yep, you were. But because you showed up and treated us all to dinner, you are forgiven."

As he said, so easy, so natural, no drama. And once again, he caught himself imagining her in his life for a period that exceeded the short weeks they had left together. And that scared the shit out of him. When he thought of the future, he was supposed to think of the company, their projects, bigger and bolder, not about a woman or romantic entanglements. He'd never been able to imagine having a long-term partner, someone permanently in his life. But, dammit, he kept catching flashes of her in his future.

Terrifying.

Fox took a deep breath and was grateful to see his car pull up, enjoying the thrill on the young valet's face of having his hands on the wheel of such an exceptional vehicle. Fox opened the passenger door for Ru and picked up the hem of her dress so that it didn't catch in the door before he pushed it closed. He walked around the hood to the driver's seat, slipping the young man a substantial tip. Feeling both tired and wired, he was about to pull off into the surprisingly busy traffic on Main Street when Ru's hand on his thigh had him looking over at her.

In the shadows cast by the yellow streetlights and the passing headlights, he saw her serious expression. She rubbed her jaw with the fingers of her free hand, and Fox knew that she was looking for her words, the best way to say something he knew he wasn't going to like hearing.

"I'm never going to ask you for something you can't give, Fox," she quietly stated. "I've gotten all your messages loud and clear. You don't want a relationship, and I'm flying to Australia in a few weeks. You don't have to keep reminding me that we don't and will never have a relationship, okay?"

What else could he do but nod?

But what if, somewhere deep inside him, maybe, possibly, he wanted that?

Ten minutes later they were back at Calcott Manor, and Ru, in the galley kitchen of the apartment, poured herself a glass of water and walked across the living room onto the balcony. It was where they always sat. Why would anyone want to be inside when the night was so magical and sensual? The sea provided the music, the stars the decoration and the air was both warm and fragrant. Hatfield, and Calcott Manor, were fast becoming two of her favorite places.

"Dinner was more enjoyable than I expected it to be," she told Fox as he sat down beside her on the armless, super-comfortable couch. His hand found her thigh, and Ru looked down at his long fingers, the raised veins on his big hands. She wondered if he realized how often he touched her. Sometimes it seemed he was unaware he was, and she wondered if was, subconsciously, looking for a connection.

"Well done on not rising to their stay-in-the-country comments," Fox told her.

It had been hard, but she'd bitten her tongue and

deliberately changed the subject. It helped that Fox was there and that they'd all been determined to enjoy the evening at the excellent restaurant. But her parents weren't subtle people, and she'd seen the hope in their eyes that Fox was the man who'd make her settle down, who'd keep her safe and corralled. There was no chance of that—not even Fox could wield that much power over her.

Ru had had a stern, get-real-now talk with herself earlier while she dressed for dinner, reminding herself that she couldn't be tied down, put into a box— she needed freedom as much as she needed air to breathe. That was why she had broken engagements, why she had dumped more than a few serious boyfriends back before she'd learned not to let things get serious. They were all lovely men, but they had one fatal flaw in common: they all needed more from her than she could give. Commitment. For her to have a nine-to-five job, to live a conventional nine-to-five life in a single, unchanging location.

Fox didn't expect that from her. As he kept telling her, he just wanted her help in the office and a few more weeks of good sex. Then he'd let her go without any drama or fuss. Annoyingly, the idea of him waving her off with a smile on his face made her heart hurt. But leaving was what she did, who she was.

She ran away from men who wanted her to stay. And wanted to stay with the man who expected her to leave.

Ru was distracted from her tumultuous thoughts

by Fox pulling her hair back and dropping a soft kiss on her neck, his tongue flickering gently against her skin. Her blood heated as his hand lifted her dress, sliding under the cotton to caress her bare thigh. This she knew…the thrum of her blood, the bold beat of her heart. Making love with Fox was what she was good at—what they excelled at—and Ru was happy to push her wild thoughts and pulsing emotions aside to focus on physical pleasure.

Fox sat up, leaned over her, and his hand caressed the curve of her bottom. Her stomach twitched, and her insides quivered. Fox's mouth came down to hers, and his tongue slipped between her lips, spinning her away on a fire-hot band of lust and want.

Yes, this she understood.

Fox's finger slid under the band of her panties and stroked the folds of flesh beneath the insubstantial fabric, his touch so gentle but so erotic. Her hips tilted, and she reached up into his touch, silently urging him to increase the pressure, but his movements were unhurried. While they'd had lots of fast, hot, up-against-the-wall and in-the-shower sex, tonight he seemed determined to go slow, choosing gentleness and tenderness over heat and urgency. She wasn't sure she felt comfortable with him slowing down. Heat and passion were easy to understand, but these gentler emotions? Not so much.

Fox removed his hand, pulled her up and tugged her dress over her head, looking down at her matching lacy white underwear with obvious approval. He dragged his fingers across the swell of her covered breast. "So pretty," he told her.

He took his time removing her bra and panties, painting her skin with kisses as he dropped the lacy garments. In contrast, he wasted no time divesting himself of his clothes.

But instead of pushing her down into the comfortable cushions of the overlarge couch, Fox dropped to his knees, his shoulders forcing her thighs apart. He kissed his way down her torso, laving her nipples and dipping his tongue into her belly button, gently nibbling on her hip bone. This was sexual teasing in its purest form, she decided. But it wasn't enough...

She needed the heat of sex to burn away her inconvenient thoughts about him and their relationship, to remind her heart that her libido was in charge. Going slow gave her too much time to think, to wish for things that had no possibility of materializing. No, fast was better.

Heat and intensity... She needed to be with him, completed by him, and have Fox, hot and thick and desperate, inside her. Half sitting up, she curled her hands around his biceps and dug her fingernails into those big muscles. She waited for him to look up and into her eyes. When he did, they blazed a bright blue, filled with heat and desire. And desperation. He was a man on the edge.

He was someone who needed only what she could give.

"Come inside me," she told him, her voice raspy. "I need you inside me. Now."

If it sounded like she was begging, she didn't care. She was beyond playing it cool, pretending. She wanted him. Now.

"Condom," he told her, the word coming out deep and growly.

Ru felt a surge of frustration. Despite knowing she was on the pill, he had used condoms every time they made love after that first time.

"Pill," she insisted. She squeezed his arms again, silently asking him to trust her again, to relinquish control in this one thing. She had this covered—he just needed to believe. Trust.

She hadn't expected him to acquiesce, to take the chance, and Ru gasped when his hand slid under her lower back, lifted her hips and he slid inside her in one long, sure, deep stroke.

He groaned, and she wrapped her legs around his thighs, hooking her ankles just above his truly spectacular ass. She couldn't stop her hands from reaching to hold his face, seeking his mouth, their tongues echoing the thrusts down below.

This was supreme pleasure, and Ru was lost within it. When they were joined like this, they made sense, created music and painted masterpieces. Their bodies knew each other, knew when to retreat, when to push for more. Knew how to touch, to love, to comfort and reassure.

Ru felt herself climb, felt her eyes dim and her body start to shake, and she wondered, just before she fell apart, why their brains and scarred hearts couldn't be as brave.

* * *

"Your grandmother has asked me to catalog her family photographs, Fox," Aly said, sitting on the edge of a white couch in Avangeline's favorite sitting room. They were having a drink before dinner, waiting for the arrival of Paz Conway, the sculptor. Ru was excited to meet the world-renowned artist. "Your parents were incredibly photogenic."

Ru took a sip of her wine, darting a look at Fox, who stood—in a true heir-of-the-manor way—with his arm resting on the marble mantelpiece, staring down into the huge, empty fireplace. She doubted that anyone noticed the tightening of the corners of his mouth, the flash of discomfort in his Majorelle-blue eyes.

"Yes, they were an attractive couple," he replied, just on the right side of polite. "So were Soren's parents."

He'd promised Jace he'd be on his best behavior tonight, which meant not riling up his grandmother about writing her will or throwing pointed barbs at Aly.

She liked Aly, Ru decided. She was glad that she'd carved out some time to get to know her. She sensed that given time, they could become good friends. Possibly even great friends. Oh, it was obvious, to her at least, that Aly had a deeply personal reason to be at Calcott Manor—something other than receiving an organ from Malcolm—but, unlike Fox, she didn't believe that Aly was out to harm the family in any way.

If anything, Ru sensed a deep desire within Aly to protect the Granthams.

But how? And from what?

"Jason and Gretchen, Soren's parents, spent more time in Europe than they did here in the States, Aly, while Jesse and Heather were very socially active," Avangeline told her. "They entertained often and were incredibly hospitable."

Ru thought about what Fox told her about his parents and wondered exactly what type of parties they threw...

Did Fox have these thoughts? Whenever his parents were mentioned, did he automatically go...*there*? And if he did, how difficult it must be for him.

Ru looked down at her glass of wine and tightened her grip on the stem of her glass. It would be one thing to know that his parents enjoyed a bit of kink. Maybe that knowledge would be a little embarrassing, in the way it was always awkward to think of your parents as sexual people, but that on its own wouldn't have been a big deal. But knowing they'd used just legal sex workers—too young in her opinion—and that his mom's tastes were seriously dark, possibly dangerous, had to be a heavy cross to bear. And he'd kept that knowledge to himself for over a decade.

"Was your dad in good shape, Fox?" Aly asked, rubbing the biceps of her left arm. "He looks athletic in the photographs. Did he work out? Run? Was he sporty?"

Ru lifted her head to look at her new friend, surprised at the hint of demand she heard in her questions. What was she trying to get at? Why did she care whether Jesse Grantham exercised or not?

Avangeline, happy to talk about her sons, answered Aly's question. "Jesse was a runner. He went for a run most days and took part in those long, long races—" She looked at Fox. "What did you call them, Fox?"

"Ultramarathons, Avangeline."

Avangeline nodded. "He did many of those, and he won several medals for them. They are in the attic somewhere. Jason preferred books to exercise. His wife, Gretchen, was a swimmer and Soren got his talent for swimming, we presume, from her." Avangeline looked at the exquisitely carved freestanding clock in the corner of the room. It was, as Avangeline had told her earlier, a Chippendale walnut tall-case clock, dating back to the late eighteenth century. "Where is the sculptor, Jacinta?"

"It's only five to. He's not late." Jace shot up from her seat next to Ru, a hint of panic on her face. Ru cocked her head and noticed that Jace's high cheekbones were awash with color. "But I'll go and wait for him by the door."

What was that about? Why was Jace as jumpy as a cat on a hot tin roof? Shrugging, Ru returned her attention to the conversation. Aly was still talking about Fox's parents. "I came across your father's logbook, Fox. He seemed to have been a talented pilot."

"He was an *excellent* pilot," he replied. Fox narrowed his eyes at Aly. "You really are digging into our family, Ms. Garwood. What are you hoping to find?"

"I'm just trying to find out more about the family of the man who saved my life, Fox," Aly quietly replied.

"Why don't I believe you?" Fox demanded.

"Because you are cynical and mistrusting?" Aly countered.

Fair enough, Ru thought. But she understood Fox's wariness of Aly. She also got the feeling that Aly was after something. Oh, not money or something of commercial value, but information, possibly a missing piece of the puzzle. But what could it be?

Fox pointed a finger at her, his expression as cold as a polar blizzard. "I will not let anyone hurt my family, Ms. Garwood, so I suggest you tread very carefully indeed." He looked at the clock and then at his grandmother. "I'm sure I heard someone knock. I'm going to find out what the holdup is."

Avangeline nodded, and when Fox left the room, Ru picked up her glass of wine and took a long sip. The silence was broken by Aly. "I'm sorry, Avangeline, I didn't mean to upset Fox."

Avangeline waved her bony hand in the hair, an impressive diamond flashing. "Fox has been upset about his parents for a long, long time, Aly."

"Losing them both so young must've had such an impact on him," Aly murmured her agreement.

"That, too," Avangeline murmured, and Ru cocked her head to the side. Now, what did Fox's grandmother mean by that cryptic statement? But, as Fox's PA—and his part-time lover—she wasn't in a position to ask.

"What is keeping them? Dear Lord, if I am going to be made to wait, then I will need another drink. Bourbon, please, Alyson, and make it a strong one."

Jacinta walked into the impressive hallway of Calcott Manor, happy to be away from Avangeline's probing eyes. The old lady knew her far too well, and she'd raised an eyebrow when Jace walked into the room, a little unsteady on her rarely worn heels.

Ridiculously, Jace wanted to open the door to Paz, to have five minutes alone with him. To see his reaction to her flirty black cocktail dress instead of her usual jeans and T-shirt. She'd pulled her thick hair up into a casual twist, tendrils framing her face, squirted perfume between her breasts and on her wrists, and she'd spent far too much time on her makeup.

She'd made an effort…a hell of one, and she hoped Paz noticed. And she hoped she'd manage to serve dinner without any mishaps in these damn heels. Dropping the boeuf bourguignon wouldn't get her fired, but it would definitely raise some eyebrows. She didn't need her family to wonder why she was off her game.

So she'd greet Paz first, pull herself together and act like the adult she very much was.

Well, that was the plan.

Hearing his footsteps on the stairs outside, she reached for the door and, at the very last second, reminded herself to wait for him to knock. He did, and she forced herself to wait thirty seconds longer before opening the door. When she did and saw him, she couldn't help lifting her hand to her heart and sighing. God, she was so pathetic. But, dressed in smart black pants and an open-neck white shirt, cuffs buttoned, his hair brushed back from his face, he looked sexy-smart. He also held what looked to be a very fine bottle of wine in his hand.

"Hi, come on in," she told him, pulling open the ornate front door. She frowned when he hesitated and noticed his smile looked a little strained.

He thrust the bottle at her. "I hope this is okay."

Since it was a bottle of sauvignon blanc from the famous Screaming Eagle wine estate, she was sure it would be just fine. "That's nice of you," she said, wondering why he was making no move to come inside. She was also a little irked he hadn't commented on her dress, her hair or how good she smelled. It wasn't like Paz to not notice or hold back.

"Everything okay?" she asked, frowning.

"Yes…no." Paz rubbed his jaw, looking uncertain and ill at ease. "Can you come out here for a second? I have something I need to tell you, and I don't want to be overheard."

The rest of the family were a long way away, but Jacinta didn't bother to tell him that. Instead, she followed him outside, stepping over onto the old tiles toward one of the marble columns that were a feature of Calcott Manor's portico.

"I picked up the mail as you asked. There was nothing but this," Paz said.

Jacinta watched as Paz pulled a postcard from his back pocket and handed it over to her. It was just lines of code, more gibberish, and she shrugged. She'd told him that Avangeline routinely received postcards from a lover. In a bid to impress her, Paz had revealed his code-breaking skills and had easily deciphered the lines of the code on the first postcard he'd seen a few weeks ago. It had proven to be what seemed like a love letter, making them both feel a bit ashamed for intruding into Avangeline's private business. This didn't look to be any different.

"I'll give it to Avangeline later." She gestured to the hallway. "We should go—the family will be wondering where we are."

Paz nodded and Jace turned away, still annoyed that she'd gone to such an effort to look nice when he hadn't even noticed. "Jace…there's a problem," Paz said, his tone serious.

She turned back to look at him. "What do you mean? A problem with what?"

Paz nodded at the postcard in her hand. "With that."

The postcard? She flipped it over from the front—it was a mildly erotic depiction of a naked redheaded woman curled up on a chair—to peer at the lines of code.

"It's a Gustav Klimt painting, Danae," Paz explained. "Sorry, that's not important."

She lifted her eyes and frowned at Paz. "Did you decode the message?" she demanded. They'd agreed he wouldn't do that again, that it was a massive invasion of Avangeline's privacy.

Paz, to his credit, looked uncomfortable. "It's so damn easy to do," he muttered. Paz pushed his hand through his hair. "Look, I know this has absolutely nothing to do with me, and I have spent the afternoon debating whether to tell you this or not…"

"Tell me what?" Jace demanded when he hesitated.

"Shit. Look, apart from the weird message, the postcard is definitely written in a different hand from the other one. It was written by someone else."

She stared at him, nonplussed. "I don't understand."

Paz took the postcard from her and jabbed his finger at the writing. "Different writer, Jace! Look at the blocky letters, the way he digs the pen into the paper." He shrugged. "I'm an artist, and things like this stand out to me. Avangeline has two people writing in the same code to her, and—" he flicked the corner of the postcard with his index finger "—unlike the other one, this isn't a love note."

Oh, God. Jacinta felt sick. "What does it say?"

Paz hesitated, and Jacinta grabbed his arm, pushing her nails into the fabric of his shirt. "That woman is my employer, my best friend and. I will do anything to protect her. What does it say?"

Paz hesitated, sighed and then took the postcard from her, frowning. "This is a reminder that I know

396 THEIR TEMPORARY ARRANGEMENT

who your secret lover is. Would your family approve? I also know about the basement. The clock is ticking so write your will per the instructions I sent you. And I require another payment to tide me over."

Jacinta frowned. A basement? What the hell did that mean?

"Jace, she's being blackmailed," Paz said, looking uncomfortable.

"Shit." Jacinta lifted her hands to her mouth, feeling stricken. Who was threatening Avangeline? And why?

"I don't know what to do, Paz," Jacinta told him, her voice rising. "Do I speak to Avangeline about this, keep quiet, talk to the boys? What do I do?"

"Talk to us about what? What's going on?"

Jacinta spun around to see Fox in the doorway to the house, anger and fear blazing in his eyes. He folded his arms across his chest, spread his feet and glared at her, ignoring Paz. "What's going on, Jace? And don't you dare say nothing... I heard you say something about a basement, and I want to know what it was."

Knowing how impossibly stubborn Fox could be, Jacinta knew she had no other choice but to tell him. So, as quickly as she could, she explained that his grandmother received coded messages on the postcards—that the previous one Paz had decoded had been from a lover, but that this one was different, written by someone else. When Jacinta told him what this latest postcard said, her unemotional, broody boy swayed on his feet, the color draining from his face.

"Fuck!" Fox muttered, linking his hands behind his head and staring at the dark driveway and the terraced gardens. And at that moment, seeing his fear, Jacinta reached out to Paz, thankful when his hand enclosed hers, giving her the silent support she needed.

Something dark and malevolent had invaded their world, something cruel and heartless. It would cause tears and pain, possibly split open souls. This was something they would all need to face, to meet, to duel with and destroy.

But they'd weathered dark times before and would survive this storm, too. It was what they did, how she'd raised her boys. They didn't buckle; they didn't bend. Gathering herself, Jacinta took the postcard from Fox's hand and released Paz's hand. She lifted her palm to grip Fox's jaw, as she had when he was a kid and she'd wanted his attention. "We're going to go into dinner and we're not going to say a word. In the morning, we will sit down and discuss this rationally and sensibly. You will not go off half-cocked! Do you hear me?"

Fox held her gaze for a minute, but eventually, his shoulders sagged and he nodded. "Yeah, okay."

"Promise?"

"Yeah."

Jacinta released a soft sigh and nodded. She walked into the house and looked at the bottle of wine she'd forgotten was in her hand. Damn, she needed one or five glasses, immediately.

The cat is most definitely out of the bag and, for the first time in my life, I am tempted to hand this problem over to Fox, to let him and his brothers deal with it. But that would be handing over control, and that is not something I can do. This is my problem, the consequences of my choices.

I know they are frustrated with me because I won't tell them who my lover is—but our love is private, wonderful, and it exists in the shadows. It would wilt and then crumble if exposed to the harsh glare of being in the limelight and would buckle under the judgement of those who don't understand. I will spend any amount of money—and I have—to protect what we have.

It has sustained me and was, during those darkest days after the twins died, the glue holding me together. I cannot, will not, give it up.

And what the hell is the basement?

Ten

By the next afternoon, after a long-ass, brutal day that included confronting his grandmother—who kept insisting that the postcards had nothing to do with him and that she was handling it—Fox knew three things for sure.

His grandmother was being blackmailed and had sent millions in cryptocurrency— the transactions were completely untraceable— to the blackmailer for nearly a year, dammit. But the blackmailer, apparently worried that his cash cow would stop producing milk when she died, had recently demanded Avangeline make provision for him in her will, via an untraceable foreign entity registered in the Cayman Islands. Fox didn't know who was blackmailing her, or why, but he suspected that Avangeline did. And his stubborn grandmother wouldn't share her suspicions with him. Nor would she consider going to the police.

The only bright spot was that Avangeline, thank God, seemed truly baffled by the reference to the Basement. As far as he could establish, given that his grandmother was being astoundingly non-communicative and implacable— she was handling this, he didn't have to worry— someone was blackmailing Avangeline by threatening to release the identity of her long-term lover.

No, the Basement was not on her radar. Thank God. But somebody did know about it and was prepared to use the knowledge to coerce her.

But if his grandmother didn't know about his parents' extracurricular activities, then how could the identity of her lover be so damaging or embarrassing that she'd give in to the blackmailer? And in the twenty-first century, a decades-old relationship, even an affair, wasn't enough to cause an uproar or be the basis for blackmail.

Fox rubbed the back of his neck as he walked across the bright green lawn to the apartment over the garage. After hours of keeping his cool, remaining calm in the presence of his tight-lipped but panicked grandmother, he needed to talk, to vent, to rage. Ru was who and what he needed. She would give him perspective and help him make sense of his suddenly upside-down life.

On approaching the apartment, he looked toward the beach and saw her slight figure in the distance.

She stood on the shoreline, the waves rolling up and over her toes. Even from a distance, he could see she was smiling, deepening her incredible dimples. The late-afternoon sun bounced sunbeams off her hair, making her dark curls glint, and he smiled as she stretched out her arms and lifted her face to the sky, arching her back, completely open to the elements.

He'd missed her today. And last night.

After dinner the previous evening, he'd been disconcerted by Jacinta's revelations and desperately needed some time alone to think. Unable to explain what he didn't understand, he'd told Ru he needed to work late and brushed off her offer to stay. From the darkened study, he'd watched her walk across the lawn to the apartment and only turned away from the window when he saw the lights go off in the bedroom upstairs. He'd wanted to run to her, to lose himself in her, in her scent, the strength of her arms, the taste of her mouth.

Instead, he'd sat in the dark behind his desk, feet up, and contemplated his course of action.

Avangeline wanted him to butt out, but there was no way he would do that. He was not going to stand to the side and let his eighty-two-year-old grandmother deal with this on her own. Sure, it was going to be difficult to find the blackmailer without Avangeline's cooperation, but he wouldn't let that stop him.

And, dammit, he had to find the blackmailer before he revealed his parents' connection to the Basement. Because that story—the secret, salacious lives of the supposedly clean-cut, wealthy and famous all-American couple—would make headlines in a heartbeat, and the story would race around the world. Avangeline would be mortified, Jack gutted, and his family name would no longer be associated with fine dining and entrepreneurship but with his parents' sexual extremes. He would not let that happen.

Fox looked at Ru, knowing that if he walked down to her, if she took his hand and asked him if he was okay, he'd spill his guts. He'd look into her eyes, and the words would drop from his lips—within ten minutes, she'd know everything he did. The strands binding them together would tighten, and when it came time for her to leave, he'd find it difficult to let her go.

But if he left Calcott Manor today, alone, if he left her with no explanation, it would snap those strands, fray the rope. She was, as she'd told him, leaving in a few weeks anyway. He was just bringing the inevitable forward.

So instead of joining her on the beach, he'd be smart and head back to his study. He'd leave a note for her, a list of tasks she could complete while he was away, along with instructions to contact Jack if anything urgent arose. He'd tell his brothers that he needed some time away, that he'd be in contact in a few days, maybe a week.

He was going hunting—for information first. Then people.

Avangeline would be suspicious about his sudden departure, but if she wasn't prepared to explain, neither was he.

He darted another look at Ru, knowing that at any minute she might turn and see him. If he was going to leave without talking to her, then he had to do it now. He couldn't tell her, especially since he had no intention of telling Jack or his other brothers of this latest plot twist in their lives.

What would be the point of burdening them with this knowledge? Jack would have his image of his happy family shattered, Soren would start to question what he thought he knew about his own parents and Merrick would feel frustrated at not being able to do anything. No, they didn't need to know, and neither did Ru. He would deal with his grandmother's blackmailing problem himself.

If Avangeline had deep and dark secrets, then he was the one who could handle them. After all, he held the biggest secret that could rip all their lives, and the Grantham-Forrester legacy, apart. He was best placed to serve and protect, since he couldn't be shocked or hurt or disappointed much more than he already was.

He knew what he needed to do—and he knew he'd have to face it alone. Because being alone, operating alone, was how he worked best.

But to do that, he needed to leave Calcott Manor—and Ru—behind.

A week later, Fox steered his car up the hill, sighing when Calcott Manor came into view. He was home, the place he'd most wanted to be for the past week.

He pulled his car into a space in the garage and glanced at his cell phone, grimacing at the notifications of emails and texts that had appeared since he left the city. No doubt more than a few were from Ru, asking him to call her, to let her know he was okay.

Yeah, walking out on her without a goodbye—except for a note full of work instructions—and ghosting her attempts to contact him hadn't been cool. He wasn't proud of the way he'd acted, but how could he talk to her, respond when he wasn't sure he could stop himself from telling her he needed her, begging her to come to him? He'd missed her on a soul-deep, *this sucks* level.

And he hated that she made him feel so off balance, that his thoughts always went to her and that she had the power to sidetrack him.

He had a job to do, to find his grandmother's blackmailer, and he wouldn't let a woman with double dimples and stunning eyes—and a heart as big as the sky—distract him. And by the time he was done with this blackmail saga, by the time he'd cleared away this layer of nastiness hovering over Avangeline's head, Ru would be in Australia. Fox did not doubt that he'd be back to working long hours, growing Grantham International, not stopping until his surname was synonymous with luxurious hotels and fine dining. He owed that to Malcolm, and to Avangeline.

His world would return to normal. It would be Ru-free but normal.

Unfortunately, he hadn't gotten very far in his quest to track down the blackmailer. He'd considered Tommy, his parents' partner in crime, the manager of the Basement, but there was no way Tommy could know about the postcards, nor was he smart enough to set up a bank account in the Cayman Islands. The only other possibility he'd thought of was to contact his paternal grandfather, because Patrick had known his grandmother as a young woman. He'd thought that he might be able to, if he asked the right questions—there was no way he'd let him know his grandmother was being blackmailed—steer him in the direction of someone from Avangeline's past who was capable of blackmail.

So he'd flown to the West Coast, intent on tracking down his paternal grandfather, the man he only dimly recalled. His grandfather had played coy and had taken his time debating whether he wanted to see Fox or not, punishing him for not coming to kiss the ring sooner. When they did finally meet, Patrick controlled their conversation, ignoring or deflecting Fox's questions.

Fox had been forced to listen to Patrick rehash his and Avangeline's divorce, telling Fox over and over that he was never given the credit he was due for his part in making her business empire as successful as it was. That his grandmother was a difficult and nasty woman, and that she'd loved her company far more than she loved him, and he'd hated playing second fiddle. Patrick's comments stung Fox far more than they should have. Was he following in Avangeline's footsteps and making Grantham International his entire focus, to the point of neglecting his personal life?

Short answer? Yes.

Not that that meant Patrick had a leg to stand on when it came to his claims that he'd somehow been wronged. Yeah, his grandparents had had an ugly divorce, but it had happened over thirty years ago and Avangeline had paid him an enormous settlement, one of the biggest ever to make a spouse go away. The old man was rich; he wore a Rolex watch and designer threads, and his driver ferried him around in a very expensive, very new Range Rover.

Patrick also owned a bunch of properties on the West Coast, still had controlling shares in an enormous, profitable construction company and had an extremely healthy stock portfolio. He had no right to whine. He also, Fox was relieved to note, had no reason to be blackmailing Avangeline himself. Which meant that Fox could go back to pretending his grandfather didn't exist. Life was much more pleasant that way.

He'd always had the feeling that successful relationships were rare in the Forrester-Grantham family, but meeting his grandfather reinforced his suspicions. He'd detailed a dreadful marriage, rife with distrust and disrespect. Underneath the glitz and the glam, his parents' marriage had been the same—a sham. And Fox knew that as he dug deeper, as he revealed more layers, the picture would get darker and more dreadful. Possibly nastier.

And that's why he wanted to spare his brothers from what the layers revealed. He was already jaded and cynical, disappointed by his parents—he didn't need his brothers, especially Jack, to feel the same way.

Ru had no connection to his parents, no reason to be affected by any scandal involving them, except for whatever secondhand sympathy she felt for him. But keeping her in the dark was the right decision, too—he was sure of it. He couldn't keep turning to her with his problems. Not when he had to get used to her not being around.

Before he did something stupid like fall in love with her, he was going to jump on the brakes and avoid the multicar pileup just down the road. His leaving Calcott Manor and having time away from her, with no communication, was supposed to prepare himself for her being gone.

In theory, it had been, was, a good idea. In practice, it had been hell on wheels. And, judging by her increasingly irate messages, Ru didn't appreciate him not checking in. Given her complaints about her parents and control, that was rather ironic—but he was pretty sure she wouldn't appreciate him saying so.

In their temporary office, Ru was climbing walls.

She pushed back her chair, gripped the edge of her desk, and stared at the blank screen of her phone, willing it to ring. She hadn't spoken to Fox in a week, and her last communication with him had been a series of bullet-pointed tasks he wanted completed. Hurt by his abrupt departure and his lack of explanation—

or even a goodbye—she'd used work as a distraction, but she'd finished those tasks by the end of day two.

In between sending him increasingly irate text and email messages demanding to know where he was, and asking him to please get in touch, she'd been twiddling her thumbs, left adrift with nothing to do. With all the time on her hands, she'd finally gotten around to contacting his old PA, Dot, and between them, they'd crafted a very Fox-specific set of requirements an applicant needed to have before they'd be allowed to interview for the position as his new assistant.

They'd sent the list to the recruitment agencies, and Dot, bless her, had offered to weed out the applicants on Ru's behalf. She felt guilty for leaving Fox so abruptly, Dot explained. She was very fond of him, and she missed the stimulation of working in his office. She would do everything she could to find him someone suitable.

Before she left the country, Ru would drive to Long Island and take Dot out for a meal. It was the least she could do. No wonder Fox had had such difficulty replacing her—Dot was a gem.

Unlike her boss, who was currently, in Ru's opinion, a lump of very low-grade coal.

How dare he leave without explanation? Why was his phone off? And why wasn't he answering her text messages, her emails? How hard was it to say, "I'm in X. I'm fine"? It wasn't rocket science, dammit!

She was worried about him, worried that something had happened. But every time she raised her concerns about him being incommunicado with Jace—she'd taken to having coffee in the kitchen with her and Aly most mornings—she was told that Jack and Fox were in constant communication and until Jack raised the alarm, she wasn't to worry.

When Ru demanded to know whether Jace'd spoken to Fox directly, the housekeeper had wrinkled her nose and nodded. Great—so Fox was talking to his family and ignoring her. Excellent news. Dammit, it shouldn't hurt this much.

Just give him some space and time, Jace told her, but she couldn't meet Ru's eyes when she trotted out the too-pat words. No, something was up, something had happened, and it killed Ru to know that she was out of the loop. For the first time since she met him, Ru felt ignored, inconsequential and unimportant.

What had changed? Why was he doing this?

She walked over to the window and looked out onto the sparkling blue outdoor pool without really seeing it. Fox had trusted her with the information about his parents; he'd shared something deep and personal with her. They'd connected emotionally over their pasts, their messed-up-in-different-ways parents. She'd genuinely thought that he was coming to care for her, that there was something more between them than work and sex.

They liked each other—and she loved him.

She *loved* him. Shit. How had that happened?

And that was why him disappearing hurt her so

much. She loved him, and all she rated was an "I'm going out of town, not sure when I'll be back" message with nine work-related bullet points. He didn't feel what she did. And God, that hurt.

But she couldn't force him to love her, couldn't shoehorn him into a relationship. And even if he did want one, what would a relationship with Fox look like?

Ru gave that a little thought, running through his day and trying to imagine where she'd fit in it. He started early and finished late—most nights he didn't leave the office until nine or ten at night. He worked weekends, and the little spare time he had he spent with his brothers. A relationship with Fox would mean late, late dinners, maybe an hour, at most, spent together at the end of a long day. They wouldn't eat breakfast together, and he rarely broke for lunch. There would be no lazy Sunday mornings spent in bed before ambling down to a coffee shop for brunch. They wouldn't spontaneously decide to go to the movies, to an art gallery or take a stroll through Central Park.

She would spend her life waiting for Fox.

Was she prepared to give up traveling, exploring the world to settle down in Manhattan, sticking around so that she could have whatever scraps of time were left over after his long, long days? Would that be enough for her? She didn't think so.

No, she knew it wouldn't be.

Not that it mattered, since Fox didn't want a relationship in the first place. Ru closed her eyes, thinking that karma was bitch-slapping her.

In her previous relationships, her significant others had been the ones demanding more, pushing her to feel more, to open up and be more emotionally connected. The shoe was very firmly on the other foot this time around, and she mentally apologized to them. She hadn't realized how hard it was to love someone who didn't love her back.

She'd offered excuses—*I want to travel, I don't want to be controlled, I don't want to settle down*—but the truth was that she hadn't loved them enough to change. Just like Fox didn't love her and wouldn't change for her.

Okay, well, this sucked.

"Are you planning on doing any work today, or are you just going to stare out of the window?"

She spun around at the sound of his deep voice, her mouth dropping open as she watched him walk across the study to his desk. He opened his laptop bag, pulled out the computer and flipped it open, his movements unhurried and normal. He wasn't acting like he'd been away, out of touch, for a week.

Anger rushed over her, hot and sour. "Where the hell have you been?" she demanded, furious to hear the way her voice shook. "Do you know how worried I've been?"

He looked up, one arrogant eyebrow lifting. "I'm sorry. I thought that you reported to me, not the other way around."

Ru shoved her hands into her hair, feeling her heart bouncing off her ribs. She hadn't fully realized how worried she'd been until now, and she closed her eyes, thanking God that he looked as good as he always did. A little tired maybe, definitely not relaxed, but healthy, uninjured. Fine.

"I have been calling you, leaving messages, sending you emails…why couldn't you tell me where you were, that you were okay? I've been going out of my mind, Fox!"

Something that looked a little remorse flashed in his eyes before they hardened to that flat blue that told her he was halfway out of the door. "I'm a grown man, the CEO of an international business, ridiculously wealthy. Do you not think that if something serious had happened to me, someone would have informed my family?"

"We are sleeping together, Fox. We are friends," Ru said, sounding desperate. "I am also your PA—"

"But you're not entitled to know where I go, what I do, Ru."

Wow. Okay, then.

Fox placed his palms on his desk and stared at her, his expression remote. "And don't you think you are being more than a little hypocritical?"

A cold hand had its icy fingers around her heart, and Ru was finding it difficult to get air into her lungs. "I don't know what you are talking about," she told him.

"Really? Isn't dropping out and being uncommunicative what you do? Don't you hate it when your parents and friends try to keep track of you, demanding to know where you are and what you are doing?"

It wasn't the same... "That's not fair!" It wasn't, was it? "I'm—"

"You're my PA, and we're having a short-term fling. Neither gives you full access to my life." Fox looked down at his laptop, and Ru noticed his right hand was clenched into a fist and a muscle jumped in his jaw. He wasn't as unaffected as he wanted her to believe, but she couldn't understand why he was acting like this.

"Fox, please, talk to me," she asked, coming perilously close to begging. "I can tell that something happened, something monumental, and I want to help."

He closed his eyes, and just for a moment, Ru thought that she might be getting somewhere, that they might be able to overcome this hurdle. That he'd open up and let her in. Then he placed his thumb on the biometric sensor to open his computer, and the moment was gone.

"Are you or are you not still planning on returning to traveling?" Fox asked her, in what she called his ordering-coffee voice, distracted and entirely disinterested.

"Is there a reason for me to stay?" she asked him. Because if he asked her, she just might, despite all her reservations.

His shoulder lifted in a half-hearted shrug. "Not on my account. There's nothing between us but sex."

Was that really all it had meant to him? She knew he didn't love her, but she'd thought what they shared at least meant something to him. Not the sex, but the part where they'd spoken, a lot, opening up to each other. Despite spending so little time together, she considered Fox to be one of her closest friends. Maybe even her closest friend. He knew her better than anyone else.

But it appeared she didn't know him at all.

"I'm sorry you feel that way, because you mean far more to me than a casual roll in the hay," Ru told him quietly, hanging onto her dignity. "And, however much you want to deny it, we both know you *did* get emotionally naked with me, and we showed each other our scars and flaws. But for some reason, one I can't fathom, you've shut me out, pushed me away."

Fox stood up straight and released what sounded like an annoyed sigh. "We agreed that we weren't going to do this, Ru, that we weren't going to get involved. So why are you pushing this?"

Good question. Why was she? Was she simply a glutton for punishment? Was she punishing herself for all those guys whose hearts she'd kicked around, whose feelings she'd dismissed? Or did this man, as she suspected, own her heart and soul? Was he the one she wanted to be with, the person she'd change her life and alter her plans for?

Simply put…yes. She wanted to be with him, however they could make it work. She did not want to walk out of his life as if they were no more than ships passing in the night.

She took a deep breath, forcing herself to be honest, to put everything on the line. "I think I'm in love with you, Fox. I think that you and I could have something meaningful and important. And I think you are pushing me away because you're terrified to let me in."

Fox held her gaze, but she couldn't read anything in his eyes but frustration. "I don't have time for this, Ru. I don't have space for you and your feelings in my life!"

He wasn't prepared to make space, and he wouldn't allocate them any time. Okay, he couldn't be much clearer than that. At least she knew where she stood. She'd caught feelings, he hadn't and she came very far down on his list of priorities. If she featured at all.

Ru nodded once, her throat spasming as she struggled to keep a sob contained. She would not cry—she wouldn't make that much of a fool of herself. But she did need to get out of this office and away from Calcott Manor. Immediately. She wouldn't stay where she wasn't wanted.

"Your payroll department has my bank details. I'd appreciate it if you could pay me as soon as possible."

He simply nodded, and Ru saw an emotion she couldn't identify flash in his eyes. Relief? Acceptance? Whatever it was, it wasn't surprise. Her leaving, on some level, was what he wanted.

"I owe you an assistant, but Dot said she'd find you one, and frankly, I think she is far better qualified to find you a replacement than me. I've been winging it since I started here."

"I know."

Of course he did—he wasn't a fool. She gestured to the door. "I'm going to pack, call for a taxi."

It almost looked as if Fox was trying to drink her in, to commit her face to memory, but Ru dismissed her thoughts. She was done weaving fantasies around Fox Grantham. He was letting her leave—he *wanted* her to go. They were done.

Walking away from him had always been the plan, what they'd agreed on.

She'd been the one to move the goalposts, to make something of nothing. Who'd fallen in love. Her fault, her choice.

And she had to live with the consequences.

Eleven

Instead of returning to take up residence on Shellie's couch, Ru went back to her childhood home in Bay Ridge. She trundled up the steps to the front door, her heart as heavy as her hastily packed, battered, stuffed-to-the-gills backpack.

This was the house she'd been brought back to when she was three after her two-week stint with her disturbed kidnapper. This was the house she couldn't wait to leave. She'd walked away from the people who she thought were trying to stifle her, whom she'd always believed were trying to control her.

Now, she was starting to wonder if she'd been wrong—if she'd been so desperate to break free that she'd confused love with control, protectiveness with paranoia.

Ru rang the doorbell, smiling when she heard the soft shuffle of her mom's footsteps behind the door. The door opened, and Ru caught the joy on her mom's face, her instinctive smile. Her mom was so damn happy to see her...she always was.

"Baby girl," Taranah said, opening the door and then her arms. Ru dropped her rucksack, shot a strained smile at her dad—he'd appeared in the hall, holding a cup of coffee—and stepped into her mom's embrace, inhaling the familiar smell of her perfume, mixed with a faint whiff of the menthol cigarettes she was forever trying to quit.

"Mom, you promised you were going to give up smoking," Ru chided her, stepping away from her mom to kiss her dad.

"Down to three a day now," Taranah told her, lugging her backpack into the hall.

Three an hour, maybe. Ru rolled her eyes at her dad before shoving her fists into the front pockets of her jeans and shifting from foot to foot. She glanced at the stairs.

"Can I..." She hesitated. "Can I stay?" She was conscious of the burning sensation behind her eyes, her wobbly chin. She hadn't cried, not when she was packing her clothes at Calcott Manor, not when she said goodbye to Jace and Aly, nor on the train ride back to the city.

But here, faced with the two people who loved her first, who loved her the most, tears started to roll down her face.

"You never have to ask that, Ru," her dad said, placing his big hand in the middle of her back. He steered her into the living room, and Ru fell into her usual seat, the corner of an overstuffed cream-colored couch. George, their huge tomcat, looked at her from the window seat, stood up and stretched before padding over and settling himself on her lap.

All she needed now was a Coke float and she could be sixteen again. Her dad settled in his chair and sent her a concerned smile. Ru brushed away her tears and stroked George, enjoying his rumbling-tractor purr. Ru caught movement out of the corner of her eye and saw her mom walking into the room, a can of soda in her hand and a glass half-filled with ice cream.

Oh God, more tears.

Ru slowly ate her ice cream float. Her dad picked up his book, and Ru craned her head to read the spine. It was, as she thought, a tome on World War Two—her dad was obsessed and read anything he could on the conflict. Her mom worked on a cross-stitch, a beach scene, and the TV played in the background.

It was so normal, so restful, and for the first time in years, fifteen or more, she didn't feel like jumping out of her skin just from being here. It wasn't Hong Kong or Lima, but it was Bay Ridge, Brooklyn. Her parents' lives might not be exciting or compelling, but they'd worked hard, raised her and were involved in their community. They'd made their home here in this diverse community, a place that was regarded to be the "real" Brooklyn, filled with native, hard-core

New Yorkers who welcomed immigrant families to their slice of the Big Apple.

Her parents' lives were peaceful and productive, and they deserved more credit she'd given them.

Ru placed her glass on the side table next to her and gently lifted George off her lap. She placed her forearms on her thighs and stared at the coffee table, piled high with her mom's gardening magazines. "I owe both of you a huge apology."

Shock chased confusion across their faces. "What for?" her dad asked, placing his book on his knee.

"In case you didn't notice, I hate it when you check in on me, when you demand to know where I am, what I'm doing, whether I'm safe. It only recently occurred to me that I've never had to worry about that with you—you're always here. You have relationships with your neighbors, and if there's a problem with you, they'd let me know."

They looked at each other, puzzled. "We're not sure what you are trying to say," Taranah stated.

Ru stared down at her bare feet in her flip-flops, thinking it was time to change her pink nail polish. "Last week, Fox disappeared on me, and I couldn't get hold of him. I didn't know where he was, what he was doing. Intellectually, I knew he was okay—I would've been told if he was hurt or injured—but not being able to reach him freaked me out." Ru closed her eyes and sucked in some air. "He came back today, and when I called him out on it, he told me I was being hypocritical, expecting him to check in when I couldn't be bothered to do that for you. I associated your needing to know where I was, what I am doing, with a need to control me."

"We just want to be involved in your life, Ru," her mom said, fiddling with a skein of bright blue thread.

Her dad shifted in his chair, his expression revealing his discomfort. He frowned at his wife of more than thirty years. "We probably pushed you too hard, tried to make decisions for you, tried too hard to keep you close. And by doing that, we pushed you away."

"It's not unusual for parents to want their children close, Ru," Taranah added, a touch defiantly. "I don't entirely agree with your father. I think you overreacted more than you needed to, took every comment and made it more of a big deal than it warranted."

Had she done that? Yeah, probably. She'd been so determined not to be controlled, to live her own life without allowing anyone to cage her in again, that she'd given them the minimum amount of information. She'd become locked into the idea that they wanted too much, and she'd punished them for being pushy by giving them nothing.

"I'm not going to come back to the city for good, not yet." How could she live here knowing that Fox was across the river and she couldn't see him? No, she needed time and space for her battered heart to heal—if it ever would—and she couldn't heal in New York City. "I do still want to travel. I'd like to see Australia and more of Europe…"

Even if she and Fox were together, she'd still

want to travel, she realized. She had a goal to see the whole world, and not completing her travels would be something she'd forever regret. Well…here was a tiny upside to walking out on Fox, and she'd take it. He wasn't the type who'd settle for seeing his girlfriend every four to six months.

Oh, what did any of it matter? She'd told him she thought she was in love with him, and he'd allowed her to walk away. That was proof positive that he didn't love her back. There was no point in indulging in ifs and buts.

"I'm going to leave again," she told her as-always aghast parents.

Taranah threw her hands up in the air, instantly frustrated by her statement.

"Mom, hold on…just listen, okay?" She released a long breath and pushed her hair off her forehead. "You were a lot more affected by my abduction than I was—"

"How can you say that! You were taken!" Taranah said, immediately distraught.

"Mom, I was three. I don't remember it, but you do." Ru's eyes burned with tears. "I'm sorry I never realized on an emotional level, how awful it must've been to not know where I was, whether I was safe, especially after you'd lost me once. In my desire to not be controlled by your fear, I've hurt you by not telling you I was safe, where I was and what I was doing. I'm going to try to do better."

Her mom started to speak, but her dad interrupted

before she could. "Thank you, Ru. We appreciate that."

She and her mom butted heads—they were both emotional, but her dad knew always knew where to draw the line and how to stop a conversation from escalating. It was a great skill, and she sent him a smile of appreciation. "I am sorry," she told him, knowing that he bore the brunt of dealing with her mother's fears.

He shrugged and nodded before changing the subject. "Since you're home with your rucksack and talking about traveling again, I presume it didn't work out with Fox?"

Ru shook her head, biting the inside of her lip.

"Your fault or his?"

There was no criticism in his voice, so she shrugged. "His, mine, ours. I told him I thought I was in love with him, but he told me he didn't have the time or space for me in his life."

Her dad winced, and her mother frowned. "How dare he! What is wrong with the man? I cannot believe he did that!"

Ru knew that some of her mom's abject disappointment was because she'd hoped Ru's relationship with Fox would give her a reason to stay close—in the same city, at least. Ru caught her father's eye and saw his amusement. "You can't force love, Taranah," he told his wife, but he kept his brown eyes on Ru.

Ru nodded. It was, after all, what she'd been telling herself, repeatedly, since she left Calcott Manor.

But man, how she wished she could.

* * *

Fox walked into the enormous kitchen at Hatfield and headed straight for the coffee machine, desperate to get some caffeine into his system. To stop himself from thinking about Ru, from missing her, he'd worked until well after midnight, only stopping when his eyes ceased focusing. Then he lay in bed, staring at the ceiling until the sun painted light across the horizon. Needing to move, he'd run along the beach for eight punishing miles, and he was now paying the price for too much exercise on too little sleep and food.

He threw back his first espresso and jammed his cup under the spout for another hit. He looked out of the kitchen window to the paddock behind the house, fighting the urge to go find Ru and to beg her to stay.

She'd told him she loved him, that they could have something meaningful. What did she mean by that? Would she consider relocating back to the States, moving in with him—

No! She'd left, and he was going to let her stay gone. That was what they'd agreed on, and he wasn't going to let his emotional heart override his brain. He and Ru were a nonstarter...

He and *anyone* were a nonstarter.

How could he love her, love anyone, when he couldn't know, or trust, anyone on a deep, fundamental level except for his family? And even then, trust could sometimes be a shaky thing. He'd thought he knew his parents, but his perceptions about them had been blown out of the water in his early twenties. He thought he knew his grandmother, had been convinced there were no skeletons in her closet, but she had secrets she was prepared to pay millions to keep buried.

How could anyone really know someone else, and if you couldn't know them, how could you trust them? Love them?

"Why don't you just put your mouth under it and do it that way?"

He turned to see Jace and Aly sitting at the kitchen table, staring at him. He pushed his hand into his shower-wet hair. "Morning. Sorry, I didn't see you there."

He saw the disbelief in their eyes and couldn't blame them for being skeptical. They were difficult to miss. Carrying his second espresso, he pulled out a chair and dropped down, stretching out his long legs.

"So?" Jace asked.

He looked at her, keeping his expression blank. Jace had never been shy about expressing her opinions, and he knew he was in for a grilling about Ru's departure. "So?" he parried.

She narrowed her eyes at him, in the same way she had when he was ten or twelve. Unfortunately, it still made him squirm. "She left yesterday," he admitted.

"We know," Jace retorted. "She came to say goodbye. Why did she leave, Fox?"

He lifted one shoulder in what he hoped was a super-casual shrug. "She was another temporary personal assistant in a long line of them."

"Bullshit."

Fox recoiled at Jace tossing a curse. He could, without exaggeration, count on his fingers every occasion Jace had resorted to swearing: when he and his brothers jumped from the hayloft into a too-flimsy pile of hay, resulting in Merrick breaking his arm. The time Merrick dared to come home drunk and behind the wheel of his car—she'd been furious that night, and rightly so. When Jack and his girlfriend had a pregnancy scare when he was seventeen. The other night when she heard that Avangeline was being blackmailed.

He'd made her swear, and he was not proud. "Jace, we agreed that nothing would happen between us. Unlike Soren, I'm not retiring, and I don't have the time and space for a relationship. And Ru still wants to travel."

"You can make time and space. You don't need to work all the hours in the day. The world won't stop turning if you fall in love, Fox."

But his world would if he took a chance on Ru and, sometime down the line, she disappointed him. His parents had, and so, in a way, had Avangeline, by putting herself in a position to be blackmailed. Why wouldn't she tell him who was sending her the postcards? What was she hiding? Why was she so very secretive?

Like his parents, she had led a secret second life. Why couldn't people just be open and honest?

"Ru is like that," Jace said, and it took Fox a moment to release he'd spoken out loud. "That girl doesn't hold much back."

"She doesn't tell everybody about her past, but she doesn't keep it secret, either," Aly agreed.

Fox frowned. "Are you talking about—" He stopped, wondering if they were on the same page. If they weren't, then he didn't want to betray Ru's confidence.

"Her abduction," Aly confirmed, nodding. "She told us the other day about how her quest to keep her past from influencing the present has backfired."

Fox leaned forward, fascinated. Then again, everything about Ru fascinated him. "What do you mean?"

Aly looked at Jace, and when she nodded, Aly continued. "She said that while she's loved traveling and doesn't want to give it up entirely, she can't keep using it as an excuse not to engage with the people who love her. The people she loves. She said she's tired of running away, that she wanted to see if she could stick, maybe stay."

His girl had changed her mind about the way she wanted to live her life, was brave enough to put her heart out there, and it sounded like she might be prepared to compromise the way she lived her life for him. She'd even said she loved him—that she might love him—and he'd responded by pushing her away.

Yeah, he was a prick.

"I'm scared she'll disappoint me," he admitted quietly, voicing his biggest fear. He met Jace's eyes and saw the sympathy in them.

"But what if she doesn't, Fox? Are you prepared to lose the best thing that's ever happened to you on what I think is a remote possibility?" Jace asked him. "She's lovely, Fox, and perfect for you. And so damn brave to stick her neck out for love."

And you aren't. Fox heard Jace's unspoken words, and they held the sting of icy needles in a blizzard. Was he prepared to lose her? Yesterday, he thought he was. Today, after a miserable night and awful morning, he wasn't so sure. He didn't know if he could live with her, but he was equally convinced he couldn't live without her.

His phone rang, and Fox pulled it from his back pocket and frowned when he saw that it was Dot calling him. She probably had some ideas for her replacement, but he wasn't up to thinking about a new assistant yet. He'd call her back later. Or tomorrow. Or next week.

"If you do decide to ask Ru to marry you, don't give her the emerald," Aly stated.

Both Fox and Jace stared at her, their faces slack with shock. "What did you say?" Fox demanded as his hands started to shake.

Aly looked at him and shrugged. "Your mom's engagement ring—don't use it. Ru won't like it, and it doesn't belong on her hand. Peyton should've kept it." Aly pushed her fingers into her hair and looked at

Jace, then Fox, looking miserable. "I'm sorry, I'm just repeating thoughts that are popping into my head."

"Malcolm's?" Jace asked, placing her hand on Aly's arm, who nodded.

Aly shrugged. "I don't think he wanted her to return the ring. I think Malcolm feels like it is hers."

If Malcolm and Peyton had married, Fox would've been okay with her keeping his mom's ridiculously rare ring. But they'd broken up, called off the engagement before Mal's death, and it was right that she'd returned it. So what was Aly going on about?

Fox looked at Jace, feeling a little stupefied. "Did you tell her about my mom's ring?"

Jace shook her head. "No. I barely knew your parents—they died a few days after I started working here. All your mother's jewelry has been in a vault for as long as I can remember. And your grandmother doesn't discuss your parents with anyone."

Fox forced himself to think, pushing away his emotion to be analytical. Right, Aly hadn't told him anything she couldn't find out with a little digging. "Malcolm was engaged, and he gave his fiancée my mom's ring. She returned it. Both stories made the papers."

Aly didn't drop her eyes. "Fair enough. But you and I both know that, should a discussion about rings come up, Ru would far prefer the black opal. She's a colorful girl, and it would suit her. Speaking of which, why is it called a black opal when it's so red?"

What the hell was she talking—

Fox felt his eyes widen, and his jaw dropped as Aly's words brought a memory sharply to mind. More than a decade ago, he and Malcolm accessed the storage box so that Malcolm could retrieve the emerald ring for Peyton. While they were there, they'd decided to do an inventory of the jewelry for insurance purposes. Their mom had adored fine gemstones, and doing the inventory took some time.

In among the pink and yellow diamond bracelets and rings, sapphires and ruby pendants, and emerald, diamond and sapphire earrings, they'd found rare gems, too—red beryl and alexandrite, tanzanite, Paraíba tourmaline, and Kashmir sapphires.

They also found a still-wrapped jewelry box, and after ripping off the gold paper, they'd discovered the opal ring in its velvet box. After a brief discussion about the unusual and impressive ring, they'd put it on the inventory and moved on.

After Malcolm's death, he and Jack returned the emerald ring to the safety-deposit box—it took two people to access it—but they didn't do any more than toss the ring in with the rest of Heather's collection. And nobody had accessed the safe-deposit box since then. Nobody knew that the opal listed on the inventory was classified as a black opal, but it was actually red, shot with blues, greens and purples. Vibrant.

The only other person who'd laid eyes on that ring beside him was Malcolm. Malcolm, who'd picked it up and said that only a colorful girl could wear such a colorful ring. Malcolm...whose liver now resided in Aly.

No. No damn way. It wasn't possible. It wasn't scientific… But Fox couldn't help thinking that he'd received a message from his brother, a heavenly kick up his back side.

"How do you know about the ring?" he asked, his voice cracking.

Aly spread her hands and shook her head. "I don't, Fox. But your brother did." She shrugged. "Like Soren and Malcolm's secret gesture, I felt compelled to mention the ring."

She looked away from him, and Fox wondered what else she was chasing, what other knowledge she had, what she was keeping to herself and what she was truly after. Because there was something bigger at play than Malcolm's memories, another reason she was here. He felt the urge to dig, to pull away the layers to find the truth.

But, right now, he had a bigger compulsion, a more important quest.

He had no idea what sort of relationship he and Ru could have, what with his work and her traveling, but they'd work it out. They had to, because he didn't just *think* he was in love with her—he knew he was. And his life was incomplete without her.

The cherry on top was that somehow, and in some weird way, his older brother was rooting for him, them, given his admittedly ghostly assurance that everything would be fine.

It had better, because if this didn't work out, he'd kick Mal's ass when they finally met up again.

And God, he thought as his phone lit up again, why was Dot being so persistent?

Fox parked his car behind a van and looked across the tree-lined street to take in Ru's parents' pretty town house. He was in a lovely part of Bay Ridge, just a five-minute walk from the waterfront. He rather liked this area—all the town houses looked spacious and light-filled, but also welcoming and, yeah, homey.

He wiped his hands on his thighs, admitting he was focusing on the house to avoid thinking about how he was going to approach Ru, how he was going to handle what he was sure would be a tricky conversation.

The hell of it was, he wanted Ru in his life, and he was prepared to make time and space for her but, while he thought she'd appreciate the gesture, he doubted a conventional relationship would work for them. Oh, there would come a time—maybe in a couple of years—when they'd need to conform. Kids and their routines and schooling needs would force them into doing that. But right now, a typical domestic routine wouldn't work for them. And look at him, thinking about kids without breaking into hives!

Specifically, a nine-to-five relationship wouldn't work for Ru. And he wasn't prepared to do anything to scare her off, to make her run. So he'd had to come up with something a little more creative...

He'd tell her he loved her, that was a given, and that he wanted her in his life long term, another nonnegotiable. But how they managed their day-to-day lives was what was making him sweat.

That and the thought that she might not even want to talk to him. Well, tough. He'd spent a few days in hell, and he was done hanging out there.

Fox left his car, locked it and walked across the street and up the path leading to the front door. His first stop today had been her friend's apartment, but Shellie had told him that Ru wasn't with her, and she'd thought she was with him. Not knowing how else to contact her—calls to her phone went to straight voice mail, making him fear that she'd blocked his number—he'd begged Shellie to give him her parents' address. So here he was, about to throw himself on their mercy. He needed them to tell him where to find Ru.

If they even knew.

He wouldn't be surprised if Ru had caught the first international flight she could get on. He could see her doing that.

Fox rang the doorbell and practiced his opening line. *I'm looking for Ru, any idea where she is? I've lost your daughter—can you help me find her?*

Just keep it simple, he told himself in a silent pep talk. *Tell them she's not answering her phone or returning your messages—yeah, yeah, the shoe is on the other foot and it pinches like hell—and you need to talk to her.*

So when Ru opened the door, dressed in a thigh-length, bohemian-print, halter-neck dress that left her shoulders and arms bare, he nearly swallowed his tongue. She wasn't wearing any shoes, and she'd changed the color of her toenails from pink to an acid orange.

"What are you doing here?" he demanded, his voice croaky.

"Uh…my parents live here. What are *you* doing here?" she retorted, and he ran a hand over his face. *Get a grip, Grantham.*

"Can we talk?"

Ru folded her arms across her chest and looked belligerent. "About what? And no, I'm not coming back to work for you. Talk to Dot if you want an assistant—she's handling that for me."

"I know. And I did. And I don't need an assistant. I've got one."

Ru looked put out. "Well, that was fast. Who? How did Dot find her?"

Fox realized that he was still standing on the porch and that he must look like he was trying to sell Ru something. Which he was, kind of—himself. "I'll explain if I can come in."

Ru stared at him for a little while, as if debating whether that was a good idea. What seemed like years later, she opened the door and stepped back so that he could walk inside. She shut the door behind him, and he looked around. To the right of the hall was a sitting room filled with comfortable-looking couches.

"Are your parents here?" he asked, sliding his hands into his pants pockets.

"No, it's their morning to play bridge. What do

you mean, you've got a new assistant? How did Dot find one so fast?" she demanded, sounding put out. He noticed that her eyes were red and she looked as tired as he felt.

"She didn't find me a new PA. She's coming back to work for me," Fox explained. This wasn't what he wanted to discuss, dammit. "She's bored and doesn't want to be a stay-at-home wife."

Ru looked gutted. "Are they getting divorced? They just got married!"

"No," Fox said, placing a hand on her back and leading her into the sitting room he could see from the hall. "She's very happy with her marriage, but her husband is a detective, and she spends a lot of time on her own. She's agreed to return to work if she can come in at nine and leave by four."

"And you said yes," Ru said, sitting down on the edge of one couch's plump cushions.

Fox shrugged. Dot would be more productive in those hours than anyone else, including Ru. She was scary efficient, and they worked together well. Besides, he didn't intend to spend as much time in the office as he did before.

"I'm happy everything is working out for you," Ru said. He knew she'd probably intended to sound sarcastic, but she actually just sounded sad. And he'd made her feel that way.

Fox looked at the sturdy coffee table, decided it could take his weight, and sat down in front of her,

her knees between his legs. "You know it's not, Ru, because you're not in my life."

"You told me you didn't have space for me," Ru countered.

A very fair point. "It was one of my more asinine comments," Fox admitted. "In my defense, I was— still am—reeling from the news I got the night we had dinner with Avangeline. Can I tell you about it?"

He wanted to, not only because he trusted her, but because he couldn't imagine *not* telling her. He didn't want there to be any secrets between them.

"What would be the point, Fox?" Ru cried. "I'm leaving for Australia. We're done, and we'll probably never cross paths again."

Nope, it wasn't going to happen that way. "I know you are leaving, but we're not done, and our lives will most definitely be crossing again—hopefully merging." Her mouth fell open at his pronouncement, but before she could comment, he told her how Avangeline was being blackmailed, about the postcards and his worthless trip to see his grandfather.

When he stopped talking, about ten minutes later, Ru lifted her hand to her mouth, looking gobsmacked. "Wow. I did not see any of that coming."

"Me neither," he admitted, feeling exhausted. He looked down and noticed his hand on her knee—he must've placed it there subconsciously. It belonged there, he thought. He belonged with her.

"My biggest worry is that I still don't know who sent the postcards, who knows about the Basement and who is threatening to expose my parents," Fox admitted, feeling sick at the thought. "I do not want my grandmother and brothers finding out about all of that."

He felt embarrassed by his bobbing throat and the burning sensation behind his eyes. "My grandmother, thank God, still has no idea about the Basement, and I intend to keep it that way," he said, his voice turning hard with determination. "I intend to find out who is blackmailing her, and when I do, I'm gonna rip him apart."

"Any ideas on how to do that?" Ru asked him. "And how can I help?"

"I might need your hacking skills," he told her, waiting for her reaction.

She didn't hesitate. "You've got them. What are your brothers doing?"

He didn't answer her, and after a little while, her shoulders slumped. "You haven't told them, have you?"

"No. They don't need to hear about it, or be hurt by this. This is something I have to search for myself, do by myself and resolve myself. With your help."

Her eyes locked onto his, and Fox couldn't look away. "Fox, this isn't your burden to carry alone. You are doing your brothers, particularly Jack, a huge disservice by not telling them. They have a right to know, a right to help protect this family, to protect Avangeline. And they'd want to help you—they wouldn't want you to deal with this on your own."

He knew she was right and felt a prick of guilt. "I'm trying to protect them!" he insisted. "I need to handle this myself."

"Because that's what you've always done, right? You've always handled everything yourself. You are so very used to being alone, to going it alone, that you'd rather be isolated than ask your brothers for help. My darling man, that's crazy talk."

"I can't do it, Ru, I can't change and let them in."

"You did it with me," she told him, placing her hands on his knees, her expression soft, her face lovely. "If you can learn to trust me, you can trust your brothers with this and ask them to share the burden. Keeping secrets is a habit, Fox, one you can change. You've already started."

He shrugged. "I keep telling you things because your eyes are a truth drug. My brothers don't have the same effect on me," he joked.

Ru touched his jaw with the tips of her fingers. "I don't want you dealing with this on your own, Fox. Please tell them."

He held her hand against his face, his throat closing with emotion. "I can't deny you anything, Ru. So, yes, I don't like it, but I will tell them everything."

"Okay…good." Then she swallowed, closed her eyes and scrunched up her nose.

"I cannot believe I am asking this again," she said, keeping her eyes closed. "But will you love me?"

God, she was so brave, so open and prepared to live life, no matter if it hurt her or not. "Yes."

He watched her face as she took in his answer, enjoying her initial joy, then a hint of wariness. She opened one eye and squinted at him. "Are you sure?"

"Yes, I will love you. Today, tomorrow, sixty years from now."

Ru rubbed the back of her neck, trying to be sensible. He wished she'd stop. "You said—"

"I said many stupid things," he interrupted her. "I love you, I want to be with you, I want a relationship with you, I can and will make space for you in my life."

Ru stared at him, and the next minute he had a warm, wonderful, fragrant bundle of woman in his arms. While the coffee table could take his weight, he wasn't sure it was up to holding another hundred pounds. So he picked her up and sat down on the couch, keeping her on his lap. Her lips met his, and passion flared between them, as it always did, fast and furious. He explored her mouth and pushed his hand up and under her dress to explore her slim, silky thigh. He couldn't wait to remove her dress, bury his face…

Ru pulled back, her hand stopping his journey to her panties. "God, we can't! Not on my parents' favorite couch!"

He banged his forehead against her shoulder, releasing an audible groan. Ru sent him a cheeky grin.

"How long until they are back?" he asked, a little desperately. "We could go up to your room."

Ru shook her head, amused. "Oh, *no*. I definitely

would not be able to enjoy making love to you in my childhood bedroom."

Making love—he liked the sound of that. But he would far prefer to be doing it instead of talking about it. Ru swiped his mouth with hers and rested her head on his chest, releasing a happy sigh. "I guess I should cancel my ticket to Australia."

Fox tensed. Right, he'd reached the tricky part. He stroked his hand over her head, enjoying her soft hair. "What if you just change it, Ru?"

It was her turn to tense up, and he shook his head. "No, sweetheart, don't jump to conclusions. Just hear me out, okay?"

Ru sat up to look at his face. "Okay, I'm listening."

He couldn't mess this up. "I love you and you love me, agreed?" When she nodded, he carried on. "But I think you also still have a yearning to keep traveling, to complete your odyssey around the world."

She frowned. "I would give it up for you, Fox."

He appreciated the thought. "But I don't want you to, Ru. And, while I wish I could say that I'd change my working habits instantaneously, I think it might take me some time to get into that groove of working less, being less obsessed with my work. I don't want you to give up everything you love and be sitting around waiting for me to come home. That's not fair to you."

"So what do you propose?" she quietly asked.

"That we a little time to be together, to enjoy and solidify what we have. I'll work a little, and we'll play a lot. In between, we'll try to figure out who is blackmailing Avangeline."

"That sounds like heaven. What happens after that?"

"Then you go to Australia, stay for a few months, and you either come home or I'll fly to you," he told her. "I've set up an account for you with the travel agent we use—all you need to do is send an email and they'll get you wherever you need to be, whether that's flying first-class or on a private plane."

"I'm not flying first-class or adding to carbon emissions by flying private," Ru told him, aghast.

Maybe, maybe not. "Explore Australia, then go to Europe. And I'll fly to you, as often as I can. While you get your travel bug out of your system, I'll get Dot to train me to work less, to help me find some work-play balance so that when you do come home permanently, we're a hundred percent ready to live together."

"My money's on Dot," Ru told him. "I'll give her six months to whip you into shape."

He dropped a kiss on her bare shoulder. "I'll missing you so much, I'll be ready in three." And that wasn't an exaggeration. He was utterly certain he'd miss her like crazy when she was away. But if she didn't go, she'd regret it for the rest of her life.

"There will always be travel in our lives, Ru," he told her. "I can't wait to explore new countries and cultures with you, with our kids."

Delight softened her features. "You want kids with me?"

He shook his head. "No, darling, I want *everything*

with you." He shifted her knee, dug into the pocket of his pants and pulled out a ring, the opal he'd retrieved from the safe-deposit box yesterday, accompanied by Jack and Merrick. He'd endured a crapload of ribbing during the ordeal, but it had been worth it.

"I'm hoping you'll want this as your engagement ring."

Ru took the ring, seeming fascinated by its colors. "It's stunning, Fox." She slipped it onto her ring finger and held it up to the light, watching as the colors danced in the sunlight streaming in from the window behind him. "Was it your mom's?"

He nodded. "But it wasn't one she wore or even knew about. It was giftwrapped, complete with a bow, so I doubt she bought it for herself." He explained how he'd discovered the ring and how much he'd always loved it. "But if you don't like it, I'll buy you something else."

"It's unusual and lovely and colorful. I've never given engagement rings much thought—"

"Even though you've had a couple," Fox teased her.

Ru punched his shoulder, but he saw amusement dancing in her eyes, in the way a smile kept trying to lift her lips. None of her previous engagements had worked out, because she was his. It was simply the way the universe worked.

"So, yes, please."

"To the ring or to getting married sometime in the future?" Fox asked, his tone turning serious.

She cocked her head to the side and smiled, and

Fox would swear that, just for a minute, his heart stopped. "To you and me, to marriage and kids and the future. To now. And to everything."

This, he realized, was joy. Happiness. And he'd found it in a free spirit with a personality as big as the sun.

* * * * *

Don't miss any of the Dynasties: Calcott Manor

Just a Little Jilted
Their Temporary Arrangement

Available now!

Plus Jack and Peyton's story
Available August 2023

COMING NEXT MONTH FROM

DESIRE

OH SO WRONG WITH MR. RIGHT & THE MAN SHE LOVES TO HATE

OH SO WRONG WITH MR. RIGHT
Texas Cattleman's Club: The Wedding • by Nadine Gonzalez
Commitment-shy photojournalist Sasha Ramos is the latest in her family's long history of runaway brides. But when her sister's upcoming wedding triggers her need to flee, businessman Nikola Williams will give her *all* the delicious, sexy reasons to stay...

THE MAN SHE LOVES TO HATE
Texas Cattleman's Club: The Wedding • by Jessica Lemmon
Wedding planner Rylee Meadows strikes a deal with professional wedding crasher Trick MacArthur to keep him from ruining the festivities. But their instant attraction brings out Rylee's wild side...and may lead to wedding mayhem!

THE RANCHER'S PLUS-ONE & STRANDED WITH A COWBOY

THE RANCHER'S PLUS-ONE
Kingsland Ranch • by Joanne Rock
Their one-night stand ended in treachery. But when Levi Kingsley reunites with PR whiz Kendra Davies to solve his latest family scandal, can they tame their explosive chemistry before revenge—or seduction—ignites all over again?

STRANDED WITH A COWBOY
Devil's Bluffs • by Stacey Kennedy
Passion ignites when millionaire cowboy Beau Ward and done-with-love city girl Nora Keller are stranded together in a tropical storm. But hot nights tangled in bedsheets will create their own raging emotional tempest when their lustful adventure leads to something more.

RAGS TO RICHES REUNION & THE LOST HEIR

RAGS TO RICHES REUNION
by Yvonne Lindsay
Oh how the tides have turned! Once wealthy Hyacinth Sanderton is back in town. And her brother has asked poor boy turned millionaire Drummond Keyes to hire her. But can Drum betray his friend by allowing a sexual entanglement with the one pampered princess he's always desired?

THE LOST HEIR
by Rachel Bailey
Heath Dunstan has just inherited billions—and it's his last one-night stand, forensic accountant Freya Wilson, who's tracked him down. Heath agrees to accept his fate and end his relationship with Freya. But rules are made to be broken...

You can find more information on upcoming Harlequin titles,
free excerpts and more at Harlequin.com.

HD2in | CNM0423

Get 4 FREE REWARDS!

We'll send you 2 FREE Books plus 2 FREE Mystery Gifts.

FREE Value Over **$20**

Both the **Harlequin® Desire** and **Harlequin Presents®** series feature compelling novels filled with passion, sensuality and intriguing scandals.

YES! Please send me 2 FREE novels from the Harlequin Desire or Harlequin Presents series and my 2 FREE gifts (gifts are worth about $10 retail). After receiving them, if I don't wish to receive any more books, I can return the shipping statement marked "cancel." If I don't cancel, I will receive 6 brand-new Harlequin Presents Larger-Print books every month and be billed just $6.30 each in the U.S. or $6.49 each in Canada, a savings of at least 10% off the cover price, or 6 Harlequin Desire books every month and be billed just $5.05 each in the U.S. or $5.74 each in Canada, a savings of at least 12% off the cover price. It's quite a bargain! Shipping and handling is just 50¢ per book in the U.S. and $1.25 per book in Canada.* I understand that accepting the 2 free books and gifts places me under no obligation to buy anything. I can always return a shipment and cancel at any time by calling the number below. The free books and gifts are mine to keep no matter what I decide.

Choose one: ☐ **Harlequin Desire** ☐ **Harlequin Presents Larger-Print**
(225/326 HDN GRJ7)   (176/376 HDN GRJ7)

Name (please print)

Address   Apt. #

City   State/Province   Zip/Postal Code

Email: Please check this box ☐ if you would like to receive newsletters and promotional emails from Harlequin Enterprises ULC and its affiliates. You can unsubscribe anytime.

Mail to the **Harlequin Reader Service:**
IN U.S.A.: P.O. Box 1341, Buffalo, NY 14240-8531
IN CANADA: P.O. Box 603, Fort Erie, Ontario L2A 5X3

Want to try 2 free books from another series! Call 1-800-873-8635 or visit www.ReaderService.com.

*Terms and prices subject to change without notice. Prices do not include sales taxes, which will be charged (if applicable) based on your state or country of residence. Canadian residents will be charged applicable taxes. Offer not valid in Quebec. This offer is limited to one order per household. Books received may not be as shown. Not valid for current subscribers to the Harlequin Presents or Harlequin Desire series. All orders subject to approval. Credit or debit balances in a customer's account(s) may be offset by any other outstanding balance owed by or to the customer. Please allow 4 to 6 weeks for delivery. Offer available while quantities last.

Your Privacy—Your information is being collected by Harlequin Enterprises ULC, operating as Harlequin Reader Service. For a complete summary of the information we collect, how we use this information and to whom it is disclosed, please visit our privacy notice located at corporate.harlequin.com/privacy-notice. From time to time we may also exchange your personal information with reputable third parties. If you wish to opt out of this sharing of your personal information, please visit readerservice.com/consumerschoice or call 1-800-873-8635. **Notice to California Residents**—Under California law, you have specific rights to control and access your data. For more information on these rights and how to exercise them, visit corporate.harlequin.com/california-privacy.

HDHP22R3

HARLEQUIN
PLUS

Try the best multimedia subscription service for romance readers like you!

Read, Watch and Play.

Experience the easiest way to get the romance content you crave.

Start your **FREE TRIAL** at
<u>www.harlequinplus.com/freetrial</u>.

HARPLUS0123